SECRET ATONEMENT

SECRET ATONEMENT

CAYCE POPONEA

Edited by
ELIZABETH SIMONTON

Cover Designer
JADA D'LEE

SECRET ATONEMENT

A man with big ambitions trying to stand out. A woman living in New York, trying to blend in. A romantic recipe for disaster.

Ian McLeod has waited and planned for the moment he took over the Family after his father's death. Stepping over his grave and onto a path, which may lead him to more than expanding the Family holdings. What happens when a business meeting to purchase a coffee shop turns into an encounter with a beautiful girl and a ruined shirt? Can he show her the beauty in his dark world or will the one person he trusts kill his chance at happiness?

Heather Murray has a deep admiration for men involved with the Mafia. Knowing her romantic ideations for the organization can have disastrous consequences, she chooses to follow her heart and the man who has captured it, into the unknown. What happens when meeting the family turns into a dose of reality, complete with a reminder of how she will never fit in?

Secret Atonement is the fifth book in bestselling author, Cayce Poponea's, Code of Silence Series. If you enjoy suspense-filled Mafia romance, then you will love this book. Join Cayce as she leads you on a journey filled with alpha men who know what they want and have no issue taking it. Secret Atonement's passion filled pages, with twists and turns you never saw coming, will leave you breathless and craving more.

CHAPTER ONE

IAN

A DULL ACHE throbbed behind my eyes; nausea fills my empty stomach, accompanied by a wave of dizziness and incredible fatigue. The result of having enjoyed myself a little too much last night, between the alcohol and an ample supply of beautiful women, I made the most of my time at the wedding of Declan and Katie Malloy.

Glancing out the airport window as the hurricane force winds blew the torrential rain in a sideway direction, flooding streets, and intersections. Gray clouds loomed like a blanket over the city, the storm shutting down the airport and delaying our departure. When I first arrived, the captain apologized profusely, assuring us the moment the closure was lifted, he would get us in the air and on our way to New York City.

The busty attendant asked if she could get me anything, I took the sexy tone in her voice as an invitation to test out the theory of a good orgasm curing a headache. With a quick fuck in the bathroom and her phone number slipped inside my jacket, my hangover, as well as her suggestion of giving her a call, was a distant memory.

Thunder rumbles overhead, shaking the chair I sat in and sending

Anna, Dominick's wife, closer to his side. He pulls her close, taking her hand in his, as he placed a gentle kiss on the top of her head.

Anna is a beautiful woman, one who makes those around her feel comfortable and welcomed, ready to save the world with acts of kindness and a gentle smile. Dominick had shared his struggle to win her affections and, ultimately, her hand in marriage. Nearly losing her to the pitfalls of his bachelorhood, and the sacrifices he makes as the leader of his Family.

After the meeting Declan Malloy called, uniting the largest Four Families in the international Underworld, much like Lucky Luciano did for the Five Family's of New York in the 1930s. I sat down with Dominick to discuss extending my holdings in the States. He had been concerned with the recent activity of a smaller Family in New York, wanting to secure his territory and the safety of his wife and children.

"Ian, this is one of the buildings I want to show you. It's a warehouse I use for storage. It wouldn't take much to convert it to meet your needs."

He hands me his tablet, security footage scrolling on the screen. In the first window is the exterior of the building, nothing special, just some bricks held together by a shit-ton of mortar. The second, showed an open space with a multitude of windows, a cement floor, and metal pillars in the center. I had a few buildings back in Scotland which looked exactly like this. Every Family had a few of these, for storage and other things.

"The second building is in Manhattan, housing a well-established coffee shop on the first floor and room for more storage on the second. Frank Ciccone, runs the place, but is looking to retire in Boca."

Frank had been a member of another Family for a number of years, using the money he earned to purchase several properties back in the day. He allowed them to be utilized for a minimal fee, and was now looking to liquidate his assets, including his penthouse apartment not far from the coffee shop.

"The employees are part of the deal; Frank won't entertain an offer which doesn't ensure they keep their jobs."

Sliding my finger against the screen, I scroll to the image of the coffee shop in question. A white marquee with red lettering, spells out Aroma. The building appears solid, and the books show a decent enough profit so as not to attract the attention of the government

"How many workers are there?"

"Not sure, my concern has always been focused on the second floor. I'll show you when I take you there tomorrow."

The rain trickled to a stop as the skies cleared and the wind died down enough for us to leave Chicago. Anna curled into Dominick's side a few minutes into the flight, her body still recovering from the birth of their new baby, a little girl. I watched as Dominick held his wife, running his fingers over her shoulder as she smiled up at him, her delicate features reserved for his pleasure. A part of me envied them, wanting what they had. Although I'm not sure I would want to fight to have it, going against my family's expectations to have the kind of love they shared.

"Ian, you're a handsome man. Why isn't there a girlfriend or wife at your side?"

Anna Santos possessed poise and grace, a beautiful face, and a kind heart. But beneath her sweet smile was the mind of an investigator, one who stopped at nothing to get the truth out of you.

"Protocol dictates I thank you for expressing an appreciation for my good looks. Common sense tells me to tread lightly as your husband is in the room."

Sending a teasing eye toward Dominick, his face breaks out in a smile while Anna waves him off as indifferent.

"My obligations as the head of my Family provide me with little time to have a steady girlfriend. The lack of what I consider qualified candidates hasn't made my search any easier."

A soft smile plays on Anna's lips, her eyes shift slowly to Dominic's, her cheeks redden, sending a clear message of her understanding of my struggles.

"The same Family has a firm set of rules for any potential woman I would consider marrying."

Her smile drops, and her brow bends in confusion. "Rules? What kind of rules?"

Anna moves her body forward, separating herself from Dominick's side, laying her hand on his thigh as she gives me her undivided attention, Dominic covers her hand with his own, an act, I would wager is done on autopilot, his body's need to be near her.

"Forgive me, I forget not everyone in our world has knowledge of how my Family works, nor the stipulations the men have been given for seeking brides."

Adjusting in my seat as the steward places drinks on the table between us, Anna thanking him as he hands her a bag of cookies.

"Many hundreds of years ago, an arrangement was made between the McLeod's, the Malloy's and the McFarland's, who possess a thimble full of royal blood. They agreed to share the lineage with the McLeod's by exclusively marrying their daughters to McLeod sons. Over the years, the McFarland women have become brash and somewhat conceited, climbing over one another to capture the eye of a McLeod male. My mum has made her choice in who should give her grandchildren, but I couldn't bring myself to marry one of my best friends, Finley McFarland."

Anna's eyes grow wide as she recalls the wedding from the night before, how I danced with the spitfire redhead when her boyfriend, Brion, had to take a phone call. "That's right. Finley told me the two of you grew up together, along with Kirk Darrow, the man who went missing."

I held a straight face as I listened to Anna speak of Darrow, my former Underboss. His disappearance was more of a stab in the back, one I plan to return as soon as possible.

"Yes."

I held the anger in my voice to a minimum, no need to show how much my blood boiled inside my veins. His betrayal carved a wound in my chest and set me up for retribution from the Malloy Family. Luck had been in my favor as word reached Declan Malloy's ears, tales of how I dealt with the dirty hands on my father's payroll. Their blood stains on my hands glowing like Neon signs, sending out a warning for the rest of the world as to how far I was willing to go to protect what is mine.

"So, you can understand why Finley and I are better kept as friends."

Reaching over, Anna pats my hand; her gesture is warm and welcomed just like her smile. I can see why Dominick pursued her so diligently.

"No one has ever caught your eye, made you nearly take the plunge?"

Anna's face crinkles in suspension, her doubt in my lack of female attachment is comical. Not a single woman has ever turned my head long enough to think about a future with her. Weddings, in general, do not interest me and most of the ones I've attended have been out of obligation, any attention I captured has resulted in a moment of pleasure, mostly on my part if the woman wasn't quick enough to find hers first.

"No, not yet."

Last night, I caught the eye of a waitress, Darcy, or Marcy, I can't remember. While she was a hellcat in the sack, she was also predictable and dull with her conversation. I'd tossed her cab fare and sent her on her way. No promise of tomorrow or call when I was in town.

"What happens when your mom becomes more insistent on you choosing a bride?"

Tipping my head back in a laugh, her inquisitiveness resurfacing like the slice of a sharp blade, quick and unexpected. Anna was the type of woman I needed, one smart enough to ask the right questions, yet clever enough to know when to back away. Sadly, beautiful and witty didn't always coexist in the women I've met, one sacrificed for the other.

"Then I will do as expected and spend the rest of my life with a woman I don't particularly care for, producing an heir or two. Until then, I will enjoy as many beautiful women as I can."

* * *

PIANO MUSIC FILLED THE SURROUNDING SILENCE, THE VEST AND BOW tie-clad bartender dried a low-ball glass from behind the bar, sending me a friendly smile as I took a seat.

Low lighting from above combined with rich furnishings gave the illusion of this being an intimate setting. A solid piece of granite took the place of the traditional glossy wooden top while its dark veins and curved edges gave the space a modern look.

The bar is empty except for a leggy blonde perched at the end of the long wooden structure, a half-full glass of wine resting between her manicured fingers. Long hair scorched at the ends, a result of too much bleach and lack of a good styling. Her short skirt highlighting her slender and sexy legs, the black material ending where the leather of her chair began. She has a look about her: hungry eyes on the prowl. Sharpened talons, ready to sink into the skin of some poor bloke's back, taking away the continents of his bank account and his dignity. She sizes me up with her blue eyes, adding the total cost of my clothing and how much she can milk me for inside her head. She won't be the first to try to use her assets to get what she wants, too bad for her I'm no amateur at this game.

The bartender lays the glass and towel on the counter behind him, plasters on a smile and a kiss-ass attitude, and moves in my direction.

"Good evening, Sir. Can I get you a beverage?"

Removing my money clip from my pants pocket, I keep the blonde in my peripheral vision. Pulling off two one hundred-dollar bills and placing them chastely on the bar, I look at the bartender.

"Macallan 25."

His eyes widen at my request and the blonde shifts in her chair, clearly familiar with the eight hundred dollar a bottle scotch. Women like this are predictable and disposable, useful enough to swallow your cum, but not much else.

The bartender eyes the money on the counter, bracing his hands on the edge of the bar, taking in a deep breath. "I'm sorry, sir, but you will need another hundred if you wish to enjoy that particular scotch."

To any ordinary man his stance would appear harmless, a way of getting comfortable while remaining professional. However, I'm far from ordinary, and this con man is about to have his game played against him.

I toss two hundred more on the bar; the greedy bastard scoops it up and turns to retrieve my scotch. I let him think he has pulled his con, out smarted another over privileged asshole out of his money. Earlier this afternoon I stopped and had a drink with Dominick, the same beverage costing me one hundred dollars.

"Business or pleasure?"

As if on cue, the blonde makes her move, ready to carve out a little slice of the pie for herself before the idiot behind the bar takes all the cash, and she is left with nothing but a bad hangover from her cheap wine. This was almost too easy, and I feel slightly guilty for what I'm about to do, not enough to stop me, but enough to bring a winning smile to my face. Her breathy voice whips across my cheek as she pushes her right tit against my arm. The bartender places a paper napkin on the bar, covering the hotel logo with my glass of scotch, nodding his head as he steps away to resume drying the clean glasses, but not before he takes an appreciative look at the blonde who is practically in my lap.

"Must I choose one?"

Lifting the amber liquid to my lips, the smell of oak and citrus hits my nose, reminding me of home. My family has owned a controlling interest in the Macallan distillery since it brewed its first batch, one of the few legit businesses we owned. I don't bother to look her way or turn my body in her direction. I'll allow her to hunt me, giving her enough sense of dominance so she fails to see the warning signs before it's too late.

"Baby, you can do anything you want."

"I usually do." Downing the glass, I signal the bartender for another. He leans over, taking my glass while giving me a knowing smirk. My bastard of a father once told me money was the root of all evil with sex and greed its lifelong companions. Where you find one, the other two are always lurking in the shadows.

Take, for instance, the bartender, he has seen and heard everything, yet has the gall to look at me, just as the blonde beside me is doing assuming, he can con me. My gut tells me the two of them aren't working together, although by the way his eyes flash to the blonde's hand on my suit, he either wants to fuck her or fuck her again. But Blondie is too stupid to look past his uniform to see his worth, giving the money he is trying to get from me; the prick is pulling some serious numbers on the side.

"Shall I charge this to your room, sir?"

He hovers the clear bottle over my glass, his hand steady so as not to spill a single, expensive drop, waiting for me to give the go-ahead for his charade to continue. The blonde beside me takes a drink of her wine and it wouldn't surprise me if she spent two minutes on her knees behind the bar, sucking his fucking dick for a free drink.

"Not this time."

Grabbing the back of his hand holding the bottle, I force him to tip the neck far enough for the liquid to come rushing out, filling my glass to the brim, the motion spilling a healthy portion to the napkin below.

"Sir, you—" He attempts to pull back, bending his knees, his body slumping against the bar due to the pain I'm inflicting.

"Next time you want to steal from someone, make sure they didn't have the same fucking drink a few hours ago, and for a third of the price!" Pressing harder against his digits, an oath of pain falls from his lips. Wrenching the bottle from his hand, I toss it onto the floor behind the bar, the sound of shattering glass causing the blonde to jump and spill her wine, her scream echoing in the room and irritating my nerves.

"That one is on you."

Downing the contents of the glass, the bartender stares wide-eyed and rubbing his wrist, beads of sweat begin to surface on his forehead. Narrowing my eyes in a glare, daring him to do something stupid like a call for security. Grabbing the wrist of the trembling blonde, knowing full well she doesn't have enough common sense to run from the situation, instead she will do anything I ask of her.

I head for the elevator, her heels click against the tiles, nearly tripping a few times as I don't shorten my gait for her. Sliding my key into the lock on the panel, Dominick has a relationship with the owners of the hotel, getting me the penthouse for as long and when ever I need.

The blonde presses herself into the corner of the lift, trying her best to hide the conflict in her mind. Her chest rises and falls with her labored breathing, her body telling me she's turned on by my bravado, yet scared shitless by it as well. Her eyes peruse me, sizing me up to evaluate if I'm worth the effort or if she should start screaming the second the elevator doors open.

"You do this often?"

Her voice is sexy but lacks the confidence she needs to chase away the fear she has rolling off her. I want to laugh at her, tell her to go home and stick with the little boys she is accustomed to playing with. How she should listen to the tiny voice inside her head, screaming for her to tuck tail and run. But I don't, I want to see how far she will take this, test the boundaries of her comfort level.

"Ride in an elevator? Occasionally."

I watch as she stiffens her shoulders and slides her body closer to mine, her lack of self preservation will play to my advantage and we will see if the smile she believes to be sexy will remain on her lips or replaced by angry words when her plan falls apart.

"No, not the elevator." Rounding my body to stand in front of me, her voice drops to a level I assume she thinks is sexy, most likely practiced and perfected in front of her bathroom mirror, and has worked on a multitude of horny and desperate men. Walking her manicured fingers along the edge of my jacket, trying her best to look alluring beneath her artificial lashes. "Finding the hottest bitch in the room and taking her upstairs."

I've always been a man who appreciates a confident woman, one who knows who she is and compliments you instead of competing for your attention. This girl, who I'm uncertain whether I want to know her name, is the latter, searching for a man who can take her with him, one who needs to show his colleagues he can snare a beautiful woman. My expression remains stoic, giving her no clue how her plan to seduce me is working. Something I am willing to gamble she isn't used to, given the clientele she is familiar with. My guess is she has gone after boys who want to be great men, but lack opportunity or the balls to go after what they want.

Opening the door to my room, an invitation to see where this road takes her. Her bottom lip trapped between her teeth and her confident eyes tell me how she envisions giving her best performance and winning my attention. Her confidence in her oral skills and the value others before me have given her enough hope she will be successful in landing my affections, or a fictional pregnancy she conjures up when I fail to call her after tonight.

Sadly, there will be no long aisle waiting for her, no church filled with flowers or the friendly faces of family and loved ones. This door leads to my enjoyment, and a lesson learned for her.

She looks behind her at the entrance to my room, wondering if she should proceed. If she were smart, she would hand me an excuse and get as far away from me as she can. But as she turns back, her eyes betray her, the blue orbs full of dollar signs and lust. I've given her ample opportunity to back out, but she has chosen to play with fire and who am I to deny her the chance to get burned?

With my tie buried in her clenched fist, an anchor for her to hold on to, she pulls me forward, pushing out her chest as a distraction in an attempt to confuse me

"Tell me, did you take a class to learn how to talk like that?" Extending the tip of her tongue out, brushing it seductively against the ridge of her front teeth. "Did you hear how much women like me are turned on by a foreign accent?"

Pulling my tie from her hand, questioning if she is this stupid or if this is a stalling tactic, a way to conjure up enough nerve to go further.

"I went to school, yes. But not to learn how to speak."

I push past her, not caring if she follows or presses the button for the lobby. Removing my jacket, allowing her to see the Glock I have tucked in the waistband of my trousers, before draping it over the back of the couch in the center of the room.

"So, this is real?"

Waving her fingers in my direction, a disbelieving look in her eyes. I don't give a shit if she believes me or not, my lineage isn't up for debate, as it plays no part in what will happen next. Crossing my arms over my chest, I wait to see what she does next. A seasoned professional would make the first move where a girl playing in her mum's shoes will want to keep talking, needing time to quiet the nerves pulsing in her ears.

"I've always had a thing for a man from London."

I could correct her, spell out for her how I'm from Scotland, but she will want to know more, and, it's none of her fucking business.

"Love how you guys pronounce your words, all sexy and shit."

Reaching behind her neck, she releases the tie of her dress, the fabric sags around her waist, her eyes never leaving mine as she pushes the black garment to the floor around her feet.

"I bet you could make me wet just by saying my name."

Stepping over the discarded fabric, her naked body inches closer. Her breasts are a decent size, dark nipples with a silver piece of jewelry through each one. Slender hips swaying with each step, blood red fingernails matching the glossy set of lips covering her teeth. Her blonde hair moves with each step; several curls caress the top of her breasts.

"Say, Destiny."

I don't take orders from many people; I can count on one hand how many have the privilege. The girl in front of me isn't one of them, no matter how creative she tries to be in changing her name.

"Get on your knees."

Unfolding my arms, I reach for the buckle of my belt. It's time to see what this bitch has to offer, and how quickly I can get her out of my room as her appeal from the bar is waning fast. The clang of my belt has her licking her lips, yet she remains standing before me as if waiting for me to scoop her up and take her to my bed. While I know nothing about this girl, I know my will is stronger; she needs me and not the other way around.

There's determination written all over her face, but the glistening skin at the apex of her thighs lets me know she is eager to taste me, have me swelling in the confines of her mouth, devouring me until I find my release.

Her eyes flash to my hand buried in the material of my pants, my fingers close to my cock, but not quite touching, an allusion I'm creating to push her further. Taking one final, timid step, she does as I say and drops to her knees like weights attached to them.

She licks her lips again, the red stain smearing on her pink tongue. The thought of the sticky shit on my junk is unappealing, something I want nothing to do with. Removing my hand from my pants, the handkerchief my mum insists I carry—a mark of a gentleman in her opinion—gripped between my fingers.

"Wipe your lips." Tossing the white square at her, I doubt this is what Lady Greer had in mind when she instructed me to offer it to a woman; thankfully she isn't here to judge. Destiny looks to the monogrammed square, and then back to me, with a shrug she complies, wiping several times until the color has faded to a dull pink stain.

Inserting my hand onto my pants, I wrap my hand around my now erect cock, stroking it twice, watching her vibrate as she waits for her first glimpse of my manhood.

"Open," I command, keeping my cock hidden from her view, heightening her arousal and giving me a bigger slice of entertainment. With a swallow, she complies, opening her mouth wide and sitting back on her heels.

Allowing my pants to dip down and moving the tales of my shirt to the side, I give her the first glance at what she has been waiting for.

"Oh my god! You're not circumcised."

Her reaction surprises me as a snorted laugh leaves my lips. With eyes wide she reaches out to touch me, it's as if she doesn't believe what is right in front of her.

"I've never seen one like this." Her index finger touches the skin covering the head, pushing it toward me, and then allowing it to slide back into place, repeating the process twice. Her fascination with the foreskin my parents chose not to remove is wearing thin on my nerves. I need her to suck my cock, not fucking play with it.

"Open your fucking mouth."

Her body jumps at the harshness in my tone, and she drops her hand back to her side, opening her mouth wide enough for me to slide my dick inside.

Her mouth is warm and wet as I venture in, her eyes wide open as I hit the back of her throat, gagging her enough to fill the corners of her lids with tears. She pulls back, collecting herself and swallowing hard. I suspect my lack of circumcision isn't the only thing she isn't accustomed to, it's clear she is used to dealing with much smaller cocks.

Adjusting her position, she reaches up to wrap her hand around the base of my shaft shoving the whole thing back into her mouth, minus the several inches which are too much for her. Bobbing her head as she sets a rhythm, her hand coming up to meet her lips. Destiny is all teeth and fake moaning, something I find boring and predictable.

Closing my eyes, I picture the girl from last night, the softness of her curves and the tattoo of an angel on her lower back. I'd taken her hard from behind, slamming my cock into her as she buried her face into the pillow, using her fingers to play with her clit as she searched to find her release.

Destiny was the polar opposite of Macy; one girl needing a good fucking while the other, the one tugging on my left nut, was out to fuck me over.

"You like that, baby? Your fat cock in my throat." She questions as she runs a flattened tongue on the underside of my shaft. Her voice crashes through my visual of the night before, pissing me off as she threatens to rob me of my release.

Placing her face between the palms of my hands, casting her a look I've used to separate a few panties from their owners, "What I would like is for you to shut the fuck up and suck my cock."

Before she can close her lips, I push into her mouth, past the waiting tongue and porn star lines, hitting the back of her throat as I push my way past her gag reflex. I didn't bring her up here to get to know her better or discuss the important things in our lives. She knew the second I pulled her off the barstool I wanted sex. Perhaps this will teach her to stay in the circles she is familiar with, leave the men, such as myself alone until she can handle the tiny dick school boys who fall for her bullshit lines and empty compliments.

My thrusts into her mouth grow sloppy while her saliva drips down her chin from the angle I have her head tilted in. She attempts to say something, and the vibration from her throat is enough to push me over the edge, my cum pulsing in spurts down her throat. As I pull out, a final burst catches her chin, mixing with the saliva creating a look of milk escaping her mouth.

Pulling my pants up, I step away from her, retrieving her forgotten dress from the floor and tossing it in her direction, landing on the couch beside her. Reaching into my pocket, I take out my money clip and slip off a few bills to send her on her way. She was a disappointment, giving me no better results than I could have achieved alone in the shower.

When I turn back around, her ass is in the air, knees buried in the cushions of the couch. A large tattoo of a leopard cover the majority of her back. Wanton eyes look back at me over her shoulder, as she wiggles her ass and plays with her clit, ready for me to fuck her. I have no interest in the over used pussy she is willing to give me, or even a repeat of the lackluster blowjob. Shaking my head, I clear the distance and toss the money on top of her crumpled dress, "Get dressed and get out."

"Are you fucking serious?" Destiny flips her body around as she shouts her disbelief for my demand. "I suck your dick, and that's it?"

I ignore her ramblings, she isn't worth a retort or the critical review I have for her lack of decent oral skills. My phone vibrates in my pocket, not caring enough to excuse myself or thank her, I answer the call as I challenge her with my eyes to say something.

"Hello."

"Ian? Hey, it's Finley. I didn't catch you at a bad time, did I?"

Hearing the voice of my best friend in the world causes a smile to tug at the corner of my lips. Not bothering to turn away to hide the conversation, or attempt to conceal the fact the caller is female.

"Baby, it is never a bad time when you call." Leaning back against the bar, I wished like hell I had grabbed the bottle from the bar instead of tossing it to the floor.

"Baby? What the fuck, Ian, you got a girl with you?"

"Unfortunately." Locking eyes with Destiny, she haphazardly tugs her dress over her hips, giving her every reason to believe my disgust has her name written all over it.

"Tell her to leave, or do you need me to be the pregnant wife who has gone into labor?"

"No, lass, I'm free to talk with you. How is your evening going?"

Destiny stumbles to put her heels on, shooting large daggers in my direction as she mumbles something about dried cum on her neck. Gathering the money I gave her, she looks at the bills in her hand and flips me off with the other as she stomps in the direction of the elevator. A smile grows on my face as I raise my middle finger in her direction; turning my back as the elevator doors close taking her back to the streets where she belongs.

"Got a call a few minutes ago I thought you might want to know about."

Dropping my tired body into the softness of the couch and letting my head fall back, I let out an exhausted breath. "From who?"

"Uh-uh, you know I keep my sources confidential. But, Ian, Darrow has been spotted in Italy."

Finley works for my mum, has since she was old enough to have a job. Where her beauty is abounding, her ability to kill a man with her bare hands is just as impressive. She's smart as fuck, constantly watching and learning from the men in our world, including keeping a few wagging tongues on her payroll.

"He with one of his whores or—?"

"He's with his mum. They were spotted leaving the train in Florence."

"How old is the intel?"

"Twelve hours, maybe less."

Darrow is as smart as he is deceptive, and I know he will take his time as they slither north, keeping his face hidden in the shadows and his name off the lips of the locals. I know where they are headed; the bottom dwellers would seek refuge in Florence and ultimately my villa.

"I haven't told Brion, my loyalty lies with the Family."

Finley had fallen hard for Declan's underboss, and he with her. But her dedication to our Family ran deep. It was never a question whose side she would stand on.

"I'll speak with Patrick since Declan is still on his honeymoon. See if I can get the hornet's nest stirred up."

"Okay, I'll let you know if I hear anything else. Enjoy your new lady friend."

"Trust me she was neither my friend nor a lady."

"Awe, poor Ian. You have such a talent for picking winners."

Another thing I love about Finley, how she isn't afraid to bust my balls, she is comfortable enough in herself and her abilities to stand up to me and most of my men. If she wasn't like my little sister, I would have married her in a heart beat.

Ending my call with Finley, I send off a text to Darrow. While he was cunning, and a self-proclaimed mastermind, he was shit compared to me on my worst day.

> I handled the Malloy's. You owe me for the fuck up in Chicago. I'll be in touch soon.

I didn't expect an immediate response, but less than a minute later my phone buzzed as I looked out over the New York City skyline.

> Sorry, Ian. You name it, and it's done.

Tossing my phone to the side, the events of the past few days catching up with me, rendering me both exhausted and excited. Darrow and Destiny could be soul mates, both out to screw everyone in their way. Perhaps if I didn't have the plans I did, I might be inclined to introduce them. Looking back at my phone, disappointment wraps around the thoughts in my mind. Darrow had been my friend almost as long as I have known Finley, the three of us enjoying one adventure after another. Everything changed when I chose not to take Finley as my wife, effectively handing her to my younger brother Blake. I assumed Darrow would keep his sworn loyalty to me, following my order by killing Blake and saving Finley from a life of horror. Instead, he had joined forces with Blake, taken the side of my enemy, and forced my hand in marking him as a traitor. Swiping my thumb against my screen, locating the contact I recently updated, I waited a few seconds for the call to connect, my heart falling slightly as a familiar voice answered.

"Hey, you got a minute? It's about Darrow."

CHAPTER TWO

HEATHER

I LOVE the smell of steaming milk. How the infused air creates millions of tiny bubbles, each bursting at the right moment to release the almond scent they hold. Although I am not fond of what the steam does to my hair; dampening the strands and making it appear as if I haven't washed it in a week. I'll take the trade-off as the calming effects are worth an extra shower after work.

"Heads up, Heather, Satan's spawn is here," Danielle, my coworker, and best friend whispers from beside me. The annoyance in her voice makes me shiver, and the hairs on the back of my neck stand up, ruining any Zen the foam had created. I don't have to turn around to know who was standing in line at the counter; I could feel the daggers hitting my back. Sweeping my limp bangs to the side, I bite the bullet and turn around to deliver the cappuccino I'd made.

"Here you go, Tony."

I slid the hot confection to the pea coat wearing man with blonde hair, his smile electric, and manners impeccable. Tony came in every day, purchased the same drink and left a sizable tip before he joined the other regulars in the far corner.

"Thanks, Heather," he winks, taking the saucer from my hand as he slips me the folded-up money. "You keep this for yourself this time." Tony knows we split all the tips, something we've done since the day I started. While I would love nothing more than to slide the money into my pocket and have a little extra at the end of my shift, I couldn't look at Gabe or Danielle in the eye if I did.

"Enjoy your coffee." I offer as he taps the counter twice before turning toward the others.

As much as I hate it, I've avoided the inevitable long enough, sucking in a deep breath, I turn and face the owner of the daggers who has taken her place at the counter.

"Welcome to *Aroma*. Our special today is two for one cappuccino."

Gabe, our new guy, rehearsed greeting was out before I could catch him. Knowing who stood before him and the level of wrath she could deliver, I should have been quicker.

"I know where I am, and I don't drink coffee." Slamming her oversized bag on the counter in frustration, the metal buckle clangs against the glass as she glares at Gabe over the top of her knock-off sunglasses. Destiny has an unhealthy obsession with animal prints, specifically leopard; evident by the skintight dress she painted on today. Huge hoop earrings dangle from her earlobes, the length of them spanning to the tops of her shoulders. Danielle surmised she must wear them to have somewhere to hook her ankles while whatever guy she is with fucks her in the ass.

"I want a latte with skim milk and two *Splenda*'s."

Holding up two fingers, showing off her new manicure in addition to the clarification she feels Gabe requires.

Bethany Palmer, known on the streets as Destiny, came in every day with the sole purpose of making my life a living hell. Originally from a small town in the Midwest, she and her older sister ran away from home the minute Bethany turned sixteen. According to rumors, the pair grew up in a devout Christian home, complete with a Baptist minister father and cookie-baking mum.

Bethany changed her name to Destiny when she and her sister discovered life in the big city was expensive, and they could earn more money by entertaining men than waiting tables. Destiny was always on the prowl, looking for the next deep pocket to crawl into and feed off. Her love of knock-off fashion is rivaled with her obsession with the regulars who sat in the corner. It's no secret she's hoping to one day get a better return on the blowjobs she boasts about giving them, landing one of the guys who laugh at her when she isn't listening.

"It's okay, Gabe. I've got her." Destiny's temper has cost us a fair number of employees. She berated anyone who questioned her choice in a latte when she claimed not to drink coffee, believing somewhere down deep the milk canceled out the caffeine. "It's time for you to take a break, anyway."

Danielle slides her drink across the counter, tapping my hip with hers letting me know she put full sugar and whole milk in her cup, with a double shot of espresso for good measure.

"On the house, Destiny."

She's so predictable, hand her something free, and she is instantly your best friend, willing to tell you everything going on in her life.

"No sugar, right? You know I don't eat sugar."

"Made it the same as always, just for you."

Her eyes brighten, and I know a story is about to come spewing out of her mouth. Just like the steamed milk, Bethany was full of hot air. It's always the same: how she snagged a rich guy the night before and how much money he spent on her, the fancy restaurant he took her to, what penthouse she spent the night in, and lastly how small his dick was. According to Destiny, every man who had money also had a tiny dick, unless of course, the man attached to the appendage was sitting at the table of men in the corner. Made men, in her opinion, did everything big, including growing monster cocks.

Sucking the straw between her lips, her cheeks hollow from the force of her suction as she closes her eyes, letting the chilled liquid enter her mouth. I have to look away to keep from snickering, hoping she doesn't suck as hard when some poor guy's dick is between her lips. Holding back a laugh when I imagine the dick starting out large, only to be severed by the *Hoover* lips she possesses.

"Oh god, that feels better."

She barely takes a breath as she begins to spill the exploits from last night's encounter. I half listen to her tells us of the guy who found her in a bar, bought her several drinks, and then had dinner sent up to his room. How he showered her with money and diamonds, watching the sun come up over the New York City skyline.

"Oh, and I have to grab Cindy a hot tea."

Cindy is her older, and slightly wiser, sister. Last year Cindy found the wrong guy to take her to his penthouse. Instead, he dragged her behind a dumpster in an alley a few blocks north, beat the shit out of her and left her for dead. He broke a few ribs and gave her a concussion, but it was the slash across her face and left eye that woke her up. Now she works for the dry cleaner owned by Frank, my boss. She spends her time in the back, with more steam than I can imagine, keeping her scarred face hidden from the world.

"Three-fifty," Danielle tells her as she rings up the beverage. The bell on the door chimes and the air fills with the rancid cologne as the other pain in my ass swaggers through the door.

Destiny hands over her card, continuing her story of how the guy from last night had called her several times this morning, wanting her to be in his penthouse when he returned from his meeting later this afternoon.

"You got another card? This one was declined."

Destiny's face pales and then flushes hard with anger. "That's impossible; you fucked it up! Scan it again."

Danielle swipes the card again, but the same red warning flashes at the bottom of the screen. "Sorry, girl. It's declined again." Sliding the bankcard across the counter in Destiny's direction.

"What the fuck? I'm not your girl. I have a name, and you better learn to use it." Tossing the full cup of iced coffee in Danielle's direction, she and I both move to the right as the cup hurls by us, smashing against the wall and the tile below.

"Hey, hold up, Shorty. What's the damage here?"

Mayo, a street thug from the neighborhood, whose real name is Malcolm Hayes, walks up beside her, sliding his arm around her shoulders and pulling her in. He's dressed in his usual gold and black, representing the gang he wishes would let him in. It's a miracle he hasn't been jumped for being stupid enough to wear their colors without being a member. He comes in a few times a week, scavengers around for any crumbs Frank will let him have. He and Destiny are a lot alike, both trying to be someone they aren't. Where Destiny wants to be the eye candy for one of the guys in the corner, Mayo wants to be a player for one of the local gangs. Too bad he is too stupid to realize the name they tagged with him is a pun and has no street creds attached.

"Oh hey, baby. Where have you been this morning?" Destiny has no shame as she purrs in what she thinks is a sexy tone, knowing Mayo will fall to her feet, letting her scratch him behind the ear like the lap dog he is. Willing to do whatever she needs just to get a little taste of her. I wonder if it works for anyone else? Or are the men she boasts about composed of more imagination than actual flesh and blood?

"Waiting to see your beautiful face."

Destiny uses the attraction Mayo has for her to get what she wants from him. I know he hasn't managed to sleep with her yet as he would have bragged to anyone who would listen how he bombed a shorty. She has him convinced there is a chance, but when she is in here with her friends, they laugh just as loud as the made men do about her.

"Is there a problem, Heather?"

Frank Cicconi, my boss and owner of *Aroma,* stands beside me. He is a massive man, measuring well over six-feet and closing in on two hundred and fifty pounds. His Italian heritage is evident in his dark hair and olive skin. Catch him in a bad mood, and he'll share with you how fluent in Italian he is and how despite his advanced age, his fists work just fine.

For as hard-core as he is, he has an enormous soft side as well, always helping people in need. I came in one afternoon on my way home from school, and he offered me a part-time job. I never planned on staying as long as I have, but when life handed me a shit sandwich, Frank let me work full time.

"No problem, man. Baby girl here got excited when she saw me and knocked over her drink." Mayo wears a gold bandana tied across his forehead, the flap of it draped over his left eye. He reminds me of a movie character from the eighties instead of the real guys who run the streets.

"That right, Heather?" Frank's eyes flash to mine, crossing his arms over his chest, his massive size intimidating, to say the least. But his heart is as big as his body and would have no issue tossing the pair of them into the street. Rule number one for working at *Aroma,* you didn't see anything. No matter who walks through the door or what they said or did, when anyone asks you what happened, you play stupid.

"Yes, Frank. It was an accident." It was my rehearsed response; anytime something went down in here, it was always an accident.

"Here," Mayo hands over a crumpled twenty-dollar bill, and I have to question where he got it as he doesn't have a job. "Let me pay for her order," Frank questions it too as he eyes Mayo cautiously, nodding his head to Danielle to go ahead and take the money. He turns to walk back to his corner, stopping briefly to greet a couple who had come in earlier and were now holding hands and looking over one of those tourist maps. Frank lowers his body into his chair, his years of hard living evident in the grimace he tries to hide, he raises an arm and points to the table of empty cups, "Heather, the boys need a warm up."

Destiny's eyes light up, and I know what she is going to say before she opens her mouth. Spinning around as fast as I can, hoping to avoid adding yet another issue to the list she has with me already.

"Hey, Heather, I need to ask a favor from you." Glancing over my shoulder, the smell of the steaming milk keeping my nerves at a decent level. I didn't bother to say anything as I knew what she wanted.

"When you get finished making those, let me take them to the table."

The trouble with Destiny is she spends too much time focusing on her next con, and not enough figuring out her shit. Relying on her good looks and willingness to screw for money, instead of being smart and finding her own way.

Granted she was dumber than homemade dirt, but she had the potential to be self-supporting. Those guys in the corner had many girls they kept on the side, but when it came to taking a girl home to see their mum, and more importantly Mrs. Santos for Sunday dinner, Destiny would never fit in.

Where Mayo has eyes for Destiny, she had her whole world centered on Dominick Santos. When he married Anna, her world shattered to hell, and she refocused her energy on the table of regulars she thinks can make her happy.

"You know I can't do that, Destiny. Frank would have my ass if I let a customer serve his guys."

"Ugh, you're such a bitch."

Pushing past Mayo, she looks at the table of guys one last time before she propels open the glass door and storms out.

It's always the same with her; from the first time we met she has chased the golden ticket, trying to win the affection of a powerful man. On one side, I can completely agree as I too have romantic ideations of the men involved with organized crime. On the other, I understand the inner workings of the Family, how the women who were chosen to stand beside these men had the approval of the Patriarch of the family. While the men provided, the women protected the close-knit inner circle, using their heads to choose the right lady, instead of lust.

Everyone who has lived in this neighborhood for a decent length of time knows this place is a favorite hangout for members of the Mafia. It's part of the reason I've stayed here so long, the nostalgia, and mystery surrounds me in every corner. Frank himself is a semiretired hit man, occasionally working for Dominick Santos. He holds a self-titled role of Public Affairs for the Santos Family, squashing rumors in the street before they build merit.

The walls of *Aroma* are filled with photos of celebrity actors who have come here to get a feel for the roles they were about to play. A number of authors have sat down with Frank, listening as he feeds them bullshit stories they could have found on the cinema screens in Hollywood, getting juicy tidbits they can twist and turn onto paper. One day he came in, pulled his gun from his jacket and emptied the magazine into the surrounding walls. When a well-known director sat down with him a few hours later, he told him the bullet holes came from a rival Family, one he purchased the shop from. We all had a good laugh about it after the guy left. Frank was been given the store when Santos had a man who couldn't pay for a job they'd done for him. I never understood why people would seek out men like Frank and Mr. Santos, only to be surprised when they wanted payment for their services, taking pieces of you when restitution wasn't paid.

I can remember listening to the stories my father would tell my mum and me about his time as a member. All the exciting things he did for the Family, the places he visited and the people he met. The number one thing he told me about men in the Mafia was if you couldn't impress their mum you needed to walk away. My mum said he gave it all up to be with her, raise me and live a peaceful life. She spoke fondly of their time in Scotland, how they defied the odds and let their love blossom. Yet there was always a sense of sadness in her eyes, one she would brush off as a piece of dust, telling me everything was all right.

Not a moment went by my father and mum didn't tell each other how much they loved one another. When my dad became ill, my mum quit her job to take care of him, spending as much time as she could before we lost him. Ironically, she ignored her own health, and by the time she was diagnosed with cancer during a trip to the emergency room, it was too late, and she died three months later. My father was heartbroken and slipped into a bout of depression. He made me promise I would someday take their ashes back to Scotland, so they could return home together He died on a Thursday, the ring my mum wore on her pinky clenched in his hand. He left me with a small insurance policy, but his medical bills, and living in New York, had taken the majority of it quick and I had to leave school and begin to work full time. Now their urns sit on the mantle, their picture and rings between them. I hope to fulfill my promise someday, find the place my mum spoke so fondly of and return them to the land they loved.

"Excuse me, gentleman." Placing a fresh cup in front of each man and picking up the dirty ones as I went. Tony pushes a tip into my apron pocket, his attempt once again to get me to keep it. "Let me know if I can get you anything else."

Danielle and Gabe were huddled at the end of the bar, the spill from earlier now clean and the smell of pine mixing with the aroma of fresh coffee. Piling the dirty cups and saucers into the sink, it doesn't take a second before the pair make their way over and join me.

"Heather, tell Gabe he worries too much."

Focusing my attention on the dishes, ignoring the bait Danielle dangled before my face, she was a smartass and loved to goat people into engaging in her game. Gabe is a big guy who is scared of his own shadow, afraid one of the guys behind us is going to shoot him for looking at them wrong. "Gabe, you worry too much."

Danielle's mouth drops as she looks at me, "I'm serious." Slapping my shoulder with her soapy hand, bubbles fly in several directions, a few land in her hair causing us both to snicker.

"He's freaked out about Santos coming by this afternoon."

Leaning back to look around her, Gabe has his head down and a frown on his face. His dark curls drifted onto his forehead, giving him more of the boyish charm I admire about him.

"Seriously, Gabe?"

Keeping his eyes trained on drying the clean dishes, shrugging his shoulder to avoid a real answer. I stop washing the cup in my hand, letting it drop back into the soapy water and fall to the bottom of the sink with a thud.

"Gabe, you have nothing to worry about. He's bringing some guy he knows to look at the building. Santos has been trying to sell several properties he owns to welcome some new blood into the neighborhood."

Gabe raises his head, shifting his green eyes in my direction. "You swear, Heather?" His voice doesn't match his mammoth size, and I want to hug him and take the sadness from his green orbs.

"Mark my words, the two of them will come in the door, say hello to Frank and head directly upstairs. They won't even know you are in the room."

Gabe looks to the door at the end of the counter, its black paint, and Franks warning, giving nightmares to even the bravest soul. Rule number two of working in this shop; never, under any circumstances, go upstairs. I have my suspicions of what is up there, but no one except Santos and Frank knows. Gabe is so freaked out by the door at the end of the room; he won't get any closer than the end of the counter, worried something would jump out a grab him.

"Okay, but if I get killed before I meet my future wife, I'm holding you responsible."

* * *

STARING DOWN AT THE CASH IN MY HAND, EVEN AFTER THE DECENT tip Tony and the other guys left, I barely have enough to buy myself a decent dinner and the subway ride home. Frank gave us the afternoon off so Santos and the potential buyer could have a private look around. On the one hand, it was great, an afternoon to myself with nothing to do. On the other, I could use the money as rent was due in three weeks. After my father died, the landlord made me sign a new lease, increasing the monthly rent by eighteen hundred dollars, it took everything I had to make it each month.

"Heather, toss the pastries from today into the alley, let the homeless have a treat tonight."

Frank may have killed his fair share of men, but he also looked out for the folks in the neighborhood. He had a shed built out back so the homeless could have somewhere to sleep when it rained, and he was a primary sponsor of the youth sports teams.

"Already did," I called out to him, keeping the two I stuck in my bag a secret. Frank had no idea how close to joining the homeless I was. For the past few weeks I'd been searching for job openings outside of New York, somewhere I could afford a little easier, maybe go to school as I planned.

Frank sat in his chair in his office, a tiny, cramped area he could barely turn around. The top of his desk was layered with papers and a single, dust-covered lamp, which worked half the time, hung limply over the corner of his desk. His black, thick-rimmed glasses are dangling from his right hand, the need for them remained in this office, and out of sight from the guys out front.

"Good girl. Now get out of here."

Grabbing my cup of leftover cappuccino, I toss my bag over my shoulder and head for the door. If I'm lucky, I could stop by the market and get home in time to watch one of those cheesy afternoon movies, getting lost in the drama of someone else's life.

Pushing open the door, I called over my shoulder letting him know I would lock up. Just as I turned back around, I smacked into something solid, the lid of my cup popping off from the force, the hot liquid covering the front of my white blouse and dousing whatever I hit.

"Shite, are you okay?"

Two solid hands grab hold of me, knocking my cup to the side-walk below. The shock of it finally registers, as I jumped back from the burn on my chest, pulling the soiled fabric away from my burned skin. Scanning my eyes up the body of my victim, his white shirt, and silver tie now stained brown.

"Oh my god, I am so sorry!" Searching around for something to help clean him up, pulling my used apron from my bag. "I wasn't paying attention, and—" I've read about love at first sight a million times, watched it play out by some of Hollywood's most talented actors. But to experience it, to live it first hand, is nothing in compari-son. Time stops, and the world around me fades into the shadows, my breath leaves me as my need for oxygen has left me along with my ability to think.

"I'm fine, are you okay?"

Blue eyes, like two identical sapphire stones, glisten back at me. Coal black hair, combed back in a relaxed style, a moderate smat-tering of facial hair masking the chiseled jaw of this incredible man.

His deep voice, thick with the accent my parents worked so hard to cover, wrapping me in a level of comfort I thought I'd lost.

"I'm all right," I mumble, my thoughts coming back to the present as his grip on me tightens. "Embarrassed, but fine." I laugh, nervously. Shifting my attention to the man beside him, I see a familiar pair of topaz eyes looking back at me, his amused grin bringing an additional layer of embarrassment.

"Mr. Santos, always a pleasure." Extending out my hand, but quickly recoiling as I remember it is covered in sticky coffee.

"Mr. Cicconi is waiting inside for you."

Dominick nods his head in affirmation, his eyes trained on the man I'd plowed into, a broad smile curling up the right side of his face as he pushes past me and into the door of the café. A gentle breeze sends my bangs into my eyes, a harsh reminder of how horrid I look at the end of my shift. Lifting my sticky hand, pushing the damp hair out of my face, clearing my view of his perfect face.

"I'm sorry, I didn't catch your name?"

His hand extended out in my direction, my eyes drift down past his tailored jacket, the fit created by skilled hands and not an assembly line, to his long fingers. Dark stains mar the edge of his white cuffs. Thankfully, the black and silver watch on his wrist appears to have avoided the catastrophe of running into me. My embarrassment increases as I realize I've been staring at his hand for far too long, sweeping my eyes to his, with as much confidence as I can muster.

"Heather." My voice cracks, fueling the blaze of embarrassment burning inside me. Sliding my hand in his still outstretched fingers, an uncontrolled smile takes over my face. "Heather Murray."

Tightening his grip on my hand, a hint of mystery sparkles in his eyes, as the tip of his tongue comes out to lick his lips, and I watch, my breath hitching inside my chest as the trail he makes caressing the tender flesh, leaving a glossy shine in its path.

"Heather, a beautiful Scottish name for such an exquisite young lass,"

His accent is familiar, yet much stronger than my father's was which I contribute to the years he spent in the States. Butterflies dance in my belly as he says my name and I can't help but imagine what it would be like to have his whisper it into my ear as he loves me, completing the fantasy I've created in my head.

"My name is Ian McLeod." The base in his voice shakes the very core of me, filling certain crevices with a need I'd long forgotten. Caring for my father had chased a fair share of men from my door; the ones who'd lingered for any amount of time weren't worth the effort or loss of sleep I would've had to sacrifice too much in order to keep their attention. However, judging from the way my body reacts to Ian, I'd be willing to give up a few hours of sleep to spend a little time with him.

Ian breaks the bubble as he looks down at his shirt, a single stream of coffee drips off the edge of his tie and I know it's ruined, not even Cindy could get the coffee stain out.

"Mr. McLeod, I've ruined your shirt. I'm so sorry; I swear I can replace it." Using the apron in my hand in an attempt to dry off any remaining streams of coffee. "I assume you are staying with Mr. Santos during your visit?"

It didn't take a rocket scientist to figure out Ian was the leader of another Family. Santos was a smart man and would want to sell to a someone who would bring something beneficial to the table.

"I'm staying at a local hotel." Reaching out, he stills my hand with the apron, dipping his head to the side in order to capture my attention. "If you're sincere in your apology for ruining my shirt, then you'll agree to have dinner with me tonight, in my suite."

Saying no to a request from a man in Ian's position isn't good for my health. Besides, I can't deny the attraction I have for him. And while I know the encounter most likely will be brief, and no promise of any future, I still want to. The eternal romantic side of me begs to live a little, allowing a man in Ian's position to touch me and make me feel like a woman again. I'm about to tell him how much having dinner with him would thrill me, when the voice I dread more than anything comes from my right.

"Hey, baby, are you following me?"

Destiny prances over to us, her ankles protesting the height of her heels against the uneven pavement of the concrete, her walk resembling that of a newborn fawn. Recalling the particulars of the story she shared with Danielle and I earlier about the rich guy she landed last night. As much as I wanted to convince myself her story was fabricated inside her mind, a fantasy created by the desires locked inside. All the facts added up and matched perfectly to the man standing before me.

With the way I internally cringe every time I accidentally touch her hand as I give her a cup of her non-coffee latte, there is no way I would consider being in the same room as the man she fucked last night.

"I'm sorry, Mr. McLeod. I don't think your girlfriend would approve of my company."

Pulling my bag, and a considerable chunk of my dignity off the ground, I shoot him a polite smile as I prepare to walk away. "I'll make sure to have a new shirt and tie delivered to your hotel room before you leave. The penthouse, correct?"

I don't wait for an answer; the humiliation, which borders on anger, builds the tears blurring my view of the street before me. I've never envied Destiny, felt sorry for her, hated the shit out of her, but never envied, at least not until this moment.

CHAPTER THREE

IAN

"You HAVE four thousand square feet of open space, plus two private offices in the back. Loft-style space over the back half of the building."

Dominick picked me up early this morning, showing me all the places he told me about and was anxious for me to see.

"I've taken the liberty of inviting one of the local gangs my Family uses for distribution and some cleanup, to meet the new owner."

Closing the lid to his briefcase, the agreed upon sale price in cash for this and two other buildings tucked away.

"Pretty presumptive, don't you think?" Standing to my full height, the single light bulb dangling from the low ceiling, casting its harsh glow to the table before us. Tiny dust particles float in the air as Dominick rises from his chair and hands the briefcase to one of his men beside him.

"Call it intuition, but something told me you would be happy with what I had to offer."

Dominick had a team of men with him, something I traditionally did back in Scotland. But here in the States, I assumed the risk would be low, and told my men to stay home and have a little time to themselves. Climbing the steps, I checked out the ceiling and the lack of available exits as we inch higher, I was beginning to regret not having some muscle on my side. Dominick's men reached the top of the stairs first, opening the metal door and moving to the side. Casting a final look around, I step over the threshold. My gut said I could trust the Santos family, but my father's voice in the back of my mind reminds me he wasn't a Scot, and therefore came with a forked tongue.

Inside the room was a long table, with high-back chairs on all sides. A pitcher of water and several glasses rested in the center, a plate of pastries and fruit to the left.

"Gentleman, I appreciate you coming on such short notice. I'd like to introduce you to the new owner and Boss of your territory."

Four sets of brown eyes looked back at me, each wearing matching yellow and black ball caps with MSS on the front.

"Ian McLeod, this is T-Bone, he is the leader of this group and the man you'll call if you have an issue."

The large black man with a dragon tattoo on his neck stands up and offers me his hand. I noticed the gold ring on his index finger, another dragon with red-jeweled eyes.

"Nice to meet you, brah."

"Pleasure."

Shaking his hand, I kept my face neutral, another lesson my father taught me. Men will judge you on the firmness of your handshake and the validity of your word, keep your face tight and make them guess what you're thinking, keep your word and they will never question your authority. T-Bone isn't the first gang leader I've had an affiliation with, but just like the others before him, he knows to stand and acknowledge me. Failing to do so would be a sign of disrespect, earning him a bullet between his eyes. It doesn't matter if I don't appeal to him, the unwritten rules are clear and violating them isn't a thought in his mind. Tucking myself into a chair close to Dominick, I pull out my cell and send a message to Cadan, the man I chose to replace Darrow before I left. I'd assumed, when I made arrangements to see these properties with Dominick, it would be between the two of us, maybe a representative with his financial interests. Never in a million years did I think I would have a sit-down meeting with a group of gang members fresh out of the gate.

"Gentleman, considering your substantial interest in the neighbor-hood, and the business changing hands, I felt it necessary to bring everyone together from the beginning."

Dominick Santos was a polished, confident, and intimidating indi-vidual, much like his father, Antonio. My dad hated Antonio, said he was too soft with his men and his wife and Family. I found him to be a solid leader, one who passed on his knowledge to his son, a man I had no issue doing business with.

"I can assure you, the McLeod Family is nothing like what you were used to dealing with when the Gallo's ran things."

Alex Gallo, the former Family leader, had fallen into a pit of his own making. His need to be in the top position, caused him to lose everything, including his life. He crawled into bed with the wrong people, plotting against Dominick's family to gain more territory, but it had backfired. Not surprising, my father looked favorably on Gallo, blaming the Santos when Gallo turned up dead in his jail cell. Yet, he kept his distance instead of confronting Santos and sticking up for his alleged friend, claiming he felt our Family's interests needed to stay in Scotland. The truth was, my father lacked any real courage, hiding behind his cruel words and actions, terrorizing his Family and associates, building fear in the people closest to him.

I, however, didn't agree with most of what he did and the moment I walked away from his grave, I began seeking out avenues to broaden our assets. Changing the way our Family did business, and how I presented myself. Growing this beard, something he detested, enforcing his belief a proper man shaved every day. I wanted nothing to do with his brand of proper, or any of the other idiosyncrasies he attempted to give me.

I purchased the estate of Velenići Porchelli, an Italian Family who had taken on the Malloy Family and lost. I tried to buy the property he owned in the States, but Dominick had beaten me to it.

As Dominick boasted of how things would change, I watched as T-Bone, and his men, nodded and spoke quietly to each other, light gleaming off the gold outlining their front teeth.

"What do you think, Ian?"

Shifting my hips in my seat, dragging my thumb across my prickly chin, each time I felt or saw my beard, it was like sending another rot in hell message to my father. Drifting my eyes in Dominick's direction, the edges of his lips lift in a smirk. By the way he leans back in his seat, he assumed I hadn't been paying attention as he spoke of the way the men at the table conducted business. How they had grown up in the neighborhood and suffered several losses of men who had inspired them, taught them how to defend what was theirs and leave their mark behind. Leaning my upper body over the table, I fold my hands together as if in prayer; looking directly in the eyes of the man across from me "I believe you and I have more in common than you think." Nodding in T- bones direction, punctuating my point, his smile vanishing and eyes squint in confusion.

"How you figure, Mick?"

Anger stirs in my chest, causing me to clench the back of my teeth to control the rage which was brewing rapidly. With the pleasantries over, he was baiting me, sizing me up to see how far he could push me. A lesser man would have back peddled, complimented the shit out of him and crawled into the fetal position in the corner. I had never been that man, never been allowed to show emotion, or let anyone around me smell the putrid scent of fear radiate off me. According to my father, it came down to who was the bigger man, and proving it to the rest of the world. Time to show him who owned the bigger dick at this table.

"First of all, it's Jock and not Mick, show some fucking respect and learn some god damn geography." The guy sitting to the left of T-Bone snickers, tips his head to the side and sucks air through his teeth.

"Something funny, motherfucker?"

Before he can answer, I slam my right hand over the tip of his fingers, the blade I keep inside my sleeve scoring his flesh. His cry rings out as he attempts to pull his hand back, crimson droplets forming a pool of blood on the table. T-Bone looks to the injured man, motioning with his head for him to leave the room. The pussy wastes no time as he jumps to his feet, holding the bleeding digits to his chest, hitting the metal door and running down the steps. T-Bone's eyes return to mine, showing no real concern for the man who left the room.

"You must get a lot of pussy with the way you talk."

His attempt to chase away the tension in the room is clever but unappreciated. I'm not my father, and I'll be damned if I let him think I can be easily swayed with a cheap ass compliment.

"Why don't you ask your mum?"

His eyes dilate, and I know I found the crack in his defenses. I can sit here all day, going toe to toe with him until I have him launching himself across the table. This isn't about hurtful words, this is about boundaries and how far you're willing to go to cross them.

"You believe we are the same. How Mic—McLeod?"

It's the best white flag I'm ever going to get. Wars are won by the number of small battles you have in your favor, gaining ground by not backing down. He knows he is outnumbered when it comes to brains and quick wit, what he doesn't know, and hopefully never will, is how defeated he is when it comes to how under-manned he is.

"The color of your uniform, yellow. The same color my Family chose hundreds of years ago to represent us. The tattoo on your neck," Shrugging out of my jacket, I roll up my left sleeve. "My family crest, the crown we hold and the pride in our Scottish blood."

Tapping my fingernail to the enamel of my teeth, "What's with the gold?"

T-Bone huffed and shook his head. "Back in Africa, where our black asses come from, gold is as common as water, nothin' special. But in our neighborhood, that shit is everything; your name, your status. It separates the nobodies from the somebodies. We all were born broke, so we tryin' to die rich, that's why we will never let this gold shit go."

"And the letters on your hat? What do they mean?"

"Market Street Saints. It's where we all live, and Saints because we are trying to save our streets from the other Sets who think they can walk on the sidewalk and not in the street."

I understood where he was coming from. Walking on the sidewalk meant you felt like you belonged, walking in the street kept you as an outsider, with no real business being there. This was a turf issue, protecting what they felt was theirs.

"Tell you what..." Studying T-Bone's face, watching his team as they moved their heads back and forth between his and mine, each man waiting for a signal this had turned sour, or a new deal had been struck. "I like your cantor, as a sign of good faith, I'm willing to make you and your associates an offer. For the next six months, you take an additional ten percent for yourselves on everything you sell for me. An additional twenty percent on any new business you bring with repeat purchases. You keep my property safe, and we will discuss this again in six months. Do we have a deal?"

T-Bone studied my face for several minutes; I could see the war raging in his eyes, questioning the complete stranger sitting before him. The man offering more money in his pocket and into the mouths of those he was responsible for feeding. But to trust a man he didn't know, one with apparent influential ties, was risky. More time than I'm comfortable with passes, his eyes slanting as he continues to study my face. Just as I'm about to stand up and walk out, a triumphant smile splits his face.

"All right White Boy, you got a deal."

* * *

"I HAVE ONE LAST PROPERTY TO SHOW YOU BEFORE WE HEAD TO THE coffee shop." Dominick couldn't believe I had offered the Market Street Saints such a huge increase over what they earned working for Gallo. I was using my father's belief in the greed of people and their lust for money to make things easier for my transition. While I hated my father and most of what he stood for, I did appreciate the lessons he left me from the failures he experienced, and the ramblings he learned from his father.

"It's an apartment building a developer I know recently finished, but not before being arrested for fraud. The investors are scrambling to sell the building, for a fraction of what it's worth."

Dominick knew me too well, I loved the smell of desperation in business. It's what I'm good at, something my father never took advantage of. His need to keep his thumb on the pulse of the people who feared him instead of finding new ways of making the Family prosperous. I, on the other hand, loved the thrill of a good gamble, tossing the dice and seeing what lady luck handed you.

"Are you one of those scrambling investors?"

Pulling his attention away from the stalled traffic, the humorless smile on his olive-colored face tells me he is as smart in business as I am. Always have an ace in the hole and an exit to take when the shit starts to rise.

"They chose to seek out more... traditional financing,"

Shaking my head, I turned to look at the pedestrians walking past on the sidewalk. Most people assumed men like myself and Dominick dealt in drugs, guns and women. Which we did, but it wasn't all we invested our time and money in. I would challenge anyone to find a product hands like ours, haven't touched.

"But when the bottom falls out." He begins.

"We are the first ones they call." I finish, humor laced in my reply.

Dominick pulls up to a tall glass building, the front resembling a hotel you would find in South Florida or the Mediterranean. Sandstone pillars divided tall archways while elaborate drop lighting graced the front entrance. Large wooden doors blocked anyone from seeing the interior lobby, and oversized metal handles granted entry onto the first floor.

"There are ten apartments left, including the penthouse. I won't waste your time by showing you anything other than the best. The owner is eager to sell, but not willing to give it to you either." Pulling an odd-looking key from his pocket, he waves it over a black pad which was positioned to the left of the door. A red light shifts to green as the click of a lock sounded within. "Each resident has their own door key like this, programmable to open automatically as they approach in the event of rain or snow."

"No doorman?"

My mum had always been a stickler for having a man open a door for her, something my father taught, but never performed. She instilled in me everything he wasn't, swearing to make me the man he could never be.

"They are in the process of hiring. Dragging their feet a little until the penthouse is sold."

The lobby reminded me of the home we owned in Edinburgh. Elaborate gold finishes with pale blue accents. While I didn't care much for the décor, my mum would feel as if she died and gone to heaven, having a flair for French Provincial furnishings.

"There is a decent level of security here, closed circuit television and twenty-four-hour armed guards."

My silence says it all, any security a place like this could provide would be nothing compared to the firepower I have on the way here. I'd been foolish to take this trip alone, my business sense clouding my better judgment and I imagine my father laughing from his seat in hell.

"The floors are Italian marble, something I suspect you know a little about. But the view is what sets this place apart from the rest."

Reaching the elevators, Dominick presses a button on the same small card he used to open the front door.

"The remote is fingerprint critical, with the only override coming from your authority or a preset password with security."

Gold accented doors open in a silent motion, as soft music is pumped overhead. Lady Greer will be hard pressed to find any flaws with this building once a doorman is hired of course. The doors close just as quietly as they opened, and I barely feel the motor engaging.

'Good afternoon, Mr. Santos. Penthouse, arriving.'

My surprised eyes flash to Dominick, his cheeky smile shining back at me, "Fastest elevator in the continental US. Twelve floors in less than fifteen seconds. Automated greeting for those who need to have their egos stroked."

Lady Greer would be one of those who felt the need to have her name announced, even if it was by a computer. Lord knows I love my mum and would do anything in my power to make her happy, but she did have a challenging nature. She came by it rightfully so, having to deal with the cruelty my father handed to her. His hate filled vitriol cutting her to the quick, but never breaking her.

The elevator door opens, revealing a stark white hall with a single door across the marble tile. I felt better knowing the lift didn't open into the penthouse, allowing a place to add additional sentries. My mum wouldn't care for the sterility of the all-white, something she would hire a team to fix for her. Dominick opened the door to the penthouse, no key or magic pad this time, something else I would change before I allowed my mum to sleep even one night inside. Black and white tile, laid down in an intricately designed pattern, graced the foyer. A solid black marble table rested in the center of the pattern. The chandelier which mimicked the design of the floor, hung from the cathedral ceiling.

"Eighteen-foot ceilings, highest the building codes will allow, are throughout. Blue-tooth enabled instruction for everything from the microwave to the blinds and even the soaker tub in the master bath. Four bedrooms and five baths. This particular unit comes with a butler and chef, a daily maid service is available for a nominal fee."

My mum would rather cut off her own arm than have someone she didn't select herself cooking and cleaning for her. She would love the grandeur of the space, the view from high above everyone else and access to the endless shopping the city provides. Her birthday was in another month, and this would be something she wouldn't expect. Plus, it would give Finley an excuse to stay in the States and closer to Brion.

"What's the asking?"

"Three million."

"Million five, all cash, and you can keep the hired help. My men will be here in a matter of hours and will need full access to the security program."

Dominick had his phone to his ear as I turned from the mid-city view. Allowing him some privacy, I stepped onto the balcony, the sun shining down on the white painted exterior. Several topiary trees, in decorative planters, greeted me from the side. A statue of a Greek goddess stood to watch over the vegetation, another feature my mum would appreciate.

Leaning over the railing, I could see the back of the building and the remaining construction materials being packed away into a large truck. The men were working as a team to clear the area, making the remnants of their efforts disappear like the for sale sign in the front lobby. I wondered how far Market Street was from here, did the men I had on my payroll pass by on the sidewalk? Or did the shiny new exterior send out a warning, intimidating them with high-tech barriers?

"Cash offer accepted. And if you're willing to go up to two million, there is one more apartment left on the third floor. You could use it for legitimate income."

"One million-eight," I retorted, not tearing my eyes from the cars below. I would keep the apartment below a secret from the watchful eye of my mum. I could have an area for me and my needs while I was here on business. Most every man in my position had a place he kept to himself, letting a few beautiful women lay their heads and other parts of their bodies, keeping your hobbies out of the wife's view.

"Come on, Ian. Tell me you can't afford two hundred thousand more?"

Turning from the activity on the street, we were up too high to hear the majority of the chaos from below, one less thing for my mum to find wrong with her gift.

"My ability to afford it or not, is none of your concern. I countered your offer. It's up to you to take it or leave it."

Blue eyes locked with topaz, another battle for dominance, and the winner getting the better deal. "Fine you cheap Jock. A million-eight."

* * *

"IF YOU WANT A DECENT CUP OF COFFEE, THERE IS ONLY ONE PLACE you should ever go."

As we pulled out of the parking garage, Dominick points out where the corner store and bakeries were located. Turning the corner, my cell vibrates in my pocket. Pulling it out, I look at the screen to see a message from Cadan McCord, my new Underboss. Growing up on the streets, the youngest of twelve brothers, he learned to fight for every morsel of food he ever ate. He went to work for my father when he was twelve as a lookout for the authorities, then moved up to a collector when he turned eighteen. The bastard loves to fight, picking up as many rounds as he can down at the arena. Women flocked to him with his coal black hair and blue eyes; his tough guy bravado didn't hurt his love life either.

> Hold on to your knickers. I'm in the air.

I snickered at his choice of words. Cadan had an incredible sense of humor, quick witted and a card-carrying smartass.

"Everything okay?"

Pocketing my phone, I nod my head. "Yes, perfect." Focusing my attention on the car in front of us, a mail truck with their caution lights flashing as the postal carrier delivers packages to one of the shops on the street.

"Good, cause we're here."

Dominick pulled his car to an abrupt stop, tossing the keys to a kid who came running out from between two parked cars. As I opened my door, I caught the smell of ground coffee and something sweet, reminding me I'd skipped lunch and it would soon be dinnertime.

"I have something for you upstairs. A little house warming gift for your new purchases."

The brick building stood in the center of the block, a date stamped in the sandstone over the entry. Three iron café tables and chairs sat in front, planters filled with flowers decorated each side of the entrance.

"Mr. Santos." A deep voice called from my left. An older man, mostly bald, waved in our direction, stopping Dominick in his tracks as we headed toward the entrance.

"Hey, Benny. You win the lotto yet?"

"Fifty dollars last week." He announced proudly, his yellow smile covering his face as he removed his glasses, his hands landing on his hips. The pride on his features is inspiring, reminding me of the little things in life worth celebrating. I loved the neighborhood already, with its friendly faces and easy banter. Looking over my shoulder one last time at the pair, I anticipate the day when Benny shares his news with me, and how just as Dominick is doing, I will tease him about buying a bridge or two from me.

I never heard the door open, or saw anyone leave the building, the laughter shared by the two friends on the street holding my attention until it was too late. Something firm hits me in the chest followed instantly by the burn of something hot and wet on my chest and hand. My mouth opens to cuss the fucker out when I'm meet by a set of hazel-green eyes. Words fail me as I stare into the face of an angel. Dark hair pulled back in a serious ponytail the ends taunting me with a bouncy curl, sleek bangs covering her forehead. She is much shorter than me, nearly a foot if I had to guess. Her lips look so soft, and I wonder for a moment if she would allow me to kiss her?

I listen as she tries to apologize for ruining my shirt, offering to have it replaced, as if I give a shit about a fucking shirt. I'm about to tell her to forget it, not to bother with a replacement, when the devil on my shoulder kicks me in the head and reminds me this would give me an opportunity to see her again. I hear her breath catch when I ask her name, and I'm grateful she isn't immune to my accent. Heather is so goddamn beautiful, and I have to know more about her. Where she lives? If she has a boyfriend? Discreetly, I examine her left hand; I'm thrilled when I see it is absent of a ring.

My moment in heaven soon descends into hell as I hear the voice I had to toss into the streets last night. It's clear by the exchange between Destiny and Heather they share a hatred for one another, one which began long before I walked into either of their lives. Heather shows her strength when she stands up to the both of us, making it clear she knew the common factor between Destiny and myself.

"Heather, please wait," I call out gently, trying my best to avoid touching her as not to send her running down the block. Cautiously, I remove the distance between us, keeping Destiny in my peripheral.

"It's true, I met Destiny in my hotel bar last night. She is not, nor will she ever be, anything to me. I never asked her to come upstairs with me, she came willingly and of her own accord."

"Just a fucking minute!" Destiny interrupts, pushing my shoulder with both hands, her intent to scare me missing the mark by miles. "I came—"

"No," I command firmly, my hand raised, finger pointed to emphasize my point. "You need to be quiet. Your mouth was of better use as my future kids swimming pool."

Destiny's eyes grow wide as laughter breaks out from several people gathered around. Her face is red with anger and her mouth hangs open in disbelief.

"But... "

Done with this conversation, never having to work so fucking hard to get rid of a girl in my life. "Apparently last night meant more to you than it did to me, but you knew the second I pulled you off the barstool, I wanted one thing from you. And just to be clear again, you fail miserably at giving a blowjob."

Heather covered her surprised gasp with her hand as Destiny screamed something unintelligible. Several onlookers laughed and pointed fingers at a retreating Destiny, taunting her on her lack of oral skills.

"I'm sorry," thumbing over my shoulder, "about her and the things you had to hear."

"It's fine," shaking her head as she adjusts the straps on her backpack. "Destiny and I have never been friends."

She stares down the block, a far off look in her eyes and the remnants of unshed tears drifting back to where they originated. My actions, although unintentional, have made her cry, something I swear to myself I will rectify.

"From the little I know of her, you aren't missing much. Listen, I'm serious about dinner, and not at the penthouse of that hotel. I have a flat not far from here, I'll give you the address, and if you will allow me, I will try to make this up to you."

Pulling an old receipt out of my jacket pocket, I jot my new address on the back, reaching forward and grabbing her hand holding the strap of her backpack. My fingers tingle as I touched her delicate skin, the sensation radiating up my arm and into my chest. Her warmth sets me on fire, creating an addiction in me, making me crave more of her. But this isn't the right time, and I have to remind myself to tread lightly, repair the riff before building the foundation.

"I'm glad I bumped into you today, Heather. And I hope to see you soon."

I sent her a half smile and a wink, the one I've used to land myself in more pussy than I can count. I need to leave her with something good, and there is no better feeling than being turned on sexually. Rejoining Dominick as he stands a few feet ahead of me, silently shaking his head.

"Can't say as I miss that shit."

"What, talking with a beautiful girl?"

"No, seeing the bad lay from the night before, ruining the tail you're chasing today."

Opening the door fully, I was tempted to look over my shoulder at Heather, but I don't, I've given her something to consider, turned up her internal temperature and stolen her breath away. Instead, I focus on how I'm going to impress the hell out of her, make her forget the unfortunate encounter with a card-carrying bottom feeder.

Dominick showed me the coffee shop and introduced me to Frank, the current owner, an OG from the early days. The walls were covered with the framed faces of famous people beside the crusty bastard.

"Frank, I have to tell you, this," motioning to the frames covering the wall, "Is fucking brilliant. You took the negative of what we are and do and gave it an edge of mystery and a beautiful price tag. This is Marketing 101 at its finest."

My mum insisted I attend university, much to the chagrin of my father who never found higher education to be of any real benefit. His philosophy of having complete control, mixed with a fair amount of backstabbing was all a leader needed.

"Honestly Ian, I can't take all the credit, I was banging this broad one day, and she had some daytime show on, as I was getting dressed, I listened to one of the actresses talking about using her flaws to her advantage and it hit me. I came back here and started talking loud enough for people to hear the bull shit stories, since there were rumors already, I made them bigger, and gave them a face."

The bullet holes in the wall added another level to the story, one that would win over any skeptics as to the validity of this being a mafia owned business.

"And the employees, do they know this is all bull shit?"

"Heather and Danielle do, but Gabe," shaking his head, an amused grin framing his face. "Is a big guy and an even bigger pussy.

You can't pay him to get within ten feet of that door. Most days he is waiting for the bullets to fly, or Al Capone himself to walk through that door." As laughter fills the room, the mention of her name made me itch to know if she would take me up on my invitation?

"Another thing you should know, Ian." Frank leans back in his chair, the smile long gone and a serious bend between his eyebrows. "I noticed you speaking with Destiny, a word of warning with that one."

"Too late, Frank. He tagged that bitch last night." Dominick interrupted, a snicker in his throat and a cheeky grin on his face. Jumping out of the way as I position my fist to back hand him.

"Then make sure you see a doctor for a shot of penicillin as that dame is a Piranha. But Heather is a good girl, always on time and doesn't put her nose where it doesn't belong. She is no stranger to the lives we live, but she isn't some whore you can fuck around like you did Destiny."

"What do you mean she isn't a stranger to this life? Is she your girl?"

Frank shook his head fiercely, a scowl on his lips, "She is like a fucking daughter to me, as far as the life she has, it's her story to tell." Leaning his body in close to mine, his cold eyes and serious stare, "But heed my warning, fuck her over and there will be a real killing these walls can brag about."

I chose to ignore the disrespect his threat held, every man has to have something to protect, give him a purpose in getting out of bed in the morning. His defense of Heather added fuel to the spark she had ignited inside of me. Locking eyes with Frank, a silent agreement exchanged between us. I understood his need to protect her, yet he knew the shaky ground he was treading on, and my limit was vastly approaching.

Dominick had settled in and was enjoying the battle lines being drawn. My day had been too long, and with the shitty events from last night smacking me in the face, I was ready to shift gears. Without moving my gaze from Franks face, I changed the subject.

"Dominick, you mentioned something about a house warming gift. I'd say it is time to wind this up as I have a young lady to impress."

My intentions had been made clear, if Frank chose to say anything further, he would force my hand, something I doubt he would ever do.

"Frank, did my guys deliver the crates?" Dominic inquires, not lifting his eyes from the phone in his hand. Rocking back and forth on the heels of his shoes as if the question is rhetorical.

"Early this morning, fucking Mayo tried to follow them upstairs."

Puffs of smoke rose from Frank's cigar, his eyes squinting as he motioned to the ceiling, a silent huff leaving his chest as the edges of his lips curled up in a smile.

"He still hanging around? Thought for sure he would have stayed away after I lit his ass up last time." Dominic tucks an arm under the other, his phone momentarily forgotten.

"You didn't scare him enough to make him quit chasing after Destiny. Motherfucker would crawl through sharp glass to sniff her pussy. Besides, he's still trying to hang with those Market Street boys."

Frank slides his eyes in my direction as he mentions the gang, a worried look on his face.

"Don't worry, old man, Ian had the pleasure of meeting T-Bone and his men. Ian showed them whose dick was bigger and gave them a sweet offer to come work for him."

"This Mayo, anyone I need to worry about?" Things had gone too well up until this point and my gut screamed at me to dig deeper.

"Nah, Mayo is a wanna-be. He thinks he's tough, but as soon as someone calls his bluff, he backs down. Parades around here like a goddamn peacock, trying to get into the pants of half the girls on this street. Destiny drops him a bone every once in a while, enough to keep him interested and being her errand boy."

I've known my fair share of Mayo's, enough to know never turn a blind eye to them.

"Hey, if you ever want to piss him off, call him Malcolm. Come on, let me show you what I have for you upstairs."

CHAPTER FOUR

HEATHER

AROMA IS BUZZING with the news of our new owner as I walk through the door. Danielle pried me for information to fill in the gaps of the rumors she heard about the altercation between Destiny and myself.

"I heard she tossed a drink in his face when he held the door open for you."

I smile at the memory of the last man who held a door open for me. My father set the bar high for what I should expect in a man. How he should carry himself in public, hold a decent job, and provide for my every need.

"But most of all, Heather, look at how he treats his mum. Does he visit her regularly, buy her trinkets for her birthday, and make sure she has what she needs? Then, if he is good with his family, make sure he opens your door. A man who can't remember to open a door for a lass doesn't deserve her time."

The last thing I needed was to have this much gossip running around with not even a thimble full of truth to it.

"Destiny did not throw a drink in his face, nor did he hold the door for anyone. Neither one of us was looking where we were going, and we collided. The lid to my cup wasn't secure, and my coffee splashed on his shirt. End of story."

Danielle searched my face for any hint of dishonesty. Gabe interrupted her exploration when he questioned if Mr. McLeod was as hot as he sounded?

"I mean, you said he came in with Santos and that man is F-I-N-E fine. It would make sense if Ian was just as delicious." Fanning his face, a blush coloring the tips of his ears and cheeks.

"I didn't notice. I was too busy apologizing for ruining his shirt."

Okay, it was mostly the truth, I did ruin his shirt, and I did apologize. But would hell split wide open with the lie I told about not noticing how incredible he looked? Those eyes of his; deep, dark pools of sapphire blue drawing me in and fusing us together. How I watched his pink tongue poke out as he licked his bottom lip. Or how most of the night I thought of what those long fingers of his would feel like on my skin, sliding into places that would cause me to scream his name. But the best part, the thing I can't get out of my mind, was how he said my name with his thick accent caressing every syllable. He gave those three vowels the most amazing sound, wrapping my body in layers of wanton need.

"Ugh," Danielle retorted, tossing the towel she used to dry the counter at me. "You're useless. I need steamy details."

Catching the towel before it could hit my face, the bell over the door sounded announcing another customer. Dread filled my chest as Destiny walked into the shop. Frank stood from his table full of regulars and came over to where she stood beside the counter.

"Destiny, you've been coming in here a long time, and while we appreciate the business, the way you acted yesterday can't happen again."

Her eyes widened as her mouth gaped open. "What about her?" Pointing in my direction.

"Don't play with me, little girl." His words threatening, full of unsaid ramifications if she chose to ignore his warning. Only a fool would turn a deaf ear to him. "Order your drink and be on your way."

Frank nodded in the direction of the door as it opened once again. David from the flower shop down the block came in carrying a huge vase of white roses.

"Morning everyone."

David swayed into the shop like he did most mornings, a smile on his face and a song on his lips. In all the years I've worked here, I've never seen him in a bad mood. He and his wife, Gloria, own the flower and gift shop at the end of the block. Their son, Darius, the leader of the neighborhood gang.

David made his way to the front, carefully placing the vase on the top of the display counter, his signature smile working overtime.

"Oh my god! How did you know I would be here?" A not-so-subtle Destiny reached over to take the card, a Cheshire grin on her face.

"No, ma'am, not today." David moves the vase to his left, away from her reach. "These are for the lovely Heather."

My heart leapt in my chest as I realize he meant me. No one, outside of my father's funeral, has ever sent me flowers. I've imagined what it would be like, rejoiced when it happened to Danielle last year when Stavros sent her roses on her birthday.

Destiny's elation turns to a scowl as David slides the flowers to my waiting hand. I have no clue who they are from, and I don't care. They are so beautiful and smell incredible.

"How fucking pathetic, you have to send flowers to yourself."

Even the brutal disdain she shot in my direction didn't tarnish the moment. Pulling the card from the plastic holder, Gloria's perfect penmanship scrolled across the tiny square.

Heather,

Meeting you was the highlight of my day. Even the ruined shirt didn't cheapen the memory I have of seeing your beautiful face for the first time. Please say you will come for dinner? You have my word I will conduct my self as a perfect gentleman.

—Ian

"Heather Murray, you little liar. You so made an impression on Ian McLeod." Danielle stole the card from my hand, holding it above her head as her eyes danced in wonderment. Gabe stood off to the side, an equally mischievous smile on his face as he motioned for her to hand it to him.

"Wait, Ian sent those..." Teeth clenched, index finger directed toward the white blossoms in my hands. "To her?"

A myriad of emotions flashed over Destiny's face. Mouth opened and closed like a fish as she fought to find her words. My heart pounded as I waited for the venom to spill, the evil living inside her could come out and ruin everything it touched.

Grabbing her purse from the counter, the rest of the room forgotten as she turned on her heels, hitting the door with a loud thud, "He fucked with the wrong bitch!" Stomping off to the left, shoving past everyone in her way, as she hurried down the sidewalk.

Laughter sounded from the table of regulars, Frank's face was red as he doubled over in his chair. Mumbling something in Italian to the men at the table as he pointed to the door. Destiny's outburst is enough to remind them it was time to get to wherever they needed to be as chair legs rubbed against the polished floor.

"You know," Gabe turned from the front of the counter, hand on his hip and a confused look on his face. "This is one time I'd love to know the real story behind what just happened in this room." Circling the index finger of his free hand in the air to his left.

"Because that," pointing in the direction of where Destiny stormed off. "Is a girl who got a taste and wants a whole bite." Swinging his finger to the vase of flowers on the display cabinet, "and those are from a man who needs to get the bad taste out of his mouth."

Gabe's words didn't surprise me. Last night after I got home, I sat on the sofa with my head in my hands, the black bag with a new dress shirt and tie between my feet, the high-end store logo facing me. I played the event over and over in my mind, breaking down each frame and analyzing every second of it. It was evident by the possessive way Destiny verbally pawed at Ian something sexual had happened between them, and while I had zero claim on him, I couldn't get passed the chemistry and prominent pull I felt between us.

I needed to know more about Ian McLeod; not the velvet feel of his accented voice or the depths of his blue eyes, but who he was as a person. My Google search surprised me less than Gabe's observation, confirming what I had already suspected based on what I'd witnessed on the street.

Ian Reid McLeod, son of Shaw and Lady Greer McFarland-McLeod, born July 17, in Edinburgh Scotland. He is twenty-six years old, graduated from Oxford with a degree in business, and holds three medals in boxing in Scotland. Due to his father's death, he sits at the number three position of the richest men in the United Kingdom. As I scanned down the page of all the charitable work he has done in the past six months, I came across a link to the wedding of Declan Malloy, Syndicate leader in Chicago. I'd heard my father speak of Declan's grandfather, Thomas, and how he owed the man a debt he could never repay.

Clicking the link, I waited as the page loaded, my borrowed

internet connection from the hotel across the street not as fast as I would have liked. The photo showed a group of four men, all dressed impeccably in designer tuxedos and genuine smiles, beautiful women stood off to the side. On the far left I recognized Drew Kumarin, the leader of the Russian Syndicate. He was recently spotted at a Detroit Northman's hockey game, and buying up abandoned properties in downtown Detroit, according to the article, he had landed himself in the middle of an FBI investigation as one of the properties had been at the center of a RICO case.

Next to him, Patrick Malloy, former leader of the Malloy Family, his proud smile splitting his face in half. Declan, the obvious groom by the different tuxedo and shiny new ring on his finger, stood beside him. On the end was Ian, one arm around his friend Declan, and the other with a glass of amber liquid. Zooming in on the photo, I could make out a ring on his middle finger, I couldn't see the details, but the shape reminded me of something I'd seen before.

As I looked at the others in the photo, I noticed the Malloy's each had a ring on their pinky, a Claddagh by the looks of it. Drew had one on his index finger, flat on the face, with something engraved in the center, but the photo was too pixilated to make it out.

Was this attraction I have for Ian, a result of my ideation for the ultimate bad boy? Would I still feel the same if he was some ordinary guy with deep pockets instead of the leader of the Scottish Underworld?

"You're probably right, Gabe." Removing my apron and moving around him, my shift was over, and I needed to get out of here. "But I ruined his shirt, and my mum would come back from the dead and beat me if I didn't right the wrong. I'm going to drop off the new shirt and tie at the front desk of where he's staying and then go home to watch terrible television."

Another half-truth; I was going to drop off the box at the address he gave me, but I had to sell my television in order to afford the shirt and tie. The whole truth, I would go home and figure out how I would keep my head above water for the remainder of the month.

* * *

PALISADES TOWERS, THE LATEST 'IF YOU HAVE TO ASK YOU CAN'T afford' high-rise apartment building in the city. Speculation ran like wildfire when the original owner was arrested and charged with fraud. He later disappeared from his holding cell in the middle of the night, his body, like Jimmy Hoffa's, never to be found. The building and the circumstances surrounding it had Mafia written all over it.

I can appreciate the splendor of it, admire the grandeur of the architecture in the design and feel of it with its perfect balance of feminine and masculine features. Walking slowly, I pass the fountain in the center of the circle drive and admire the statue in the center. The modern impression of a kissing couple, their bodies curved around one another, giving the onlooker the impression of eternal and unending love.

I'd wanted to attend school to become an architect, but the need to care for my sick father negated my attendance. I was glad to have been with him during his last hours, reminding me of how much he and my mum loved me.

Squaring my shoulders, my feet feel heavier as I grow closer to the massive entrance and the two men dressed in suits who stand guard. I wouldn't allow them to intimidate me, show them a sliver of the cold fear coursing through my veins.

"Good evening, gentleman. I'm sorry to bother you, but could I leave this for Mr. McLeod? I'm not sure which unit he lives in." My rambling reveals the first sign of my nerves taking over, making me feel more like an idiot and less the confident woman I need to project. "Could you make sure he gets this?"

The man on the left shoots a glance to the one on the right, but remains silent. The man on the right lowered his sunglasses, a half-grin shattering the stern look he wore ten seconds ago.

"Ms. Murray, Mr. McLeod is expecting you. If you will follow me, please." Turning his body, a quarter turn, he reaches his right hand out for the ornate handle. I shouldn't be surprised, but having a complete stranger know your name, especially in this city and dealing with the type of man behind those doors, my warning bells sounding loud and clear.

"Excuse me, how did you know my name?" Remaining firmly rooted, I refuse to step inside the building until I knew what I was up against.

"My apologies, Ms. Murray. My name is Cadan McCord; I'm an associate of Ian's. We've been expecting you."

His accent is as heavy as Ian's, although not quite as powerful in ruling my reaction. My mouth is braver than the rest of me as Mr. McCord's name was not unfamiliar to me. Cadan made the news a few years ago when he was arrested for attempted murder after beating a man half to death. My father once told me it wasn't what you know, but what you could prove, as the charges were dropped a few weeks later.

"But how do you know I'm Heather Murray?"

Cadan removed his sunglasses, the cocky grin shifting to a serious line. "Boss said to look for a beautiful set of hazel-green eyes and raven hair, attached to a gorgeous lady." Gesturing with his free hand to the box tucked under my right arm, "Bringing a new shirt and tie to replace the one she ruined."

Glancing to the box and back to Cadan, the half-grin returns as he pulls the door open, allowing the sound of music to escape. If the interior was any reflection of the exterior, I knew I would stand out like a turkey in a rainstorm, gawking at the masterpiece inside.

"Great."

Stepping forward, I pull the box from under my arm and holding it out in his direction. "Since he is expecting a new shirt, you can give him the box and I'll be on my way."

Cadan looked from the box back to me, ignoring the offering and motioning for me to step inside. It was pointless to argue, one way, or another I was going to see Ian and give him the shirt. Might as well do it under my own power, and fully conscious.

As incredible as the exterior was, the lobby left me speechless and the worry of what waited me left momentarily as I perused the room. Soft tones with gold accents, all beautifully combined to give the place the feel of elegance. A Louis V inspired desk sat against the far wall, two men with headsets watched what I assumed were security monitors, as their eyes never rose to follow me.

"Ms. Murray?" Cadan called my attention as he stood with an arm against the frame, preventing the elevator door from closing. "Mr. McLeod is waiting."

Nodding my head, knowing the sooner I give this to him, the sooner I can leave all this behind and continue with my life. As I entered the elevator, I turned around expecting Cadan to enter behind me. Instead, he wished me a good evening as he released the door and disappeared behind the blue and cream inserts.

'Ms. Murray, penthouse, arriving.'

Startled by the automated voice above my head, looking around for the security camera but coming up empty. Closing my eyes and leaning my head against the wall, a humorless laugh escapes my throat. Of course, he would be in the penthouse, all the way up top so he could see the world below. A way to impress any potential female companion he may seek to pursue.

Quicker than I anticipated, a soft tone sounded, and the doors opened to reveal a relaxed Ian McLeod standing on the other side. Gone was his tailored suit and dress shoes, in their place was a soft gray sweater and dark-wash jeans and sock clad feet. The combination made his eyes more vibrant and his hard persona less rigid. A smile found his face as he stepped forward, hand raised to greet me, "Heather." I caught a whiff of his cologne as he placed a kiss to each of my cheeks, lingering on the second side a little longer than socially acceptable. "I'm so glad you accepted my invitation."

Sliding his fingers down the side of my arm as he backed away slowly, the tingle from yesterday returns and eases the nervousness that had been brewing since I arrived. His eyes drop to the box under my arm, reminding me of the reason I was here.

"Thank you for the invite, it's very kind of you, but I can't stay. I brought you a new shirt and tie. I had to guess on the size, but the receipt is in there, so you can exchange it."

Ian's eyes never left mine as he takes the box from me, "Heather, I have a thousand shirts, more than I will ever wear. I will have my staff return this in the morning and get your money back. Tonight, I want to have a nice dinner and get to know you better."

Tossing the box on the black entry table, he interlaces our fingers and guides me to the next room. The warmth of his hand makes me forget to admire the décor and focus on the toothy smile he has for me.

"I called in a favor and had a few of my favorite dishes prepared for you to enjoy. Frank told me you love the deli on Fifth, so I had Cadan pick up a few things."

A kitchen bar sat off to the left, marble countertops and state-of-the-art appliances completed the modern look. To the right, a staircase ascended to the second floor, the windows beyond providing a view of the buildings and the bridges the city is famous for.

"The weather is beautiful this evening, so I thought we could enjoy dinner on the balcony."

Three sets of French doors opened to the stark white exterior. A cloth covered table sat just beyond the doors, where silver domes sit atop several dishes, making me curious what his favorite dish was.

Passing through the living room, more of the same French influence from down in the lobby decorating the spacious area.

"You're our first guest, so you'll have to excuse me for not planning this better." His admission, though meant to be light-hearted, made me pause and consider. He never denied being with Destiny; on the contrary, he was brutally honest about her. So, who was the 'our' in his admission?

"I thought you were staying at a hotel. Who lives here?"

"I stayed at the hotel the night before I met you."

"When you slept with Destiny." The words were out before I could stop them. I slapped my hand over my mouth, shaking my head in disgust.

"I'm sorry, Mr. McLeod. I have no right to say anything about you and your choices."

Pouring two glasses of wine, the crimson liquid flowed freely into the crystal glass. "My name is Ian to you. I'm glad you brought up the subject of that repulsive girl as I had planned to clear the air regarding her." Handing me a glass and pulling out my chair, inviting me to sit down.

"I went to the bar at the hotel to have a drink and then head up to my room. The barman tried to pull a con on me, and when I caught him, I also attracted her attention. I allowed my anger to get the better of me and took her up to my room. No names asked, no promises of tomorrow. With the way she carried herself, I assumed she expected something quick and dirty, which was what I needed."

His version of what happened was the polar opposite of what she described. It made me question what else she had fabricated to make herself look good?

"When we made it upstairs to my room, she removed her clothes and something inside me shifted. I ordered her to get on her knees, she complied, and when I was finished, I made her leave."

He leaned back in his chair, not a hint of embarrassment or regret for what he did on his face. "I can see by the look in your eyes, Destiny told you something different. I'd appreciate it if you would share those details with me, if you don't mind."

Reaching for my glass of wine, needing something to ground me, I lick my lips and take a sip.

"Well, for starters, her name is Bethany Palmer. Destiny is the name she gives to the men who take care of her, giving her money and such."

Ian nods his head but doesn't comment, his eyes dance between mine as he leans forward toward me.

"She comes in almost every morning, flirting with the regulars and bragging about the new guy in her life."

"When you say flirting with the regulars?"

"The men who work for Frank and Mr. Santos, and well, I suppose now you." Gesturing in his direction.

"Danielle, the girl I work with, thinks she is trying to work her way up the ladder, starting with the Earners who sit with Frank in hopes of stealing Mr. Santos away from Anna."

Taking a drink from his glass, his silence tells me he understands what I mean.

"Yesterday, she came in like normal, except she was talking about the incredible night she had previously. How he, or apparently, you, took her to dinner and made passionate love to her by the light of the moon; all roses and candlelight with promises of happily ever after. When she showed up at the same time you did... "

"You assumed I was Mr. Hearts and Rainbows?"

"Something like that," I giggled, his choice of words fitting the moment.

"She was in the shop when your flowers—" The realization hit me hard; I had neglected to thank him for the roses. "Oh my gosh!" Grabbing his hand lying on the table, "I forgot to say thank you for the flowers. They were a welcome surprise, and I loved them, but you didn't need to."

Gripping my hand in his, lacing our fingers together, he brings my hand to his lips, kissing my knuckles.

"I felt the need to make you smile, something I plan to do often."

A thousand emotions flooded my head, a hundred reasons why I should pull away and tell him goodbye. It was the way he made me feel, made me crave his eyes on me, his hand touching me, which made all those reasons fade to black.

"Bethany assumed they were for her." My voice barely above a whisper, afraid to pop the bubble we were in.

"Frank told me," his face leaning toward mine, lips so close I could feel his breath wash over my cheek, my breath hitched from the heat radiating between us. "Heather, you know who I am, what I do?"

"Yes, with a little help from Google."

Recalling the write up on the death of his father Shaw, knowing how devastating my fathers death was to me. "And I'm sorry about your father."

Ian's eyes turn cold at the mention of his father's name, and I swallow hard as I pull back slightly.

"Thank you, but my father doesn't deserve your condolences." I can tell by the bitterness in his words there is a story behind the hurt; I don't dare question it, just as I won't admit to the loss of my parents.

"I'm sorry, Heather. I didn't mean to be short with you— "

"It's fine," I interrupt, not wanting to make the situation worse. "You were saying... about me knowing who you are and what you do?"

"Yes," he nods his head, grabbing my fingers once again.

"And you're not frightened by it?"

"Why? Should I be?"

Ian leaned away from me, severing the electric current growing between us. For the first time since I'd arrived, he looked uncomfortable, worried.

"No, at least I don't want you to be, but things in my world can be overwhelming and challenging at times. I want to show you where I live and the people I love, let you see the real me. Not the leader I have to be for my Family, but the man who wants nothing more than to kiss you and hide you away from the rest of the world."

What should have registered as creepy and stalker-ish, made me want to straddle him and kiss his face off.

"But I want to do this right and think with the head on my shoulders."

Just as I was about to toss caution to the wind and ignore his suggestion to go slow, the sky opened up and began to rain down on us. Ian grabbed my hand and the bottle of wine, running back into the shelter of his penthouse.

The sound of the torrential rain hitting the cement, combined with the laughter I couldn't stop if I wanted to, left me giddy and back in Ian's arms. In a single, magical swoop our lips collided, soft and tender. He kissed me as he backed me against the frame of the couch.

Laying me gently down on the stuffed cushions, his lips never left mine as he covered my body with his. Moving my hands to his hair, the thick, wet strands gliding through my fingers. As his tongue slid across my lip, asking for permission to enter, I pulled a moan from his chest when I tugged at his hair.

Maneuvering his leg between mine, the feel of him hard against my hip made me want to toss caution away once again and see if he felt this good inside me.

Ian's hands roamed over my body, keeping to my sides and back. I tried pushing my chest into his when he palmed my ass. Instead, he pushed his erection harder into me. Just as his fingers dipped under my shirt, heating up my already scorching skin, his cell began vibrating in his pocket.

"Fuck." Leaning his forehead against mine, "I'm sorry. I have to check it."

Nodding my head in understanding, I was grateful for the interruption, as this wasn't me. I didn't sleep around with men I barely knew.

"Hello, Mum."

Moving off the couch, I pushed back my wet hair and headed for what I hoped was the bathroom. I needed a minute to collect myself, clear my head of the lust filled haze clouding my better judgment. After drying off, and giving Ian plenty of time to finish his call, I combed my hair with my fingers and wiped the smeared makeup from under my eyes.

Ian had closed the French doors, our dinner still sitting in the rain, long forgotten when he first took my hand.

"I'm sorry. I promised you dinner and instead talked your ear off. According to my mum, I will never find a good girl with such rude behavior."

His eyes held embers of the raging fire we created earlier. Crossing the distance, his touch warm against my chilled skin.

"But I believe this time she is mistaken."

Looking at his chest, not willing to return to where we left off, and not trusting myself to resist him. Ian places his finger under my chin, bringing my attention back to his face.

"I brought you here, to the home I purchased as a gift for my mum for her birthday. To show you the place you've carved out for yourself in here." He flattens my hand out, placing my palm over his beating heart. My own flutters at the mention of his mum. My father's advice playing in the back of my mind. "I'll pick you up tomorrow night, take you somewhere… dry."

Ducking my head against his muscular chest, the gentle sound of his laughter filling my ears. "What do you say, Heather? You willing to take a chance on me?"

CHAPTER FIVE

IAN

The smell of her perfume lingers as I welcomed the first rays of the New York morning. Sleep had taken me to dreamland filled with images of Heather and I back in Edinburgh, her laughter filling my home with the warmth it has lacked for so many years.

I wanted to tell my mum, when her call interrupted us, of the girl who had practically fallen in my lap. How she set things off inside of me, shining her pure light into the dark spaces I thought were lost to the bitterness my life had created. But I changed my mind at the last second, wanting to include this news when I showed her the penthouse I'd purchased for her. Let her see how happy Heather made me, and how prosperous I had become without the shadow of my father looming over me.

"Ian, should I contact Ms. Murray's landlord, or do you plan to move her in here with you?"

Shooting a glare at Cadan, his phone in one hand, a cup of what smelled like coffee in the other. He and I have been friends long enough he knew when I found a woman I want to spend time with on occasion, I would take care of her living expenses, and make her life revolve around my schedule. But Heather was different, and while I did want to have her at my beck and call, I knew this relationship was going to be so much more.

"No, but you can return the box on the table and get her money back."

Cadan's mouth dropped, his left eyebrow dipping down in a questioning stare, "I thought you liked her?"

"I like her very much. Which is why you are tossing your cup and we are going to the shop to talk some business."

Cadan remained rooted as I pushed past him, blinking several times as he allowed what I said to sink in. Maintaining my stoic expression, I wasn't willing to show my hand and divulge how much she meant to me. "I need some decent coffee, served by an insanely beautiful lass, before we blow the minds off a few of our new employees."

Dominick had given me the name of one of his contacts down at the harbor. I sent Cadan and a few of the guys down there last night to work out a plan on getting our merchandise past customs and into the warehouse I'd purchased. When he arrived, he sent back word about coming across one of the boys who used to work for my father as a lookout. They struck a deal to have him work for us, while maintaining his job at the docks, keeping an ear open to anyone stealing something that didn't belong to them.

Aroma was a full house when we walked in, the line to the counter at least fifteen deep. Heather and Danielle flew around one another like a team of dancers, working together to get the customers their much needed dose of caffeine.

"I'll grab us some coffee and meet you upstairs." Cadan went to step behind me, catching the attention of one of the girls. As he excused himself, I placed the back of my hand against his arm, making him stop his progression.

"I've got this. Go have a seat with Frank and the lads, I'll be there in a second." Not waiting for him to agree, I stepped around a table of what I assumed were college students, their books piled around them, their laughter directed at the one with cream on his upper lip.

Rounding the edge of the counter, the young man from yesterday is at the register, sending me a double take before a smile grows on his face. Frank had shared a little on each of my employees including how Gabe was a huge pussy where Danielle was a ball-buster. Heather held a special place in his heart, with her unwavering kindness and respect for everyone.

"Morning, Gabe."

"Hey, Boss Man." He tossed over his shoulder as he hands an older woman her change, along with a huge smile, asking when she was going to leave her husband and run away with him. Danielle spins around just as I'm about to grab the coffee pot, nearly colliding with her. "I'd tell you to get the fuck out of here, but since you sign my paycheck, I'll get out of your way." She laughed, as she shoved a muffin into a brown paper bag, handing it to a little girl who was holding her mum's hand with the other.

Heather stood with her back to me, the whirl of the blender making it impossible for her to hear what we had said. My heart yearns for her, my body craves to touch her, kissing her like I did last night, ignoring any phone calls this time.

Her dark hair is pulled back in the same ponytail from before and I find myself envious of the light overhead as it touches the edges of her curls, giving off a silver hue, making her look more angelic than she already is. Crossing my arms over my chest, I bask in the delight of watching her line a glass with chocolate syrup, as she waits for the blender to finish crushing the ice. Our eyes meet as she looks over her shoulder, lips curling into a contagious smile, one which pushes me off my voyeur post. Wrapping myself around her from behind and burying my nose in the nape of her neck, I let the concentration of the perfume I woke up with fill my nose. She spins to face me, my hands resting on the counter on either side of her, trapping her against me.

"Good morning."

"Hey," reaching up she plants a kiss to my lips as I pull her closer. "I didn't expect to see you today."

"Why is that?"

"I," she starts and then looks at my chest quickly. "I assumed you would be tied up with business." Her eyes flash back to mine, a hint of sadness lingers as she reaches up to caress my cheek.

"Well, you are correct, I do have business to handle. Fortunately for us, my meeting is upstairs which gives me plenty of time to deliver this."

My lips cover hers, my hands reaching up to caress the sides of her face, shielding this moment from any prying eyes. Sucking on her bottom lip, I can feel her smile fall as my tongue passes the inner line of her mouth, tipping my head to the side to get a better angle. My fingers move from her face to the back of her head, granting me the freedom to feel the silky strands I envied earlier.

A push from my right pulls me from the essence of Heather, her frustrated moan telling me I've affected her as much as she did me.

"Don't stop on my account." Danielle winks as she takes the drink I interrupted Heather making.

With a sigh, pulls herself away, grabbing the next ticket in line and begins to pour coffee and different syrups. "Can I make you anything before your meeting?"

"I need two coffees."

"Wow, double fisting it already?"

"No, love, one is for Cadan."

"Anything special, or are you a hardcore drinker?"

"Just beans and water for me."

"I'll keep that in mind." Pulling two cups from the tower she had in front of her, she pours the coffee into two cups and then secures a lid on each one.

"Two coffees, black." Hands outstretched, her eyes bright with happiness and I know I'm responsible for the flecks of wonderment floating around in her smile.

"Dude, my girl asked for a latte. Now you best get her what she wants, or we are gonna have a problem." Turning to my right, I see a tall man with the bill of his ball cap turned to the side, a white bandana wrapped around his head, the long edge covering his right eye. There is a dusting of hair at the tip of his chin and along his side-burns. Under his left eye, three specks of ink resembling teardrops running down his face. A silver ring dangles from the septum of his nose, a yellow bead in the center.

"She asked for a latte, and that is what I'm charging her for."

"It says here coffee, and my girl don't drink no coffee." Tapping his finger against the register display. Destiny stands smugly beside him, a look of challenge smearing her features. Cadan comes to the side of the pair, pushing his body into the small space separating them. "No need to get upset. My friend back there will make her whatever she wants."

The punk looks Cadan up and down and I assume by the way the corner of his lip turns up in disgust, he assumes the tailored suit belongs in one of the offices down the street and not at the table in the corner.

"You need to step back outta my face, before you get your Armani- wearing- bitch ass -hurt." His head bobbed side to side as he closes the distance separating them, his index finger hovering danger-ously close to Cadan's eye.

Rounding the counter, I need to step in before this guy buys himself a one-way trip to the emergency room.

"I've got this." Gripping Cadan's shoulder, motioning to the cup of coffee on the counter. "Head upstairs and I'll meet you there."

Cadan nods his head, backing away and grabbing the cup. This guy has no idea how close he came to having a bad day.

"What're you gonna do, Mick?" Spitting the last part at me as I see Frank move into my peripheral vision.

"Watch your mouth, Mayo."

So this was the infamous Mayo, the spit of a boy parading around as a man. From the way Frank spoke of him, I expected some skinny-crack-head looking punk. This motherfucker standing before me, trying to be all knight in shining armor for some common street whore looks more like one of those geeky bastards who spend more time in their mums living room, masturbating to World of War Craft instead of chasing a set of real tits.

"Hold on," raising my right hand to clarify. The door to the shop opens and in walks the Market Street Saints, each dressed in black from head to toe, part of a gold t-shirt poking out of the collar. The same ball caps from before sitting on their heads.

"Are you fucking serious? You're walking in here tossing ethnic slurs around, to the wrong nationality I might add, bitching about how your girl doesn't drink coffee, yet she orders a drink with coffee in it. Threatening my staff and getting in the face of a man who could rip your fucking head off in the blink of an eye. And your name..." Shaking my head, I turn to Frank and laugh, "Is fucking Mayo?"

"Don't talk about my fucking girl, know what I'm sayin'?"

"Don't talk about your girl?" Feigning mock surprise, looking at Frank with eyes wide from fake astonishment. "Whatever you want, motherfucker. I won't say a fucking word about how stupid she is for ordering a coffee drink when she doesn't drink the shit. Or how she was on her knees two nights ago, sucking my fucking dick down her throat while she fingered herself."

"Fuck you, man, my girl does what she needs to do. Know what I'm sayin'?"

"What she needs to do? What, you not enough of a man to take care of her? Your mum not give you enough allowance?"

One of the men standing beside T-Bone, the one whose fingers I cut, snickers bringing Mayo's attention behind him.

"Hey, Cuz." Mayo extends his hand, making an odd shape with his fingers, and then clasps his hand with T-Bone, finishing with a man hug.

"You need my help today?" Mayo questions as if this is something he regularly does.

"Nah man, you know it ain't like that."

Tuning out the conversation as I don't give a fuck what the affiliation between Mayo and T- Bone is. Frank motions toward the ceiling, reminding me of the meeting I called late last night.

"Let's get this shit started." Grabbing my coffee from the counter, I lock eyes with a nervous Heather. I don't like the look on her face, seeing anything but happiness looking back at me pisses me off.

"Hey, Heather?" Motioning her with my index finger to come to me. She's hesitant at first until I reach my hand out for hers, pulling her over the counter, and placing a kiss to her luscious lips. "Do me a favor, bring up a tray of coffee in an hour."

Heather shakes her head vigorously. "Rule number two, employees are never allowed to go up to the second floor."

"Well," kissing the back of the knuckles on the hand held in mine. "You're not just any employee, you're my girlfriend. Ian's rule number one is, he needs to see you as often as possible. Including behind the door upstairs."

My label brings the life back to her face, capturing her bottom lip between her teeth, and smiling her megawatt smile. "One hour, lass." Slowly releasing her hand, I send her a flirtatious wink over my shoulder.

Frank has directed the Market Street guys to the stairs., the sound of their shoes squeaking against the hard wood of the steps. Just as I'm about to follow behind them, I turn around one last time.

"Oh, and Mayo?"

He looks up from his place at one of the tables, Destiny sitting beside him, her phone in her hands. "One more thing I won't talk about," pointing my index finger at my left eye. "How your tattoos are running from all the crying you just did."

* * *

"GENTLEMAN, THANK YOU FOR DROPPING EVERYTHING AND MEETING with me today. I assure you this will be worth your while." Putting my cup on the table, motioning Cadan to open the hidden panel on the wall.

"It's my understanding your organization has primarily made money from drug sales. And while the money is good, it has the potential to be much better."

Cadan places two guns on the center of the table. "These are rifles made in my Family's factory. I've arranged to have two deliveries per week, with the opportunity for more, depending on how quickly you can sell these."

T-Bone picks up one of the rifles, twisting and turning it around in his hand. "This the only style you have, no hand guns?"

"Let's see if you can handle this first shipment, and then we can move on to more variety." Cadan slaps his personal gun on the table, making T-Bone's eyes grow wide with envy.

"My Family has plenty of products: guns, booze, you fucking name it. Sell what we have here in a week, and we will discuss our next move. Go ahead and keep this one, take her for a test drive. What do you say, T-Bone?"

T-Bone looks around the room, shoves the gun into the top of his pants, and then slides down into the chair. "I say, I'm ready to make some fucking bread."

CHAPTER SIX

HEATHER

LAUGHTER ECHOED from the table of college kids who come in every Saturday, taking up a table for hours, and pretending to study. I never questioned why they came here, instead of the trendier coffee house a few blocks over. I assumed they were like the rest of the crowd and came in hopes of seeing an infamous criminal. Whatever their reasons, they were lousy tippers and left a mess behind.

Stacking their discarded notes and torn napkins on the tray, all while mulling everything Ian said around in my head. Destiny and Mayo sat close together two tables away, his head down as she gave her opinion of the earlier altercation.

"They see you as a punk now. You should have done something, showed all of them I'm your girl."

Mayo was far from the tough guy he pretended to be, constantly looking for ways to catch the attention of Market Street's leader. I'd heard Frank, and the guy's, mention how he would never survive once he got in.

Destiny begged for a life where she would be taken care of. One where she was able to walk down the street with an air of importance, wrapped around the arm of a man she felt powerful enough to cling to.

Then there was Ian and his public declaration of how he labeled our relationship. He reminded me of my father; his ability to switch back and forth between the enforcer he had to be with the characters he dealt with and how gentle he was with my mum. I won't lie, a thrill shot down my spine when he turned and kissed my hand, hitting me hard and fast, much like the progression of this relationship.

"When you're finished daydreaming about your hot new boyfriend, come help me clean the display case."

Danielle stood across from me, removing the trash and dirty dishes from the table near the front door, a glint in her eye. I knew she wanted to talk instead of clean. She was my closest friend and always had my back, particularly where Destiny was concerned.

Using the reflection of the window, I glanced at the couple still huddled in the corner. Destiny doesn't even try to lower her voice as she continues to berate Mayo for his lack of stepping up for her. I almost feel sorry for the guy. He tries so hard to fit in around here but has always chosen the wrong crowd to associate with, especially Destiny.

"Come on; I know someone." Destiny jumps from her chair, the force of it slamming the back of the wooden chair into the wall behind her. Mayo glances around wide-eyed, but ultimately rises from his seat and allows her to pull him past me and out the door.

Setting the tray of dirty dishes on the counter, Gabe is already elbows deep in soap and hot water. He hates switching out the pastries and cleaning the display cabinet so much; he volunteers to wash and dry the dishes by himself. Danielle is on her knees pulling out the cookies and croissants. She prefers a stale cookie to a fresh one, and Frank lets her have as many as she wants. After filling a bucket with hot water and soap, I join her as she shoves the last of her chocolate chip cookie into her mouth. I give her time to chew and swallow, pulling the last of the lemon cake and placing it on the counter. I'll divide it up in a minute and take it upstairs for the men to enjoy.

"How long have you known Ian?"

Turning to face Danielle, her sad, disbelieving eyes look back at me. I can feel the hurt rolling off her, and it bothers me to see her this way.

"Oh, come here." Pulling her close, I lock her in a tight hug. Most of the time she is tough as nails, but I understand how she feels. "I swear to you, I never saw him before yesterday."

Danielle nods her head against my shoulder, pulling back before Gabe can see any weakness. She prides herself on being the strong one. Growing up with four older brothers, she learned to tuck away her emotions, hiding them deep inside so no one could see.

"But you did see him last night? At his hotel, right?"

Shaking my head and handing her a clean rag, "No hotel. He purchased the penthouse Frank needed to sell, said it was a gift for his mum."

"Heather!" She exclaimed, eyes wide as saucers and the beginnings of a traitor smile growing on her face. "Are you kidding me?"

Danielle is well aware of my requirements in men. I'd received a few eye rolls from her as we sat one evening eating sushi and drinking a bottle of cheap wine at her house, swapping stories.

"No, she phoned him while I was there. He took the call, didn't even send it to voicemail or ignore her."

Her smile elongated as the sadness vanished like the morning fog, her hands dipping the rag into the soapy water.

"And he's Scottish, just like you. I'm sure that made his mum happy."

Danielle had poked fun at the way I said certain words and phrases. At first, it bothered me, and I would avoid talking, but one day she started asking me questions about my family and if I missed living in Scotland? She was surprised when I told her I had never stepped foot out of New York City before. Using my rag to scrub bit vigorously, my lame attempt at avoiding the question.

"I, um..." I start, guilt building in my chest. "I didn't tell him."

Danielle stops her scrubbing, glances my way quickly, and then resumes. "Too busy getting naked?"

I can't blame her for the assumption. Ian is a powerful, wealthy, and handsome man, his thick accent is a head turner, and I imagine helped separate a few ladies from their panties.

"We kissed a little, but nothing more." Tossing my rag into the suds-filled bucket, taking a deep breath as I steadied my resolve. "And I never mentioned being Scottish."

My father once told me to keep my mouth closed and eyes open, never letting anyone know more than you need them to. Danielle knew where my family was from, but not what my father did or why they left. She didn't know how broke I was or how close I was to being homeless.

"Why not?" Stopping her scrubbing, staring at me with confused eyes. "Information like that would have been the third word out of my mouth."

"Really?" Feeling slightly agitated. "You start every date off with, 'Hello, my name is Danielle, and I'm Italian'?" Resuming wiping out the cabinet, huffing the remainder of my frustration out.

"Okay, okay, you have a point, but you forget I'm only half Italian," Her voice softens as she places her hand on my shoulder. "But hey, imagine how much it will make him smile when you do tell him."

* * *

STANDING AT THE BOTTOM OF THE STAIRS, THE TRAY FULL OF COFFEE and lemon cake shakes slightly as I contemplate taking the first step. For years I've ignored the door at the end of the room, creating a solid wall in my mind where the black painted wood rested.

Danielle made me swear I would take mental pictures of every nook and cranny and report back to her. Somehow, I knew the apprehension I felt as I took the first step would erase anything I tried to remember. Muffled voices from above carried down the narrow staircase, none of them I could distinguish from the other.

My hand shook as I raised it to knock, butterflies racing around in my gut, begging to be set free. With a deep breath and a silent prayer to whoever was listening, I rapped my knuckles hard enough to silence the conversation on the other side. Forks clinked against the stack of plates from the shaking my body was experiencing.

The click of a lock sounded seconds before the bright smile of the man who had walked into my world and changed it forever greeted me. It didn't matter what he did, or why this meeting with known gang members was going on behind closed doors. What did, at least to me, was how his smile made me feel. How it effortlessly calmed the shaking, erasing all the anxiety and filling me with a feeling I couldn't quite label.

"You're three minutes late," he winks, taking the tray from my hands. "But I'll let you make it up to me tonight at dinner." Whispering in my ear as he turns and places his hand on the small of my back.

I'm not sure what I expected to find once I crossed the threshold of the room. Certainly not the polished table and captain's chairs, flat screen television and several couches around the room. Dark shades covered the tall windows; bucket lighting spread a warm glow around the room.

"Gents, I assume all of you know who this beautiful lass is?"

I've seen or spoken with the majority of the men looking back at me. Darius, or T-Bone as he is known on the streets, tips his head at me. Last year he and a few of the others kicked the shit out of a couple of guys who assumed they could harass Danielle when she was leaving the shop. Frank paid him to keep an eye on the homeless guys out back, making sure the cops didn't run them off.

"Guys, help yourself to the lemon cake and coffee. If you prefer something else, I can have it brought up."

"This is fine, love. If they want something different, they can grab it before they come up here next time." Several snickers sounded around the room as just as many hands reached out to take a plate of cake.

"How did you know lemon is my favorite?"

Ian's breath washed over my cheek, the sweet smell a mixture of his coffee and what I assumed was a breath mint.

"I didn't, but in truth, the lemon doesn't sell as well as other items. I can't stand to toss food in the trash."

"You know, you and my mum are a lot alike. She has a use for everything, even the day-old bread our cook bakes. I bet the two of you will get along famously."

"I get it from my mum. She used to tell me when she was a girl she saw too many families going without."

Emotion caught in my throat as I thought of her. How she hummed as she kneaded dough in the kitchen, too stubborn to buy the kind in the store. She and my father preferred to stay at home and enjoy each other, instead of eating out at any of the many restaurants in the city. I was in my teens before I had my first fast-food hamburger with my friends, finding it dry and tasteless.

"I can assure you tonight you will have your fill. You are far too beautiful to go without. Choose any restaurant you want; I will get us a table."

"Thank you, Ian." Flashing him a grateful smile, moving closer into his embrace. "But my favorite place in all of New York is a tiny Greek restaurant, not five blocks from here."

* * *

Dancing Zorbas should have been a city landmark as it's been around since the nineteen-thirties when the original owners came over from Greece. The tiny restaurant reminded me of Aroma, with its intimate size and celebrity photographs covering the walls. Everyone who works there was a member of the Nakos family. Tons of people tried to apply, but the family held firm and didn't let outsiders in.

"So, what's good here?"

"Everything." Ian smiled as he glanced over the top of his menu, sending me a casual wink which warmed my belly. Dancing Zorbas was always loud with the clanging of dishes and the raised Greek voices, calling out instructions and, if I dared to guess, a few arguments. It's my experience most ethnic families are passionate about one another, and passion can get loud.

"Ian McLeod, I didn't know you were in town."

Stavros Nakos, in all his olive-skinned glory, stood at the end of our table. First time I brought Danielle to eat here, she spilled her drink several times as she absently watched him. He was handsome, with dark hair and eyes, a thick Greek accent and the most prominent hands I have ever seen on a man, Danielle letting it slip what she wouldn't give to have those hands on her.

Ian stands from the table, adjusting his suit jacket as he faces Stavros. Both men are equal in height, and while both are dangerously attractive, I find myself pulled toward Ian.

"Stavros, my friend, I mean no disrespect. My business is expanding. Santos sold me a few properties, nothing too close to you and your Family."

I swallow hard as the conversation continues, knowing anything I hear must be forgotten and never repeated to another soul. Focusing my eyes on the plastic menu on the table, I raise my hand to cover my ear as to minimize the details discreetly.

"Heather?" Jumping as my name is called, Ian's fingers touching the hand I have over my ear. Looking to the two men, smiles and hints of amusement at my jitters crease the corners of their eyes.

"Didn't mean to spook you, lass. This is an old Family friend, Stavros."

Extending my hand, I practically hold my breath to keep the tremors inside. Until now, I had never associated the Nakos with organized crime, however with the way Ian had apologized and what I knew of the organizations, it made perfect sense.

Stavros takes my hand, leaning over and placing a gentle kiss on my knuckle. "Some things never change my friend, always showing up with the most beautiful women."

A throat clearing in the background grabs my attention as one of the waitresses attempts to deliver some water.

"Anita, aftoí eínai oi filoxenoúmenoí mou. Párte ó, ti théloun sto spíti." (Anita, these are my guests. Get them anything they want on the house.)

"Ah, Efcharistó." (Thank you)

I'm unable to hide my shock at hearing Ian respond in Greek, his Scottish accent giving it a new twist.

"It is nothing, McLeod. Perhaps we too can do some business soon."

The wait staff brought over several dishes, octopus and a plate of cheese they set on fire and shouted, "Opa!"

Ian and Stavros spoke for several minutes, thankfully keeping the conversation in Greek. Just as I was convinced the discussion was becoming heated, they laugh and shake hands.

"Heather, please forgive me, I have stolen your and Ian's time long enough, I wish you a good night." Leaning over, he kisses my cheek. "He is a lucky man; you come find me if he misbehaves." Hiding my reaction to his teasing, I hope all of what he whispered is for shock value. I share my most innocent smile, thanking him for the wonderful dinner and the welcomed feeling his family provided.

Stavros does a tour of the room, stopping at each table as he laughed and patted men on the back and shook hands. He kisses the cheek of several ladies and gives money to a couple of children, who run off to feed the gum ball machine beside the entrance.

"Are you finished? I need to stop by the shop; I left something upstairs I need tonight."

Ian reaches across the table, sliding a piece of bread through the sauce remaining on my plate, and then popping it in his mouth. Something I watched my dad do to my mum's leftover plate at least a thousand times.

"Yes, thank you for dinner."

Laying my napkin on the table, the music overhead increases as the staff begins to dance in a large circle around the room. Ian leaves a large tip under his wine glass, bidding Stavros and the rest of the staff a good evening, tucking me under his arm as he leads me back to his car parked at the edge of the curb.

I didn't bother to ask what kind of car it is, or why he would need a car if he doesn't live here full time. Instead, I take in the smell of new leather; melting into the comfort the high-end seats provide and enjoy watching the city as we pass it by.

"You know, for someone who is used to driving on the opposite side of the road, you've adapted well."

Ian tosses me a quiet smile, laying his hand on the inside of my thigh, squeezing slightly, but not removing it.

"Not my first time driving in America, but thank you for the compliment."

Ian removes his hand as the car decelerates and he shifts gears, turning the corner with a little more speed than I prefer. In a flash, he pulls into a parking space, navigating the car as if it's an extension of himself. He leans over my lap to look at the building Aroma is housed in. His body so close to mine I can feel his chest expand with his breathing.

"Brilliant, the lights are on upstairs, Cadan is still here. Come up with me; it will take just a moment."

Ian jumps out of the car; his fluid movement is impressive considering his tall stature and how low the car rides. Adjusting his jacket as he rounds the front of the car, his eyes do a quick scan of the surrounding street. Opening my door, he extends a hand to assist me out of the car, pulling me close as my feet land on the sidewalk. The air swirling around us is filled with promise, happiness like I haven't felt in quite a while. His face is mere inches from mine, eyes full of want and desire. His arms circle me, pulling me impossibly closer to him. There is no fear, no apprehension, as I raise myself up and plant my lips against his. I welcome the warmth surrounding me, filling my belly with the desire to take this kiss much further. Painting my tongue along his bottom lip, I'm surprised when he backs away.

"Come on, Heather. The sooner we get upstairs, the sooner we can finish this."

Movement from the side of the door catches my attention, making me gasp and Ian turns to look at me. I watch in horror as Mayo emerges from the shadows, a gun in his hand, the barrel shaking wildly as he points it in our direction. Ian pushes my body behind him, pinning me between him and the doorframe of his car.

"Do yourself a favor, mate. Put the gun on the ground and walk away."

"Fuck you, Mick. You and your fucking boy upstairs disrespected me in front of my girl." Mayo motions nervously upstairs, his body twitching so severely, making the gun move with it.

"Your girl? Is that what she made you believe? You know Bethany isn't the type to settle for a guy like you, not when there are so many like me walking the streets." Ian's words are laced with humor, punctuated by the chuckle which drifts out as the words settle in Mayo ears. Fear grips me deep inside, making me question the validity of Ian's sanity. His lack of concern is unnerving, leaving me stunned in silence.

"Shut up! Don't you call her by that name, she is Destiny."

Mayo's shaking has shifted from being nervous to pissed off, looking down the dark and empty street. Using the sleeve of his shirt, he wipes his mouth and nose several times, his eyes wild like a caged animal, beads of sweat forming on his brow and upper lip.

"Her name is Bethany, and she is a fucking hood rat, passed around the neighborhood like a fucking joint. She isn't yours or anyone else's girl."

Tears well in Mayo's eyes, the truth of what Ian is telling him registering in his mind. Bouncing back and forth on his feet, he begins to shake his head. His face contorts as the tears start to roll down his face, and the gun he is holding dips down slightly.

I can feel Ian reach into his pocket; I don't have time to consider what he is looking for as several things happen at once. The alarm on the car I'm pinned against starts blaring, echoing a shrieking sound off the surrounding buildings. The incessant beeping startles Mayo, making him lose his grip on the gun. As it's falling to the ground, he manages to catch the handle against the trigger causing the gun to fire and Ian's body to slam back against me before dropping like a lead weight to the ground. Blood is pooling on the dark street around him as Mayo runs as fast as he can in the opposite direction.

"Ian!"

My scream joins the alarm of the car bouncing off the brick and mortar around me. My knees hit the pavement as I reach out for his head, feeling around on his neck for a pulse. I find one thankfully, just as the front door to the store opens and Frank, Cadan, and a red-haired girl I've never met come rushing out.

"Cadan, he's shot, you have to help him!"

Frank moves over to me, pulling my body against his chest as

Cadan calls his name, asking him if he can hear him in Gaelic. When Ian doesn't move or respond, Cadan pulls something from his pocket and points it at the car, silencing the alarm. He proceeds to pick up Ian, draping him over his shoulder and runs back into the building.

"Did you see who shot him?"

Frank mutters into my ear in a tone I've heard on a handful of occasions when speaking with Santos.

"Mayo."

My voice laden with anger as Frank pulls me toward the door. I know once I cross the threshold there will be no turning back for me, no way out even if I beg for it. Men like Ian, and Santos, don't involve the cops or visit an emergency room, even when they are more than likely dying from a gunshot. A doctor will come, one who is either on the Family's payroll or lost his license for questionable practices. Either way, everything, including what happens to Mayo, will be handled behind closed doors and without any help from the authorities.

CHAPTER SEVEN

HEATHER

Ian

Blinding pain, the kind served up by Satan himself after refusing to do his bidding, shot through my head and right shoulder. The pungent smell of good scotch swirled in the air surrounding me, making me crave the incredible flavor. Braving my unknown surroundings, I cautiously force one eye to open.

"He's waking up."

A hand on my right arm squeezes tight, as the room comes into focus, although spinning slightly from the blinding pain. Frank is hovering over me, a bottle of my favorite scotch posed in his hand. Finley is standing beside Cadan, her hands covered in what I imagine is my blood.

"Aye, Ian. What do you remember?"

Finley wipes her hands as she moves closer to my head, she's had the misfortune of stitching me up more times than not.

"Fucking Yankee bastard shot me."

Turning my head to look at my burning shoulder, my shirt and jacket have been removed and are nowhere in sight. The skin around the dark hole in my flesh is already starting to bruise. The pain is concentrated to the front of my arm, and I suspect the bullet is still inside my shoulder. Finley's equipment lays assembled and ready, including a syringe full of pain medicine she won't be using.

"The way his hands shook, he scared the bullet out of the goddamn barrel and into my bloody arm. I twisted hard when I heard the shot, to avoid the bullet hitting Heather. I landed on the sidewalk with the side of my fucking head."

My heart dropped as I searched the room for her, until the warm hand squeezed my arm again, bringing my attention back to the pair of hazel-green eyes I adored so much.

"Are you okay?"

Attempting to sit up, her worried eyes grow large as Cadan moves forward and pushes me back down. I would fight him, but I suspect he is the reason I'm lying on this table. I'd forgotten my gun when I left to take Heather to dinner. When Mayo crawled out of the shadows, I knew I had to either scare the shit out of him or gain unwanted attention from the neighborhood. I took a chance Cadan would be upstairs and investigate the blaring car alarm.

"Not so fast. Finley hasn't had time to remove the slug from your arm."

Nodding my head at Cadan, I hold out my uninjured hand for Heather to take. I watch carefully as she moves around the table, her eyes focused on me and not the open gun cabinet on the wall. Her body tells me everything her mouth never will; how she has noticed the guns and drugs, and the lack of police or an ambulance. She is either planning to run at the first opportunity or too terrified to utter a word.

"I'll be all right, love. Finley is a professional at patching me up."

"You scared me." She whispers as she lays a gentle kiss to my lips, holding onto the moment a little longer, savoring the satisfaction that I'm still alive. Leaning back, she motions over her shoulder. "Who exactly is Finley?"

Her jealousy is refreshing, and it stirs a smile on Finley's lips. "Finley McFarland is one of my best mates in the world. She works for my mum and is our in-house Bone Saw."

Heather looks into my eyes, her beautiful orbs searching mine for any traces of a lie, which is a waste of time as she will find nothing but honesty and respect for her there. She nods, but remains silent, turning her head to an approaching Finley who now has a set of gloves on her hands and a syringe full of shit she doesn't need.

Heather wraps my hand tightly in hers, bringing our interlaced fingers to her mouth where she places several kisses against my knuckles. My eyes lock with hers as Finley lowers the needle to the wound.

"Finley, you can put that shit right back where you got it."

"Ian, she needs to numb you up before she takes out the bullet." Gripping her hand tighter, I send her a reassuring smile. "Finley needs many things to get the bullet out, shit for pain isn't one of them."

Heather starts to open her mouth to argue, but Finley interrupts. "Don't worry yourself any, Heather. I offer, but this mental bloke refuses every time."

"Ian, this isn't a time to be brave," Heather reprimands, her face flushing with agitation. "Let her give you the medicine so she can do her job."

"Love, I know you're concerned with my pain, but you have nothing to fear. Besides, pain is for pussies." Finley was accustomed to my bravado and didn't waste any time digging into my wound in search of the slug of lead. The red-hot fire burned through my shoulder, causing my teeth to clench and a bead of sweat to form on the back of my neck.

The pain takes me back to the day I learned how cruel my father truly was. Shaw McLeod possessed an ego much bigger than his abilities could reconcile. He was always trying to outdo or scam the guy next to him, using the disguise of staying ahead, and being productive in a dog eat dog world.

"Heather, do you remember the other night when you offered your condolences on the death of my father?"

Finley scoffed at the mention of him, her love for the man even less than mine. Heather's eyes flash in Finley's direction, narrowing her eyes in what I assume is irritation due to her clear disdain for the man.

"How about I tell you a story, and then you will understand why Finley and I hate him as much as we do?"

Heather grips my hand tighter, a compassionate smile coloring her lips as she nods for me to continue.

"It was my seventeenth birthday and my father's idea of celebrating was a business trip which included my half-brother Blake. I was young and naïve, insisting Darrow, and Finley come along. I should have been suspicious when he wanted to leave in the middle of the night, not waking my mum or taking any of his men with us. He piled us all into one of his cars and drove until the sun came up. As we pulled into a small village, he parked the car outside of a rundown hotel and restaurant. I was the only one, besides him, who was awake, so he told me to come inside for a minute."

Fire blazed in my shoulder as Finley pushed the muscle to the side as she searched for the bullet. My vision blurred slightly as the pain increased and my stomach threatened to expel the dinner I had enjoyed with Heather. Swallowing down the bile in my throat, I focused on the beautiful face of the woman who, in such a short time, had made everything much better.

"We walked into the abandoned building, and it was then I received my first real taste of apprehension; the feeling you get on the back of your neck screaming to turn and run. I ignored the gooseflesh, believing in my heart my father could stand up to anyone, feared nothing, and would protect his family to the death."

Heather's face blurred slightly as my focus shifted to the ceiling above. Living through this nightmare once had been more than enough, but she needed to understand where all of my hatred comes from.

"I never saw the man waiting in the shadow or reacted quickly enough when I was grabbed from behind, a hood placed over my head and something hard knocking me unconscious. When I woke, my hands were bound behind my back, my ankles tied to the legs of the chair I was sitting in. Light filtered in from a couple of dirt-covered windows, the thickness of the grime rendering it impossible to see much of anything. An overwhelming smell of stale earth and urine flooded my nose, forcing me to breathe through my mouth. Looking around the dark room, I saw Finley tied to a table, her mouth covered and her green eyes full of fear. Darrow dangled from his arms above his head, his chin touching his chest and a thick chain was wrapped around his wrists, blood dripped from his bottom lip onto his shirt. Blake sat in a chair beside me, his eyes wide with fear and tears coating both cheeks."

The sound of metal hitting metal rang out beside me, Finley's eyes flash to mine as she mouths an apology to me. We've never spoken of the events of that day, not while it was happening and not once since it has been over.

"Three men stood against the far wall, each dressed in black with masks covering their faces. I took a good look at my surroundings when I noticed my father sitting on the floor against the far wall to my right. His hands were tied but his feet were free, a nasty cut over his eye, blood running down the left side of his face. Our eyes met as he tilted his head back against the wall, a sinister smile creeping slowly on his face. My father yelled for me to keep my mouth shut and not to tell them anything.

My mind was wild with questions, why were we there? What did these men want and how did they know my father? None of the men made a move toward any of us for a while, and I was too scared to open my mouth to question anything, so I kept my eyes drifting from one person to another as time passed by. Darrow finally opened his eyes and raised his head, shooting daggers in my father's direction. It was evident something had transpired during the time I was out between him and my father."

Looking back, knowing what I do about Darrow, I know for certain I would have done something to turn the pain on him. Make those bastards come after him instead.

"The man on the end was the first to move, walking in Finley's direction and pushing the table she was strapped to against the wall, making it impossible for her to see me and vice versa. Next, he stood in front of Darrow, raising his hand; he backhanded him across the face rendering him unconscious once again. Blake began thrashing around as the man turned to face us, whipping his head back and forth as his body jerked with his sobs. The second man pushed off the wall, taking significant strides to join the first. His dark eyes looked down at Blake, and then he raised his hand and hit him with enough force to knock him out."

At the time, I was afraid for Blake, worried they would hit him hard enough to kill him. Too bad it was wasted energy on a man who didn't deserve it.

"He asked if I was going to cry like Blake, but I ignored his question and tried hard to figure out if I had met him before. I couldn't place the accent, but he was definitely not Scottish or Irish, but also not American with his broken English. I remained silent, hoping he kept his hands to himself if I don't show any fear. My father demanded I remain silent, telling me not to speak a single word; I refused to look in his direction. I trusted my father, took what he said to me as the best way to survive this. These men were foreign to me, I don't know what they wanted, but I refuse to be the reason one of us died. The first man lowered his head to align with mine, his dark eyes reflecting back at me. His breath made me want to vomit from the rancidness of it while broken and chipped teeth hide behind chapped lips. He asked if Finley was my girlfriend or if I preferred Darrow instead. He tried to get a rise out of me, but I refused to give him the satisfaction of knowing how much his words angered me."

A scoff sounds from Finley's chest and I know what she is thinking. She and I are too much alike to be anything other than friends and the thought of us being a couple is comical.

"My silence didn't sit well with the pair as the man with the bad breath grabbed a chair from behind me. The tip of the leg smacked the side of my face as he maneuvered it, flipping it around and straddling it with his body. He joked with the second guy how pretty boys like me don't settle for one girl, instead, I must have them lined up around the corner. I didn't flinch or feign interest in where the conversation was headed. I'd watched my father long enough to know they are baiting me, trying to see where my boundaries lie, so they can pounce and get the information they want out of me. But I assumed my father would intervene before that happened. He had a plan, he always had a plan. I just had to remain silent, allowing my father time to get his thoughts together before he sprang into action. The man stood from the chair, swinging it behind him, raised his foot in the air, and then planted it firmly in the center of my chest. The air in my lungs was knocked out as my back slammed into the concrete floor. I coughed several times as the burn filled my chest, the sweet feeling of air filling my lungs once again. He pulled at the hem of my pants, sliding a knife along the seam until he reached my mid-thigh, where my position hindered him from going further. Shoving me on my side, he pulled at the material of my pants, sliding the knife further up, slicing my skin in the process. My body jerked of its own volition, catching the eye of my father. He looked at me with cold eyes and said pain is a state of mind and I could choose to accept what my brain was telling me or I could fight like a man. The next slash of the knife lands across my right nut, the pain like nothing I had experienced before. Nausea rose in my throat as the edges of my vision blurred and darkened. My father shouted at me how pain is weakness leaving the body and for me to ignore it and keep my mouth shut."

My mum had to take me to a specialist to make sure I didn't have any permanent damage. For the next two years, I had to jack off into a cup to check my sperm count. Having an heir was an important part of our Family and my inability to produce a son to take over when the time came would have been detrimental to the McLeod's.

"The man against the wall grew tired of listening to the pep talk my father recited to me as he kicked him in the side and face several times. Over the course of the next several hours, they bounced back and forth between us, delivering crushing blows and various cuts with a knife. Darrow struggled in his chains, but they left him alone. Blake may have woken up, but he was too big of a pussy and kept eyes closed. Together, two of them righted my chair, and waves of dizziness floated over my body. They asked my father if he had seen enough and was ready to tell them where their money was? My heart sank as I realized this was related to him cheating someone out of what he owed them, or stole from them. It was always a game to him, even when it came to his family. My father refused to tell them anything, spit on the floor and sneered something about a dead dog. Moving away from my father, the man cleared the distance between us, kicked my chest and once again slammed me to the floor. He threatened to start cutting me apart, break me down into little pieces and bury me beside the dog. My father stood to his feet; the coldness in his eyes something I will never forget. He told the man to go ahead, he had other sons. His words shattered me from the inside out. I watched as he leaned against the wall as if not a care in the world as the man picked up a hammer and slammed it down on my shin, breaking my leg in three places. I owe my life to Finley as she took advantage of them not paying attention to her and placed a call to my mum."

Having my balls cut open was nothing compared to the pain I felt when he admitted how little he cared for me. He had spent his life screwing a multitude of women in order to have a long list of sons to choose from. Too bad I was the only one with the proper bloodline to run the Family.

"Just before I lost consciousness from the pain, the doors to the building crashed open, and bullets rang out, killing all three men. Finley splinted my leg and held pressure to my groin until she managed to get the bleeding to stop; our family doctor was waiting for us once I got home. My mum was so furious with my father she threatened to divorce him and take everything away. He denied his involvement, claiming he had been ambushed. Years later, I learned he had double-crossed the Romanian Family on a shipment of guns. They had warned him what would happen if he failed to deliver, but as usual, his head was full of himself."

Worry, hurt and sorrow reflected back at me in Heather's eyes. Her gaze never wavered as I told her the gory details of my first experience at becoming the leader of this Family.

"Almost there, Ian," Finley assures me through the grimace on her face, a strand of hair falling into her face. The burn in my arm increases as I feel her reach the bullet, clamping onto a piece of it with the tool in her hand, and the sensation changes as she begins to pull it out.

"Cadan, I need more gauze."

Heather grips my hand tighter, fear filling her hazel-green eyes, her concern for me a genuine comfort, something I didn't think I would ever need. As odd as it sounds, even to me, I feel safe when she is around. I feel the moment the bullet is out, the negative pressure I've felt increases, and then instantly decreases, and I'm able to unclench my teeth and take a deep breath.

"Ready for the fun part?"

Heather's eyes snap away from mine, the grip on my hand tightening. She watches intently as Finley pours powder into the open wound.

"Here we go." Finley has never been fooled by my straight face, and balls of steel attitude when it comes to this. She knows how deep my hatred of my father runs, her explanation for my reaction to pain, or lack thereof. Witnessing how Heather internalizes my pain, catalogs my reaction and remains by my side is confirming what my heart and head feel for her.

The click of Finley's lighter is all the warning I get before the scent of burning sulfur fills the room, followed by the smell of singed flesh. Cauterizing the wound is the quickest way to close it, keeping the infection to a minimum. It doesn't make it hurt any less. Finley knows I feel pain, the kind that hurts more than some bloke taking a shot at you. She knows what it's like to hear how you are nothing in the eyes of your father.

"Okay, love, you will live. The bullet is a small caliber, and you're too fucked up to die," she teases. Bandaging my wounds has never been a time where we have become serious, taking the pain for what it is and not giving it any power.

"Heather, can you get him some water and something sweet, please?"

I know Finley doesn't trust Heather, I wouldn't expect her to. However, she is trying to let her in, make room for her in our world, as I know, she has water and sugar pills in her bag. She is giving her an out, an opportunity to run and never look back.

"I'll be right back." Heather kisses my lips, squeezing my hand before releasing it. Looking at Finley, she nods her head before turning and walking toward the door. With a final glance over her shoulder, she hurries out the door, the sound of her footsteps vibrating off the floor.

"I hope she returns, Ian." A sad smile touches Finley's lips as she finishes cleaning the blood from my arm and chest. "I can see how much you care for her."

Frank turns from his post at the window. "She'll come back. Heather is a smart girl, knows more than most about this life." His protective nature for her was honorable, taking the role of her protector seriously in the absence of her father.

Despite Frank's confidence in Heather, only time will tell if she has the strength for this life. For now, I have something much bigger to focus on.

"Cadan, get T-Bone and his men over here. I need to have a chat with them. The gun the bastard used was the one you gave him."

CHAPTER EIGHT

HEATHER

I watch the teeth of the knife slice through the yellow cake and sugar glaze. Using anything and everything to get my mind off what Ian told me of his father and the lack of reaction on his face. No one was immune to pain, not to the level he demonstrated earlier. Not once did he flinch or wince, just kept his eyes focused as if in a trance. I'd heard of people meditating, finding a focal point when women are in labor, but this was something else entirely.

I would have to Google the two men Ian spoke of, his half-brother Blake and the one he called Darrow. I cannot fathom the level of pain Ian endured at the hands of his father, and it was no wonder he didn't want anyone to feel sympathy for him. However, after listening to Ian tell his side of the story, I wondered if he had anything to do with his fathers death?

Balancing a plate of cake and several bottles of water in one arm, I made sure to make plenty of noise as I climbed back up the steps. Sneaking up on men like Ian was a recipe for disaster, much like getting caught eavesdropping on their conversations.

"I brought enough for everyone!" I shouted, perhaps a little too loud as I neared the top of the landing. The door was opened several inches, and I could make out Cadan standing by the windows, his cellphone to his ear, his free hand on his hip by the gun I didn't notice before.

Finley had given Ian a sling for his arm, cleaned the blood up off the table and packed her instruments away.

"I hope you're hungry, Finley. I hate for good food to go to waste."

Setting the dishes on the table, Finley reaches over to help me with the water. The atmosphere in the room is different, the tension remains, but has changed. I can tell Finley doesn't trust me, and justifiably so, as I'm not one hundred percent sure about her either. I'll allow time to clear any confusion, let her witness with her own eyes how much I care for him.

"You sure you want to get involved in all of this?"

Finley grabs my hand as the last bottle is placed securely on the table. Cadan doesn't wait for an invitation as he scoops up two slices of cake and starts shoving them into his mouth.

"Don't really have a choice now, do I?"

I could have run when I went downstairs, but it would have been useless, as Frank knows where I live, and I have nowhere to hide, even if I wanted to.

"There is always a choice." Her words are hard, a firm warning of what is to follow. "But hear me now; fuck my family over, and even Ian himself won't be able to save you."

Just as Ian refused to give into the pain, I stand firm in her attempt to scare me. I've dealt with girls like her, protecting their place in the food chain of organized crime, keeping in good favor with the man at the top.

"I don't need Ian, or any other man, to save me. As far as fucking you," looking her up and down. "Never batted for the home team, don't feel like starting now."

Finley pulled away, an unreadable expression on her face. She watched me for several seconds, a myriad of emotions flashing in her eyes. As Frank reached in to take a slice of cake, pushing his way between us, Finley turns to face Ian, a smile growing on her face.

"I like her, Ian."

My father once told me to never let anyone see how afraid you are, how it gives them power over you, sets you up for failure. I could talk a good game, stand up to the biggest of opponents, but I won't lie, not even to myself when I say how relieved I am to have passed the best friend test.

"Glad I have your approval." Locking eyes with Finley, her silent response is in the green of her eyes. Even a blind man could see how much he values her opinion, ready to dump my ass if I didn't make the grade.

Ian reaches over, taking my fingers in his. "Thank you for coming back upstairs."

I knew our time was limited as he and Cadan would have to find Mayo and deal with him. You can't be in Ian's shoes and let something like this go, or the men in your employ will develop doubts about your ability to handle your shit. Wherever Mayo took off to hide, he was taking his last few breaths, as his time on this earth was limited.

"Let me take you home, it's late, and I have some things to do before I let this arm rest."

My heart sank a little at the mention of my home instead of his. I tried to reason with myself he may want to go home and handle Mayo at his penthouse, but the implication still stung.

"Don't worry about me, I don't live far, and you need to rest."

"I'm not letting you walk home by yourself at this time of night, love. Especially after what just happened in the street."

"I'll take her, Ian." Frank offers from the back of the room. "I give you my word she'll get home safely."

Ian opens his mouth, and then closes it again, the war raging within etched across his face. He knew he had a job to do, but somehow, in this tiny window of time, his focus has changed, alternated to include me in his priorities.

"Aye," his voice laden with worry, surrounded by the pain he denied himself to accept. "I'm grateful for the help."

Warm fingers enveloped my chin, his thumb brushing across the skin of my bottom lip, eyes so blue the depths of the ocean stood in awe of their color. Each pass of his gaze like a pen stroke on a sheet of parchment, immortalizing his thoughts for reference in the future.

"I'll see you bright and early in the morning."

* * *

THE RIDE TO MY APARTMENT WAS SURROUNDED IN SILENCE, NEITHER one of us wanting to discuss how much tonight had changed things for me. While I was no stranger to the criminal element, I was no expert either. Things in the Underworld had a habit of changing without a moment's notice. Loyalties could be shattered and, once defined, lines blurred like the pages of a wet magazine. There was one certainty in all of this, one guarantee I couldn't deny. Ian was going to find Mayo, and either he would kill him himself, or he would find somebody to do it.

Frank refused when I told him I was fine to walk upstairs by myself, instead double parking and daring someone to make him move. While his days of earning his living illegally were mostly gone, his reputation remained fresh in the minds of those in the neighborhood.

"Heather, you don't need me to tell you to be careful. You're a smart girl with a good head on her shoulders, one who can read the signs and know when to get the fuck out."

Frank's pearls of wisdom rattled around in my brain as I got ready for bed. Too keyed up to crawl under the covers, I grabbed my mum's picture off the mantle and settled into the cushions of the couch. I missed her smile, the way she made me feel better no matter what was going on around us. How she greeted every stranger on the street with a kind hello and a free smile.

"I think you'd like him, Mum. He's Scottish and, just like daddy, he has a love of family."

Tracing my finger over the glass, imagining for just a moment it's her raven hair I used to curl around my finger. Oh, what I wouldn't give for five more minutes with her, to have the opportunity to ask her how she separated the two men my father was. The kind and loving gentleman he was with her and the cold-blooded killer when he was with his men? Did he, like Ian, ignore everything around him and focus on what was important for the Family?

Cradling the frame against my chest, the clank of her ring hitting the metal edge. When I was a little girl, she would tell me how someday when I met the man of my dreams and had children of my own, she would give me the ring. She spoke in awe of marrying for love, and not a sense of duty. I never had the opportunity to ask her what she meant as someday never came.

"Good night, Mum," I spoke gently, placing a kiss on the cold glass. "Please keep him safe."

I assumed I would spend the night tossing and turning, chasing sleep just out of reach due to my fear for Ian's safety. When the alarm blared, causing my eyes to open wide, rousing me from a sound sleep filled with dreams of castles and dark-haired knights on white horses, I knew I was wrong.

It was important for me to continue as if this were any other ordinary day. Instead of crawling under the sheets and hiding from the twenty possible scenarios running through my head, I needed to stick with my routine and get my ass to work. While the chances were slim, they weren't zero as to the possibility of someone witnessing what happened and calling the authorities. Shootings occurred every day on the street, some were talked about while others lay as silent as the corpse left behind.

Ian was the new guy on the block, and people around here didn't know his reputation, or how open their mouths should be. I could feel it in my soul; all of it was about to change. Ian McLeod was about to make a name for himself, one that would go down in the history of the city.

Frank was waiting in his car when I exited the building, still double-parked with his engine running. I should've known he'd be here, feeling a sense of duty to the new man he was calling Boss. When Santos sold the business, he offered more than bags of coffee beans and state-of-the-art equipment. Frank would leave soon, joining his extended family in Florida and spending the remainder of his days on a sandy beach with a fishing rod in his hand. Until then, he will continue working for Santos, his sense of duty overriding his need for retirement.

"You look as if you slept well."

"Are you saying I usually look like shit?" I teased, knowing full well what he meant.

"If you're fishing for compliments, toss your hook toward your boyfriend."

* * *

NOTHING APPEARED OUT OF THE ORDINARY AS FRANK PULLED INTO his parking spot outside the shop.

Even the blood, which had pooled on the sidewalk under Ian's still body, had vanished in the still of the night.

Danielle and Gabe stood behind the counter, each with an early morning cup of coffee in hand and the remnants of sleep in their eyes. Gabe noticed me first, his confused eyes flicking between Frank and me, unsure of what to make of the two of us coming in together.

"House special is orange cappuccino. Come get me if Destiny shows her face today." Frank calls out as he heads upstairs, slamming the door behind him.

Danielle hands me a cup of coffee, a blank expression on her face. I know she won't be silent for long; her inquisitive personality is too strong to let it go.

"Ian and Cadan left about twenty minutes ago. He said to tell you he would be back in about an hour, and to give you this." Pointing to the white box on the counter, its cardboard surface I failed to notice earlier.

"T-Bone and his guys have been standing on the corner for the past hour, almost as if they are preparing for war."

Picking up the box, I shake the contents back-and-forth, whatever is in there is solid or packed with no wiggle room. "No war today, just doing what they are paid to do."

Danielle looks surprised, and I question if she's heard what's happened, but I won't assume she's playing stupid, allowing her time to tell me what she knows.

"Did something happen? Did a hit go out?" Shrugging my shoulders, "Don't know, guess we'll find out." Taking my coffee and the box Ian left me, I walked around the counter and took a seat at one of the tables. Inside the box is a brand-new phone, a note stuck to the top.

Heather,

I can't have you not owning a phone, leaving me

unable to speak with you whenever I want. Don't worry about the bill; consider it restitution for putting up with me.

—Ian

I knew this was coming, gifts were a part of being with a man in Ian's position. Tiny reminders of how much he cared, pre-planned apologies for when he had to break his word, all part of the big picture I'd chosen to include myself in. Assuming Ian placed his name in the contacts, I locate his number and sent him a text thanking him for the generous gift.

The bell over the door rang, announcing the arrival of most of the regulars. However, today instead of occupying their usual table, they each grabbed a cup of coffee and headed upstairs. I pretended I didn't notice, choosing to ignore the static in the air as if a spring storm was brewing on the horizon.

Just as my nerves settled and the morning rush had dissipated, in walked Destiny in her post-salon glow. She, like most of the women who lived around here, had a standing appointment at one of the four salons in the neighborhood. Hair, tanning, and nails so long you questioned how they could wipe their own ass, were a common appearance. Most of it financed by the men upstairs.

I had never been big on that level of grooming, a simple shower, and a good hairbrush was all I ever needed. Besides, my pale skin would be lobster red after only a short time in one of those tanning beds. And those nails wouldn't last long dishing out coffee and pastries as fast as I do.

"Morning, Destiny. Your usual today?" Gabe stood ready behind the register as Destiny placed her bag on the counter. Danielle walked over to the house phone, pressing the numbers to ring upstairs.

"I'd like a cup of tea, since my new man is from Scotland."

I didn't bother to look at her or acknowledge the bullshit coming out of her mouth. Either she really had met someone last night, or she was trying her damnedest to bait me.

"Milk and sugar?" Gabe asked her as he punched the keys on the register. "Gross, who puts milk in their tea?" I wanted to laugh at her, pointing out her clear disregard for the delights of others. I wanted to explain to her in detail how my mum served tea every afternoon with cream and sugar. Instead, I chose to ignore her, and turn around to make her requested tea. Using the techniques my mum taught me if Bethany wanted an authentic cup of tea she was going to have the best.

But as I turn back around, poised to call her name, I found her face-to-face with none other than Finley. And by the look in Destiny's terrified eyes, it wasn't a social interaction.

Finley grabs Destiny by the arm, tugging her close to her body as they head for the door. "Sorry, Heather, *Bethany* doesn't have time for tea today, she has an appointment with a friend of mine."

The pair head out the door where they join two men waiting on the sidewalk. A second later, a black SUV pulls up to the curb, and Destiny and Finley climb into the back seat. Danielle joins me as I watch them drive off, the sound of a powerful engine roaring down the block.

"How did they know she was here?"

"Finley said to call her if she showed up."

Turning back to the busy street, the normalcy of life in New York City playing out as if nothing happened. Sadly, Destiny had played a game she couldn't win, poked a sleeping dragon one too many times.

CHAPTER NINE

IAN

IT WAS Darrow who came to me one evening and pointed out the high demand for weapons in the world. My father scoffed at the idea, feeling we should supply our own with the guns we made, and not send them out into the hands of our enemies, something I should have learned from previous dealings with the Romanians. His old-school way of thinking was what kept us from growing like the Malloy's or exploring new territory like the Kumarin's. He was content to sit back and live off the sweat of the farmers and small earners. Had it not been for my mum and her royal blood, we would've fallen years ago. All that was behind me now, I would take us and stand among the top-grossing Families, securing a future for myself and, more importantly, honor in my mum's eyes.

According to Cadan, Market Street Saints gave little pushback when I demanded to see them just before three in the morning. I suppose some of it had to do with the incredible amount of money they had made from the guns I gave them to sell.

While having the Market Street Saints in my employ was good; I've never been one to trust openly. It was possible they were responsible for the attack on me earlier. I've learned through conversation, Mayo bragged about wanting to join the gang, willing to do anything to join their ranks. It didn't escape my attention, Mayo wore Market Street colors and had the gun Cadan gave T-Bone.

Looking over the New York City skyline, holding a glass of scotch in my hand hoping to numb the throbbing pain in my shoulder. The endorphins had long worn off giving me a taste of the real severity of my injury. I longed to have Heather here, her unique scent surrounding me, lending me a moment of reprieve from the truth that is my life. How peculiar my meeting her had been, coming at a perfect time when I had convinced myself my life was complete. Looking back, I can admit my life was utter shit. Yet one woman, one incredibly beautiful, perfect woman had righted all the wrong in my world. And I would be damned if I let one angry little piss ant ruin it.

"Ian, the guys are here."

"Let them in, Cadan."

Chugging back the remainder of my drink, sitting the glass down with a clank against the glass of the table.

"Gentlemen, I'm not going to insult your intelligence by asking if you know what happened a few hours ago. What I am going to do is demand to know your involvement."

Five sets of eyes looked around my condo, clearly impressed with what they saw, as they looked around the room. T-Bone took a step ahead of his men, removed his ball cap and tossed it on the table.

"I heard about what went down; word is the motherfucker popped you and ran." Looking over his shoulder, he motions with two fingers, silently instructing the others to remove their ball caps, dropping them to join his on the table. It's a sign of respect, just as shaking my hand the first time we were introduced; T-Bone respects my position.

"We know he was wearing our colors, false flagging like he was one of us. But the motherfucker who shot you ain't one of mine, and he wasn't none of my business until he stole from me."

"I know who shot me, and I know why. Pussy is a powerful thing, and I've been trapped by the chains which come along with it more than a few times. But no whore is worth dying for, no matter how well she sucks your cock."

T-Bone huffs and shakes his head, "Well, G, sounds like you ain't found a good hoe then. Got a few bitches I could send over to ya." I chose to ignore his offer. This meeting wasn't about scoring some ass or bragging about the size of your dick. This is about exchanging information, without giving anything up.

"So Destiny is one of your girls?"

"Fuck no, that bitch has been passed around more times than a murder weapon. Ain't a dick in the 347 she ain't sucked or fucked."

"Funny," I countered, "You would think with all the practice she's had she'd be better at it." Raising an eyebrow at T-Bone, letting Destiny suck me off wasn't a memory I would necessarily cherish.

"Listen, cuz, I'mma be straight with you. The shit that went down didn't come from our house. We appreciate how you've come in and taken care of things. We like our arrangement as it is, benefiting both of us."

Pointing to the stack of ball caps on the table, "All this black and gold shit aside, we ain't stupid. The only color that matters is green."

And there it was, everything I needed to know without a single drop of blood being shed. I'm sure I could ask around, find someone willing to sell me the whereabouts of Mayo's hiding place. But by the look on T-Bone's face, I had a feeling I was about to find out. Something deep inside told me T-Bone was telling the truth. At the end of the day he, like me, was a businessman with the responsibility of making the best decision for the family.

"Our business dealings benefit us both, and for now, I'm satisfied they can remain as they are."

T-Bone nodded his head, extended his hand out to me as if to shake, "Sure you don't want me to call up one of my bitches for you,

G?" The side of his mouth curled with a curious smile. Another test of my boundaries and how far he could successfully push me.

"I think I've got that covered, but thanks."

"Alright, brah, suit yourself." After shaking my hand, he bends over to retrieve his ball cap, pausing for a moment before he adds, "Last year when I took a bullet, one of my homeboys stopped over at the deli on Fifth Avenue. Dude up in there has a good chicken sandwich covered in fucking mayonnaise."

With the same swagger he came in with, T-Bone left the room with his men in tow. And while he showed me, and his men the type of loyal leader he is, he also gave me a glimpse of the kind of ally I had in him as he dropped Mayo's location without looking like a fucking rat.

* * *

I WASN'T SURPRISED TO FIND THE DELI BUZZING WITH ACTIVITY. Tables filled with drunk bar-hoppers shoving carbs down their throat to absorb the alcohol they had consumed. Cadan and I sat outside the restaurant in my car, watching a few people milling around the entrance before going inside. At the end of the block sat two black SUV's filled with my men ready to jump in if shit went bad.

"Corner booth, by the bathroom." Cadan opens his door; his attention fixed on the bastard attempting to hide in the bright yellow of the aged seat covers. His abnormally pale skin is counterproductive in his efforts to lie low, and I now understand the name he was given. Fifties music plays softly overhead as we walk in behind a pair of couples. Cadan had come here once before to pick up food for Heather, which unfortunately was ruined by the rain. Knowing eyes surveyed us, comparing the way we present ourselves to the legends they have heard. As we near Mayo's table, his head is buried in his hands, instead of watching his surroundings. I'll give him some credit, as a much lesser man would have been miles away by now. Cadan sits beside him as I take a seat opposite him.

"Hello, mate." Mayo's head pops up; his body pushes back in an automatic retreat. Cadan wraps an arm around him, leans into his ear as he squeezes the back of his neck, "You should have run when you had the fucking chance."

Cadan releases his neck, shoving him into the window at the end of the table, the collision making a thud which gains the attention of a couple on the street. Mayo holds his throat, his face red and eyes full of terror.

"Welcome to Fifth Street diner; my name is Amy..." The waitress stands in awe beside Cadan, his good looks and the tendency to flirt his ass off getting him more free shit than anyone I knew, besides myself. He reaches out to take Amy's hand; placing her further into the hormonal haze he is creating. Judging by her gaping mouth and trembling fingers, I'd wager a sizable amount her panties are soaked, and her brain is mush.

"Amy," Cadan sings in the voice he uses on most of the females he encounters. "What a beautiful name for an incredible woman." Pulling her hand to his lips, his eyes locked in hers like a snake hypnotizing its prey before it strikes. "Tell me, Amy, what is a girl like you doing in a dreadful place like this?"

Amy's soft, pink tongue pokes out and moistens her lips as her eyes blink, clearing away the strands of cobwebs clouding her mind, "I'm sorry." She stammers as she realizes how close Cadan is to her. In a quick motion, she pulls her hand back, averting her eyes to the menus in her hand.

"The special today is a grilled chicken sandwich with fries and a drink for nine ninety-nine. I'll give you a minute to look over the menu." She squeaks, disappearing as fast as her feet can carry her.

Glancing over my shoulder at a shocked Amy as she stands beside her coworkers who are apparently consoling her as they each try to hide the looks in our direction. Turning back to a proud looking Cadan who is relaxed in his seat continuing to flirt with her.

"You're going to hell for that." I point at Cadan whose smile falls from his face when his eyes shift to mine.

"What? I was being — "

"A fucking asshole." I finish for him, trying to keep the amusement out of my voice. Cadan turns back to Mayo, nodding his head in Amy's' direction, "Lass's are odd creatures; wouldn't you agree?"

Mayo looks from Cadan to me as if searching for the answer to his question. My shoulder has started to ache, reminding me I have shit to do and a beautiful girl of my own to see. "You're wasting your breath, Cadan. Mayo still has his fucking cherry in his hip pocket and doesn't have a clue about women. Do you, motherfucker?" His lack of answers and refusal to look us in the eye spoke volumes to not only his fear, but of his status of being a virgin.

"He doesn't know how to deal with some cunt who has her hand up his ass telling him what to do and say like a child's sock puppet." Mayo raises his head in defiance, a flash of anger shining in his eyes. Boys like Mayo believe what they are told, too scared to stand up and be a man, one who dominates the relationship and the pussy.

"Hand me your phone, Mayo." Folding my body forward, my hand palm up in his direction. "I'm going to show you how easy it is to get Destiny's attention and make her forget you ever existed."

Scrolling through his contacts, I find her number and dial it using my phone. Pressing speaker, I place my phone on the table and lean against the back of the booth. Cadan nudges Mayo's arm, a Cheshire grin on his face.

"*Hello?*"

"Hello, darling, it's Ian. You busy?" Silence follows my question, a smirk forming on Mayo's face. A part of me feels sorry for the sick son of a bitch, lost in a world where a girl he pines for returns his affections, giving all of her love to him.

"Never too busy for you, Ian. What did you have in mind?"

I watch the light in his eyes dim as Mayo hears the change in her voice, the wanton need wrapped around my name. She doesn't bother to question how I got her number, or why I'm calling so late. Just as the night in the bar, she knows the reason behind my call. "You on your knees with your ass in the air, that pussy all wet and ready for me."

No hesitation, not even a hint of reservation passes as less than a second later she answers, *"I can be at the hotel in fifteen minutes."* Mayo hangs his head as I end the call, shoving my phone in my pocket and sliding his toward him.

Cadan wraps his arm around Mayo, "As I said, mate, odd creatures."

I've met plenty of men like Mayo, trying with all their might to fit into shoes that are too big for them. Making the mistake of following advice given to them by fools. I didn't need to hear the story of how he got here; I knew the second he let Destiny have his ear to chew on, the boy was headed for disaster. I never thought he would attempt to take me with him. He allowed his desire to bury his dick in her to cloud his better judgment and sentence him to death.

My cell buzzed in my pocket, a message from Heather thanking me for the phone. I was concerned when Frank mentioned she didn't have a mobile phone and how she wasn't in a position financially to afford one. Being with me would change all of her money problems as no girl of mine would ever go without. Cadan and I walked Mayo out of the deli, making sure plenty of the locals on the street saw us toss him into the back of a waiting SUV. By the time the sun set on the new day, my name would be known on the streets, and Mayo would be the Devil's problem.

* * *

Cadan had done a remarkable job soliciting for men from around the city to help with our organization. With just a few phone calls, he had thirty armed men in a warehouse, many who had worked for Gallo in the past and hadn't been able to secure employment. Stoic, yet respectful faces greeted me as I entered. I needed to carve out time to sit down with each of them and have a conversation, making them aware of my expectations. Finley stood in the corner, arms crossed over her chest, as she glared at a trembling Mayo. He had plenty of reasons to be frightened, staring into the faces of those he betrayed. Market Street was here, out of respect and a taste of revenge.

Closing the distance between Mayo, and myself I reached out and removed the tape securing his mouth, not giving a shit if his skin came with it. He winced as I tossed the tape to the floor, a trickle of blood spilling from his top lip.

"Do you know why we are here?" Taking in the room full of men behind me His eyes wide as he shook his head violently back and forth,. "Aren't you happy to see your boys over there? Haven't you been begging to be a part of their ranks?"

"I..." he starts as I kicked his chair, the rage inside me reaching its boiling point.

"You what? Where the fuck is your badass attitude you were spouting off the other day? Or do you save that shit for when the whore you're trying to fuck is around?"

We both knew the answer, the big fucking tears he let run as we left the deli was evidence of it.

Ignoring the mumbling words dripping out of his mouth, more watered-down versions of how he saw the truth. I motion for my men to string him up; it's time for Mayo to pay for his crimes. He thrashes like a fucking fish as they attempt to wrap his ankles in chains, his crying giving me a fucking headache. Cadan has a short fuse for bull-shit, and it's clear he is approaching his limit as he walks over, pulls the chain out of the guy's hand, tosses it to the ground and picks up the hook instead. With the same swing he uses when he boxes back in Edinburgh, he drives the hook into the soft part of Mayo's foot between his ankle and heel. Mayo screams so loud; I'm surprised the glass in the windows doesn't shatter. Cadan pulls the chain links through the ring at the top of the ceiling until Mayo dangles a few feet from the floor. His shirt is ripped from his body, revealing a set of nipple piercings, skull and crossbones on each side of the puckered flesh. Thug Life is tattooed across the bottom of his stomach, earning a chuckle from me.

"Thug?" T-Bone scoffs, amusement filling his voice. "Mother-fucker, the closest to the hood you ever got was watching Fat Albert cartoons on your momma's television." A round of laughter sounds from the men behind me, a few words spoken too low for me to hear creates more jeers, and a few oaths.

"I bet if you pissed on his tattoo it would run off." More laughter sounds as Cadan locks eyes with me, our faces mirror images of each other, each lacking joviality. He knows how serious I am, not being one to prolong the anticipation of what is about to happen.

"Tempting, but I prefer this approach," landing a punch to Mayo's side, he followed it by the slash of his blade severing the skin, three lines of crimson drips down his chest muting the old English lettering scrolled on his stomach. Mayo cries out in agony, his body jerking with each sob. Cadan grows tired of his cries, rolling his eyes as he rips a dangling piece of Mayo shirt shoving it into his mouth.

"Thank you, Cadan. Now the bloke can listen to what I have to say."

Bending at my knees and bringing myself eye level with Mayo, I push the center of his forehead. The force makes him swing backward and then return, causing the chains holding him to moan with the movement. "You might be interested to know; I didn't have you brought here because you shot me. Not that what happened could be credited to you as you did, after all, drop the gun."

I hear Finley snicker from my left, but keep my focus on the pleading eyes of Mayo. "I've been shot at more times than you've woken up with a stiff dick. Stabbed and kidnapped, had limbs broken and nearly drowned. But never, in all those other attempts, did they take from me what you have."

Pushing his forehead again, using a little more force as sweat beads roll down Mayo's chest and neck. His head hits the brick wall behind him, slamming him back in my direction. "See, I have this insanely, beautiful woman who loves nothing more than straddling my lap and wrapping her arms around my neck. The problem is, I can't hold her close to me, making her feel like the lady she was born to be. Not to mention, how for the foreseeable future, she has to do all the work, when I want to slide between her thighs, which is not my style at all. When I have a girl under me, I control her pleasure, her every breath, and the way she shouts my name as she begs me to let her come."

The more I talked about my lack of ability to love Heather the way I wanted, the angrier I became.

"Raise him up!"

My father never sheltered me from the ways he obtained information from the people who were under him. While his methods were ancient, they fucking worked. My personal favorite, and the one I chose to introduce to Mayo, would include the piercings in his nipples. Attaching the clamps running to the battery on the floor to his right nipple, the jolt of juice causes him to rock back and forth. "Awe, come on you big pussy. Isn't that the purpose of those things, to direct a little pain to your fucking dick?"

Finley's cell rings as I'm about to attach the second clamp, distracting me as I release the clamp and instead of gripping the metal of his piercing, I slice off the entire nipple, resulting in both falling to the floor.

"Ian, your other guest showed her face. I'll be right back." Finley taps my good shoulder as she passes us. Looking at the severed nipple on the floor and then back at me, she shrugs her shoulders, and then bends over, picking up the battery clamp and digs it into his skin, sending his body into a series of jolts.

"Thanks, love." I praise her, placing a kiss to her temple. Finley will always have a deep place in my heart. I may not care for her as I do Heather, but both women are a constant in my world.

My shoulder throbs, pissing me off more, as I had never had an injury act this way. Cadan shoots me a questioning look, trailing his eyes to my shoulder and back again. There's no need to lie to him, Cadan has the nose of a bloodhound when it comes to afflictions; able to tell if his opponent is seriously hurt or ready for more.

"Hey, T-Bone. You ever have the occasion to box?" Looking past me, Cadan ignores my obvious pain, giving me the time I need to get myself together. Looking over my shoulder, the motion pulls at my wound bringing on a wave of nausea and causing my vision to blur slightly. T-Bone looks to each of his guys, then shakes his head in denial. "Brilliant. Come on, let me show you how we do it in Scotland."

Cadan moves his feet into his stance, landing a few quick jabs to Mayo's ribs. "Don't you need gloves?" Cadan stops his movements, Mayo's body swinging back and forth like a practice bag. Sharing his signature grin with the room, "No, lad. Gloves are for wankers to wear during the winter."

While Cadan shows T-Bone the finer points of UK boxing, I slip outside to my car, retrieving the medicine bag Finley made for me and tossing back the antibiotic she worried I might need. I found a bottle of painkillers, slip a pair into my mouth and chase them both down with water. When I dropped off the mobile phone earlier, I told

Danielle I would return in an hour, but I'd managed to slide past that time nearly an hour and a half ago. Letting Heather into my world placed me in a position where my life was no longer my own. I owed her an explanation and chose to do so by sending her a text message.

> My meeting has gone longer than I planned, I'm sorry, and I will make it up to you.

Just as I was about to go back inside, she returned with an answer, bringing a smile to my face and easing the pain in my shoulder.

> Your work is important, and while I miss you, I understand.

Heather Murray had no idea how well she fit into my life. I couldn't wait to introduce her to my mum and show her the benefits of being with me. With an overwhelming need to see her again, it was time to end this shit and get back to her. My shoes echo off the cement as I walked back in, a new determination in my steps and pull in my chest. Cadan was still showing T-Bone his jabs, but Mayo's eyes are closed and his body limp. He had either passed out or died from all the pounding Cadan and T-Bone have thrown at him.

"Wake that bastard up; I want him to feel how pissed I am." Cadan picks up a bucket of water, splashing it against Mayo's chest, his eyes flying open as he began to struggle against the material in his mouth. Cadan reaches over tugging the fabric and in one swift motion, rips it from his mouth

Finley returned from her errand, a tied-up Destiny in the corner, her makeup stained eyes pleading with me.

"She showed up at Aroma?"

Finley nods as I entered the room, hands hooked on her hips and a satisfied look on her face. "Aye, spouting her mouth off about some new Scot in her bed. She was loud enough to give your Heather a good grin."

Looking to a struggling Destiny, "Really, do I know the poor bloke?" Finley grinned at the cavalier undertone in my rhetorical question. Destiny didn't know how to cut her losses and fade into the shadows. She was willing to lead Mayo into the lion's den, while she sits in the stands and tosses raw meat into the ring.

"You know something, Finley? Since this bitch loves to run her mouth so much, let's give her an opportunity to tell Mayo how everything he has done for her was for nothing."

Cadan and T-Bone had righted Mayo, sitting him in a chair close to Bethany. Finley reached over, ripping the tape off her mouth, a line of snot falling down her face, as her eyes pleaded with mine. Mayo's head dips to his chest briefly before Cadan reaches over, pulling it back up by tugging the hair at the back of his head.

"See, Malcolm," I started, pointing two fingers at his face. "There is no need to call you Mayo or her Destiny for that matter, as the pet name is a tease and not anything related to what you earned. And since Bethany is a whore, it doesn't really matter what we call her, now does it?" Glancing in Bethany's direction giving her a taste of the bite in my voice.

"You have spent your life trying to fit into a circle when you're shaped like a god damn square. You made the mistake of listening to the mental ramblings of a woman, who needed revenge for an affair which never happened, leading you to believe there was something between the two of you. And after the phone call earlier, you now know how much she used you." Pain washed over his face. The kind that would haunt a man forever, killing him slowly as he dove deeper into the thick of it.

"And you," rounding on a shocked faced Bethany. "What is so

wrong in your life you needed to have me killed? A man you barely knew and yet wanted so badly. Willing to risk the life of the only man in this world who seemed to give a shit about you." Tears rolled down her face, fear evident in her eyes. She remained silent, her face contorted as she held back her sobs.

"Heather." Malcolm rasped out, blood trickling down the corner of his mouth, running like a small river onto his chest.

"What about Heather?" Bethany shook her head violently, tears flowing down her face like a waterfall after a spring rain. "I said, what about Heather?" I demanded, the pain in my shoulder returning, fueling the fire I need to become the savage bastard my father created.

"Tell him, baby. You owe me." Malcolm begged, the life in his eyes dimming with each labored breath. "Tell him why you hate her so much."

Bored with Bethany's inability to open her mouth, Finley grabs a handful of blond hair and pulls it hard enough to earn a scream. "Next time, I yank it out. Now talk." Bethany winces as Finley tugs harder, driving home her point.

"She always wins." The words are barely out as her body convulses into sobs. Her breakdown goes unnoticed as an enraged Finley continues. "Wins what?"

Bethany's eyes look to me, fondness and longing swim amongst the terror and pain. "My, God, how pathetic. You can see it in her eyes. She's still mooning over you." Finley was right, Bethany had a dangerous fixation on me, too stubborn to give up and move along when I tossed her out.

Bethany stiffens her back and swallows her tears, and for a moment I'm convinced this breakdown has all been an act. Leaning to the side, she wipes her face on her shoulder and with resolution in her eyes, "Frank, Tony, all the guys adore her, making sure she has what she needs and not making her suck their dicks to get it. Then there's you. I thought I had my chance at the life I want, but then you saw her, and you were just like the rest of them. Falling for her smile, tripping over yourself to get at her."

Finley is back in her face in a snap. "How fucking stupid can you be? Relying on a man, instead of finding your own way in this world." Bethany's confession found the wrong ears as Finley was one of the most independent women I knew. She stood toe to toe against every man in my Family, proving she was just as tough, and twice as strong.

"And you fell for this shit?"

Malcolm began to laugh which rapidly turned into a coughing fit, blood pouring from his mouth. Shrugging his shoulders, "I love her, man."

Cadan lets go of his hair allowing Malcolm to spit blood on the floor, no doubt the result of a few broken ribs. "Oldest game in the books, mate. You should have known to get the pussy first before taking a shot at a man you have no issue with."

Having heard enough fucked up shit for one day, I pulled the Glock from Cadan's waistband, firing two rounds into the center of Malcolm's head. Bethany screamed, and started crying for someone to help her, "Somebody shut her the fuck up!" I demanded, waving the gun at her as my frustration increased.

"I've got this." T-Bone moved around me, pulling a bag from the back pocket in his jeans. "Bitch crossed the wrong motherfucker when she stole my gun." Untying her hands from around her back, Bethany tries to fight him, but two of his men join him, holding her left arm out to the side.

"Just so we're straight, Ian was right; you can't suck dick for shit."

My eyebrow lifts in question as his brown eyes flash to mine, a hint of regret edging out around the need for revenge. "Shorty comes to the crib, acting all friendly and shit. She walks up to me like we's cool, takes the blunt from my hands and motions for me to follow her to the back room. We get back there and she starts taking off her clothes, riding up on me like a fucking pro. I bomb the shit out of her, and she is letting me do anything I want. I pop off a nut, and she jumps up and starts sucking off one of my homeboys. Everything is going great until she decides she needs a minute. One of my other shorty's takes her place, and I don't give her a second thought until I get ready to go collect some bread. When I can't find my piece, I nearly tear the crib up until I remember Bethany letting me fuck her in the ass as she hung out the side window of the bedroom, not two feet from where I laid my gun down."

"The gun Malcolm used to shoot me with."

T-Bone nods his head, "No disrespect, but when she stole from me, she made all of this shit my business, and I ain't about cutting off the fucking hand trying to feed me."

"None taken," offering my hand to him, he takes my digits and shakes firmly. Respect is a curious thing, some feel it is a given, while others demand it be earned. An oath both parties believe benefit them the most. T-Bone and I understand one another, and while we are from different circles, we have mutual respect.

"Everyone knows she is a whore, so when they find her body beside a dumpster, cops will add her to the list of junkies who OD'd in this city." T-Bone ties a tourniquet around her arm, pulling a syringe from the bag in his hand, he injects the contents into Bethany's vein. Her eyes cross and roll back in her head. Giving hot shots to junkies, who either owed some dealer money or pestered him to death for better shit, was a common practice. I'd heard horror stories about how they convulsed and suffered until the heroin finally killed them.

"Gentlemen, clean this up and check in with me later."

Waving the gun in Malcolm's direction, a chorus of "yes sirs" sounded behind me as the guys sprang into action. One of the larger men knelt down to close Malcolm's eyelids, just as T-Bone grabbed his wrist. "Leave them open." Everyone, including myself, stood still as the pair locked eyes, weighing the severity of the interaction. "Motherfucker deserved to die. He needs to watch the Devil come for him." I wouldn't discredit his beliefs as I have a basketful of superstition of my own. Signaling for my guy to comply, I hand Cadan his gun back, "Let's get out of here. I have a girlfriend to spoil."

CHAPTER TEN

IAN

HEATHER

I didn't need to turn around to know Ian was behind me as the air clicked with static electricity. Tiny hairs stood up on the back of my neck. Not in a scary way, but in the way it feels to have a man wrap his arms around you from behind, move your hair over your shoulder, and nibble at the sensitive juncture of your neck. His cologne permeated the air around me, filling me with a higher level of comfort than the steamed milk. I could still taste him on my lips, feel the way his fingers drifted softly across my face as he took his time kissing me, fueling a desire in me, one only he could ignite. I close my eyes as I feel his fingers play with my ponytail, curling the ends around his hand as he presses his hips into me. A moan vibrates from his chest, against my back.

"The sway of your hips is making it extremely difficult to maintain my self-control and not bend you over this counter, claiming what is mine." Nipping my earlobe with his teeth, burying his nose into the shell of the tender flesh, his deep inhale of air tickles the skin on my neck, creating a moan in me to match his. His actions both thrill and make me nervous. My body craves more, begs him to touch me, kiss and even bite harder. My brain, however, is waving red flags, screaming at me to think about what he's doing, and how many other women have heard his sweet words and devilish lines.

The rational side of me, the one who goes to bed early and says her prayers, wins out as I turn to face him. "Mr. McLeod, you can't come back behind the counter, my boss will have a fit." I'm rewarded with a clever smile and loving eyes. But it's the flush of his skin and pink of his cheeks that makes my smile drop and my hands reach up to feel his skin.

"Ian, you're burning up." Every time I touch him, I bask in the heat he has naturally, but this is different. Where his warmth is usually welcomed to cast away the chill of my day, this is the heat of a fever, one not created from kissing my neck and talking dirty to me.

"Are you trying to say I'm hot?" Wagging his eyebrows, he cups my face with his free hand. Glancing around to make sure no one is within listening distance, I pull his hand away.

"Ian, I'm serious. You're pale, and your skin is hot."

"I know, Heather." His voice is deep and serious, and I can hear the exhaustion in the thickness of it. "I'm tired and my lack of sleep last night is catching up with me. And you're right; I do feel as if I'm fighting something."

The bell over the door announces the arrival of a new customer. Ian looks over his shoulder but doesn't let my face go. Shifting my eyes over, I let out a sigh of relief as Finley walks in the door, followed by Cadan and several other men, a few I recognize from the neighborhood.

"Aye, just the person I need to see." He calls out to Finley, as Cadan, who is leaning over the counter, motions for Danielle to come closer to him. She tried to hide how she found Cadan attractive yesterday when he came in. I suppose he was a handsome man, with his dark hair and green eyes, thick lashes and a killer smile, but

Danielle had an on again off again boyfriend. She was currently wondering if they were off as he had ignored her recent text messages. Danielle, much like me, was a sucker for a strong, handsome man, especially one with connections to certain organizations. Finley smacked Cadan in the back of the head as she walked around him, the pair exchanging a look which was directly related to the flirting he was shamelessly doing with Danielle.

Where Ian has exhaustion written all over his face, Cadan looks as if he could take on the world, or at least Danielle. So many questions floating around in my head, a kaleidoscope of scenarios of what may have happened to Mayo. Rumors started popping up in hushed whispers on the lips of a few afternoon customers. Ian's name had joined the ranks of Mr. Santos, solidifying his position as someone who was not to be messed with. Soon, men and women alike would seek him out, trying to carve a notch in his world for themselves. I wouldn't fool myself into believing there wouldn't be more girls like Destiny who walk in here and try to catch Ian's eye.

"Hey, can I steal you away for dinner later?"

"Of course, but wouldn't you rather crawl into bed and sleep for a week?" Ian pulls me closer, returning his mouth to the shell of my ear. "Crawling into bed to sleep should never be uttered together where you are concerned." A traitor chill runs down my back, leaving a wake of heated lava in its path. Damn him and his ability to control my body the way he does, expertly playing me like a seasoned musician. I'm swimming in deep waters when it comes to Ian and the life he lives, full of pitfalls and hidden dangers. And the biggest risk, the one which would become the largest threat, is what he is capable of doing to my heart.

"Dinner sounds great." I agree without hesitation. While those girls will come, and chances are, there will be many; I plan to enjoy every minute I have with him.

"Brilliant, I'll pick you up when I'm finished for the day."

Finley comes to stand beside me, pulls out a cup, fills it with hot water, and then grabs a tea bag, depositing it into the hot water.

"You ready for me to look at your shoulder?" Ian nods solemnly, grimacing slightly as he kisses my lips once more, reaching behind me for a cup of his own. Finley smacks his hand, motioning with a tip of her head for him to go upstairs. She pulls down another cup as he places a kiss on the back of her hair, bringing a speck of a smile to her face. Cadan joins him as he rounds the counter, a cup of coffee in one hand and a knowing grin on his lips. Danielle either promised him something enticing, or she told him in three words or less what he could do with himself. Either way, his face held a blanket of pride, with a chunk of victory tucked into his hip pocket. Ian cast a final look over his shoulder as Cadan opened the door, Frank, and Tony fresh on their heels.

"Heather if you plan to be in his life, you will need to learn how to brew a cup of tea. His mum, Lady Greer, sets her watch to tea time and judges a person's character on how well the tea is made." The perfect opportunity to share my family history was laid out before me, but something told me, perhaps my father's warning of trusting too freely, giving your secrets away before they benefited you, kept my mouth closed and my knowledge inside my head, save for a time where it would truly matter. Finley complimented the brand of tea we had, admitting she would never have suspected an American store to offer it. After my father passed, Frank come by to visit, making sure I was handling things well and seeing if I needed anything. He commented on the tea I served him and had me order it for the shop when I went back to work. Finley grabbed the cups and a plate of pastries Danielle had put together, "Someone will ring you if we need anything."

Hours after Finley closed the door to the stairs, a pair of police officers came into the shop, Joe Ferrezzio and Jamie Ricco. Both had been in many times, selling information to Frank or picking up money

Mr. Santos owed them. Joe was tall, muscular, and had all the quali-
ties of a player which is why he attracted the attention of Danielle so
long ago. I know they went out a few times, but according to her,
nothing had gone past a good night kiss.

Jamie was just as tall, with a slender build and kind eyes. He, with
his wife and three kids, live in the same building I do. The pair
constantly fought, mostly about money from what I could understand,
but occasionally a girl's name would get tossed in the cruel words and
gut-wrenching insults. I'd overheard him mention a few times how
unhappy he was, yet too worried about her taking away his kids to do
anything real about it.

After they ordered a black coffee and Joe flirted shamelessly with
Danielle, they took a seat by the window. Jamie appeared upset,
agitated as he sat drinking his coffee. Joe tried to engage him several
times, but Jamie kept his attention focused on the pedestrians on the
sidewalk. Frank came downstairs just as they were leaving, greeted
them and offered them something to eat and a fresh drink.

"Have to take a rain check, Frank."

"Oh, something going on we should know about?" Jamie pulled
Frank to the edge of the counter, leaving a short distance between the
pair as he attempts to hide the conversation.

"Bethany Palmer was found behind a dumpster a few blocks
over."

"Any sign of assault?"

"This wasn't a rape or beating; we found track marks on her arm
and between her toes. She had a few burns on her wrist, but the
Coroner feels those may have been self-inflicted."

Frank shakes his head, his face contorting in disappointment. "I
knew she was into a few destructive habits, but shooting up was never
one of them." Jamie places his hands on his hip, the creek of his
leather belt increases the tension as his fingers rest on the edge of his
holster. "She's been arrested twice for drug possession in the past year

in Manhattan. Both times at a high-end hotel where security was called due to a disturbance."

Joe pulls out his phone as Jamie's eyes flash back to the window. "I'm headed over to tell Cindy about her sister's death."

My heart breaks for Jamie as his voice cracks when he says her name. A few years ago, when Cindy was attacked, Jamie was the cop who found her. He was there as they placed her in the ambulance, riding with her and staying while they bandaged her up. Jamie did everything in his power to catch the guy, but no arrests have been made. If I were to think about it hard enough, it seems to me; it was the same time he and his wife started having issues.

"You tell her if she needs anything to give me a call." Jamie nodded his head. With a long face, he slipped his hat back on and headed out the door.

Frank and Tony spoke in hushed voices, pulling money out of their pockets and agreeing on something. I wasn't stupid enough to believe Destiny's death wasn't a direct result of her involvement in Ian's shooting. She may not have pulled the trigger, but she certainly loaded the gun with the amount of conniving she'd done. As Joe and Jamie get in their car, Duane Carter, the owner of the funeral home six blocks over steps inside. I cringe as he scans the room, from the first day I met the man, he has given me the creeps with the way he looks at me. Tony and Frank walked over to where he stands, Frank extending out a hand to shake, no doubt slipping him enough money to make the problem with Destiny go away. I'm about to turn away when a thought hits me, Duane isn't here because of Destiny. He would have picked her body up from the alley and contacted her sister. No, he is here for another reason, one I hadn't considered until now. Duane helped Frank make more people disappear than Houdini, and if my suspicion is right, that someone today is Mayo.

"Can you believe she's dead?"

Startled, I turn back to Danielle surveying the expression on her face. Her eyes are fixed on the door where Joe had exited. With the rag in her hand, she aimlessly wipes the same spot repeatedly, her ponytail swaying back and forth.

"If what they say about her doing drugs is true, then I guess it was only a matter of time. It would certainly explain a lot of things about her."

"Do you think Mayo was supplying her?"

"It's possible, I guess." It was a complete lie; Mayo was many things and tried to be so much more, but he didn't have the courage to approach a drug dealer, much less be one.

I know Danielle's about to break it into a thousand questions as to what Mayo's role in all this was. She's worked here longer than I have and should know by now to follow rule number one. As I'm about to remind her of it, the door to the stairs opens wide, Finley leading the pack of men. Ian is the last to come down, the sling he wore earlier nowhere in sight. His face looks better, less ashen and feverish, almost normal. Cadan is laughing about something and sends a wink in Danielle's direction. It doesn't have the same effect as earlier, no girlie giggles or blushing. Too bad for Cadan, Danielle will always have a soft spot for Joe.

Finley rounds the corner, grabbing another tea bag as she fills her cup with hot water. "Do me a favor, Heather," not bothering to look up as she makes her tea. "Don't let him exert himself. I've changed his antibiotics, so he should be on the mend."

"Finley, I have one mum I don't need two." Ian rounds the corner, slips past her and wraps me in a tight hug. It feels good to have both arms around me; his unique scent floods my senses, and I can't help but fall into his embrace.

"I'm quite acquainted with your mum. I'm sure I speak for her when I say, take it easy." Finley's reprimand has some serious bite to it; it's evident she's been a caregiver in his life for quite a while. Her stony features give him no leeway, not a crevice for him to charm her.

"On the contrary, Finley. Mum would insist I spend a glorious evening with this beautiful creature. Which, by all measures, I intend to do."

Finley is about to open her mouth when the ringing of her cell stops her. Pulling it from her pocket, a smile like I've never seen graces her lips. It's clear as day, whoever is on the other line is important.

"Tell Brion I said hello, *Mum.*" Turning her back to him, she waves her hand over her shoulder, while raising the phone to her ear and whispering into the receiver.

"Who is Brion?" I question into his chest, not ready to let him go. Having him this close felt incredible and all-consuming.

"He's her boyfriend. He lives in Chicago, but I suspect he's making a trip to New York."

"Chicago? Wow, that sucks." The words were out before I considered the situation. Ian and I lived half a world away from each other, with no guarantees of how permanent his visits would be.

"Not really. He works for an associate, so she gets to see him as often as she'd like. I imagine he's calling to tell her he's arrived." Ian pulls back against my protest of wanting just another minute surrounded by him. I could stay here forever lost in the essence of him. "Which ironically gives us the entire evening alone. How about I finish my day and meet you at my penthouse in two hours?"

* * *

SOFT MUSIC FILTERS THROUGH HIDDEN SPEAKERS AS IAN OPENS THE door to the penthouse for me. The fresh aroma of meat cooking lingers in the air as he closes the door behind me. Raising his hand to my cheek, his eyes scan my face as a hint of a smile crosses his lips before he lowers his head, placing a somber kiss on my lips.

"I hope you're hungry. Cadan oversaw picking up our dinner, and he has a healthy appetite."

Ian grabs my hand, his fingers intertwining with mine, leading me out of the foyer and into the main room. It's been a few days since I was here last, but so much has changed. Gone is the black and white sterile feel, in its place are rich fabrics complimenting the windows with majestic curtains. The walls are painted a robin's egg blue, and crown molding has been added. The once masculine and linear furnishings, now look as if they belong in a museum highlighting the turn of the century.

"What happened in here?"

Ian lets my hand go long enough to light the tall candles housed inside the ornate holders. The Queen Anne mahogany table takes up a massive amount of real estate. Two place settings adorn the end of the table. Ian fills two crystal glasses with wine as I take in the splendor of the room.

"Wasn't this room white a few days ago?"

Ian smiles but doesn't drop his focus from the glasses of wine. "Yes, they were, but I know how my mum is, she would have hated the black and white. I called her decorator, who happened to be in New York at a trade show, and she and her crew did all of this yesterday."

I was impressed, normally work like this took weeks, not hours, to complete. Having the resources to do something like this would be amazing.

"The windows are incredible."

"I suppose," shrugging his shoulder, handing me one of the glasses of wine. "My mum is quite particular about her surroundings. She has the same fabric in all the homes we own, same furnishings and all."

Holding his glass in the air as if to toast, I follow suit, admiring the look of happiness on his face. "To new beginnings, a prosperous business, and the most beautiful woman I know."

"Cheers," touching my glass to his, I raise the crimson liquid to my lips, savoring the delightful flavors as they caress my tongue. I'm not surprised at how good the wine tastes, considering his family's ownership of several vineyards, another discovery during my perusal of Google.

Ian places his glass back on the table, his tongue slipping out to savor the last trace of wine on his lips. His actions leave me feeling heated, adjusting my position to gain some friction, clenching my thighs together in hopes of a little relief.

"I thought it might be nice to let you sample a few of my favorites from Scotland."

Ian pulls four aluminum flat pans from a handled shopping bag. There's no logo on the front, but I suspect he had Cadan visit McClain's, an old pub over off Fifteenth that serves traditional Scottish fair, with a new special each day. Like most of the ethnic places in this neighborhood, the owners were immigrants who settled here several generations ago.

"Now, I'm not sure if it will be as good as the stuff I get back home, but it will give you an idea."

The Ian standing before me was unlike the one who spoke with Mayo or even the one I'd met in the street. This Ian was carefree, dressed in jeans and a long-sleeved shirt, completely relaxed. I didn't have the heart to tell him I'd tasted the food he loved from Scotland, made from the tender hands of my mum. This was important to him, a piece of his life he wanted to share with me.

McClain's was decent enough, but the real joy was listening to Ian speak of how he could eat his weight in Scottish eggs, shortbread, and stovies. Ian refused to let me help with the cleanup, giving the excuse of the staff taking care of it. I chose not to protest, instead refilled my glass and wandered off to enjoy the view through the windows of the dining room.

Twilight had faded into the horizon, its purplish hues hanging on the last ounce of dusk, surrendering to the dark of night. I could see my reflection in the glass, appreciate the happiness Ian put in my eyes. He filled his glass once more but didn't pick it up, choosing instead to stand behind me, pulling my hair to one side.

"I love how your perfume lingers." Touching the end of his nose to the skin of my neck, I can feel and hear him suck in a deep breath, committing to memory the fragrance he found there.

"I can't wait to taste you," he places an open-mouthed kiss on my neck, causing shivers of arousal to ignite the embers I tried so hard to kill earlier. "Every time I see you."

Pulling the collar of my shirt to the side with his left hand, exposing my shoulder, while his right hand seeks out my breast, kneading it through the layers of my shirt and bra.

He nips at the skin of my shoulder, pinching it between his teeth and then soothing it with his flattened tongue. Releasing my breast, he threads his hand into my hair, wrapping it around his wrist and tugging it tight to the right, opening my neck for him to lick and suck.

Releasing my hair, he reaches around, cups my chin in his hand, turns my face over my shoulder and devours my lips. Our tongues come together like two trains on a collision course, desperately seeking one another. A groan escapes my throat as Ian's hand trails down my neck and collar, past the material of my shirt and bra, grasping my right breast in his large hand. Fingers knead the tender flesh as his thumb circles my nipple, bringing his digits together creating sensations which shoot directly to my clit. I attempt to back away, intending to put my glass down before returning to the intensity he is creating. Instead, he grabs my right hand, slamming it to the glass of the window. "Don't move your hand, Heather," he growls, his eyes dark with lust.

The crystal glass in my other hand trembles from the need I have for him, I so desperately want to set the fragile container down for fear of breaking it. "Keep that glass in your hand, and the wine inside, I'm far from finished with you." I can see his eyes in the reflection of the window, commanding and hungry, never leaving mine as his lips once again find the skin of my neck. My nipples are hard from his continued ministrations, and I feel as if I could climax from his touch alone. I can feel the edge nearing, the burn in my belly starting to increase, as my knees get weaker, the glass in my hand grows heavier.

My mouth opens as the edges of my vision starts to blur into a white haze, my breathing labored and urgent. I'm so close I can almost taste the sweet fragrance of my impending orgasm. But as my body starts to shatter, Ian releases my nipple, moving his hands lower to the button of my jeans, unclasping them and shoving down the zipper as he moves his left hand through my saturated folds. I'm stunned at first, and a fair bit pissed off he would leave me on edge and not let me tumble over. All is forgiven when he trades my nipple for my clit. He slides two fingers inside me, pressing his thumb hard onto my swollen and needy nerve, allowing me to shatter into a million pieces. I cry out as the euphoria surrounds me, the feeling of absolute calm and relaxation filling the space between us. Sex has never been like this, intense and all-consuming; ironically while my clothes remained on.

He removes his hand from my jeans, the moisture of my climax wet on his fingers, leaving a heated trail as he caresses the skin of my pelvis. Keeping our eyes locked in the reflection of the glass, he brings his fingers to his mouth, sucking them clean as he straightens the collar of my shirt. Leaning my forehead against the glass, Ian moves to the table, his fingers still buried inside his mouth, picking up his discarded glass of wine, savoring the flavor of me until the last possible second as he brings the glass to his lips. I want nothing more than to clear the distance between us, toss the glass to the floor and strip him naked. Pushing away from the window, I have every intention of taking him as he took me, when the sound of his cell pierces the surrounding tension.

Ian pulls the phone from his pocket, glancing at the screen, and then answering in Gaelic. I pretend I don't understand what he is saying, knowing how dishonest it is, but feeling too good to care. He listens intently, then says to call him back when they arrive. Ending the call, he looks at me, "Sorry, love. I have to take care of something, and I'm back with you."

I expect him to go into another room or exit onto the balcony, but he doesn't. Instead, he motions me toward him, opening his arms in an invitation to snuggle into his protection.

"It's Ian. I have some information you're going to want to hear."

CHAPTER ELEVEN

IAN

Doing what I do, it's beneficial to have knowledge of any skeletons hiding in the closets of your friends, and particularly your enemies. My father passed the ones he had down to me in the hours before his death, his involvement no longer relevant. One had me questioning the man closest to me, fueling my decision to send my half-brother Blake to the States and Darrow to follow behind with orders to kill him. What Darrow didn't know, is how his betrayal forced me to contact Cadan, arranging for him to take out Darrow.

The most significant and damaging skeleton my father shared with me, involved the Malloy's and a secret, which would have imploded the Family if it got out. I'd chosen to keep what I knew to myself, that is until Darrow turned his back on my Family. When his loyalties changed, so did mine. Now, he could deal with whatever hell the Malloy's rained down on him.

Holding Heather close, I silently celebrated inside my head as my plan formulated. I would settle the score with my father's transgressions against my mum, while allowing the Malloy's to have the closure they didn't know would be coming. Declan Malloy wanted revenge for the shooting of his wife, Katie, and the tragic death of their unborn child. Patrick, his father, had dealt with the kidnapping of his wife, Christi, years ago before they were married. He had made sure the parties involved died for their betrayal, all except one.

Raindrops cascade rapidly down the glass of the window while the memory of Heather's orgasm causes my cock to twitch. I hadn't planned on taking her like that, but when she stood in front of the window, the allure of her became too great. I had to stake a claim to her, leaving no doubt in her mind who she belonged with.

Lightning off in the distance followed by a deep rumble of thunder startles her, sending her deeper into my side. I now understand how Dominic felt when Anna did the same thing back in Chicago as we waited for our plane. How he subconsciously caged her in his arms, protecting her from whatever caused her fear.

"There's a trip coming up I'd like to discuss with you."

Just as the sound of the thunder causes her to jump, the vibration of my voice elicits the same reaction. She tries to pull back, but I hold fast, not willing to let the warmth of her body leave mine.

"You're leaving?"

Her voice cracks, the disappointment evident in the sadness of her words. I hate how the sorrow in her voice sounds, something I can smash like a fucking bug on the floor.

"No love," pulling my fingers through her hair, losing myself in the silky strands, as the scent of her shampoo drifts up into my nose. "We are."

Heather pulls back, extricating herself from my side, this time I allow her. Pieces of her dark hair fall to her shoulders, her hazel-green, disbelieving eyes, stare back at me. "Excuse me?"

Unable to hide the smile her defensiveness brings out, I reach for her hand, needing to touch a part of her, have her warmth and goodness surrounding me. "Hear me out," I plead, turning my body to face hers, grasping her hand in mine. "Finley has done everything she knows to do for my shoulder, but she and I both agree it would be best for me to see my family physician. Cadan contacted him, and he is visiting Italy, but wants to have a look at the wound."

"I can't, Ian. I'd love to, but I can't miss work." Her mouth says no, but the rest of her body screams yes. Leaning over, she grabs her glass and downs the remainder of her wine. I watch with fascination as she tips her head back, allowing the last drop of the crimson good-ness to fall on her tongue and down her throat.

"Correct me if I'm wrong, but you work for me, yes?"

Heather's body heaves as she takes a deep breath, no doubt considering her response carefully, tasting defeat on the horizon. I can see the conflict in her features, confused between what she knows is the truth and something I'm not privy to. The longer I'm around her, the more I want to know about her, dig deeper into her soul.

"You are," she exhales. "Which makes things worse." Setting her glass on the table, looking back at me over her right shoulder. "People will say you're playing favorites."

Reaching over, I take a hand full of her silky strands and let them fall, admiring how the shine of her hair soaks in the light of the room, each strand falling in perfect harmony with the one before. Looking up, my gaze locks with hers, "So if I brought Danielle over here, made her come against the window, and then offered to take her with us, you'd feel better?"

Fire, rage and something I wasn't certain I could label, develops in her eyes. Her nostrils flare, and her breath hitches when my quirked eyebrow remains in place. Heather Murray has a possessive side, one she caged me within. I could never fault her for it as it mirrored my own in regard to her. I would, however, use it to my advantage.

"If you want to be with Danielle like that, I have no reason to stand in your way."

She tries hard to cover the crack in her voice as she lies through her teeth. Adjusting her shoulders, she dons a complacent attitude, or perhaps she was fishing for a definition or clarification of how I viewed us.

"C'mere."

Some battles aren't worth winning, not when the price of victory includes the shredded emotions of someone you care deeply about.

"I want to share with you the home I have in Italy, the people in the village and one of the wineries I own there. Then after my doctor takes a look at this shoulder, I want to show you where I grew up, let you taste authentic Scottish food, visit with my people, and introduce you to my mum—as my girlfriend."

It's funny how ten letters seem insignificant when they float around aimlessly, but align them together and create a word. One stowed away in the heart of a young girl, or the internal workings of a beautiful woman. Either way, it has allowed a speck of a grateful smile and the exhale of a held breath to relax the girl who completes my world.

"I don't have a passport or..." Her mistake was out before she could catch it. She didn't need to finish her statement; I knew where this is going. Pulling out my phone, dropping my eyes to the screen briefly as I unlock it and select the number.

"I need you to arrange for a passport for Heather, and an open return ticket from Edinburgh. Make sure it's first class and on my desk in the next few days." I don't wait for the argument Cadan undoubtedly has for me as I pocket the phone and admire the look of surprise on Heather's face.

"You can give me a thousand reasons why you can't go. Tell yourself just as many on why you should stay behind. We can sit here all night and argue the various points you have cataloged in your beautiful mind. Or you can let me spoil the fuck out of you, treating you the way I know you deserve." I rub my nose along her jaw, kissing my way down her neck, inwardly cheering as her body surrenders and the sweet taste of victory floats in the air.

"And we can spend the rest of the night enjoying one another, instead of fighting a battle you know you want to surrender to." Dropping my voice lower, a dirty trick I've used on more than one occasion, I nip at the sensitive skin on the edge of her ear. "One simple word, Heather. Say what we both know you're holding in."

I can feel the moment she gives in, letting her body follow her heart as I'd hoped she would.

"Yes."

"Mmm, good girl."

Leaning her back on the couch, I have every intention of making her come again, bring her to the edge of insanity and give her the level of pleasure which will make her forget her name. My lips capture hers, dominating the speed and intensity of the kiss. My hand slides under her shirt, my fingers dipping under the lace of her bra, surrounding the delicate flesh of her breast. Her nipple pebbles instantly, her soft moan spurs me on. Her tiny fingers find the back of my neck, gripping the short hair and tugging hard enough to pull a moan from me, the pain taking a direct path to my cock.

"Ian," she pants as I pull back to remove her shirt, needing to feel her skin against mine. Her eyes are full of want, hands reaching for me as I pull her up, and grab the hem of her shirt.

"Shh," I warn her, letting her know with a sly grin how much she is going to enjoy this. With a return smile, she raises her arms above her head, giving me an unhindered path to getting her one step closer to naked. As her hair falls to the soft skin of her back, her shirt hanging loosely between my fingers, my cell rings in the tone I have set for my caretaker in Italy. I feel her body sag, the aggravated sigh leaving her ample chest. I consider ignoring it, letting it go to voicemail and dealing with it later, but Roberto would never call if there weren't an issue.

"Yes?"

"Mr. Ian, it's Roberto. I apologize for the call, but something has happened you should know about."

Handing Heather her top, I stand and walk to the French doors, the rain still coming down fast enough to keep me inside. I can see the reflection of the room in the glass and watch in awe as Heather tucks herself into the cushions, attempting to ignore me.

"It's fine, Roberto. What's the issue?"

Roberto and his wife, Margareta, have worked at the villa since the moment the first owners walked through the door. The pair worked tirelessly and for little pay until Velenići Porchelli was killed in his bed by a psychotic woman out for revenge for wrongs against her. Roberto had Margareta run into town in the dead of night to report the murder to the authorities. I'd heard stories from the men who worked for Porchelli of how the woman, in a crazed state, marched around the house demanding to be recognized as the new leader of the Family.

"Mr. Darrow phoned from the train station needing the car to pick him and a guest up. I hadn't received word from you of any expected arrivals"

Darrow was moving faster than I anticipated. Either he was spooked by something or being rushed by his travel companion. I'd bet my left nut it was the latter.

"Go ahead and send the car. Let them have the guest rooms on the second floor. Tell Margareta no special meals and the sheets get burned when they leave."

"Of course. Anything else, sir?"

I'm about to decline when I catch Heather reach over and fill her glass with more wine. "Yes, pretend to misplace the keys to my wine cellar, Darrow has a taste for my private stock."

Ending the call, I watch Heather as she tucks her feet under her body, using the cell phone I gave her to keep herself occupied. I can't wait to take her to Italy, walk with her through the rows of grapes as I let her taste the incredible wine we make. I want to watch the sunset from the balcony of my bedroom, as I love her until the sun rises the next morning. By the time I was able to acquire the property, the vineyard was overgrown and in near ruin. It had taken several seasons before the vines began to produce. Today, my vineyard has brought me an excellent return on my investment and has won many awards.

With Darrow feeling comfortable enough to seek shelter at my villa, he would feel safe enough to stay as long as I allowed. Giving me the opportunity I need to set my plan into motion. Raising my phone to my ear, I watch as Heather laughs silently at something on her screen. I hear the phone ring twice before the gruff voice answers.

"It's done."

CHAPTER TWELVE

HEATHER

HAVING NEVER LEFT NEW YORK, this would be my first time on an airplane. I'd barely slept the past few days, attempting to rationalize with myself why this trip was a good thing and not something to fear. It was more than my anxiety about being thousands of feet up in the air, sitting in a tube with several engines full of highly flammable jet fuel attached to the belly. It was all the guilt I allowed to move into my mind, clouding the rational side of me and making me momentarily forget this was part of being with Ian. In the end, I reminded myself it was an opportunity to give my parents what they had asked of me; taking them back home where they could rest in peace.

Danielle nearly bounced out of her skin when I told her where I was going, begging me to let her take me shopping over on Jamaica Avenue. Her excitement reminded me how foolish this was, I didn't have the funds to shop at a thrift store, much less the trendy places she frequented. Gabe didn't understand why I didn't ask Ian for money to shop with after all it was his mum I would need to impress. I waved him off, telling the pair I didn't feel comfortable approaching him for money, as the relationship was still new. Gabe pointed out Ian had purchased my cell phone; so a few hundred dollars more wouldn't make much difference. I argued it was Ian's idea to get the phone, not a request on my part. Danielle finally relented when I gave her my best pouty face and begged to borrow some clothes from her.

Ian was pleased with himself as he took in the surprised look on my face as he slid my passport and first-class ticket across the counter, grinning like the cat who ate the canary when I held the papers tightly to my chest, cradling them like a new born baby unable to believe he had pulled off the impossible. The glint in his blue eyes sparkled back at me as he leaned over, removing my hands from my chest, and pulled me closer to him. The smell of him covers me, filling me with a heat, which travels from my head to my core. He requested I spend the night before we left with him in his penthouse, but a call late in the afternoon caused him to cancel. Although, he did promise he would make it up to me while we were away.

Making sure I had everything I needed, I checked my purse for my identification and passport. I had looked three times since I put them in there last night, terrified I would get to Italy and then be turned away when I couldn't produce the proper documents. Double-checking the two containers which held my parent's ashes and my mum's ring, reminding myself this was the justification for allowing Ian to take me on this trip. My father spoke fondly of the home they first shared, and I hoped to have time to locate it, see the place where I was conceived for myself.

Ian called to tell me he would pick me up around lunchtime at my apartment, but since we weren't leaving until midday, I chose to work the morning shift, earning at least a little money as I didn't have an exact return date. He wanted me to meet his mum, Lady Greer, who was currently on holiday herself. He assured me she would be on a plane the moment he let her know I had arrived.

* * *

"WHY ARE YOU HERE?" DANIELLE STOOD INSIDE THE DOOR, HER HAIR still wet from her early morning shower, hands on her hips and a disbelieving look on her face. "You're supposed to be sleeping beside your boyfriend, exhausted from all the crazy hot sex he is giving you."

"He had to cancel last night, and I already told you we aren't leaving until noon."

Danielle crosses the room, her backpack hanging off her left shoulder. "And you came here instead of his penthouse? You could have snuck into his bed and given him a wake-up blowjob." Subtlety had never been one of Danielle's strong suits. She had tried several avenues to coax a hint out of me as to how far Ian and I had gone in our relationship. I didn't have the desire to tell her of my frustration at every interruption we encountered as we attempted to go further.

"Do you really think sneaking into anything involving Ian is a good plan?" Danielle shrugs her shoulders, grabs a cup from the warmer and fills it to the brim with fresh coffee.

"While you make a good point, I'd bet money he wouldn't be angry if you showed up naked in his bed." Blowing gently across the top of her coffee, "Put a gun in your face, maybe, but not mad."

Just as the morning rush died down, Ian and Cadan walked in like a pair of runway models. Wearing his signature suit, eyes hidden behind sunglasses and a severe look on his face, Ian took my breath away. His bright smile greets me as he lowers his glasses, revealing those sapphire blue eyes which make me melt. Brilliant white teeth light up his face and remind me how incredible his kisses are. Rounding the corner of the counter, he doesn't disappoint as he delivers a soft reminder, his cologne adding a layer to the comfort he brings me. "Hey, love. I'm sorry about last night," his hand reaches up to cup my cheek. "I'm going to make it up to you, starting now."

* * *

PULLING INTO THE AIRPORT, I ASSUMED WE WOULD PARK THE CAR IN long-term parking and walk to the terminal. However, when Cadan passed the turnoff and headed to a side road, my heart began hammering in my chest. He took three more turns, driving past several older hangers owned by airline companies I recognized from television ads. Finally, he pulled the car into the open door of the last hanger, putting it in park, but leaving the engine running. Several men dressed in black suits came to stand on either side of the car, and I notice tiny white cords tucked behind their ears. They stood still as statues, not bothering to say hello as Ian and Cadan climbed out of the car. Ian lent me his hand as I cautiously step from the vehicle.

Ian takes my hand in his, squeezing my fingers as he leads me toward the steps of the plane. I'd assumed we would take a commercial flight, never in my wildest dreams would I have thought he would rent a private jet.

"Mr. McLeod." A man, I assumed by the uniform he wore was the pilot, greeted Ian. The two shook hands before he invited us to board the jet. With shaky legs, a mixture of apprehension and excitement, I took my place behind Ian as he climbed the steps.

Considering the sleekness of the exterior, the inside of the cabin had to be incredible, however what I found as I reached the top of the stairs made my breath hitch and my pulse quicken. I had been impressed with his penthouse, but it was nothing compared to the luxuriousness of this space. Cream leather seats, embossed with a scripted letter M, a stag and a crown on either side in heavy thread. Tiffany blue blankets, lush and thick, were rolled neatly and resting in the center of each chair. High gloss varnished wood covered the floor, reflecting the soft lighting of the candle sconces. But it was the oil painting hanging in the rear of the plane which impressed me most.

A strikingly beautiful woman, with hair the same shade as Ian's, sat in a high-back chair, her expression neutral as if bored with sitting for the artist. A stern looking man stood to the right of her, his cruel looking eyes, surrounded by lines of wisdom and worry, stared back at me. In an instant I knew, Ian hadn't rented this plane, his family owned it. A chill found my spine as I looked into the painted eyes of whom I can only assume is Lady Greer. Suddenly, I was afraid to touch anything; too worried she would reach out and smack the back of my hand in reprimand.

"Sit anywhere you want, love." Ian's voice sends a shiver down my spine, making me jump as if he could read my thoughts. Embarrassed by my overactive imagination, I take the first seat on my left, tucking the blanket gently in my lap. Cadan sits across from me, tossing himself into the seat as if it's his living room, reaching over and taking the blanket from my lap, he throws it along with his to the sofa across the aisle.

"Always hated those fucking things, sheds like a motherfucker all over your clothes."

Ian sits down beside me, a bottle of amber colored liquor in his hand. Raising the wooden armrest, he reaches in and pulls out three glasses.

"Since this is your first flight, I think it calls for a little something to take the edge off." Normally I would have declined, as I'm not a huge drinker, but he was right this was my first flight, and I was considerably nervous. Cadan leaned forward as Ian poured the alcohol into glasses, his anticipation almost childlike, as if receiving his favorite brand of ice cream.

"Heather, I'm glad you're on this trip, this bloody bastard would have made me drink the cheap shit otherwise." I suspect Cadan is teasing as nothing about Ian struck me as cheap. He handed me a glass, the smile on his lips making it almost possible to ignore the sound of the engines increasing.

Cadan held his glass high, signaling a toast. "To meeting Lady Greer and all it entails." Something about the way he said it, and the look he and Ian exchanged, made my heart stammer a little, and question the choice I made to take this trip.

"Really mate?" Ian tossed his blanket at Cadan's head, the pair of them laughing at the inside joke. "You make my mum sound like a fucking troll, chasing all the beautiful women away." Cadan is laughing so hard he nearly spills his drink.

"Keep it up fucker, and you won't get another drop." Ian turns to me, removes the glass from my hand and places his fingers under my chin. "I can see it in your eyes, Heather, you're worried about meeting her. I can assure you she will love you and she will see what I do when I look at you." The softness in his voice as he recites the latter makes my heart come alive, and all the worries I've accumulated vanish into thin air. His touch is hypnotic as I barely feel the plane gaining altitude.

Ian excuses himself to take a call, and I question if he will be able to keep his promise of this trip being about us. The thought is barely born, and I instantly feel guilty. It's not like I don't understand what's involved with a man who is a syndicate leader. I've heard all the stories and seen far too much heartache, but I know, in the end, I can handle this life he lives.

"Heather, please accept my apology, my joke was in bad taste earlier. I assumed you'd be more like Finley, and less like some other girls he has dated."

In my mind, Cadan is digging a bigger hole for Ian rather than helping him out, as I never gave a thought to the women who had come before me. How I wish I could find where they had failed, study their flaws and avoid them at all costs. Knowledge like that is a double-edged sword, as discovering their shortcomings also gives way to knowing their strengths, making your inadequacies more apparent.

"You're good for him, Heather. Ian's right, Lady Greer will take a shining to you."

Cadan takes the bottle of scotch, ignoring his glass and began drinking straight from the top. He offers the bottle to me, but I shake my head and settle into my seat. Ian returns a short while later, only to be called away several more times. I pass the time by looking out the window at the bank of clouds, which seemed to sail below us. I wondered if the clouds were to open if I could see the ocean? When Ian gets up for the fifth time, Cadan pushes a button on his armrest, and a flat screen television descends from the ceiling.

"I have some business to attend to, order any movie you want, even those in theater now." Knowing this was a long flight, and Ian would be pulled away for most of it, I perused the selection and settled in to enjoy some of Hollywood's delight. Sometime after the movie started, my tired eyes began to droop. One moment I was watching a chase scene through the streets of LA, and the next I could hear faint whispers about the Malloy family.

"You plan on telling him the truth, or at least what you understand to be the truth? Shaw wasn't always the best at keeping a story straight you know."

"Cadan, I'm well aware of what my father was capable of, the lengths he went to in order to make himself look good. I need to set the precedence with Malloy, take advantage of the guilt he feels for killing Blake. He needs to know the truth, and she needs to pay for every crime she has committed against this Family."

CHAPTER THIRTEEN

IAN

I KNEW Heather was no stranger to the rules of my life, yet the knowledge didn't keep her from wanting to be with me, sacrificing more than I think she's aware of to be here. While I knew she didn't fully trust me — a definite characteristic on her part—I had plans in motion to show her how exceptional she was to me. Gaining her trust with actions instead of words.

Her excitement camouflaged her need to remain neutral; unimpressed as if this was an occurrence she witnessed every day. Her apprehension decorated her face as she climbed aboard my plane, even she didn't realize how much her body shook as I took her hand in mine.

"Ian, remind me. Did your family build or purchase this home?"

I recall with perfect clarity the first moment I laid eyes on my villa. The Tuscan inspired exterior, with its native Italian shrubbery surrounding the entrance. Granted the roof leaked, the foundation was crumbling, and the vineyard was all but destroyed, it still held no greater beauty than seeing it through Heather's eyes. She would find out eventually the real story, how Porchelli's death was one I justified as karma. Porchelli was a man whose evil was second only to my father's. He too thrived on the tears of those whose lives he destroyed, always plotting and planning for his next strike.

"I purchased the Villa, Scotland is my home," I admit, as I turned her face to mine. "It's where my heart will always live." Looking deep into her eyes, hoping beyond all hope she understands the depth of my statement. I am Scottish to my core, my loyalty to my Family runs through my veins and to the marrow of my bones. And she, my beautiful Heather, is part of that family.

The hues of twilight reflect in her eyes, helping to hide the shadows of exhaustion creeping onto her face. She tries so hard to be brave, convincing herself she doesn't need anyone, but the truth, as I believe it, is she needs me as much as I need her. I am so grateful I waited for her, ignoring my mum's insistence on taking a bride. Somehow, deep inside, I knew Heather was out there, waiting—just like me. Now that I found her, not only do I plan on never letting her go, I'm going to give her everything she's ever wanted and more.

"I've arranged to have your room on the same floor as mine. I don't want you to feel uncomfortable in one of my homes." Even with the pale light, I can see the sadness in her eyes, her mind questioning why I would do this and not instantly have her in my bed. It's clear she doesn't understand or have a concept of how much she means to me. By this time tomorrow, Heather Murray will know the depth of my affections.

"However, if you feel or have any need to come to my room, the door is always open. There will never be any pressure or ultimatums, only the assurance your needs will be fulfilled." It's slight, and I know she's not aware of it, but the glint in her eyes and the hitch of her breath tells me she is intrigued. It won't be tonight as I have far too much to do, but soon she will be right where she's always belonged.

"Unfortunately, this trip isn't all about pleasure. In a few hours, I have additional guests arriving for a short stay." The spell is broken, and with a slight twist of her head to clear the cobwebs, her mask returns.

"Finley will arrive in the morning and is anxious to take you shopping in some of the best shops in this part of Italy." When I met with Finley yesterday, she laughed in my face when I told her of my plans. She reminded me people who don't have money to pay for rent, have even less to buy frivolously. She shared with me the conversation she overheard between Danielle and my Heather. How the beautiful blouse she showed up to work in was on loan from her best friend. Her advice was not to allow Heather to decline, to give her instructions and perhaps a little bribery; show her the benefits of being with a McLeod. She reminded me if I wanted her to be a queen I needed to treat her as such. Pulling an envelope from my inner pocket, I tug her hand from her lap and turn it palm side up.

"Here is three thousand euro, and a credit card with no limit." Her head is shaking, and she attempts to pull her hand back. I knew she would react like this, but I'm prepared.

"Heather," I caution, gripping her wrist a little tighter. "I failed to prepare you and supply you with information on the types of events we would encounter. Therefore, it is my obligation to compensate you and make sure everyone who sees you, agrees you are the most beautiful woman in the room." She's gracious enough to understand how important this is to me, foregoing any thoughts she has to refuse. "Ian, you don't have to say such sweet things. I'm happy to be with you and see the places you find special. It's understandable a certain standard of dress would need to be met and thank you for the help."

Mr. Roberto pulls the car into the circular drive as Heather tucks the envelope into her purse, beside her passport. I watch in amusement as she's checked several times for her documents once we left customs. She's never traveled before and doesn't understand how easy it would be for me to replace it. I'll let her have this to focus on in hopes she's able to ignore what's about to happen. Roberto opens the door, and as I exit the car, Margareta is standing on the steps with her hands on her hips. I can tell by her face she is none too happy by the guests who are, hopefully, asleep inside my home. Standing from the car, I dip down and kiss the cheek of my housekeeper.

"Margareta, I'd like you to meet Heather Murray," extending my hand into the car, wrapping my fingers around Heather's tiny ones as I help her to stand. "She is the special guest I told you about, make sure she has everything she needs."

Heather pulls away from me and walks closer to Margareta, extending her hand as she begins to climb the first step. "It's a pleasure to meet you, ma'am." Margareta can be a cold and distant person, she's cautious and untrusting, with good reason.

All these years later, after Porchelli's death, she still holds a bit of loyalty to him. I expect her to be hostile, mumbling crass words in Italian under her breath, but as Heather takes the final step and comes face-to-face with her, a speck of a smile crosses her lips as she throws her arms around Heather, thanking God over and over in Italian.

* * *

As the sun breaks through the trees surrounding my property, I stand on the edge of my balcony, admiring the view I paid so much for. Heather did not come to my bed last night, not that I anticipated she would. Margareta pulled her into the house and set about to feed her every morsel of food she could. Once she felt satisfied Heather would not starve, she took her upstairs and tucked her safely into bed. I finished my calls and welcomed the Malloy's, who arrived just after midnight. Patrick questioned as to why I insisted he bring his wife Christi, and his brother-in-law, Caleb, but I assured him all would be told in due time. Declan eyed me cautiously but chose to remain silent, taking his new wife, Katie, upstairs to bed. I bid them all a good night and found myself lying beside a sleeping Heather for several minutes, soaking in the essence of her, and then kissing her good night. As I exited her room, I found Margareta standing in the hall, using a stack of clean towels as a ruse to fool me. She didn't have to say a word, and chose not to, simply sending me the smile I hadn't seen in many years. Just as I suspected, Heather has charmed her way into Margareta's cold heart.

"Good morning," I swear I could feel her enter the room before I heard her beautiful voice. Her presence made the world seem lighter and less evil. "Morning," I turn to greet her, unable to control the need to touch her. Setting my coffee cup down, I pull her into my embrace, surrounding myself in the calming essence of her. "Did you sleep well?" Heather pulls away, but not before kissing me squarely on the lips.

"You must have some voodoo shit around here; I slept like the dead." The joy in her voice makes my heart react, clambering around in my chest like a jolt of lightning. She was happy, genuinely happy, because of me. I hadn't made anyone smile out of pure emotion in a long time.

"No, love. I believe it has to do with being awake far too early and staying up way too late because of me. This trip is the least I can do to help you recharge your batteries."

"You're right," her eyes find mine, truth written within the orbs. "And I thank you."

"It's my pleasure, Heather. Now, let's go grab some breakfast before Margareta has my head for keeping you away from the table." Taking her hand in mine, her genuine laughter echoes off the walls and dances in my ears. I wish this moment could last forever, and I could ignore the duty I have and the job which awaits me downstairs. The smell of food cooking hits us as we descend the stairs. The morning sun is shining through the stain glass windows along the staircase, giving an ethereal glow to her beautiful face.

"Ian?" A male voice calls, collapsing the bubble created between the two of us. Patrick Malloy stands at the bottom of the stairs, a coffee cup in one hand and a questioning look on his face.

"Aye, my friend, I assumed you would sleep until noon with the late hours you kept."

His gaze leaves mine and settles on Heather's face; a questioning head tilt as he takes her features in. Anger rises in my chest at the audacity of him admiring what is mine. I'm quick to rein it in as Patrick has the Empress of all syndicate wives in his beautiful Christi.

"I'm afraid sleep hasn't found me, too much unease as to why I've been summoned here with my family." The Malloy's and the McLeod's have a mutual understanding of the power each Family possesses. I've no doubt Patrick had to sit on his hands letting Declan call me in regard to the death of my half-brother, Blake. His ability to relinquish the reins has not come easy. A fact made clear by his tone, saying he's trying to hang on. "Forgive me my manners, Ian. Jet lag has indeed claimed hold of me."

Landing on the final step which separates us, even on level ground, I'm still a few inches taller than Patrick. A small part of me, the ounce of my father which remains in my blood, gloats at the height difference, rejoices in the non-existent victory.

"No apology necessary, may I introduce you to my beautiful girl-friend, Heather?" Pulling her close, giving a warning of possession that's not needed nor welcomed judging by the lack of response on Patrick's face.

"Heather this is—" Before I can finish the introduction, her hand is out to greet him much like last night with Margareta. However, this time it's my turn to have my breath hitch as her words hit me in the gut.

"Patrick Malloy, it's a pleasure to finally meet you."

CHAPTER FOURTEEN

HEATHER

The photo in the Chicago Sun-Times did him no justice. His Irish heritage burned brightly in the red highlights in his dark hair, a sprinkling of silver decorated the edges near his ear, a few more were scattered throughout the scruff of his facial hair. But it was his sea-glass; green eyes which caught my attention and made my back straighten. The chiseled cut of his chin reminded me of my father, and the way his devilish smile began on the left side of his face, giving the receiver the impression he was unamused.

"Have we met? Because I never forget a beautiful face."

I felt foolish, having learned everything about this man from newspaper articles and the tail end of conversations among the regulars. Patrick was rumored to be a dangerous man, lethal in his ways of dealing with those unfortunate souls who crossed him.

"Not formally, but I found the announcement from where your son was recently married. Congratulations by the way."

"So, you've never met him?" Ian held me close as he waved his free hand back and forth between Patrick and I, the look of relief coloring his features. A half-smile curled the left side of Patrick's lips.

"All right, gentleman. You can stop the pissing contest." Three sets of eyes turned toward the approaching lady, auburn hair surrounding a heart-shaped face. Green eyes, which would make the Emerald Isle jealous, and lines of wisdom surrounding each orb. Her slender hands surround a white porcelain cup, the sun dancing off the enormous diamond on her left hand.

"Christi," Patrick steps away from me, shoves his hands into the pockets of his slacks. "I thought you were still asleep."

Christi closes the distance and leans over to allow Patrick to kiss her cheek. "After all these years of marriage, you should know I don't sleep well unless you're beside me." Patrick moves behind her, molding his body to hers. I'm envious of the love they share, how even when she catches him in the actions of being a man, she loves him just the same.

"And this must be Heather; the young lady Margareta has raved about to anyone who would listen this morning."

Christi Malloy intimidated me as much as she impressed me. Being married to a man with the reputation Patrick has, she possesses an enormous amount of confidence and determination.

"Good morning. Yes, I'm Heather." Christi gives me a quick once-over, then shoots a wink in Ian's direction.

"Ian, you won't mind if I borrow Heather for a few minutes, correct? It will give the two of you time to get your rulers out and see whose mickey is bigger."

Not waiting for him to reply, she reaches out to take my hand, pulls me off the last step and down the hall. Nearly stumbling twice, I look over my shoulder with wide eyes at a stunned Ian and a laughing Patrick.

Christi leads me into a room at the end of the hall; sunlight fills the space from the open doors along the wall. Multicolor flowers, in a variety of shapes and sizes, decorate the patio. Sheer linen curtains hang from the edge of the lanai, waving in the gentle morning breeze. "Come and have breakfast with me and get to know one another. My daughter-in-law, Katie, should be joining us soon. If my son lets her out of bed that is."

For the second time in such a short period, my eyes grow wide in shock. Her brazenness is rivaled by that of her husband. "Oh, don't look so surprised, I'm not immune to the charms of the men we keep. I have two sons who are as handsome as the man who helped create them, and I know what kind of power they wield with those charms they inherited."

Christi sits on the sofa, pouring what I assume is coffee into her cup. "I presume by you being here, and the staff in a tizzy about you, that you know what you're getting into." Taking a seat, the nervousness I felt when I walked in collapses like a poorly made souffle. Christi was a lot like the other wives I met, married to powerful men with secrets to keep.

"And I presume by you saying, 'getting into,' you mean the world of the syndicate?"

Christi raises her cup to her lips, stopping as she looks over the edge, "Great, you're one of *them*." Shaking her head as she takes a sip, her eyes closing in disgust.

"One of who?"

Setting her cup on the table, she leans over and glares at me in disbelief. "One of those who thinks by slapping a pretty word on something, it somehow changes the meaning. Syndicate, mob, mafia; it's all the same thing. Grown men making a living by unconventional means. You can dress a piece of shit up in lace and leather, still doesn't change what it is."

I couldn't hide the amusement on my face. The more time I spent with Christi, the more I liked her.

"This is a criminal Family you're spending time with, just like mine and Patrick's, along with Declan and Katie. Our men do bad things, sometimes for good reasons and, sometimes, because it makes them feel better. I can tell by the look in your eyes you're okay with it. Able to adjust your sails when things go bad and keep moving. That's good, and a skill you will definitely need. But you love him, and that can be a double-edged sword."

Holding up my hand in protest, I stop her. "I don't love him; we haven't known one another long enough."

"Don't fool yourself, men like ours live in a fast-paced world. Falling in love instantly and making lifelong decisions comes naturally to them. They don't proceed lightly, but when they find it, they don't waste time on someone else's rules."

I wasn't certain how I felt about what Christi said. On the one hand, I knew her relationship with Patrick came about at warp speed, Declan fell in love and married his wife in less than six months, while Anna made Dominick wait a few months longer. Still, all the marriages done within the syndicate, I knew, did indeed move fast. But just as the engagements lasted a fraction of a second, it didn't take long for the first dose of reality to get lodged in throats. Usually caused by a scorned ex-lover who hadn't been able to land the coveted title of wife. Something I was already all too familiar with.

"You may not believe he has deep feelings for you, and you are justified in your doubts. I see a lot of myself in you: independent, strong and not afraid to get your hands dirty. Which according to my sources will come in handy when you meet Lady Greer." My interest is piqued as she offers to fill my cup. How her option on Lady Greer mirrored that of Cadan's from yesterday. I've been around these people long enough not to go begging for more information than they are willing to give.

"According to Ian, his mum will love me."

"Oh, I'm sure he believes she will. Ian is her only biological child, and speaking as a mother myself, he can do no wrong in her eyes.

Add in her insistence on everyone calling her Lady Greer, and how she seems to live in the eighteenth century with the old traditions and class status. You, my dear, have an upward battle on your hands."

* * *

THREE BLACK MERCEDES SEDANS WAITED FOR US IN THE CIRCULAR driveway. Men in dark suits, with eyes hidden behind sunglasses, stood at open doors to take us to Florence. Ian gave the two men he assigned to help me firm words, or at least I assumed they were, as he spoke in Italian. By the way his voice sounded, along with his fingers hitting the center of their solid chests, I am fairly certain the words were of warnings and not of having a good trip.

Christi, Katie, and I would ride in the middle car with three guards in the first and third car in the convoy during the one-and-a-half-hour trip to the city. Patrick refused to be shown up as he also had words for the guy selected to drive our car. Declan was too busy kissing Katie to bother with anyone else, threatening to keep her upstairs in their room instead of allowing her to join the rest of the ladies.

Ian turned to help me into the back seat of the sedan, surrounding me in his arms as he gave me a final goodbye.

"I want you to have fun. Use the card and money I gave you."

"I'll try, but only if I find something I love."

"I don't care what you purchase," kissing along the shell of my ear, his tongue grazing the tip of my lobe.

"Although, if you happen upon a lingerie store, feel free to buy two of everything, that way when I shred it off your glorious body you'll have a spare."

His words, and the way his body felt against mine, lingered in my mind for the majority of the trip. How the muscles in his chest constricted as I ran my fingernails up his spine. But the best part, and the singular thing which made me smile like a fool, was how the scruff of his beard prickled my face as he kissed me with purpose.

Christi would pull me into the conversation occasionally but left me to my thoughts for the most part. Florence is a city rich in history and architecture, incredible churches and museums. As we passed through one of the streets, I hoped we would get an opportunity to have a look around. When the car stopped, and two of the guards from the first car got out and went inside a large store, I knew sight-seeing was a no-go. Less than a minute later the pair came back out, holding the doors open for the shoppers inside to come out. Those exiting, stood on the edge of the sidewalk trying to see who was in the waiting cars. I wasn't a stranger to what was happening; I'd heard a few of the regulars mention how they did the same for Anna when she wanted to go shopping and not be disturbed.

"All right, ladies, let's go give our husband's credit cards a heavy work out."

I wasn't stupid enough to correct Christi Malloy as to my not being married to Ian. She, like Anna Santos, held a level of authority. While not as high as Patrick or Ian, significant nonetheless.

Two guards opened the car doors for us, and Christi climbed out first. Several people, who remained along the sidewalk, pointed and took photos with their cell phones. She smiled and gave money to a woman who sat on the side of the building. As I passed by, I noticed her feet were disfigured and missing several toes. I reached into my purse to give her more money, but the guard who Ian had spoken with stopped me, dropping several bills from his pocket into her hands.

Once inside a pair of sharply dressed women stood at attention, their hair pulled back in a severe bun. Their smiles were painted on, and I suspected as fake as the mannequins behind them. Christi walked over and shook hands with them, exchanging pleasantries, and accepting their offers of a bottle of wine.

Katie and Christi collected an armload of clothing and went into a dressing room. I walked around the store, feeling the material of several shirts, a few skirts and the leather of a couple of handbags, but nothing stood out begging me to try it on and take it with me. By the time Christi and Katie had tried on and paid for their purchases, the crowd outside had thickened.

"Who do they think we are?" I hadn't meant for the question to leave my lips; I was far too grateful to be included in the trip in the first place.

"Mr. McLeod is an influential man in this town; his winery employs a number of the locals, he donates to charities and has helped with a few of the schools and churches. Word travels fast among the residents of your visit. They want to show their appreciation and meet the woman Ian has chosen to be by his side." Hearing this rendered me speechless and left me feeling quite overwhelmed. As we left the store, my mind reeled as several people reached out to touch my arm, joy-filled faces staring back at me.

By the time we pulled up to the next store a few minutes later, I had composed myself enough to take the lead as we exited the car. The crowd wasn't as large, but I suspected it would grow before we left. Once inside, I made it a point to choose several pieces. If spending money in the local stores cast a positive light on Ian, I would do anything I could. Christi and Katie joined me as I tried on the clothes I chose. As we finished and made our way to the register, I found my purchases had already been paid for and placed in the waiting car.

Scanning the faces of the three guards beside the front entrance, "who paid for my things?" The tallest of the three stepped forward, lowering his head to address me. "McLeod's ladies do not pay when he sends them shopping." Straightening my back, mentally chasing away the growing number of faceless women who had preceded me. Ian never claimed to be a saint, and I had never questioned the number of relationships he had before ours.

Movement to my left pulled my mind back to the here and now, Christi and Katie had joined me, a knowing look on both of their faces. Grabbing my shoulder in a supportive grip, Christi leans into my left side and gently reminds me. "Like I said, Heather. A double-edged sword."

I recognized several faces as we left the store; this time I held my hand out, allowing several to kiss my hand as the guard to my left handed out coins. A group of children ran up to us, smiles wide and speaking rapidly in Italian. Another guard came from behind, giving them fistfuls of candy. They laughed and ran off, enjoying the special treat in their tiny hands.

As we pulled up to the next shop, I questioned if Ian had done more than warn the guards to protect me and pay for my clothing. Inside the double glass doors were rows and rows of intimate apparel: garter belts, stockings, bras, and corsets lined the shelves. Recalling Ian's request, I filled several bags and, no doubt, the bottom line for the owner of the shop with my excessive purchases.

Climbing into the back of the sedan, Christi voices her need to stop and have some lunch. While I wasn't hungry, I was ready to take a break and grab something to drink. The ride to the restaurant was silent, giving evidence to how tiring the morning had been. Incredible landscapes made a beautiful backdrop as we drove to our next desti-nation. A massive iron gate greeted us as we pulled onto a winding road, pristine foliage lined the sides of the road, giving way to what I thought was an estate at first.

Pulling into a circular drive, I noticed black canopies, their edges wrapped around brass bars, attached to the white building. Contrasting lettering was scripted across the center of the awning, my Italian too limited to understand the title. My attention turns to a row of people dressed in pressed uniforms, with long white aprons wrapped around their waists.

"Ladies, Mr. McLeod has closed the restaurant until this evening and encourages you to sample the local freshness." Just as the previous stops, our car pulled to the curb and the guards open the doors. Again, I take the lead as we walk up the steps, shaking hands with each member of the staff.

Inside the décor is much different from what I expected; several long tables with benches on one side of the room. Open wood beams line the ceiling, while iron chandeliers hang from several of the rafters, giving the place a soft feel.

"Ladies, if you will follow me?"

The hostess, whose name I didn't catch due to my perusal of the room, waves her hand in the direction of the back of the restaurant. Stepping between accordion style doors, the room opens into a circular design. Matching iron sconces hang unlit against three of the walls, the light from the windows more than enough to sufficiently brighten the room. A cloth covered table takes up a good chunk of the space, a bowl filled with lemons and green leaves sits in the middle.

"Would you look at this?"

Katie moves to opposite side of the room, stepping out into the tiny courtyard, a bubbling fountain in the center. "This reminds me of the hotel Declan, and I visited in Greece."

She had shared a few stories of how incredible her recent honeymoon was. Christi subtly questioned if a grandchild would be on the way anytime soon. Katie is smarter than she looks; quickly changing the subject to something sweet Declan did for her. Three waiters served a variety of dishes including mussels, fresh fish, and pasta. Mouthwatering sauces and the most incredible pizza I have ever tasted.

"Mr. McLeod offers a bottle of his newest wine with his compliments." The label was blank, but the white wine had a hint of sweetness with a citrus blend. "This is incredible, can I purchase a case to be shipped back to the states?" Christi raises her glass up, admiring the color as she questioned the attentive waiter.

"My apologies, Mrs. Malloy, this particular selection has not been named and therefore is not for sale. However, I can let the winery manager know you enjoy it and he can contact you when it is available."

"Oh, that's okay, I happen to know the owner's wife. I'm sure she can get me a case or two if I asked nicely." There was no stopping the smile that crept across my face, hearing the title from her did something to me, creating a warm and comforting feeling inside.

"If there is nothing else, may I bring in dessert?"

"Oh Lord, no. I have no room for dessert, but if the guys want some, feel free to serve it to them."

Our waiter nodded and bowed, collecting our empty plates, and then leaving the room.

Christi picked up her wine glass, holding it just shy of her lips. "Good call, Heather. I have absolutely no room for another bite."

Katie agreed as she rubbed her stomach, pushing her unused silverware to the side. "That fish was to die for; I had to stop myself from ordering another one for myself."

"Well, if you like, I can get the recipe from Ian when I have him ship a boatload of wine to Chicago."

Katie smiled as she tossed her napkin in my direction, regretting the motion as it caused her stomach to hurt.

"Speaking of Ian," Christi began, tilting her glass slightly in my direction. "How about we get out of here and find out why he had us come all the way to Italy when one, he lives in Scotland, and two, insisted Caleb come with us."

CHAPTER FIFTEEN

IAN

I HELD my breath until the bumper of the last car disappeared, swallowing down the longing feeling bubbling up in my chest. All of this was foreign to me as I've never needed to have a woman this close to me or felt the need to protect one in the way I do Heather.

"Ian, not that I mind time away with my wife, but I do have business to attend. So how about we discuss what was so urgent you needed us for." Declan stood beside me, arms crossed over his chest, his eyes watching the now empty drive. Not bothering to pull my eyes from the road, my heart begs me to jump in one of my cars and follow her, ignoring the bullshit which needed to be dealt with.

"Come inside, lads. I have a bottle of good scotch waiting for a reason to breathe."

When Roberto phoned to tell me of Darrow's impending visit, he understood what I meant when I said no special meals and to place the pair in the room we found useful for hiding items, or persons, we needed to be kept silent.

"Cadan, if you would assist our guests in joining us." Cadan nodded once, and then hurried up the steps, taking two at a time until he reached the landing. Stepping around Roberto, who stood with his hands behind his back and a look of determination on his face. Roberto and Margareta had waited a long time for this day. And the benefits Malloy would receive, would contribute significantly to strengthen our relationship.

As we entered the living room, Margareta opened a bottle of scotch from my private stock and set out enough glasses for everyone to enjoy. Patrick Malloy made himself at home as he took the bottle and poured everyone a drink. His brother-in-law, Caleb, stood off in the corner, checking his phone with a worried look on his face. Last night, when they arrived, he apologized for not being able to bring his wife, Paige, as she was feeling under the weather. Patrick walked over to where he stood, offering him a glass, but Caleb declined. I knew Mr. Montgomery had issues with my family, and it didn't surprise me when he refused the drink. A small smirk found my face as I asked myself how much his attitude would change when he discovered the reason he was here.

"Gentlemen, I appreciate your willingness to come so far, on such short notice. I can assure you, what I have to say, and show you, will be well worth the inconvenience." Caleb appeared to ignore me, keeping his focus between the vineyard outside and his phone. I'd allow him this one moment of disrespect, as his life was about to change.

I hear the distinct sound of my front door opening, followed by the unique tone of Finley's voice. As she rounded the corner, her green eyes bright, and face flushed from the sun, her left hand intertwined with the right of Brion, Declan Malloy's Underboss. "You weren't going to start this without me were you, Ian?"

I hadn't been sure if Finley would make it on time as she had been burrowed underneath Brion for several days. She served as a valuable witness; her attachment to my family gave her the clout needed to be in this room. "Of course not love, grab yourself a drink."

Finley was not a fan of scotch, or alcohol in general, but she would never be rude or go against something I asked her to do. Brion, on the other hand, fills his glass twice, drains the first, and then takes a seat beside Declan.

Turning back to the Malloy's, my glass in hand, the amber liquid and oak fragrance taking me back to the moment I learned the truth from my father.

"As you are all familiar, Shaw McLeod was a foolish old man. He believed his way was the only way, ignoring the sound advice from men around him. His ignorance and blatant disregard nearly cost us our family fortune many times."

Swirling the amber liquid in my glass, I take a deep breath, and then let it out in a slow and forced motion. "But not a soul in this room shed a single tear when the man took his last breath."

Dipping the glass to my lips, rejoicing as the burn dances across my tongue and into my throat. My father hated this scotch, wanted to invest money in a competitor but my mum forbade it, the ownership of the company had been on her side of the family for countless years.

"When the doctors told my mum to call in the family as my father wouldn't last the night, she sent the staff home and told Finley, myself, Blake and Darrow to come into my father's room with her." Declan tensed at the mention of Darrow's name, his hatred for what he had done evident on his face.

"She demanded he tell us the truth before he died, calling him a coward if he refused. My mum had put up with so much, spent years being disrespected by the man she married, yet held her head up high when he paraded his whores into the house she owned. For nearly an hour, he admitted to actions he had done and blamed on someone else, the lies he told and trouble he caused."

Finley reached over and squeezed Brion's hand, releasing it and making her way over to me. "But in the final moments of his life, he confessed the biggest secret of all. Something so sinister and vile and has an impact on every person in this room."

Caleb's eyes flashed to mine, it's taken me less than five minutes to grab his attention, but was he ready to hear the truth?

"I spent my entire life knowing the ins and outs of my father's affairs with various women, not bothering to hide the illegitimate children he produced. Some were adopted by men who cared, giving them a life far from the evil of their biological father. While others, a select pair, came to live with us for a time. The first you know, Blake, who disrespected your family in the worst way. He wanted to lead my Family, take over the reins he felt he was owed from my father, but his motives were clear. I'd hated him since the moment I laid eyes on him as a small child. My father knew of my intentions when it came to Blake. What I didn't know, and a part of me is glad I didn't, was how connected the second bastard child was to all of us."

I could feel my blood boiling in my veins like an eruption from a volcano contained under too much pressure. After all this time, and the death of Blake, I was no closer to a resolution than at the moment it happened. My frustration got the better of me, coming to a crescendo as the glass in my hand shattered from the pressure of my fingers. Ignoring the burn in my hand, I kick the shards of glass out of my way and move across the room to wait for Cadan's return.

"When Finley came of age, he wanted her to marry me, keeping the perfect lineage going. But I refused him, so he ordered her to marry Blake, a man she hated almost as much as I did. This union gave me fuel for my fire, and I sent him to America under the guise of expanding our operations, in reality, it was a set up to get rid of him and all he represented. I have you to thank, Declan, for handling his demise and as a token of my appreciation, I find it only fair to tell you, and your family, the secret my father kept from all of you."

Loud footfalls sounded against the tile, the screeching sound of a female voice protesting the rough treatment she received. Caleb

Montgomery stood ramrod straight as his head twisted and for a moment I thought he recognized the voice by the look on his face.

"You see, gentlemen, Rick Darrow came to live with us along with his mother when he was five. She marched into our home, set on taking over, driving my mum out into the cold. However, she underestimated the abilities of Lady Greer, mistaking her gentleness for weakness and before the first week was over, Rick Darrow's mum was a fading memory, or so we all assumed. That is until my father's deathbed confession."

Seeing Darrow's eyes for the first time in months, all the lies and betrayal lurking behind his blue orbs. It's funny how as children we're able to look past our differences, ignore the cruelty fate had presented and chose to be friends.

"For years I treated him like a brother, even selecting him to stand by my side as my Underboss. As I leaned in to hear the secrets my father saved for me, everything I knew as a child became a lie. Not only was Darrow one of my father's bastard children, but he was also a blood brother to Blake, they shared the same mum. A common whore, my father, found while on a trip to Italy to visit an associate who was in jail. According to my father, it was love at first sight for him, but I bet if we ask her, she may admit to being an opportunist, using men as she has done her entire life."

Brown eyes met mine, fear and apprehension swirled alongside each other. Her once dark hair, now a brassy blonde with ends looking like harvested straw. Her surgically enhanced face courtesy of my Family's money, but I would recognize her anywhere, and I had hoped Caleb Montgomery would as well.

"My father spared no expense getting her out of prison, ignoring those around him who said she was there for murder. He told me she touched something deep inside him, a place my mum could never reach. He gave her a home, and a way of life in exchange for keeping their sons."

I felt the moment the tension in the room shifted, heard the oath Caleb Montgomery swore under his breath as he crossed the room. "Motherfucking, Mia."

Darrow attempted to step in front of his mum, shielding her from Caleb who was hell-bent on hurting her. The fury in his eyes reminded me of the way I felt when I first learned who she was.

Years ago, when Patrick and Christi were first introduced, Patrick's sister Paige, had plans to marry Caleb. And while the marriage was arranged, Caleb's mother Eileen was not happy about the union. She plotted and planned, using a child she had with another man in attempts to kill Christi, all the while making everyone believe Mia was the legitimate child of her husband, Sherman. Their plan nearly worked, and if it hadn't been for some discrepancies on a birth certificate, Christi Malloy wouldn't be here. Mia escaped to Italy where she attempted to seduce her biological father. When her efforts failed, she stabbed him in the chest, fatally wounding him. And that's how she ended up in an Italian prison, the place where she met my father.

"You're supposed to be dead!" Caleb roared as he tried to get past Cadan. "I saw the fucking picture of your goddamn dead body."

I suspected this was how my father pulled off getting her out of prison. It wasn't the first time he would've bribed the guards to come up with some bullshit game like this. He had several men on his payroll who didn't technically exist, dead to the world around them, but alive and kicking and in his debt.

"And you're supposed to be in America with that idiot wife of yours."

Patrick and Declan were both off the couch, pulling Caleb back. Brion moved in to help Cadan keep Darrow and Mia contained. Finley stood beside me, her arms locked around mine keeping me grounded.

"Is this your idea of a joke, Ian? Inviting us to stay at your house and then bringing the fucking Irish trash with you."

Darrow always did have bigger bollocks than he did brains, getting himself into a number of skirmishes Cadan or I had to bail him out of. He felt big at the moment, hiding behind Brion and Cadan.

"Hold on!"

Raising my voice to reach him over the ruckus Caleb had created, ready to give out the punishment I had planned for him all along.

"I never invited you to this house! You, and your whore mum, pushed your way through my front door like you always do. For years, I had to endure the shit the pair of you left behind, always sacrificing what I wanted, what my mum wanted, for you, but no more."

Motioning for Cadan to move out of the way, I pull my Glock out of my holster, offering the handle to Declan. "This is the son of a bitch who shot your wife and harmed the precious baby she carried. It's time he paid the price for his crimes against your family."

Declan's jaw clenched, the muscles showing every ounce of pain he had been through. Watery eyes narrowed in on their target as he pushes away my gun and retrieves his own.

"I've waited for this moment for far too long. I held my beautiful Katie as she woke from nightmares for months after you shot her." Raising the barrel in Darrow's direction, Cadan steps away with a cursing Mia who demanded to be let go. Patrick places his hand on Declan's shoulder, "Go ahead, son. Take away her monster."

Declan shook his head back and forth, "Welcome to hell, mother-fucker!" He didn't get the last word out before he began firing the gun, the barrel jerking up as the bullets left the chamber, burying itself in Darrow's chest. Blood splattered as the third bullet found its target, his body slumping to the floor. Declan didn't stop; he continued firing the gun as he walked toward Darrow's dead body. Even when the magazine was empty, and the last shell casing bounced on the floor, he continued to pull the trigger, the clicking sound echoing off the walls.

Silence filled the air as everyone stared at Darrow, lying in his expanding pool of blood; his eyes open looking to the ceiling as if searching for redemption. Roberto stepped around Mia, leaning down to close Darrow's eyes. T-Bone's words flooded my mind as I took in his prone body.

"No, Roberto, leave them open."

Mia gasped as her attention focused on me, her face covered in streaks of mascara, running like tiny black rivers down her cheeks.

"He needs to see the Devil coming to get him."

Roberto nodded his head, stood up straight, shooting Mia a look, and then spat on Darrow. He mumbled his disgust for him in Italian, which caused Mia to bow her head as sobs gripped her.

"What about you, Mia? Are you ready?" Caleb stood with his hands at his side, the rage from earlier appeared to be gone. I compared myself to him, both of us having been betrayed by those we loved.

"Ready for what, to die? We both know you don't have what it takes to kill me. Our crazy father taught you never to hurt a woman, raising you to be a pussy instead." Pride and pleasure weaved into Mia's voice, even after all these years, she still knew how to defeat her brother.

"Maybe his father taught him how to treat a lady, showing him how to be stronger than a coward who uses fear as a measure of control. It's clear to me your mum taught you how to be a whore, using whatever you needed to, in order to get what you want." Finley stepped closer to Mia, silently challenging her to give a rebuttal and discredit the truths she shared with the room. "Thank God, her venom didn't get to him, making him the same type of cunt she made you. And while I suspect you're telling the truth about his lack of ability to kill you and make you pay for the crimes against all the Family's in this room, you forget one tiny bit of information." Finley held her hand up, demonstrating with her thumb and index finger the small amount she referred to. I was at a loss as to where she was headed with this as she had never mentioned an issue with this woman.

"And what would that be, little girl?" Mia spits the latter two words out as if they had rotted on her tongue, ignoring the calmness in Finley's manners. She was in the midst of making a grave mistake, unknowing of how lethal Finley can be.

"For one, you failed as a mum. Showing your piece of shit son how women are possessions, easily tossed when he tired of them."

"Oh, I see." Mia sneered, a look of victory on her face. "You had a crush on my son, and he didn't return your feelings. Oh, you poor, poor dear."

A chortle left Finley's throat, and I had to hold my laugh deep inside. "You are far more mental than I imagined if you think I cared about your bastard spawn for a moment. On the contrary, I hated everything about him. How he tormented young girls in our village when they didn't want him around, or how he took whatever he wanted just because he thought he could get away with it. Most of all, I hated him because of who you are and what you represent."

The smile dropped from Mia's lips as Finley moved closer, finally recognizing the danger she was in. "No, Mr. Montgomery won't hit you or cut you like the pig you are, and he certainly won't cloud his mind with the mixed emotions he would feel when you join Darrow at the gates of Hell."

Looking over her shoulder at me and holding her hand out, palm side up, she wiggles her fingers in a silent request for my gun.

"But Mr. Montgomery didn't grow up with Darrow and his brother Blake. He didn't have their hands in places they didn't belong, with torn dresses and split lips. He didn't see the hurt they caused or the family they nearly destroyed. But most of all, Mr. Montgomery never served at the pleasure of Lady Greer." Mia's eyes went wide as Finley took the first shot, her arms recoiling from the force of the gunpowder igniting, releasing the bullet from the barrel. Tendrils of Finley's red hair jerk with the motion. It's clear by the way her body relaxes as she lowers the gun; there is more to her story than she will share with the room. Finley holds her gaze on Mia's and Darrow's dead bodies, where her mouth remains closed, her eyes scream of the pain they caused her. I won't call her out on why she never came to me, as it's clear as day she felt the need to handle this on her own.

CHAPTER SIXTEEN

HEATHER

When the gates of Ian's estate came into view, Laird, the man who had driven our car to and from Florence, pressed a key on his cell phone, opening the iron partition before we breezed through. Early evening had settled on the land, coating the once beautiful landscape in shadows and mystery as we rounded the final corner. The house came into full view; the yard illuminated as if every light was inside burning. Three shadows stood on the front landing, even with the dim light and distance, I recognized Ian immediately. He stood to the left, hands in his pockets and feet spread shoulder length apart. I imagined the muscles in his jaw tightening, something he did unconsciously as he pondered his thoughts.

"Awe, how sweet," Christi spoke from her seat beside me, her voice laced with sarcasm, retrieving a mirror from her clutch, evaluating her appearance. "Looks like we were missed."

Glancing away from her face, a sliver of anticipation crawls up my back and settles into my throat. My pulse quickens as Ian descends the steps, his footing sure and his movements hurried.

"Some more than others," she muses, not bothering to hide her amusement or the entertainment she got at Ian's expense.

Ian doesn't wait for Laird to stop the car as he pulls open my door, reaching in and sliding his hand around the back of my neck, crushing his lips to mine. Warm and dominating, he pushes his tongue past my lips, searching mine out and pulling it into his, alternating between sucking and nipping. His mouth tastes of strong alcohol, rich in oak and the bite of smoke. I can hear the other men greet their wives, its faint, but their snickers are loud and deliberate. In his overzealousness, Ian has pushed me onto my back, my seat belt digging into my side. Ian lands his knee on the seat between my legs, increasing the grip on my neck as he switches the angle of his head, ramping up the level of suction on my tongue. This is a new and welcomed side of Ian I haven't been introduced to, but one I wanted to know more intimately. The prickle of his beard dances across my chin, the action making me ruin the moment by laughing.

Ian pulls back, a look of irritation flashing across his face, speckles of anger showing in the edges of his blue eyes. "Do I want to know why you are laughing at my tongue in your mouth?" Where his eyes convey his frustration, the huskiness in his voice speaks of his need for me. The passion heavy words match the need I have for him.

Planting a quick kiss on his lips. "No, I happen to love the way you kiss me." Reaching my hand up, scratching my fingernails along the thick, dark hairs on his chin. "Your beard tickles when you move your head sometimes."

His face morphs into a smile, the one I want to pretend is all for me. "I will have to kiss you more and get you used to the feel of it." Wiggling his eyebrows as he presses the release on my seatbelt, pulling me gently out of the car.

Ian told me of his aversion to a shaved face, his eternal middle finger to his late father who insisted facial hair was a sign of a poor man. I couldn't imagine him without the manly addition to his jaw adding so much to his raw persona.

Laird and two of the men from the car behind us are unloading the trunk. Ian asks Laird if there had been any trouble since they last communicated, attempting to hide the conversation from me by speaking in his native tongue. Sometimes I have the overwhelming urge to say something to him, letting him know I understand every word he says. Instead, I turn my back to them, searching the area around the car for the other couples.

Declan and Katie are nowhere to be found, the newlyweds more than likely found a dark corner to reacquaint themselves in. Christi and Patrick share hushed words and concerned looks. My pulse quickens as I catch a word or two, piecing together something about someone getting what they deserved. Christi removes herself from Patrick's embrace as she turns toward the steps, their clasped hands hanging on to the other until the last second as she tells him she will have a word with Caleb.

I turn before she can catch me eavesdropping, nothing good can ever come from being caught gaining information the Family wants to keep to themselves. Joining the men who work in silence, I remove packages from the trunk and place them in a line on the brick pavement of the driveway.

Strong arms wrap around me, glancing down I see the expensive watch Ian wears, its black face with silver trim attached to his wrist. It's too dark to see the features of the timepiece, the precision movements I admired only days ago as he played with strands of my hair.

"Over half of these bags better belong to you, or I'm taking you shopping when we get to Edinburgh." He whispers in my ear as his breath drags across the flesh of my neck, stunning me stupid.

"Half would be pushing it, given there were three of us shopping." I remind him, attempting to turn my head to capture his lips, but he keeps nipping at the juncture of my neck and shoulder.

"The others weren't told to spoil themselves, picking up things I would enjoy."

The combination of his tone of voice and the way it reached deep inside my core made me want to do everything he asked of me, giving into his every whim. His signature fragrance, and feel of his muscles as they passed over my body, fill me with visions of things I wanted to do with him and he to me.

"Laird, take Ms. Murray's bags to my room and tell Margareta to have dinner ready in an hour." With a nod from Laird, Ian picks me off my feet, tosses my body over his good shoulder and heads into the dark yard, my surprised laughter filling the night. I beg him several times to put me down, but the giggles that follow give my demands less of an edge and more of a playful nature.

Ian is a massive man, tall with broad shoulders and muscles to spare, yet I worry the strain he is inflicting on himself carrying me like this, as he runs for a destination unknown, causing further damage to the wound on the opposite shoulder.

I must admit I enjoy the view of his ass, the muscles working in tangent with the stride of his gait. How his hand grips the back of my thigh, his pinky finger dangerously close to where I desire him most.

Ian slows his run to a walk, followed by the groaning sound of an old door opening. I attempt to turn my body upright, but Ian slaps my ass hard making me yelp and tells me to settle down. He walks across the threshold, while the room is bathed in darkness, the strong smells of wood and fruit hit my nose, tickling my senses. My heart is pounding, and my apprehension is skyrocketing as several loud clicks sound off in the distance followed by the slow progression of lights coming on in the room. Ian takes a handful of steps into the space, and then sets me on a hard surface; a final loud click above alerts me seconds before we are bathed in light.

Warm hands encase my face, blue eyes flicking back and forth between mine, questioning what I am not certain. "Mother fuck, I missed you." I want to remind him I've been gone a short time but chose to keep this to myself. Ian looks at me with such longing, and I want it to continue, as I have become addicted to the way he craves me. Without warning, he crushes his lips to mine once again, pulling me tightly into his embrace. My hands travel up his chest, and I feel him wince as I drift over the wound on his shoulder.

"I'm sorry." I pull back, the passion between us temporarily forgotten as I worry I have hurt him.

"It's fine, Heather. Hasn't bothered me all day, and I won't let it start now."

Ian doesn't allow me to argue or beg him to let me see his shoulder, resuming the intense kissing he captured me with earlier. His touch is an equal measure of powerful and gentle, dominating and submissive. He knows without me telling him where to touch to elicit the moans which hide in my chest, betraying me and giving him an idea of how much I need him.

Ian pulls back, his hands falling from my shoulders down to my thighs, where he runs his hands up-and-down the fabric of my pants. "As much as I'm enjoying this, and would love to spread you out like a buffet and eat until I get my fill, I do have a reason for bringing you here."

Sitting up straight, I attempt to clear the lustful haze which has settled around me, clouding the level-headed judgment I should have on hand at all times. Ian has the uncanny ability to make me forget everything, wrapping me in an invisible bubble where my inhibitions aren't allowed to enter.

"Which is where exactly?"

"My wine vault. C'mere, I have something to show you."

Ian helps me off what turns out to be a worktable of sorts; a wooden structure with solid legs and cut marks on the top. The light from above highlights the small slashes and deeper grooves. Wrapping his hand around mine, Ian pulls me further into the room where I can almost make out the source of the wood fragrance. Down a narrow path, the dim light from above is more suitable for a romantic evening than performing any task. As we reach the end of the path, taking two steps up onto a platform, my eyes grow wide as I look over the loft-like structure and into a brick-lined room. Wooden barrels are stacked three high on each side, bars made of metal supporting each one.

Ian places me against the wooden rail, encasing his body tight against mine, moving my hair to the side as he rests his chin on my shoulder. "My wine master has been working on a new product for the winery, something deeper than a Blush but not as bold as a Merlot or Cabernet. All the flavor without the bite." His lips brush against the shell of my ear, his words whisper soft and creating a fire deep in my core. "It's taken years to get it right, but according to Laird you enjoyed it enough to have several glasses."

"He's right. I enjoyed it almost as much as Christi Malloy." The deep rumble in his chest vibrates against my back as he snuggles in hugging me tight.

"I know, Patrick had his pilot load several cases into their plane. We have one problem though."

Turning around to face him, I see the tiniest hint of a smile on his lips. His hands reach up to touch my face, running his thumb along my bottom lip. "What's wrong?"

His eyes drift from my mouth to my eyes and back again, lowering his lips to mine. The kiss this time is quick and gentle, but still has the power to make me want so much more.

"We can't agree on a name; nothing seems to fit."

"Oh?"

Moving his lips to my chin, he places a soft kiss on the skin there. "Everything Hernando suggests doesn't seem right." Running his nose alongside mine, nipping at the corner of my lip.

"I want the title to have meaning, something I hold close to here."

Placing my hand over his heart, tapping his fingers against the back of mine.

With as much love and pride he has for his mum, I assume he wants to have her name on the bottle. Lady Greer would sound formal, worthy of a well-made bottle of red wine.

"I wanted you to be the first to see the label."

Ian releases my hand and reaches behind me to a shelf I hadn't noticed before. He pulls out a wine bottle, the seal around the top missing. "This isn't the final product, but I wanted to show it to you before we leave for Edinburgh."

Turning the label to face me, all the air leaves my lungs as I read my name scrolled in red, scripted font against a white background.

"My graphic designer will do all the fancy work, giving it dimension and adding my branding."

I can feel my body shaking, the shock of him doing something so incredible for a woman he only met recently. "Why did you do this? Place my name on something with the potential to win awards and boost your sales. This is an honor you should have given to someone you love or feel deeply for."

Placing the bottle on the railing beside me, he takes both of my hands in his. "You're right, it is an honor, and one I did bestow on someone I love and care quite deeply for."

My eyes flash to his, searching for a hint of deception, a sliver of a lie hidden in his blue orbs. All I find is the truth, surrounded by the love he quite eloquently admitted to me. Christi's words come to the forefront of my mind. "*Men like ours live in a fast-paced world. Falling in love and making lifelong decisions comes naturally to them. They don't proceed lightly, but when they find it, they don't waste time on someone else's rules.*"

Where words fail me, actions speak loud and clear. I pull his face down to meet mine, kissing him with everything I have. I won't question why anymore but live in the here and now, grateful for every second I am blessed with Ian in my life.

"Thank you."

It's all I can manage as I place my forehead on his chest, afraid the emotions will bring on unwanted tears, something I don't like shedding in front of anyone, no matter the reason.

"No, thank you."

Pulling back in confusion, my curiosity overrules my embarrassment. Ian allows me to leave his embrace but remains touching me, keeping our bodies close. "Why would you thank me?"

"For starters," leaning his back against the railing, I catch the wince on his face as he adjusts his arm. "You spilled coffee on my shirt, getting my attention and showing me your beautiful face. For that, I will always be thankful."

Laying my palm over the hand rubbing his injured shoulder, I smile softly. "And second?" Flashing my eyes to his, the surrounding air is cold for the benefit of the wine, but the heat he is creating within me may ruin it all.

"For accepting who and what I am, and for the right reasons."

For the first time in forever, I feel as if I found where I belong. No longer hiding in the crowds of the city, using the unknown faces as protection from an enemy I never knew. Being with Ian, I feel as if I've found a home.

"Now, I do believe I noticed several shopping bags with the name of a famous lingerie store on the side. I, for one, am looking forward to a private viewing of what you purchased."

After the building is secured, the lights extinguished and the bottle of wine he made for me tucked protectively under my arm, we head back to the main house to enjoy dinner. According to Ian, his meeting with the Malloy's was successful, and they will head back to the States early in the morning. As we saunter along the gravel path, he tells me of Finley's arrival and how she and Brion will travel to Scotland with us.

Laird and two other men stand sentry at the door as we climb the steps, and I silently wish we could go back to the wine vault, spend the evening alone instead of in a house full of guests.

As Ian opens the door to the house, I expect to hear the loud voices of conversations going on inside. Instead, we are greeted with the smell of cooking lamb and freshly cut herbs, but the house is silent as a tomb. Ian leads me by the hand into the main room where I see Caleb sitting in a chair, a glass of what I assume is scotch captured in the fingertips of the hand draped over the arm of the chair. His eyes are hollow as he stares out the window into the black of night. Christi sits on the opposite side of the chair, her arm wrapped around Caleb, her eyes also focused on the dark exterior.

Patrick and Declan are seated in adjoining chairs, their conversation hushed, cell phones in hand. Margareta appears in the doorway, announcing dinner in the dining room. Knowing deep inside I want nothing to do with whatever is going on between the Malloy's; I take two steps into the hall before I take in the smell I can never forget.

My eyes fall immediately to the floor, an instant reaction I have when I need to avoid something unpleasant. However, this time my instincts fail me as not only do I smell the scent of gunpowder, I catch the shine of the spent casing lying against the edge of the tile in the corner, the still wet splattering of blood on the mopboard.

As elated as I was a moment ago, my heart plummets as I realize Ian sent me to Florence not as an act of love or kindness, but as a way to get me out of the house so he, and possibly the Malloy's, could murder someone.

"Are you all right, Heather?" Christi stands next to me, startling me with the touch of her hand on my arm. Her smile is intact, but concern colors her features. Borrowing her smile in an attempt to cover the fear which has gripped me, "Yes, of course. I'm sorry, I'm not used to shopping like we did today, perhaps still a little jet lagged as well."

It's a lie. I work hard enough every day to more than cover the amount of walking we did today, and I slept quite well on the plane and last night. I don't know how involved Christi is in all of this, and I'm not sure of how much I can trust her.

"Well, if his face is any indication, you won't be getting any sleep tonight." She pats my arm twice as she continues down the hall, the rest of the Malloy's following close behind and I wonder, as she walks through the tall archway of the dining room, just how involved in what happened today she is? The bigger question is, what did the poor soul who died in this room do to receive such punishment? Would Ian do the same to me when he learned of the secret I kept from him?

CHAPTER SEVENTEEN

IAN

"GOT A CALL FROM MY BROTHER JIMMY." Cadan takes a pull from his beer after returning from escorting the Malloy's to the airfield. Declan had shaken my hand, giving me his word our Families would be allies from now on, protecting each other's interests and getting together more often.

"Aye, does he need money?" Cadan is the baby of the family, living most of his life on the streets of Edinburgh, fighting was a way of life for him, it was as much a part of him as was breathing. His older brothers, Jimmy included, took to petty crimes to get the coin. Sadly, the lot of them were horrible at it, spending more time in jail than out.

"Nah, he heard talk on the streets, Gibby Macintyre is organizing a fight. Bloke says I haven't joined because I can't beat Lachie Callahan."

Cadan's knuckles were white from being wrapped tightly around the amber glass of the bottle. In all the years I'd known him, I've never seen him back away from a challenge. Lachie was a common street thug who ran his fucking mouth, using controversial tactics to win in the ring. Last year, he tried the bitch move of palming sulfur and tossing it into his opponent's eyes when he was losing. Cadan noticed it before Lachie could pull it on him, beating him till he was unconscious. A few days later we found out Lachie had fallen into debt with a group of guys, convincing them he would win big against Cadan.

"Sounds like Lachie needs money again." Cadan doesn't respond at first, capturing his bottom lip between his teeth as he sucks at a drop of beer. I can tell by the way his fingers drum against the side of his bottle he wants to ask me to go with him to this fight, but he knows I plan to spend a few days with Heather, showing her the vineyard during the day and, hopefully, christening a few corners in this house.

"Aye, and a good beating for letting my name leave his fucking mouth."

Even a blind man could see the way Cadan's skin prickled, itching to jump into the ring and remind Lachie, and his clan, who he was and what he was capable of.

"Lachie Callahan is a walking douche bag." Finley's eyes squinted as she shared her opinion on the subject. She had gone with Cadan at the insistence of Christi Malloy, the pair needing a minute to gossip or some shit. "Why do you worry what he thinks? Everyone knows you can kick his ass blindfolded."

Finley may have grown up around a bunch of guys, but she has no idea what it is like to be one. The pressure to remain on top and defend your reputation, to keep face with those around you and stand up for what you believe. Being tough is a full-time job, let someone get the best of you, and you could pay with your life.

"When and where is this fight?" I interrupt, knowing the thin string Cadan's temper teeters on, even with Finley.

"Dover's Corner, day after tomorrow."

Cadan didn't need my permission to shed his shirt and beat the shit out of anyone, least of all a snot nose bastard like Lachie. But he was loyal to a fault and knew with Heather in the house; I was more than a little distracted. Being this close to enemy territory, I needed him around, helping me out if any shit went down.

"Tell you what," pushing my glass away, I fold my arms on the table, leaning forward and closer to the conversation. "Have your brother spread a rumor you are hiding away in some broad's cunt. Let Lachie think he has a clear shot of walking away with the pot."

Cadan's sour expression shifts to neutral as he considers what I'm proposing.

"Hell yes!" Finley slams her hand on the table. "Watch the little fucker piss himself when you walk in and challenge him."

Fighting at places like Dover's Corner is simple; men show up, toss money into a pot and then start scrapping. The man left standing, in the end, is the winner and walks away with the money. There are no gloves or timeouts; rules are scarce, and the blood is real.

"Besides, Heather could do with a taste of what she is getting into." Her expression defiant, challenging me to defend Heather's honor.

"I'd say she got a mouthful this afternoon, wouldn't you agree?" After Mia's body was wrapped and taken to the incinerator, Margareta commented how the house smelled of gunfire. Finley agreed as she picked up shell casings, tossing one in the air and catching it repeatedly. She wanted to squeeze Heather, see how observant she was and if she could be trusted. A single casing was strategically placed in the hall, and all the phones, including the cell phone in Heather's purse, had been tapped.

"Hey, just like you, I have a job to do."

"She's been home for what," looking at my watch, my voice rising in anger. "Six hours and hasn't lifted anything except her fucking wine glass."

"I'm glad, Ian. Really, I am, but you know as well as I do the kinds of questions Lady Greer is going to ask."

After my father died, Mum felt the need to take a more significant role in the everyday running of the Family, assuming my dad had been correct when he said I wasn't strong enough to lead us. The day I had to call her into my office, speaking to her as a leader and not her only son, was painful but necessary. While she has backed off of me, she remains vigilant in knowing what is going on, using Finley as her informant.

"Lady Greer can ask whatever question she likes, and you can stand on the belief you serve at her leisure all you want." Locking my gaze with hers, I left no room for discussion or debate. "But you work for the McLeod Family, and we both know who is in charge."

Finley lowers her attitude, swallows hard and finally nods her head in agreement. Everyone sitting at this table, apart from Brion, has watched me take the reins of running this Family, shutting down several smaller groups which threatened to attack us. They witnessed how I stood up to them, joined forces with others, and strengthened our assets.

"She worries you are avoiding your destiny, taking too many risks like Shaw when it comes to women."

"You haven't told her about Heather, have you?"

"No, but I can't help but wonder why you haven't?" Finley's brow pinched between her eyes, voicing the suspicions swirling around in her head. When Finley first learned of Heather, I gave her explicit instructions not to discuss her with my mum.

"According to you, she shits rainbows and fairy dust. Making her the fucking perfect candidate to parade around your mum. So you can't blame me for wondering why you are hiding Heather."

Her question lingers in the air as the sound of my phone vibrating on the glass of the table. Looking at the screen, the woman in question name crosses my screen, no doubt having gotten a report from Finley about Mia.

"Cadan, call your brother. Finley, go to bed, we leave for Scotland at noon."

Standing from my seat, my gaze meets each of theirs one last time, solidifying my orders. Chair legs scrape against the tile, irritating my ears as the pair scatters off in different directions, no doubt planning my demise under their breaths.

"Good morning, Mum. Up past your bedtime, are we?"

Last time I heard from her, she called to tell me she was extending her stay with a friend of hers in Spain. Just as I stepped over my father's grave and took control of my life, Lady Greer began celebrating hers without the ball and chain of her faux marriage.

"Excuse me, Ian. I do believe I am still the parent in this relationship."

My mum was never one to stay out and frolic until the sun came up. She commanded order and repetition, being the quintessential creature of habit. She was usually up with the sun and heading to bed not long after her evening brandy, demanding the house remain as quiet as a tomb.

"One whose disciplinary role is no longer wanted or needed. Now, explain why you are calling me at nearly two in the morning. Did Victor run away again?"

Victor was her ten-year-old Scottish terrier, mean as Satan himself, with an attitude which would rival any tabloid harlot. She spoiled him beyond measure; the best food, toys, and even his own bathroom on her private jet.

"Victor is sleeping in his bed, something you should consider yourself."

"Says the woman who called her favorite son at this ungodly hour. So tell me, what's his name?"

Call me evil, but I loved getting Mum riled up, get her blood boiling as I tested her boundaries. She had become a new woman since my father died, one who laughed and enjoyed her life, taking trips to see her friends and, on occasion, entertaining a gentleman or two.

"*What is whose name?*"

"The lucky bloke who is keeping you awake." While she was free to see whom she wanted, it was my job to ensure her safety, and one I took seriously. Several of my men watched her constantly, taking out any bastard who crossed the line.

"*Oh, you're a cheeky one.*" The gravely sound of sleep in her voice is replaced with the bit of humor I'd hoped to give her. "*His name is Ian, and he has kept me awake since the night he was born.*"

Her depiction of how I came into this world, causing her an incredible amount of pain and, ultimately, rendering her unable to conceive any more children. Hours spent in labor, with tubes and wires hooked up to her, drugs which made her skin itch and her mouth dry. All in measures were in vain as she couldn't keep me in long enough. She fought infection and depression, all while caring for me and the issues, which tagged along with a premature infant. She took on these challenges by herself as my father wrote us both off when the physicians didn't hand him good news. He found comfort, as he always did, between the thighs of another woman.

"Touché, Mum, touché."

After all the years of watching my mum suffer, her heart being broken over and over, all while keeping her head up and a cloak of dignity around her, I swore to make the remainder of her life much like the time before she was forced to marry my father. Treating her like my grandfather McFarland treated my grandmother, showering her with respect and admiration, bathed in luxury and fine things, and forbidding her to worry where the money in her pocket came from or if it would be the last she ever saw of it.

"I understand you've entertained a few special guests in the villa."

Lady Greer McLeod had a natural finesse for getting you to speak the words you swore to keep secret; I had inherited this ability and expanded it by outsmarting the old gal.

"I have, the meeting was good, and they left satisfied."

"Finley tells me you look happy. Do we owe this to a young woman or the conclusion of a good business deal?"

I wanted to tell her about Heather, give her an ounce of the excitement I felt when I was around her, but I wanted her to see for herself. Witness how the smile which had been in hiding for years, was now permanently etched across my face.

"Malloy and I mended fences, forging an alliance between the Families. One which is going to be beneficial, and profitable, for both sides."

Silence hovered between the lines, hers from the cogs in her brain turning the wheels of her mind, processing the words between the lines of what I had said. For me it was anticipating her next question, perfecting the answer to give her only as much as I felt she needed to know.

"What of Darrow and his—"

"Yes, Mum. The pair were dealt with and won't bother anyone anymore, least of all the people they hurt the most."

When my mum learned of my father's affair with Mia and the subsequent birth of not one but two bastard boys, it took everything in her to face the day. Mia tried everything in her power to worm her way into Mum's home, even spreading harsh rumors, which fell on deaf ears.

"You told Malloy what Shaw confessed to you?"

"Yes, he had every right to know. Now we can put the demons to rest once and for all." There was no reason to mention how important it was to have the Malloy's as allies. Mum knew all too well the influence they had over the lands to our south. Stretching our holdings to the States would give us an edge, opening the door for shipping our products, wine, and other, not so legal, options.

"For what it's worth, thank you."

Fierce protectiveness clenched my chest, causing my heartbeat to quicken as her words found my soul. Anger gripped me as I tried to ponder where the sadness in her voice came from. "What do you mean? This alliance is something we both wanted, strengthening the pillars we stand on from the enemies my father created."

"Sweet, sweet, Ian. Your ears were not the only ones Shaw whispered confessions into. He saved one for me; one the Malloy's hoped will never be revealed."

CHAPTER EIGHTEEN

HEATHER

Purple hues of light ran parallel to the horizon, while golden beams of sunshine pushed the shadows of the night into the corners of the world, blanketing the vineyard with the light of a new day. Sleep had not found me, even after Ian came to bed. My mind was spinning in a million directions after the conversations I'd overheard. This home was beautiful, built with every modern convenience anyone could hope for, but it also had incredible acoustics, letting even the most hushed conversations rise up the grand stairwell. Hearing Ian admit he hadn't spoken to his mum about me created a myriad of questions in my mind, the answers I somehow knew I didn't want to find out. I'd made a mistake in thinking Finley was my friend, her loyalty to the Family was deeply rooted and unshakeable. In retrospect, this was a good thing, especially when it came to Ian's safety and whom he could trust. She had effectively created an invisible gully between us with the bullshit she pulled, baiting me with the shell casing, and breaking my rule of conditional trust, something I would never extend to her again.

Cadan had perched himself in the middle of those stairs as he made his phone call to his brother, aggressively telling him how he planned to knock the smug look off the face of the man who had spoken ill of him. My father had talked about the kind of fighting he was entering. I remember how he would watch boxing matches on the television, bragging about how the fights in his day were far more brutal and required more skill. My mum would wrap herself around him, glimmers of days gone by in her eyes as she settled herself at his side.

As the sun grew bolder along the horizon, I caught the movement of Margareta in the yard returning from the chicken coop at the edge of the property, fresh eggs piled in a woven basket. With a hum in her throat, she hurried her steps until reaching the stone of the back patio. Quietly as I could, I left Ian sleeping while I headed downstairs to enjoy the final moments of our time in Italy.

The house was quiet with the early hour, the ticking of the hall clock delicately keeping time as I stepped off the last stair. The smell of dough rising permeated the downstairs, making me miss the streets of New York as I walked to work. The scent was a reminder I needed to call Danielle, making sure everything was okay.

"Good morning." Roberto greets me as I step into the kitchen, a white starch apron wrapped around his waist as he cut fresh fruit on a wooden cutting board.

"Morning." Looking around the kitchen in an attempt to find coffee, the absence of its sweet aroma hitting my senses. "Is there coffee available?"

Margareta looks over the rim of her glasses at me; her hands busy cracking the eggs she collected earlier. "Not yet, Miss., I'll have it in a few minutes if you would like to wait on the veranda." Her eyes tell me she too kept a late night, crouched somewhere safe and secluded.

"If it's one thing I'm good at, it's making coffee. Point me in the right direction, and I'll be happy to get it started."

Margareta looks from me to Roberto, silence filling the air as the pair continues to exchange looks. Finally, just as I'm about to start looking on my own, Roberto points from me to the ceiling, speaking in a firm tone. His Italian, which sounded romantic yesterday, now has an edge, much like Frank when he would yell at the delivery guys. I caught a few words: boss, angry, and mother. Everything else was unfamiliar, and I suspected a different dialect than what Frank used.

Leaving the couple to have their spat, I spun around slowly and located the coffee carafe nestled against the far corner. Assuming the beans would be near, I opened the cabinet above and found what I was looking for. Cups and saucers stood to the left, while a French press sat eye level, just waiting to be used. Pulling the beans and the press down, I looked around for the sink but notice a bottled water dispenser at the end of the counter.

"Do you ever get sick of making coffee?"

So focused on filling the kettle with water, and avoiding the still arguing couple behind me, I failed to notice Finley walk into the kitchen. Her hair was pulled back at the nape of her neck, dark circles from lack of sleep forming hollow areas under her eyes. Still dressed in her pajamas, not a stitch of makeup or any sign she had showered this morning, she stood with her arms crossed and back resting against the center island.

"Not really." Casting her a brief smile, my attention monitoring the water as it filled the kettle. I wanted to say so much more, chastise her for being a backstabbing bitch, but I kept it to myself, hiding my disdain for her and the way she looked at me.

"Well, Ian likes it strong, and I need all the caffeine you can shove into my cup."

Ignoring her, I moved the water to the stove behind her, purposely keeping my back toward her.

"You okay?" Finley moves next to me, leaning her hip against the stainless-steel stove, forcing me to look in her direction, continuing to hide the anger and resentment I have for her.

"Yes, why wouldn't I be?" Locking eyes with her this time, as she has essentially backed me into a corner. Green eyes survey me, drifting back and forth between mine. The skin between her brows dips as she tips her head to the side a little.

"Oh, I don't know. If my boyfriend promised me a romantic trip to Italy, and then kicked me out the door to go shopping with strangers, I'd be pissed."

I'd assumed with Destiny's death I would be free from being baited this early in the morning. Clearly, I was wrong.

"He never promised me anything, and I knew getting on the plane he would be busy." Turning my body to face hers, "I did notice the lack of his physician being here, which is the reason he gave me for coming here. Have you even checked on his wound lately?"

Her eyes dilated in anger, lips pursing as she caught the aggression in my words. Her lips split to open just as the voice of Roberto echoes in the room.

"Mr. McLeod, good morning, Sir. Breakfast will be ready in fifteen minutes." Standing in the doorway is a freshly showered, suit-clad, Ian. His usually dark hair is slicked back, the lights above reflecting silver against the wet strands. He has cleaned up his beard as it is slightly shorter and thinner adding so much to the bad boy persona he carries so well.

Stepping around Finley, I launch myself into his waiting arms, pushing my chest flush against his. I rest my chin against the collar of his starched shirt, breathing in the scent of his cologne, relishing the way he holds me close.

"Hey." His voice calms my rapid heartbeat, a side effect of the rage I feel for Finley. "I missed you when I woke up. Why didn't you wake me?" Ian rubbed my back as I held on a moment longer, partially to aggravate the feisty redhead huffing behind me, but more to ground myself and give a reminder of how he invited me here to be with him.

"I assumed you had a late night and thought you needed your sleep." Pulling back, keeping the sharpness of his beard against my face, I bask in the prickle each coarse hair brings me. Ian separates us, his hands moving up to grab my shoulders, piercing blue eyes flash back and forth between mine.

"In the future, wake me. Got it?" Kissing my forehead, followed by my lips, he tucks me into his side as he snatches a piece of fruit from the bowl. The whistling of the kettle demands my attention, I cross the room and turn the burner off. Making the perfect cup of coffee has always centered me, chasing away the trolls which beg to be fed. Finley may be one of his closest friends, but it doesn't mean she has to be mine.

Ian made several calls after breakfast; I assumed they were business related and turned a deaf ear. Finley took her cup of coffee and a plate of food up to her room. About an hour later, the sounds of an intimate moment between two people carried down the steps. I refused to join in when Cadan and Ian made snide remarks, teasing the pair on being careful not to exceed the limits of the condom. Listening to them act more like brothers than business associates, teasing each other, gave me a reason to smile and see the pair of them in a different light.

Ian pulled me onto the privacy of the veranda, wrapping me tight in his arms as he apologized for needing to end our time in Italy, telling me what I already knew of us leaving for Scotland.

It was close to noon when Finley and Brion came downstairs, both wearing private smiles and holding hands. They shared a quiet conversation as we waited for the car to come around, with Finley letting out girly squeals when Brion touched her in certain spots. Cadan kept his eyes on his phone; a scowl on his face, which I assumed, was related to the fight he intended to attend. I wanted to ask him about the man they spoke of last night, find out for myself why surprising him was worth all this effort, but I had to leave it alone, or else I would out myself for eavesdropping on the conversation.

Ian slid into the car last, folding his tall stature into the leather of the back seat with more grace than I could ever hope for. He pulled me close, resting his left hand on my thigh, giving it a squeeze as we drove away from the vineyard.

"Next time we come, it will be just the two of us. No shopping or a house full of guests." I lay the side of my head on his shoulder as he spoke softly to me, basking in the promise of him following through with the plans he made.

"Thank you for bringing me here. I enjoyed spending time with the Malloy's." Out of the corner of my eye, I caught Finley as she swung her head in our direction, the smile Brion created earlier now flat from the name I dropped. I didn't look at her or lift my head from Ian's shoulder until we pulled up to his waiting jet.

The pilot announced our flight would take a little over four hours as butterflies began to fill my stomach. I didn't know if Lady Greer would be waiting for us in Edinburgh or if she would take one look at me and toss me out of the house.

"Fight has been moved to Baird Manor." Cadan dropped his phone on his lap, frustration filling his voice. Leaning back in his seat, running his hands up and down over his face.

"Did your brother talk with Lachie?"

"Aye. Made a trip to the cold store where he spends most of his time. Said Lachie was running his mouth to everyone who would listen about how he would have loved to show me what a beating felt like, scab up my pretty face for me." I hadn't heard the term cold store since my dad was alive. My mum would correct him and make him say corner store instead. Sometimes I swore he did things like that just to get under her skin. A thud from my left pulls me from the conversation in time to watch Finley lean over and pull her cell phone off the floor, the gold in her bracelet reflects off the sunlight coming through the windows. It's the same reflection as the shell casing and reminds me I had been left in the dark to the conversation.

"What fight?"

Ian turns in his seat, a smile splitting his face. "I'm sorry. You were asleep when we were discussing this." Motioning his hand back and forth between him and Cadan. "Tonight, we are going to watch a fight, something the men in our family enjoy from time to time."

"Heather, if the sight of blood makes you sick, you can always join me in getting ready to welcome Lady Greer back home." The last thing in the world I wanted to do is spend time with Finley even if it would earn me bonus points. "Thank you, but blood has never been an issue for me, and I want to spend as much time as I can with Ian."

"Well, if you change your mind, I have plenty of work to do." Finley settled into her seat, focusing her attention back on the screen of her cell phone, her fingers working at warp speed on her keyboard. Leaning my head against the leather of my seat, I contemplate catching a quick nap to make the time pass faster. Before closing my eyes, I give her one final look. As my eyes landed on the softness of her curls, the plane shifts to the left, making the beams of sunlight from the open windows stream across her face. Raising her hand to shield her eyes, I catch the reflection of the ring on her right hand. My body jerks forward as I squint my eyes, trying desperately to get a better view of the ring.

"Heather?" Ian lays his hand on my arm; his worried eyes search mine as his other hand cups my cheek. "Everything all right?"

My tongue feels thick in my mouth and sweat begins to gather at the back of my neck, it's suddenly quite warm in here.

"Yes," my voice squeaks and I clear my throat in hopes of a speedy recovery. "Perfectly fine, just caught off guard when the plane moved so suddenly." It's the best I can come up with and maintain the fake smile I've painted on my lips. My heart is racing with the panic I feel in my chest, the confusion as to how she would have gotten the ring overwhelming me, making me want to demand her to tell me where she got it. "Nothing to worry about, love. We will arrive before you know it."

I excused myself to the bathroom, needing a minute to collect myself. Finley gave me a brief look as I pass her seat, returning her eyes to the screen of her phone as I continued, affording me a closer look at the ring on her index finger. Securing the door behind me, I am too overwhelmed with what I discovered to appreciate the grandeur of the space. Pulling the straps of my bag open, I dove into the bottom, hunting for the one treasure I held close. Relief washed over me as my fingers wrapped around the velvet pouch at the bottom of my bag, the firmness of the single item inside chasing away the combination of anxiety and anger bubbling inside my chest. Pulling the ring from the tiny bag, I slide it on my index finger just as my mum had shown me when I was a little girl. Her last words, which echoed in my mind, her plea for me to keep the ring safe and never part with it. She told me someday I would know how unique this ring was and what it meant for my family.

As I put the ring back into the safety of my bag, the panic from earlier turns into something new, a fuel of sorts I would need to answer the burning question inside my brain.

Why did Finley McFarland have a ring exactly like my mum's?

CHAPTER NINETEEN

IAN

Baird Manor sat off in the distance, the once profitable estate of one of the country's oldest families, with its fertile fields and prize-winning horses. A generation of mismanagement and poor care had left the home, and its surroundings, in ruin. A number of hopefuls had come and looked at the property, but with the elements and the occasional squatter, the place was a wreck. The glow of the fire blazed through the cracks in the boarded-up windows, cheers of the crowd rose as the shadows of the fight danced around. Cadan bounced from side to side on the balls of his feet, psyching himself up for the battle he hoped would explode once he stepped inside. Two of his older brothers were here, waiting for the best moment to signal for us to make our presence known.

Heather's eyes were full of excitement, a bubbling energy about her. I worried when she sat up in her chair on the plane, the way her body shook, and eyes grew severe that she was about to have a panic attack. When she returned from the bathroom with the smile back on her face, and her warm hand calm as she placed it in mine, I knew she would be okay.

"Time," Cadan announced as he pocketed his phone, jumping off the low standing border which surrounded the property.

"You ready?" Squeezing Heather's hand which had been tucked inside mine since we left the States, her warmth, and softness the kind of painkiller my shoulder needs.

"I'm ready, but are you sure you're up to this?" My physician had met us at the airport, complimenting Finley on her suturing skills and how healthy the wound looked. He gave me a shot of antibiotic, assuring Heather it was just a precaution. After he collected his bag and wished us well, he sent me an email instructing me to go easy on the sutures as he could tell I had overworked them as usual.

"Lass, I'm always ready to see a good brawl."

Greg, one of Cadan's brothers, stood holding open a makeshift side door, allowing the light from inside to illuminate the ground and the noise from inside to travel out. As the brothers greeted each other, exchanging a side hug and words of welcome, Greg's eyes grew wide as he took in the beautiful woman beside me.

"McLeod." He dipped his head in respect, pushing the door open wider and averting his eyes from Heather's direction. Crossing the threshold, the sounds and smells of a heated fight hit me, bringing back so many great memories of previous events. Heather held tight to my arm as she stepped over the cracks in the wooden floor. The heels she had picked up during her shopping trip made her legs look incredible, giving her a reason to hang on tight to me. Looking around the ample space, several familiar faces appear before me, most currently on the Family payroll.

Fights such as these drew a diverse crowd from men of means, such as myself, to the workers who manned the fields and worked in my distillery. Each of us here for the same reason although not with quite the same motive as Cadan. Men stood in a circle while women dressed much in the same fashion as Heather sat on a makeshift wooden bench against the far wall. No one outside of Greg had recognized me yet, and I would play this to my advantage. Cadan stands beside me, his arms crossed against his chest. Somewhere between the door and now he'd shed his jacket and rolled the sleeves of his shirt up to his elbows. His hardened features told of his eagerness to see the end of this fight, allowing Lachie to get the shit scared out of him when their eyes meet.

A loud roar and a shower of paper tickets let us know the fight is over and the victor was not the crowd favorite. Heather pushes up on her tiptoes, attempting to see the action in the center of the crowd. Putting my body around hers, cradling her exquisite backside against me. "Hold on, Heather. The minute the real fight starts, you will have a front row seat."

Men shuffled around, tossing tickets and curse words in disgust at the result of the fight. Gibby Macintyre jumped up on what was once a stone hearth; his arms raised high in the air. "Listen up you slimy bastards! The moment you all have waited for." Gibby knew how to run a crowd, siphoning as much as he could from it until he got them where he wanted them. Like most fight masters, Gibby would receive a portion of the pot, and if I knew him as I thought, he had his hand in the side bets, something a man controlling them should not have. "Get your quid ready for the next challenger!" Cheers and boos ring out as Lachie climbs up to stand beside Gibby, dancing around like a deranged rooster, pounding on his chest like a gorilla trying to attract a mate. By the look on his face as he danced around, he felt he had this fight in the bag.

"Fucking git." Cadan spat as he had enough of the folly dance Lachie is doing. Pushing through the crowd, he rips his shirt down the front, letting the buttons fly as his steps pound against the old wood.

"Make a hole," I order, picking Heather up by the waist as there isn't a second to lose getting to the center of the crowd. My men jump into action, using their bodies to shield us from the excited spectators.

"Lachie Callahan!" Cadan roars as he reaches the center of the ring, the noise of the crowd simmers as the anger in his voice echoes off the dilapidated walls. "Get your fucking ass down here and challenge me like a goddamn man!"

Reaching the center, I place Heather back on her feet, my presences ensuring this will be an event to remember. Cadan rips at the sleeves of his shirt, too impatient to remove them in a conventional way.

"Wait a minute; you can't come in here like this." A man I'd never seen stands bloody in the center, a cut over his eye swelling, restricting his ability to see. "I haven't lost yet. That pot is mine once I win this match." One look at his shoes and pants and I can tell he is doing this for more than just bragging rights. Cadan needs this fight with Lachie, needs to show the bastard what happens when you mess with a member of our Family.

Before Cadan can do something crazy like punch the man in the face, I reach into my pocket, pull out a wad of money and slap it across his sweat-drenched chest. "Here, Lad, this is more quid than you would have walked away with. Give your spot to this man and concede."

The bloodied man looks to Cadan while whispers of my name ricochet around the room. I don't need to look in Lachie's direction to know he is quivering in his shoes. Taking the offered prize, the man reaches over and shakes Cadan's hand.

"You can't do that!" Gibby shouts, jumping down from the hearth, pulling the man back into the center. "If you walk now, you will never fight in one of my matches again."

The man looks at the quid in his hand and back to Gibby. I've never been a fan of his, found his ways of making money cheapen the core of why these fights happen in the first place.

"Macintyre, you have no say in who fights in these events. No final word on anything that goes on in this part of Scotland." I dare him to challenge me, say one word in his defense. When he remains silent, I shoot him a satisfied grin and tell the man to go home to his family.

Cadan moves forward toward a shocked Lachie, clearing the distance until the pair practically blends together. "You made a huge mistake motherfucker. Allowing my name to cross your lips."

Lachie is visibly shaking, a trait he's held since his youth. His need to be bigger than he is has landed him in more than a few dangerous situations. While he is well versed in slinging bullshit, he lacks skill backing it up.

"You should know by now anything said about me will get repeated and find its way to me. Too many times you have run your mouth, telling anyone who will listen how you can whip my ass. Yesterday, you told my brother the only way I'm able to win is because I cheat." Cadan puffs out his chest effectively shoving Lachie backward. "Everyone knows how you coat your hands with sulfur, blinding the fuck out of the man punching you." Greg and Steven, Cadan's other brother, grab Lachie by the arms, ripping the shirt off him and then dowsing his hands with bottled water. Instantly the putrid smell of rotten eggs fills the surrounding space, proving Lachie to be a cheating liar. Chatter fills the air, mummers of disbelief about what they are witnessing. "Get ready for a fair fight, one where the rules will be followed."

Several things happen at once. The crowd comes alive with side betting, and Gilbert, a short, balding man who has refereed these matches since I was little and came with my father, drew a line in chalk on the floor.

"Toes to the line, gentleman."

Cadan is the first to follow instructions, snapping his fingers and pointing at the line to get Lachie's attention.

"I want a fair fight; no kicking, no biting, and no gouging."

Lachie finally places the toe of his boot on the chalk line, his fists raised and still dripping with water. Cadan takes a jab at his face, but Lachie pulls back, walking to the edge of the crowd behind him.

"Fight me you cock sucking bastard." Cadan taunts as he takes another swing in his direction, this time the punch lands under his chin, snapping his head back and his body into the crowd.

Gleason, one of my men, shoves Lachie back into the fight. Instead of standing against Cadan, he turns back and tries to hit Gleason before he realizes who he wants to swing at. Gleason isn't fazed in the least, but a gasp from my side reminds me Heather is watching.

"Baby, I'm sorry. I need to explain what is going on." Heather shakes her head, but her eyes never leave the action in front of her. "I know the rules of boxing." Her admission brings both a smile and surprise to my face. I'd assumed she lived a simple life, free of the adventures I yearn for.

Lachie takes a swing at Cadan, but misses by a mile, using his entire body in the effort causing him to nearly topple over. Cadan delivers several blows to his midsection, each punch making his body jerk in an upward motion.

"Come on!" Gibby shouts, his face red with the exertion. Gleason looks at him, shakes his head, and then glances at me. A grin with a visible laugh is exchanged between us, both knowing this is not going to end in Gibby or Lachie's favor. Cadan has never been one to play at anything, fighting is no exception, especially when it comes to defending his reputation and shutting down a piss ant like Lachie. Growing up as hard as Cadan has, he knows when to hold back and when to lay it all on the line. This fight is no different, and I know the second he is fed up with the bullshit Lachie is handing him. Rapid fist flies at Lachie's face and body, the force shooting his head back as each punch lands on its target. Blood gushes from his nose, followed by the launch of one of his front teeth as Cadan increases the punches.

Everyone can see the end coming, Lachie is done, and Cadan is growing bored with the non-existent challenge.

"Say my name again, motherfucker," Cadan demands as he pulls his fist back, Lachie wobbling and sucking air. His fist lands in the center of Lachie's chest, sweat spraying in a million different directions. "And this will seem like a fucking good time." With a final punch to the edge of his jaw, Lachie's eyes roll to the back of his head, and he lands on the floor in a dead heap. The crowd around us goes wild as Cadan takes a step forward, rears back and spits in the middle of his face.

Hands come out, slapping the sweat-streaked back of Cadan who doesn't appear winded at all. "Come on, man, I'll buy you a drink." Cadan nods his head in agreement, stepping over Lachie's still motionless and bleeding body. Heather smiles at Cadan, offering him an excited congratulation, bringing a smile to his face as she holds his hand up in victory.

"It's easy to win when you make all the rules. You're no different from your bastard father."

Silence once again fills the room as Gibby comes to stand before me. His dark eyes glare at me, challenging me to say something. He and I have had our fair share of scrapes in the past, but tonight was about Cadan, not any lingering thorns he may have in his side.

"What the fuck did you say?"

"You fucking heard me, McLeod. You are no different from your fucking father, parading your whores around when your girl is waiting for you back at home."

CHAPTER TWENTY

HEATHER

ASTONISHMENT HELD FAST in my throat, making it impossible for me to swallow down the bile threatening to come out and forcing me to accept the bold statement the man Cadan called Gibby had made. Even if I hadn't been fluent in Gaelic, the way he pointed to me and the sneer on his face gave him away.

"You fucking prick!" Ian spat as he began removing his jacket, the dark fabric sliding down his massive shoulders, revealing the leather of his gun holster. "You dare to open your motherfucking mouth and speak of things you don't know? Talking about things which are kept behind locked doors?"

The vibration in Ian's voice gave me chills, drowning out the sorrow which cried out in my chest, begging for what Gibby said to be a lie. I reminded myself he had called me his girlfriend, traveled thousands of miles to show me where he came from, the place he loved above all others. Yet he was a man involved in the syndicate where it wasn't uncommon to have a woman on each arm and a few more trailing behind, never knowing the others existed.

"Take your fucking shirt off, you motherless cunt! I'm about to show you just how different from my fucking father I am."

I jumped as the roar of the crowd grew, silencing the sound of Ian's shirt ripping as he split the fabric down the middle, buttons flying in a dozen different directions. Gibby's eyes widen as he realizes the severity of his actions. "Heather, stay next to Cadan." Ian's eyes are nearly black as he grabs my shoulders, his gaze intense, causing my heart rate to increase to dangerous levels.

"Cadan?" The pair locks eyes, a silent conversation passing between them, their friendship of so many years interpreting the words left unspoken. Cadan tosses a single nod and crosses his arms over his chest. Several men standing behind him do the same and, as I search the room, I notice man after man following suit.

"Heather?" Ian gently grabs my chin with his fingers, pulling my attention back to him. "Stay beside Cadan. If this thing goes to shit, listen to him and get the fuck out of here."

I don't possess the level of courage needed to argue with him, to beg him to walk away from this fight or ignore how much the thought of him with another woman bothers me. Wiping the terror which fills my entire body to the side, I nod my head like one of those ridiculous toys on the dashboard of cars and force a smile to color my lips.

"Mind the shoulder," I press, swallowing hard to clear my throat of the anxiety filling the space. Threading my fingers through the loops on his pants, I pull him closer to me. "And kick his ass."

It's for the best if Ian remains unaware I understood the hateful words directed at me. Allowing him to use the embers of rage to rain hellfire down on the man with the forked tongue and less than meager common sense. I'm not stupid nor do I have fantasies about being his first and only relationship. Perhaps he ended something before coming to the States and gave his word to the girl to keep it secret. Nothing is certain in this aspect, except my unwillingness to be the side girl. If this woman Gibby speaks of is real, I have zero issues taking the next flight back to New York.

Cadan takes Ian's gun, and what's left of his shirt. The banter between them is light, and I wonder how many times they have faced a situation such as this? Unlike the prior fight, there are no side bets, no pieces of paper fluttering around the room like leaves in a winter storm. A new line is drawn in the center of the floor and the phrase toe the line alters from the way I've perceived it all these years.

Cadan gently takes my arm, pulling me to the side, and steps up on a platform I hadn't noticed before, demanding the men who occupied the spot to move to where we just came from.

"You can see better from here, and it's a mite safer too."

It's not my safety I'm worried about, although I would never tell him this. Gibby stood a few inches taller than Ian, while his shoulders were not quite as broad, he also didn't have a fresh bullet hole in his shoulder.

Watching Cadan fight the man who wronged him had brought something out in me, opening my eyes to a world I never imagined existed. I now understood how my father would scoff at the boxing matches he watched on television, how he laughed at the men who circled one another in sponsor covered athletic attire, with mouth guards and timeouts. This was raw, no gloves or firm rules, capturing my attention and forcing me to get involved, even if it was limited to shouting for my favorite to win.

"You have nothing to worry 'bout. Ian has beaten bigger blokes when he was piss drunk." Glancing over my shoulder at Cadan, I find a cheeky smile reflecting back at me. Leaning down he whispers just loud enough for me to hear, "You put up a big front, but you're shaking like a leaf. Trust me; he will be grand."

I barely hear the halfhearted instructions given by the referee when a surprised gasp rounds the room as Ian pulls his arm back, his fist connecting with Gibby's chin, sending him backward into the thick crowd. Ian wastes no time clearing the distance and pulling a bleeding Gibby off the floor as he delivers several more punches to his face. Blood and teeth bounce into the air around the two as Ian refuses to stop, his arm looking more like a jackhammer than an injured appendage.

"Call her a whore again," Ian demands in perfect English. My body stiffens, recoiling from hearing the word fall from Ian's mouth.

"Easy, darling. Gibby opened his mouth when he shouldn't have. Accused Ian of being a coward and a cheat like his father and then called you a whore."

Ian backs away from the prone man, giving him what I expect is an opportunity to gather himself. He stands up straight, not dancing around like the men I watched with my father, hands at his side, bobbing his neck back and forth to stretch it. Gibby takes his time rising to his feet, a blood-stained smile on his face.

"What's wrong, McLeod? Truth hurt?" Gibby taunts through a combination of laughter and coughing. His eyes are bright with the fight still brewing inside him, his English rough but clear to my ear. Ian responds with another fist to his chin, slamming his face to the side and causing his body to stumble.

Gibby spits blood on the floor, the sweat-soaked hair on his forehead clinging to the skin there, blocking his vision but not the sinister smile he continues to share. With wide eyes and a rebellious shout, he rears back and returns with a set of his own punches, effectively landing his fist on an angry Ian, adding fuel to his already burning inferno. Ian stands like a gladiator; his feet spread shoulder width apart as Gibby's fists land on his face and arm. While his aim is accurate, the force isn't enough to push Ian off balance. My heart sinks as I watch Ian's injured shoulder take punch after punch, yet he doesn't appear to feel anything. If it weren't for the crimson stain spreading rapidly on the bandage, I would swear they had no effect.

Gibby's punches become strained, exhaustion showing in every blow. Once solid strikes now look more like noodles tossed against a kitchen wall. His chest heaves with his labored breathing, and sweat pours down his face and body. He has nothing left as he sways back and forth, fighting for his last ounce of energy. Pulling his arm back, his fatigue is evident and winning. Crying out, he uses his entire body to deliver one more punch. Ian catches his fist in midair, crushing the man's grip in his hand. "You never could throw a decent punch." Gibby drops to his knees, the pain from his hand registering on his face, as his mouth opens and the cries of an injured animal fall from his lips. Ian doesn't ease his grip, instead, he the opposite, twisting his arm to a painful angle.

"Call her a whore again."

The rich, velvet voice, which once brought me to nirvana, is now replaced with a lethal growl, deep in baritone and making my breath hitch. Ian's commanding persona has intensified, like the floodgates raised wide open, washing away everything in its path as it covers the valleys below. From the first moment I laid eyes on him, the attraction has been combustible. Now, with the levels of testosterone filling the room, it takes everything I have not to demand the fight end so I can straddle him where he stands, allowing everyone to watch as I claim him with my body.

Ian takes Gibby by the arm, twisting harder as he pulls the defeated man closer to where Cadan and I stand. A single line of blood trickles from under the soaked bandage, but the way Ian stands before me, presenting the man who he has beaten, makes me forget all the bad shit we've gone through.

"Call her a whore again, before I rip off your fucking arm and let her beat you with it."

Angry eyes meet mine as Ian commands Gibby to do what he says. Massive tears fall from his eyes as he shakes his head in defiance. "I'm sorry," he repeats over and over, fear-riddled in his dark orbs.

"Tell her!" Ian roars, jerking the arm further.

"I'm sorry, I..." Words are replaced with high pitched cries as Ian snaps the arm back, breaking it at the elbow, and then jerking it upward receiving a second snap, causing the wide eyes of Gibby to roll back in his head. Ian finishes him by kneeing him under the jaw, sending his limp body to the dirty floor below.

"Anyone else have something to say? A rumor they heard coming from this piece of shit?"

Not a single person moved or made to open their mouths. Wide eyes take in the prone body of Gibby as his broken arm swells to the size of a melon and turns a frightening shade of blue.

"Everyone in this room knows what a lying cheat Gibby Macintyre is!" Pointing his index finger at me, his brow furrows with his angry words.

"This beautiful woman is no whore. She is kind and generous, and the future Lady of McLeod Manor!" The real meaning of his bold statement is lost on me, all I can think about is getting out of here and into his bed. Slipping my hands to the side of his face, relishing in the prickle of his beard, I ignore the murmur of voices surrounding us and launch myself at his muscled body, crushing my lips against his. Never in my life have I been this bold, so willing to lose myself in a man, but Ian is so much more than a typical male, with so many layers I can't wait to peel back.

I vaguely hear Cadan shout orders for someone to get Gibby to the hospital, how he will be lucky if he doesn't lose his arm. Ian separates us long enough to tell Cadan to bring the car around and then grasps my ass with his hands hoisting my legs around his waist, pulling my mouth back to his and commandeering my lips. The ride to his home is full of demanding kisses and intensely groping hands, moans filled with promises of what will happen once we are alone. I should be disappointed I'm missing out on the beautiful sights we pass, but Ian's hands are bringing me more delight than any rolling hill ever could.

When the car slows, Ian pops his head up to look around and flings open the door, rushing us inside. As we run down the cobblestone path to the massive front door, I catch a glimpse of purple hues in the sky announcing either the end of one day or the beginning of another. Either way, I doubt it will matter once we cross the threshold of the stone structure.

As hurried as Ian was to get inside, he now takes his time as we stand in the center of what I assume is his room, kissing me slowly as he begins removing my clothes.

"Heather, forget what Gibby said. You couldn't be a whore if you studied for ten years and had detailed instructions."

He doesn't allow me to respond as he slips his tongue past my lips, picking me up and placing my back against the softest of mattresses. Easing his fingers under my bra, moving both cups up and out of the way as his open-mouthed kisses descend toward my chest. Taking my left nipple between his teeth, causing me to jump in pleasure as he nips at the stiff peak and then releases it, chuckling to himself at my reaction. Running my hands through his thick, dark tresses, I lose myself in the way he makes me feel. I've never been bold when it came to sex, but something in the way his eyes drink me in makes me feel confident and sexy. Shoving his head down, a silent instruction for him to move lower where his attention is needed the most. Ian is a quick study and doesn't hesitate when my fingers leave his scalp to cup my breasts removing them from his mouth, tugging both nipples as I spread my knees wide, inviting him to watch as he lowers his body between my thighs. Ian's patience ran thin as the sound of ripping fabric competes with the moans I allow to fall into the space between us. My skirt and panties lay on either side of my hips, their frayed edges increasing the heat I feel in my core. His beard scrapes the skin on the inside of my thigh, making me drop my right nipple and lower my fingers to my wet folds.

"Open that pretty pussy for me." Dropping my other nipple and using my left arm to prop myself up, I watch as my fingers spread myself and his long, pointed tongue comes out to lap at my opening. The sensation of his tongue sliding up and down, combined with the way his large fingers move smoothly inside of me, reaching the spot hidden deep inside, brings out the wantonness in me.

"That's it, baby. Let me hear what I do to you."

My fingers remain holding my lips apart, giving him an unobstructed view of my clit. The need to touch it outweighs my need to watch his tongue devour me and I allow my back to hit the mattress while my fingers rub the bundle of nerves voraciously. In a move which sends me careening over the edge, Ian covers my fingers and clit with his mouth, creating a suction that is mind blowing and leaves me gasping for breath.

Ian raises his torso, wiping his drenched chin on the back of his hand as he climbs back up my body, not allowing me a sliver of time to recover. Somewhere, in the fog of the desire he created in me, I missed his pants and shoes being removed as his massive cock lays at my entrance. The way he fills me with his sizable girth makes me raise my pelvis to meet his hips, craving the friction his lips created only seconds ago. His mouth covers mine, joining his tongue with mine as he keeps time with the thrusting of his hips. One hand finds my left breast, squeezing and kneading as he drives me once again closer to the brink. I can feel the waves of my next orgasm building, the delicious burn in the bottom of my pelvis announcing its imminent arrival.

"Have to see them." Ian chokes seconds before he flips our positions leaving me straddling his hips. His hands find my breasts as my hips find a rhythm, restarting the search for my lost orgasm.

"I fucking love your tits." He admits as he pushes them together, circling his tongue around the outside of both nipples, licking the peaks like a melting ice cream cone.

"That's it, Heather, ride my cock like I know you want to. Like I saw in your fucking eyes back at the fight." There is no use denying it, no point in being embarrassed as to how good this feels. Reaching behind his head, I grab hold of the wooden headboard, forcing him to fall back against the pillows as I use the wood for leverage. I want this, need to quench the thirst he created when he defended me and show him how grateful I am to have him. As the heat begins to rise in my core once again, my speed increases as I chase the waves building behind my clit. His blue eyes study me, dark hair, now slick with sweat, stuck against his skin. Something in me shifts as I feel his hands circle my hips, helping me add the much-needed pressure on my clit.

"Come on, fuck that cock." Ian lowers his right hand to where we are joined, and in the brief time our hips aren't connected, slips two fingers against the sensitive and swollen flesh, giving enough pressure to send the pair of us over the edge. I've never experienced sex as intense as this. Never felt as free and warm as I do lying limp against his chest, trying desperately to regain control over my breathing. Ian places several kisses on the top of my head as his hand traces lazy circles on my back, lending me a helping hand into the world of sleep.

Later, when I wake in the darkened room, the sound of Ian softly sleeping and the aroma of sweat and sex fill the air. I raise my head from his chest and notice the bandage has been changed and all traces of blood from before are now gone. Not wanting to disturb him, or ruin the bubble he created, I slip out of bed and over to one of the windows across the room.

Outside the moon is high and bright in the night sky while millions of stars twinkle as the lack of ground light allows them to shine brightly. Scanning the lawn, I notice a fountain in the center of the driveway and recall seeing the same one at his penthouse in New York. Perhaps it's just a coincidence or lack of enough light, but something seems repetitive in the possible copy.

Ian stirs behind me, and as I look over my shoulder at him, I see his pants in a pile at the end of the bed. I recalled how severe my need for him was as I watched the unbridled emotion come spilling out of him, beating his enemy to a bloody pulp, all for a lie he tried to sell to the crowd. A thought crosses my mind as I recall the words Gibby used, accusing Ian of stepping out on a girl he kept here at his home. Every lie ever told has a side of truth to it, how obscure we allow it to become defines its validity. He had proclaimed my innocence at being a whore, yet never challenged the accusation of another woman.

Was there a woman who laid her head beside Ian's? If so, where was she laying it tonight?

CHAPTER TWENTY-ONE

IAN

WAKING up in the comfortable confinements of your own bed after a trip away is incredible. The sight of the woman you find yourself in love with sleeping naked beside you, priceless. Adjusting my position beside her, my shoulder throbs, reminding me of how adrenalin can be your greatest asset during a fight, and worst enemy when it's over. It fueled the rage I used to beat the shit out of Gibby and fight the pain I battled as I woke Finley to re-suture the damage my bravado caused to my wound. Cadan came in as she applied a fresh bandage with word of how Gibby had indeed lost his arm, the two breaks he suffered too severe for the surgeon to repair. Serves the motherfucker right, spewing bullshit lies to the men and women who work for me and this Family, lowering their faith in me and my ability to be a good leader.

The beating he received was a long time coming. Gibby Macintyre has held a personal vendetta against me since the moment I turned down his cousin, Erin McFarland, after refusing to take Finley for my wife. Where Erin was beautiful and had a body to die for, she lacked the scruples to turn any man away from tasting what she possessed between those sculpted thighs. Where I was far from a saint and had enjoyed more than my fair share of women warming my bed, I refused to have a common whore take the role as my partner. Gibby had chosen the wrong phrase when he made his proclamation, arousing the sleeping dragon who lived deep inside of me.

Tracing my fingers down the soft curves of Heather's side, I smile gently to myself as I watch the tiny hairs spring to life in response to the goosebumps my touch creates. I love the feel of her soft skin; how the delicate scent of her coats my sheets and makes me want her again. Having her this close was both heaven and hell; my need for her created a yearning I felt would never be fulfilled. One day I would be forced to let her sleep, but with the rapidly growing appendage I had pressed at her back, it certainly wouldn't be today. Shoving the sheets and blankets to the end of the bed and running my finger through her slick heat, I thank whatever God was watching us for making her this incredible. Raising her left leg high, allows my cock to slide between her legs and into her warm folds, rejoicing as her hand comes around and grips my hair hard enough to elicit an oath from me.

"Fuck, yes." I cry as I ease into her, resting her leg over my thigh. Grabbing her tit with my left hand and kneading the flesh there, her nipple captured in the crevice of two fingers receiving the pressure I knew she enjoyed. I find the crease of her neck and begin to bite and suck. Her hips joining mine as we searched for pleasure. I never asked her if she was on any birth control and didn't give a shit if this resulted in a pregnancy. I wanted her to be the mum of my children, to stand beside me as I continued to lead this Family. The feel of her fingers touching the top of my shaft as she plays with her clit has the question of birth control and children placed in a dark corner of my mind.

Last night as she rode me hard, I studied how her body reacted to me. Heather liked to have her clit played with, slightly on the rough side and with quick motions. Her nipples, on the other hand, loved to be licked and nipped, she became wetter when she could see my teeth playing with the hard peaks.

Heather's hand left my hair moving lower as she gripped my hip and directed the speed and intensity she needed to be fucked, remembering my commands from last night of using my cock however she pleased. I watched in awe as her hand left my hip, grasped mine and began showing me how to pleasure her tits. I knew she was close the second her fingers on her clit sped up, and the rhythm of her pelvis skipped a few times. Nothing in this world makes me hotter than watching a woman take control of what she wants, but nothing would ever compare to the moment after she finds her release, she slid out of my arms and dove for my cock, wrapping her hands and mouth around my needy dick. On her knees before me, her hazel-green, half-lidded eyes look back as she takes me deep into her mouth, moaning around the shaft, creating a euphoric effect on my balls. Up and down, circling the tip with her tongue before diving back down taking me as far as she could without gagging.

"Baby, I want back inside you," I begged as she increased her suction and massaged my balls, grazing the tight skin behind them.

"You are, Ian." She replied with a wink. She had a valid point, and I chose to let her do as she pleased, while closing my eyes and holding on for the ride.

* * *

"ARE YOU FAMILIAR WITH A PLACE CALLED ARTHUR'S SEAT?" Heather had shot out of the bed when I told her I would love to take her around the city and show her where I grew up. She bound into the shower, brushing me off when I attempted to christen the stone walls of my bathroom, reasoning there would be plenty of time for more sex after I showed her around. I couldn't necessarily blame her as I had to cut short our side trip to Italy.

"I do, it's a bit of a drive, but we can go if you like." Her eyes lit up with excitement at seeing a bunch of rocks, even after I emphasized there weren't any shops or restaurants around the area.

"It's fine; I don't need any more clothes or trinkets. I made a promise to my mum and dad I would bring them to Arthur's Seat. It's where he asked for her hand in marriage."

The way her soft voice spoke as her face reflected the memory made me want to take her there now. "Okay, how about this," pulling her into my lap. "We will stop at a couple of places along the way, eat at one of my favorite restaurants and visit a few people I want you to meet. Then, we will spend as much time as you need at Arthur's Seat." Having lived here all my life, I know every inch of this city; where to avoid and how to get past the lines the typical tourists stand in. Today, I would introduce the woman I love to the city which holds my heart, allowing Heather to see a side of me not many ever have.

Holding her hand in mine as we exit the car, my men formed a line of protection around us. The Royal Mile is a tourist hot spot, lined on both sides of the street with musicians, merchants, and food vendors. Heather's eyes grow wide as she takes it all in, her grip on my hand increasing as the crowd becomes larger.

"Ian is that...?" She gasps and discretely points to the man walking toward us, surrounded by an equally impressive security team.

"Yes, love, the Prince of Whales is a family friend. Come, let me introduce you." I want to pat myself on the back for giving her this gasp moment, ruffling my tail feathers in a prideful way for impressing her. Instead, I have far too much fun pulling a hesitant, red-cheeked, beautiful girl over to where the Royal Guard surrounds the prince. Pleasantries are exchanged, and I have no doubt within the hour, my mum will know of Heather's existence.

Lady Greer has worked quite hard keeping the lines of communication open between the Royals and our Family, holding on to her title as if it were the Hope Diamond. Security details can easily be bought, and I know for certain she has a few of his guards on her payroll.

Continuing further down the street, my men have to deflect more than few eager merchants thrusting their wares in Heather's face. No doubt they witnessed the attention the Prince of Whales had shown to her and the security she was enveloped in, seeing dollar signs dance in their eyes at the prospect of gaining her attention. Sadly, they had chosen the wrong girl to proposition, as her attention was focused more on the architecture than the cheap bobbles they tried to shove in her face. Cadan parted the crowd as we honed in on a small pub at the end of the street, paying bar tabs and insisting patrons take their meal to another venue, on us of course. Food hit our table before I had the opportunity to help Heather into a chair, another gasp moment in my hip pocket as she took in the decadent meal spread before her.

"Oh, my God, Ian. These tastes just like my mum used to make." Closing her eyes, she chewed slowly on the bite of Scottish egg she took, moaning around the flavor and causing my cock to jump in my slacks.

"Heather, you say mum not mom like most Americans, why is that?" Cadan had ordered a pitcher of beer for himself, hoarding it between his large hands, his knuckles bruised, swatting away any attempts to gain a glass from others at the table.

"Because my mum wasn't an American."

"Really?" He clarifies, "You never mentioned not being from the States." Setting her beer down on the table, she wiped her lips with the napkin in her hand.

"Because I was born in America, lived in New York my whole life."

Cadan parts his lips to ask another question but the sound of a familiar female voice derails his train of thought. "Cadan McCord!" Dozens of heads turn toward the front of the pub as a tiny dark-haired girl winds her way to our table. Cadan pushes the pitcher of beer, which once held his attention, to the center of the table. Standing from his chair, he bends slightly at the knee in order to catch her mid-flight.

"I take it they know one another." Heather jokes in my ear, leaning her body closer to mine, resting her head against my cheek.

"Leslie McCray, her father owns one of the largest producing horse farms in the country. She and Cadan have been in love since the moment they laid eyes on one another, but her father wanted more for his daughter than a street thug with no ambition. After the fight last night, and Cadan's win against a member of the family he wanted her to marry into, I suspect he feels differently about him."

There was much more to the story behind why McCray wanted to separate the two, but it wasn't something I felt Heather needed to know. Her smile is electric as she stands and claps with the rest of the crowd as Cadan kisses the life out of Leslie.

* * *

"So, LET ME GET THIS CORRECT, YOU RAN INTO HER, AND SHE SPILLED her coffee on you?" Leslie has never been a shy one, jumping head first into any conversation she encountered.

"Something like that." Heather agreed, squeezing my hand under the table, her words slurring slightly from the amount of alcohol we had enjoyed for the past few hours.

"And Lady Greer is in favor of the match?" Leslie didn't have a mean bone in her body; she was pleasant to everyone she met, much like Heather. My heart still dropped as I felt Heather shift uncomfortably in her seat as she quietly responded to her question.

"We haven't been introduced." Tension filled the air as Leslie averted her eyes to Cadan, low murmurs sounded around the room as avoidance conversations sprang up. It was time to make another stop, show her the crown jewel in my Family dynasty.

"Cadan, make sure the staff is well compensated for our unscheduled visit." Standing to my full height, I held my hand out for Heather to take.

"I trust you will speak with Mr. McCray about future dates with Leslie?" Cadan nods his head as he helps Leslie from her chair, wrapping a protective arm around her. He deserves this amount of happiness with the girl he was willing to give everything up for.

"I have one more spot to show you before we head for Arthur's Seat. A place I would spend all of my time if the Family business would allow me."

The tourist crowds had thinned considerably as we stepped out of the pub. The midday cloud cover threatened rain and likely the reason for the early retreat of the merchants along the street.

"I'll meet you back at the manor." Cadan tossed over his shoulder, his arms wrapped around Leslie as they walked toward her car.

"Take your time. I'm showing Heather my office and then heading over to Arthur's Seat."

"Arthur's Seat? Well, aren't you a bleeding romantic?"

"Shut it, McCord, it's where the lady wishes to go." Cadan shakes his head and waves over his shoulder, his body still vibrating with silent laughter.

Half an hour later, my car pulls up to the stone building which had stood here for nearly a hundred years. Every board was hand carved, and the large stones carried up from the river below. Not a single machine had been used in the building of this factory.

"Your office is in the Macallan Distillery?"

Another gasp point is awarded to house McLeod as well as one more shake of my tail feathers in a proud dance. "It is. Of all the places my Family owns, this," pointing at the painted marquee. "Is my favorite."

The earthy smell of oak and fire combined with the fresh scent of roasted grain greets us. Heather's eyes close as she takes in the unique aroma, pulling in a deep breath as she shares a smile of appreciation.

"Come on," grabbing her hand. "I have something to show you."

Our shoes echo off the wooden planks as we run down the hall toward my office. Her laughter filling the small cracks in the ancient structure, bringing life to the dust filled corners. Entering the wooden door at the end of the hall which, up until my father's death, had been a place he brought women to have sex with. A few days later, I came into the room, tossed out everything he kept hidden from my mum and made it my office.

"Wow, Ian. This place is incredible." Heather stands in the center of the room; her head tipped back as she admires the stained-glass windows that make up the circular skylights in the Bastian room.

"When I was a little boy, I used to hide in this room, pretending I was the king of the castle and my father was the evil dragon who tried to break into my home." Walking over to my desk, I pull out the bottom drawer and remove the bottle of scotch I have aging in there.

"This was the first batch I was allowed to help make. I took this bottle and hid it in the closet at the house. When my father died, and I took over everything, I placed it in this drawer. I plan to open it on the first occasion I have to celebrate."

Heather crosses the room, holding out her hand for the bottle. With the same care, you would extend to a newborn baby, she takes the bottle and reads the label.

"You know my father loved this brand of scotch. He said it was everything he loved about home in a single bottle. Mum made sure he had a glass of it for every Christmas and birthday. When I became old enough, he let me have a sip, introducing me to the water of his homeland."

Her voice cracked as she spoke the last few words, I took the bottle from her and cradled her in my arms. "I promised him I would bring them back here to where it all began." Her sobs racked her body, and she fights to get her words out. "Thank you for helping me keep my word."

Thunder rumbles overhead as I continue to hold her tight. Heather has always exhibited such a strong front that this is a side of her I'm unfamiliar with. "You never really speak of your father," pulling her away from my chest. "What was his name?"

She must realize she has shown me her vulnerable side as she briskly wipes the tears from her eyes with the back of her hand, forcing a smile to her lips to disguise the hurt she feels inside.

"I'm sorry, Ian, I didn't mean to get all crazy emotional. His name was Scott, and my mum was—"

The shrill of my phone sounds seconds before the Heavens open and pour down on the glass tiles above us. "Hold that thought, babe. I have to take this."

Grabbing her hand as I dash out of the room, the voice on the other end bringing a smile to my face.

"Hello, Mum. How is your holiday?" I feel guilty as I speak in Gaelic, fearing Heather feels out of place and lost.

"Never mind my holiday. What is this gossip I hear you have a beautiful girl in my house?"

"No gossip, Mum, I brought a woman home to meet you. Her name is Heather, and I know you will love her."

"Unless her last name is McFarland, you can hand her a broom and have her work off her room and board."

"You can meet her when you return next week. I meant it to be a surprise, but this will work as well."

"Well, Ian, the surprise is on you. My plane lands in half an hour, and I have already given the word for my staff to prepare for my arrival."

"In Scotland?"

"Yes, in Scotland, where else would I mean? Really, Ian, this young lady has you forgetful."

"Mum, she has me seeing things for the first time. And for once in my life, I know exactly what I need to do."

"Yes, yes. What you need to do is have her waiting for my inspection." Lady Greer ends the call as she always does; no bids of a good day, just a click and then a dial tone. With a grin bigger than I ever thought possible, I turn to an eager-looking Heather.

"Well, love, are you ready to meet my mum?"

CHAPTER TWENTY-TWO

HEATHER

IN LIFE, there are a number of questions, which bring about fear. Could I be pregnant? Where did I leave my wallet? Can I see you in my office?

And while I have encountered each of those questions on numerous occasions, none of them have held a candle to the amount of fear I feel from the impending introduction to Lady Greer. Was I ready? Hell no, I wasn't, not even close. But like the good girlfriend I claim to be, I slipped into his favorite smile and told him what he wanted to hear.

"Absolutely, I can't wait to meet her." From the moment Ian read her name on his phone, everything about him changed. Not to say he wasn't happy being with me because he was, but his emotions changed, and his good mood increased tenfold.

"Listen, I know I promised you we would go to Arthur's Seat, and I swear we will, first thing tomorrow. Hell, Mum loves it out there and I know she will want to show you her favorite shops and some of the tenants on our land."

I didn't have the heart to remind him this was the same thing that happened in Italy, pushing his promises to me off to the side so he can take care of others.

"It sounds great. Maybe she can help me find a good place to spread my parent's ashes." I tried to sound excited and open to his needs. The last thing I wanted to do was come off ungrateful for this trip. Ian pulled me close, his cologne calming my heart and reassuring me everything would be okay.

"If I knew we could beat her home, I would go ahead and drive you out there."

"No, really. It's okay, come on let's get out of here before the rain gets any worse." One of the many things I love about Ian is the over the top ways he tries to impress me. If I had to pick one, it would be the way he holds my hand as he drives, even as he shifts gears, his hand is wrapped around mine. Last night, as he loved me in his bed, his hands found mine, such a small thing which spoke volumes.

"Nervous?"

"No," I sigh, squeezing his fingers as I lean over and place a kiss on his cheek. In true Ian fashion, he pulls our hands up to his lips and kisses my knuckles.

"Good, you have no reason to be. Mum is going to love you as much as I do." I swallow hard at his choice of words. Our relationship has been fast and furious in the month since we met and while I knew my feelings for him reflected his, I hadn't been brave enough to return the sediment. The secret I kept from him eating away at me from inside. How could I tell him I loved him, yet kept something so big to myself?

Having arrived at Ian's home so late in the night, and then leaving so early this morning, I hadn't been able to get a good look at the exterior of the home. I assumed by the other things I had experienced with Ian: his private jet, the penthouse in New York, a villa in Florence; he had deep pockets. So why I nearly lost my breath as he circled the car around the fountain in front of the house is beyond me.

I'd seen pictures of castles on television and in books, but to see one up close is breathtaking. Rolling green hills served as a backdrop to the dark stone of the manor. Sandstone columns separate five arch-ways, highlighted by dangling chandeliers. Torch-like sconces hung every four or five feet around the first floor. A uniformed man ambled down the steps as Ian placed the car in park. "Good after-noon, sir."

Ian ducks out of the car as the man greets him, movement from my right startles me as Finley rushes the car, flinging my door open and ordering me out of the vehicle.

"Could you cut it any closer? Lady Greer landed twenty minutes ago!" Finley reminded me of the Secret Service with her clipboard and headset, wearing a polished suit and hair pulled back in a chignon.

"Calm down, Finley. You know Mum doesn't allow the car to go above a crawl. Besides, Heather is perfect."

"Perfect?" Finley gasped. "You think jeans and a t-shirt are perfect? I'll be lucky if I can make her mediocre in the time we have."

Two red-haired women stood behind Finley, their attire a carbon copy of hers down to the ring on their fingers, which matched the one I had in my bag. I wanted to confront her, demand to know what the hell was going on with their rings, but the anger her harsh words stirred inside me pushed aside my better judgment.

"Mediocre? Fuck you! I don't give a shit what you think of me, and another thing..."

The two women behind her came around and stood between us as Finley cocked an eyebrow and pointed her finger in my face. Ian rushed around the car, grabbing me by my waist and pushing me inside the house.

"Heather, I know this is a stressful time, but Finley—"

"Is a fucking bitch!" Ian couldn't hide his smile, pulling me close and kissing my forehead.

"You're right, she can be a real bitch sometimes, but she takes her job as my mum's assistant seriously."

"Taking her job seriously doesn't require her to be rude. And who the hell were the two clones behind her?"

"Those two are part of my mum's team, her ladies-in-waiting."

"Seriously?" Pulling myself out of his embrace, unable to comprehend what he was implying.

"Didn't that die out with the plague?"

"Afraid not. If Mum had her way, she would still hold court. She clings to the traditions she grew up with, holding on to the past in hopes of preserving it. Finley works hard to make her happy, so please, for me, be kind to Finley."

Ian may have said Finley, but I knew he meant to be nice to his mum, and I would. But the first chance I got, I was pulling Finley to the side and demanding some answers.

"Of course, I'm sorry for going crazy back there."

"You don't have to be sorry," pulling me back into his embrace, peppering my neck and cheek with prickly kisses. "I found it incredibly sexy, the way you wanted to go ten rounds with Finley."

"Well, Mr. McLeod," nipping his earlobe with my teeth. "The day isn't over yet; you may get your fantasy after all."

Finley and her groupies stood at the end of the hall, arms crossed and foot tapping in irritation. "If you're quite done feeling him up, we have work to do." She turns on her heels, the two clones following suit, climbing the second set of steps up to the next floor. The walls on either side of us were decorated exactly as the rooms in the penthouse in New York, even the carpet on the steps was an exact match to the rug in the foyer.

"Fiona, I need you to get the suit I had delivered this morning and place it in Ian's dressing room. Isla, I need the makeup kit in my room brought to me as well. We have a lot of work and not a ton of time."

The two split off in opposite directions, speed walking as if their lives depended on it.

"Thank God, you showered this morning as we don't have time for a good hose down." Stopping dead in my tracks, I checked over my shoulder to make sure Ian wasn't following us. Everyone had their limit, and this cocky bitch had crossed mine.

"I hope you're either talking to yourself or some imaginary friend because you sure as fuck ain't talking to me." Finley spins on her heels, an angry wrinkle in the skin between her eyes, a scowl forming on her face. Raising her bony finger in my direction once again, she cleared the short distance between us like a raging bull.

"Hold up," I warned her, my body language giving off dozens of warning signs.

"You may have a job to do, and I get it, but don't think for a single second you are going to talk trash about me, and I'm going to sit back and take it." Finley opened her mouth to say something, but I was quicker.

"Now, out of respect for Ian and his mum, I'm going to change my clothes, and run a brush through my hair. However, I don't need you, or your entourage, to make me look good. I can manage mediocre by jumping out of bed," looking her up and down.

"What's your excuse?"

* * *

WHEN IAN SAID LADY GREER HELD ON TO OLD TRADITIONS; HE WASN'T lying. The entire staff lined up in parallel lines on either side of the red carpet the doormen rolled out two minutes ago. What I assumed were the housemaids, wore gray dresses with starched white aprons and matching caps. The men, who waited at attention at the end of the carpet, wore full tuxedos including top hats and white gloves. Huge vases filled with fresh flowers stood on each side of the rug, another sat beside the wooden doors which were held open by another set of tuxedo-wearing men. The amount of pomp and circumstance for this woman's arrival was ridiculous.

As a dark gray Rolls Royce limo pulled up to the carpet, I swear I heard a collective inhale of breath from the staff. One of the tuxedo guys opens the door and a single leg steps onto the red carpet. Patent leather shoes, expensive and designer, announce her arrival as the rest of Ian's mum slips gracefully out of the limo.

"Your Ladyship." Rings out in unison by the staff, each of them bowing as she passes them on the carpet. Her blue eyes find Ian as a spark of a smile tugs at her lips. Holding out her hand, Ian dips his head down and kisses the ring on her finger. It takes everything I have not to double over laughing at all this nonsense. How big of an ego does this woman have?

"Lady Greer, I have someone I want you to meet."

I pinch the skin of my hand in an effort to control the laughter threatening to spring out of my chest. I had given my word to Ian, and if he supported this kind of treatment for his mum, who was I to question it?

"Heather, I would like for you to meet my mum, Lady Greer-McLeod. Mum, this is Heather Murray."

I wasn't sure if she expected me to bow like everyone else, but since I wasn't on her staff or gave a shit about her title, I chose not to. It wasn't hard to see where Ian got his looks as he shared her eye and hair color. She wasn't what I expected, with her dated hairstyle and conservative clothing, her collar buttoned so tight I wondered if she could still breathe. What felt like a long time passed, as she remained silent and studied my face, almost as if she was seeing something or someone in her past.

"Mum?" An anxious Ian pulled her from her scrutinization of me. "Is everything okay? Do you need to lie down?"

"No, love, I'm quite all right. The flight was dreadful, and my surprise for you is late." Taking his hand in both of hers, patting them like a small child.

"Come, Finley had the staff prepare your favorite meal." Wrapping her arms around his, she stepped past me as if I wasn't there. She continued her conversation, telling Ian of the long wait she had to endure before taking off. Ian glances over his shoulder, sending me a wink and mouthing I'm sorry. Finley kept three steps behind her, following her lead as she too ignored me.

"Ms. Murray, if you will follow me?" One of the tuxedoed men held out his arm to me, a kind smile on his pale face. "I have instructions to escort you to the dining room."

Glancing back to Ian, my heart aches slightly as he and Greer had already walked inside. Refusing to feel out of place, I turned back to the man and shared one of my best smiles. "I would be honored to walk with you to the dining room, but I didn't catch your name."

His eyes widened in disbelief, lips gaping like a fish out of water. "My name, Miss.?"

"Yes. You know who I am, so it is only right I know who you are as well."

"Nigel, Ms. Murray, my name is Nigel." Taking his offered arm, we fall into step with the rest of the staff.

"It's Heather if we are going to be friends we should at least use one another's first name." A smile broke out on Nigel's face, one I suspected didn't make an appearance often with Greer at the helm. Choosing to walk as slowly as possible, I peppered Nigel with questions about Scotland, keeping to something neutral so as not to get him into any trouble. Walking into the house, I find Ian kissing his mum's cheek as she continues upstairs, Finley and her group of mean girls close behind. Every move Greer makes is done with an abundance of grace and charm, her steps fluid as if she glided on a cloud up the regal staircase. Ian turns to face me, his bright blue eyes shining with pride and happiness. His smile is contagious as he crosses the marble tiles between us, giving a dismissive nod to Nigel.

"Hey, I thought we were having dinner?"

Ian looks at the top of the steps before leaning down to kiss me; I can only assume he is making sure he won't get caught doing something he shouldn't.

"We are, but Mum has to change out of her traveling clothes."

While I find it strange, it does fit into the insanity going on around here. All this work when the result will be the same, the food won't taste any better if you wear denim or diamonds.

"So, do we wait here, or is there something else I need to be doing?"

"Well," drawing the word out in an uncomfortable length, his eyes cast down in avoidance of me. "I'm assuming you are familiar with formal dining, but if you're not..." Letting his assumption hang in the air, too afraid or embarrassed to come straight out and ask if I knew the difference between a salad fork and a dinner fork. Not that it would matter much, either one would do enough damage to make me feel a little better about stabbing Finley in the eye.

"I may have grown up simple, but I assure you I can handle dinner with a royal." My words hold bite, and I mean every ounce of it. My mum's advice for not letting people make you feel inferior by giving them permission fills my head.

"Or perhaps it would be better if I took my meal somewhere else, perhaps with the rest of the staff?" A shift of anger flashes in Ian's blue orbs, lines form around the edges as he opens his mouth to retort.

"Champagne, sir?"

Five crystal glasses sit atop a silver filigree tray, each three-quarters full of a pale gold liquid. Bubbles float in long streams as they race to the top.

"Are we celebrating something?" Ian looks confused as he reaches for one of the flutes. The older gentleman holding the tray clears his throat as he responds. "Her Ladyship requested champagne be served instead of appetizers."

Warning bells sound all around me as something isn't right with this situation. Ian is clearly confused as to why the bubbly drink is being passed around, and it's enough for me to decline taking a glass. The man gives me a hard look, but bows slightly and moves on to the next room. Ian drains his champagne in a single gulp, setting his empty glass on a nearby table. As he turns to walk back to me, the look on his face shifts from agitation to one of shock and disbelief. As I turn to see what the source of his issue is, my breath is caught in my throat as I hear him say, "What are you doing here?"

CHAPTER TWENTY-THREE

IAN

IT WAS BOUND TO HAPPEN, and I knew damn well there was nothing I could do to prevent it. Finley had a strong personality, as did Heather, both taking their role in my life seriously. When you add in the intensity of the pressure Mum inflicts on Finley and the level of nervousness meeting her for the first time put on Heather, it was the perfect storm in the making.

Finley avoided making eye contact with me, even as she welcomed my mum home, she wasn't her typical self, full of eye rolls behind her back and clever jabs Lady Greer never understood. Today, she was all business, and it was wearing on my last nerve. She had led me to believe she loved Heather and felt she was good for me, but by the actions she exhibited, something had changed.

And the way Mum studied Heather and then failed to acknowledge her was something she had never done, even with the women who paraded into this house on the arm of my father. She acted as the perfect host, saw to their comforts and ignored the cries of passion which rose from the closed door of my father's bedroom.

My suspicions were confirmed when Mum insisted she needed to change into something more dinner appropriate, having never needed to impress anyone for the evening meal before. I didn't know how to explain all this unusual behavior when Heather questioned me, so like a fucking coward; I said the first thing that popped into my head. I needed to gain control of this and find out what kind of game the ladies upstairs were playing as I had already decided Heather would be a permanent fixture in my world. But as I turned to apologize to Heather, and ask her to have patience with me while I figured this out, another dose of gasoline hit the out-of-control fire in my life.

Erin McFarland stood inside the door. Dressed as if attending a royal ball, Erin held nothing back as she stood in her long, satin dress. Her red hair pulled back into a low ponytail, her makeup, as usual, heavy enough to make a drag queen blush. Flashing her cosmetic smile, the one she conned Blake into paying for, her attempts at seduction wasted on me.

"What are you doing here?"

Erin's eyes flash to the steps behind me, "I invited her." Looking over my shoulder, Mum and her ladies stood in the middle of the stairs. A look of deceit danced in her eyes, and I knew she was up to something.

"So good of you to come, Erin, you look lovely. Doesn't she look lovely, Ian?"

Erin played her part, blushing and lowering her eyes at the right moment, all delivered on cue and well-rehearsed.

"She looks healthier than last I saw her. Rehab appears to have worked this time." Erin had a habit of doing stupid shit when she wasn't receiving the attention she felt she deserved. During the time she was fucking Blake, she claimed several addictions just to keep him coming to her bed, desperate to have a slice of the McLeod fortune and power.

"Oh, Ian, how you tease." Erin gushed as she handed her fur shawl to a waiting staff member.

"Rehab is for people with serious addictions, I took a holiday to clear my head, and center my aura." Holding my hand out to help my mum down the remaining steps, keeping my focus on her not falling.

"Call it whatever you need, as long as it doesn't involve McLeod money."

"Ian, let's not be rude to our guest."

"You're correct, Mum." Releasing her arm, I step around Erin and grab Heather's hand. After this shit show of a gathering is over, I would need to take Heather somewhere private and explain the dynamics that make up this family.

"Gilly, I am told you made all of my favorites." Squeezing Heather's fingers, trying my best to give her some form of reassurance. I can only imagine what is going through her head as she stands here with me, feeling as if the wolves have descended upon her.

"When have you ever come home and not had a good meal in this house?" Gilly McFarland had been our family cook for as long as I could recall. She came to work for our family when Mum was a little girl, and her older sister died in childbirth. According to Gilly, she was so young she had to use a step stool to reach the stove and sink, but she came from the good side of the McFarland clan. The ones who worked their land instead of raising girls to warm McLeod beds.

"No, Gilly, you have always created perfect meals in this house."

A smile forms across her ninety-year-old face, one she shared with few people in the manor. Gilly didn't conform to the dress code or the way Mum had everyone else address her. She spoke to her with respect, but not with her title.

"Which is getting colder by the minute." Her eyes lit up as she removes the towel from over her left shoulder, waving it in the air to make us hurry into the dining room.

Wrapping my arms around Heather, pulling her closer I leaned in and whispered into her ear. "I don't know why Mum invited Erin. She was Blake's plaything for a while, but I never had an interest in her. I promise when this is over, you and I will talk."

When Heather didn't answer, I looked at her face to find her mouth ajar, her eyes dancing in amazement. Following her line of sight, I watched as the footmen finished opening the doors to the dining hall we haven't used in years. Mum had outdone herself as the twelve-foot table was covered in every piece of fine china she owned.

"Oh, my it's—"

"Ostentatious, ridiculous, and pissing me off." I finished for her, meaning every word I said.

"It's beautiful," she argued. "But why?"

My gut burned with frustration, knowing mum had learned her manipulation from all those years married to the bastard she called a husband. But to turn her skills on me could be disastrous as she would be reminded who held the reins of the McLeod Family.

"I don't know, love, but I will find out."

CHAPTER TWENTY-FOUR

HEATHER

EVERY MAN HAS a flaw in their defenses, no matter if it's a petty thief pick-pocketing on the subway, or the fireman who just rescued a group of children from a burning building. They are all human, made of flesh and blood, unable to resist the charms of a beautiful prize dangling in front of their face — Ian included. It's the only rationale I can find for her inviting Erin to dinner. Dangle a piece of juicy meat at the starving lion and watch him pounce. What she didn't count on was Ian bringing his own snack, a woman who didn't need him, but wanted him as much he did her. The difference between Erin and myself—besides the layers of makeup and false everything — was my ability to know when to walk away.

"Ian, love, you will sit beside me." Greer pointed her glove-covered hand to the high-backed chair closest to the end of the table; her nose stuck so high in the clouds I was surprised birds didn't shit in it.

"Erin, my darling, you will sit there." Pointing her index finger at the chair on the other side of Ian.

"And I'm sorry," she tossed, rolling her eyes and pointing repeatedly in my direction. "What was your name again?"

"Greer, you know her fucking name, quit being a bitch!" Ian shouted in Gaelic as Erin snapped her fingers for the footman to pull out her chair. Choosing not to get involved in the squabble, intuition telling me this meal would be over before it began, I pulled out the chair one away from where Greer stood, not waiting for anyone to help me.

"Ian, this is my party for you, and I will not have you ruin it with your vulgar language." Greer returned in Gaelic. I pretended to ignore them as I admired the painting on the walls and ceiling.

"Lady Greer, you never mentioned having the King Henry collection. I would have insisted on a meal with the family years ago." Not so surprisingly, Erin joined the conversation, her Gaelic not as perfect as I would have guessed.

"Oh, Erin, one never brags about such things. But since you asked, it was a gift to my ancestors when he gave the McFarland's our land and title."

I saw it a second before it happened, the way Ian's face turned red and his teeth clenched, before slamming his hand down on the pristine table, sending silverware in numerous directions. "We have a guest at this table, one who doesn't understand Gaelic, and it is disgusting for the two of you to carry on as if she doesn't matter."

The condescending expression on Greer's face never fell as Ian leaned over the table. "Heather, on behalf of my mum and her guest, I apologize for their rudeness."

Picking up a saucer in his hand, the design matching the color of the room.

"Erin is impressed with our dishes, which have been in our family for generations. A gift from a King who had eyes for every woman he ever met. To this day, no one is certain what transpired between one of my mum's relatives and King Henry, but he gifted her a title, this manor, and all the land which surrounds it. These dishes," tossing the saucer back to the table, the clatter erecting a gasp from both Greer and Erin. "Were a gift to shut the mouth of the girl's mum and father, ensuring the lie they constructed would be believable."

Sitting back in his chair, unbuttoning his suit jacket and leaving one arm resting on the table. "Which worked by the way, as my mum, and every female born to the line, has held the title of Lady of the Manor, and entertained countless royals on china bought with secrets."

And there was the crack in Ian's defenses; a lie told long ago which kept his family hostage. A part of me wanted to hear more of the story, diving deep into the walls of this manor and listening to what they had to say. The bigger part, the one that held my heart, wanted to climb over this table, ignoring the dishes and hug him until all the pain left his face.

"You are quick to share the parts of our past you find amusing, yet remain silent on the most important and relevant to your future. How dare you bring a girl to my home—"

Ian slams his hand on the table again as Greer had ignored his demands to speak English. Several goblets tipped over releasing a river of red wine down the baby blue tablecloth as servants rushed to save it.

"Leave it!" Ian roared, the pain in his voice echoing off the fine paintings framed in gold overhead.

"Whose house?" He demanded, fire glowing from his eyes.

"The house comes with the title. Therefore, it is mine."

"Wrong!" Ian shouts as he stands from the table, shedding his jacket and tossing it to the side. "The house and land belong to the McLeod's, as long as a title holding McFarland lives here. Everything you see here became mine the day we shoved that bastard into the fucking ground."

Ian's chest rose and fell with his labored breathing, but Erin smiled with a twinkle in her eye as she watched the pair argue as if it was commonplace.

"Yes, Ian, technically all of this does belong to you. However, you forget something important, a stipulation you continue to jump over every time I try to speak to you about it. Which is why I've invited Erin for dinner." Erin shifts in her chair as if this is the moment she has been waiting for; claws and teeth ready to sink into whichever team can carry her furthest.

"You must marry a McFarland, one who knows where she comes from. Erin is a direct descendant of the same family who was given the title I hold. It is she, not some American mutt, who I doubt could trace her heritage beyond a few decades. It's clear by her defiance sitting at this table; she lacks the proper skills and etiquette a well-bred mum would teach."

And just as all men have their breaking points, a crack in the wall surrounding them, I had mine. You could say whatever you wanted to about me, but I refuse to let anyone smear the memory of my mum. I'd held my tongue and swallowed enough bullshit today to last a lifetime.

Standing from my chair, laying my napkin across the plate before me, I hope the fury welling up inside me didn't cloud my voice and make my Gaelic sound bitter, "Lady Greer." Clearing my throat as three sets of wide eyes look back at me.

"You speak of my mum as if she were one of your servants, one too stupid or unfortunate to afford the luxury of a proper education. Born into a family, absent of the royal blood you so desperately cling to. You say I lack proper etiquette and formal skills required to sit at your table of secrets. My mum, whom you condemn without knowing, taught me many lessons before she died. One which I will share with you, in hopes it will make you a better person."

Thinking of my mum as she stirred her tea, my father reading the paper as we sat around the breakfast table back in New York.

"A proper lady is a woman who makes everyone around them feel comfortable; no matter what they wear, look like or where they come from."

Greer blinked in disbelief, her brow furrowed in confusion. Stepping away from the table, knowing my time in this house, and with Ian, has come to an end.

"From the moment we were introduced, you have treated me in the worst way, ignoring me to some extent."

Reaching for the chair beside me, the pain of leaving a part of my heart with Ian is too much to bear.

"You know, it's a good thing you carry the title of Lady, and everyone in this room has to refer you as such, because the actions you've shown me today labels you as a bitter old woman, and not the lady you profess to be."

Greer shoots her hand out to stop me, her bony fingers digging into my arm. "You speak Gaelic so well. How is this possible? And the phrase you use…" Shaking her head in disbelief, tears well up in her eyes as she tries to find her words.

Jerking my arm out of her grip, "None of you bothered to ask, so why would it matter now?"

I ignore Ian calling my name as I run out of the room. Finley and Nigel are waiting outside the door, a look of shock on both their faces.

"Nigel, you are the only one who has treated me with respect, and I thank you, but I need to ask a favor. One that may get you fired."

CHAPTER TWENTY-FIVE

IAN

"HEATHER, WAIT!"

Watching her run out of the room hurt far worse than any gunshot I'd ever experienced. Not even when a man stabbed my balls with a knife, did the pain render me as useless as I feel now.

"Let her go, son. She needs a minute to collect herself."

"Collect herself?" Looking down at my mum, her once stoic face now smeared with tears. "I need her to come back, to understand..."

Mum rises to her feet, collecting my face between her gloved hands, "how much you love her? I know. I saw it in your eyes when I got out of the car. Heard it in your voice as you spoke of her on the phone."

Lowering her head in shame, wiping the errant tears from her cheeks. "I knew this day would come, feared it more than anything," Mum admitted as she twisted the ring on her finger. "I tried telling myself you would sample your way through nameless girls until the time came for you to fulfill your destiny and marry a McFarland."

Erin remained quiet as a church mouse as I sat back down beside my mum.

"So, you got scared, and tossed your ace in the hole by taunting Heather with Erin?"

Mum grasped the goblet of wine before her, brought it to her lips and took a long drink. "Something tells me your Heather doesn't scare easily."

Leaning back in my chair, the exhaustion from it all too much to stand. "Heather is as tough as they come, she fits seamlessly into this Family. At least she did."

The creek of the door opening from the kitchen had my heart fluttering, hoping to see Heather's face come bouncing through the small door, my spirit crashing as Gilly wobbled across the floor, a large bottle in one hand and a pair of glasses in the other.

"Finley says not to come out of this room until the bottle is half gone or you're ready to act like adults, whichever comes first."

"And where pray tell, is Finley?" Mum questioned as she helped the staff clear the priceless china from the table.

"She went up to the room I made for Heather. She mentioned something about making this right."

Lifting the bottle from the table, I poured myself a glass of the amber liquid, offering one to Erin who turned up her nose. "You might want to rethink it because, as the men I work with back in New York say, it's about to get real up in here."

Mum shoved her glass to rest beside mine as I filled both glasses to the brim. Erin pulled out a mirror and lipstick from her clutch, too involved with adding another layer of gunk to her face.

"You know, out of all the eligible McFarland girls around, it still baffles me why you would want me with Erin?" Mum finished her glass and then reached across the table for the bottle, filling her glass once again to the brim.

"Because you know her so well. She was here for every holiday, and she is familiar with all of our associates."

Glancing over at Erin, who was popping her lips and making fish

SECRET ATONEMENT 263

faces into her phone, "I didn't know her half as well as Blake and Darrow did. Or most of the men who work for us, including your husband." Erin stopped mid fish-kiss and shot her wide eyes in my direction.

"She has no boundaries for who she fucks, no morals as to when or where. Hell, she gave your husband a fucking blowjob in his car with Blake and I in the back seat. When she finished him off, she crawled in the back, straddled Blake, and fucked him as we drove through town. Is this the type of woman you want as a mum to your grandchildren?"

Mum sat in her chair, drinking her scotch. Her calm demeanor should have frightened me, but I knew she was choosing her words carefully.

"Did you notice how Heather's use of Gaelic was so crisp and refined? No slang words or emphasis on the wrong syllables. How she spoke clean and unbroken, using the proper tense and verbs?"

Of all the things I assumed mum would consider, the way Heather spoke was not one of them.

"Not really, Mum. I was too focused on her walking out the door," shoving my empty glass away, no longer having a taste for my favorite drink. "But please, stay here and examine each word she used. I'm going to go find her and beg her to stay."

As the wood of my chair clambered against the tile and rug of the floor, Finley walked in through the kitchen eyeing the bottle between us.

"Not quite half gone, but enough you both will listen to me." Slamming a large file on the desk, along with a velvet pouch and her glasses she uses only to read with.

"Mum you listen, I'm going after Heather."

Finley snaps her fingers in my face; my hand reaches for my gun at the small of my back.

"Don't even think about it, Ian. Mine is closer and with your shoulder fucked up, I'm quicker. Besides, Heather isn't here anymore."

"What do you mean she isn't here? Gilly said she was going upstairs to clear her head."

Finley kept her focus on the pages in her folder, spreading them out across the table. "She did, but then decided she needed to leave. Heather took the ticket you gave her and had Nigel drive her to the airport, they left an hour ago."

"Why didn't you find me? I could have stopped her!" I demanded, the burn of tears creeping up behind my eyes. I can't recall the last time I cried, but I knew I would make up for lost time as my world shattered.

"By the time I realized what an idiot I had been in all of this, I rushed to her room to find it empty, except for her bag. I hoped she had left her passport in it and would buy us time to stop her, but what I found instead..."

Finley shook her head as she reached for the bottle of scotch; not bothering to use a glass, she tipped the opening to her lips and took several pulls.

"Instead what, Finley?" My patience growing thin as I turned for the door, intent on getting on my jet and bringing her back.

"Wait!" Finley shouted. "Give me fifteen minutes to show you what I dug up; it will give the pilot enough time to ready the aircraft."

With reluctance, I dropped my tired body into a chair. Snatching the bottle out of her hand, my eyes silently telling her to get on with it.

"Okay, so we know she said she grew up in New York and never left because of her parents, right?" Finley moved several pages as her eyes became brighter.

"Which if you think about it, is odd as everyone takes a holiday. But no, she was telling the truth. Heather Murray has never booked a ticket on any airline or train company in the States." Sliding a piece of paper out of the stack, she hands me what appears to be a life insurance policy.

"See this? Heather Murray, the sole beneficiary of a life insurance policy for Scott Murray."

Looking where Finley pointed, handing the document to my mum. "Aye, we know her father died, so what? This doesn't tell me anything new.

"Of course it does," Finley corrected as she pulled the paper from Mum's hand. "Scott was her father, not her husband, so why wasn't his wife listed as the beneficiary?"

I could see the cogs spinning in Finley's eyes. The way she analyzed things was a mystery taking nothing at face value, she was a vital asset to this Family.

"Because she died before he did, almost six months to the day, long enough for him to change the policy to include his daughter. But," Finley added as she shifted more papers. "I couldn't find the original insurance documents. There is also no marriage license registered in the States for Mr. Murray and the unknown wife."

I could feel Heather slipping away, my heart crumbling along with her absence. It would take a miracle to find her and bring her back, convince her we could be together despite my mum.

"I was ready to give up, but as Lady Greer mentioned Heather spoke near perfect Gaelic. I thought to myself if she spoke that well, she had to learn it from a native. So I dug deeper, and found this." Shoving forward a copy of an immigration and naturalization application, the names written in pen were Murray Scott Malloy and Bridgette McFarland Malloy.

"But look here," showing the copy of the typed application, the names listed were in mixed order, Scott Malloy Murray and Mallory Bride Murray. The country of birth was listed as Ireland.

"Either her parents paid the immigration people a ton of money, or found the one person who didn't care what name went on the application."

"But how does this connect to Heather? Tons of Irish immigrated to America during that time, still do."

A triumphant smile curled the lips of one satisfied Finley McFarland, the gleam in her eye making my heart beat faster and my mouth run dry.

"Look at her birth certificate."

My hands shook as I felt the sheet of paper slide between my fingers, I would have felt more secure if she had handed me a venomous snake. Perusing the piece of paper, inked images of her tiny feet, alongside her mother's thumbprint, sat below the names of her parents, Scott and Mallory Murray.

"Aye, so her parents were Irish immigrants who lied on some legal documents. They're dead and buried so what difference does it make?"

Finley reached inside the bag Heather carried with her onto the plane, pulling out a square wooden box and sitting it on the table. "Dead yes, buried, no."

Mum had continued drinking her scotch, her eyes shooting daggers at Erin who hadn't sense enough to leave when she had the chance.

"Motherfucker!" I shouted as I threw a glass from the table against the far wall, the crash gaining Mum's attention and encouraging Erin to leave the room. "She asked one thing of me, one, and I failed. She wished for me to take her to scatter her parent's ashes at Arthur's Seat."

"There is one more thing I found," Finley's voice dropped as she passed the velvet pouch to my Mum. "I caught her looking several times at my ring, so I think she already knows."

Mum stares at the pouch for the longest time, darting back and forth between Finley and the cloth in her hand.

"It can't be."

Finley nods her head, walking around to stand behind Mum as she opens the pouch. "I ran the print off the birth certificate; they are an exact match."

Mum pulls a ring from inside of the pouch; the likeness of the one she and her lady-in-waiting wear is uncanny.

"Oh, dear Lord. Bridgette, my baby sister is gone." Mum collapses into a heap of tears. Finley wraps herself around my mum, whispering words I cannot hear.

Clarity hits me like a wrecking ball, and my chest feels the brunt of it. "Mum, please tell me what I'm thinking isn't real? Tell me there is some kind of mistake and that I haven't been sleeping with my..."

I can feel my skin crawl at the memory of what I had done, the night and morning I had spent with Heather, my—oh, God.

"No, Ian." Mums head pops up, her face full of remorse. "I'll explain everything on the plane, but we have to get to New York and find Heather. There is so much she needs to know."

CHAPTER TWENTY-SIX

HEATHER

STANDING in line behind a family of six makes my heart heavy, and a few tears threaten to fall. Mentally chastising myself for allowing myself to dream of a future with Ian. I feel like some creepy voyeur as I watch the husband place a kiss on his wife's forehead. How precious love is until we don't have it anymore, taken for granted and wasted away.

"I'm sorry, sir, but the first-class cabin is full." The lady behind the counter looks as remorseful as the woman wrapped in the man's arms, her body shaking with tears.

"Ma'am, is there a way we can trade tickets with another passenger so my family can sit together?" The husband pleads, his voice cracking with emotion.

"You are welcome to ask, but I doubt anyone holding a first-class ticket will trade for your single coach seat."

"Tell me, what is the difference between the two seats, fare wise?"

The lady behind the counter hits a few buttons and then whispers, "Two thousand US dollars, sir."

Reaching for his wallet out of his suit jacket, "offer anyone willing to trade twice that."

As I look down at my ticket, the bold letters First Class Boarding stare back at me. Four thousand dollars is a lot of money, considering I was looking at being homeless and unemployed once I land in New York. That money, plus what I had from the shopping trip Ian sent me on, would go a long way.

"Excuse me, sir?" The man flashes his eyes down at me, the blue of his orbs making my heart melt as I thought of Ian and the way his eye color made me feel. "I have a first-class ticket I will sell you."

* * *

SITTING IN THE WINDOW SEAT, I WATCHED THE CLOUDS DRIFT BY, THE same blanket of billowy white, which had been laid out along the path to Italy. How long ago it all seemed, the further we went away from Scotland. Was he laughing with Erin and Greer as they planned their wedding, the arranged marriage of the century? I wanted to be angry with Ian, hate him for being dishonest about her, but I couldn't. I knew by the look in his eyes he was as floored as I was. He would forget me soon enough. I would be gone before he made any business trips back to the States, working in some small forgotten town some-where in the middle of nowhere.

As the plane landed and the gaseous man beside me pulled his bag from the overhead, I looked around in vain for my cloth bag. I tried to think of the last place I had it when I realized I had left it at Ian's house. I had been so focused on getting the hell out of there I had grabbed my passport and wallet, but left my tiny bag in Ian's room by the dresser. Perhaps I could speak with Mr. Santos or Mr. Nakos as they had business dealings with Ian, I would ask one of them to see if Ian would return my parent's ashes and the ring.

The sounds of the busy city greeted me as I stepped out of the airport, yellow taxis lined up along the curb waiting to take passengers wherever they needed to go. I have always been a subway or bus kind of girl as taxis are pricey, considering how crazy the past few days had been, I opted for a solo and expensive ride home. Late evening shadows danced along the interior of the taxi as we crossed the bridge into Manhattan. I considered going to the coffee shop, but changed my mind, as I knew the next time I went there it would be to say goodbye to Danielle and Gabe. I needed to find a new life, far away from New York and the Families who ran it. Maybe I could find a place where I could afford to go back to school, get my degree and be something my parents would have been proud of.

"Sixty-three even, doll." Lost in my daydream, I hand the cab driver seventy dollars, telling him to keep the change. He thanks me and wishes me a great day as he drives away, leaving me alone on the curb outside my apartment. Climbing the steps, I am comforted by the sounds of my building. The second floor always has the smell of curry as most of the families are from India. As I round the steps to the third floor, I can hear Mr. Nelson yelling at the television; he must be watching a game show as he is shouting out answers followed by curse words. The fourth floor is waiting for me, welcoming me with the smell of my mum's perfume and my father's tobacco. As I open the stairwell door, I see Mrs. Rocco stacking boxes in the hallway followed by a short man who isn't Jamie, her husband.

"Hey, Heather." The portly woman whose name I never knew, except as Mrs. Rocco, stands up with her hands on her hip, one of the children crawling out of the apartment after her. "I tried knocking on your door, but I'm guessing by your bag, you've been out of town."

"Yes, but I'm back. For a little while, at least."

"Good, I'm glad. Listen, I know you and I never spoke, but I suspect you could hear the arguing between Jamie and me."

Nodding my head, I continue stepping closer to my apartment

door. "Couples fight, nothing new there." I try to sound neutral, not wanting to get in the middle of anything.

"Well, you'll hear no more arguing coming from this apartment." Pointing her thumb over her shoulder. "Jamie and I have called it quits. Since the DNA tests came back on the kids, he moved over with that freak, Cindy."

The portly man took the baby from Mrs. Rocco, their eyes the same shade of green. "When they found her sister's body beside the dumpster, Jamie had to tell Cindy about her passing. He came home that night and said he wanted a divorce, he found the two of us coming out of a hotel on Fifth Avenue." Waving her hand between the man and herself.

"Yesterday, he came over with DNA results from some hair he took out of the kid's brushes and found out how long Clint and I have been together. Since his grandmother owns this apartment, the kids and I have to go live with their real dad."

Jamie Rocco is one of the nicest guys I know in the city, and the way this woman speaks so bluntly about her deceit makes me ill.

"Jamie asked me to give you the key when I get my stuff out, said he would be by the coffee shop to pick it up."

"Okay, sure. I can do that." Taking the key from her chubby fingers, I opened the door to my apartment and wished them good luck, before closing and locking the door.

Early the next morning, after sleep avoided me and tears of pain wrapped themselves around me, I decided the inevitable was unavoidable. I needed to go to the shop and say my goodbyes. As I walked down the block toward the subway, I expected things to be different, but time stops for no one or nothing, even a broken heart. Mother Nature must have decided today was a bad day for her as well as she opened the heavens and let the rainfall in buckets as I stepped onto the stairs for the train.

Aroma was one of the few shops with interior lights on. Considering the early morning typhoon and today being a Saturday, I shouldn't have been surprised. Danielle danced as she poured water into the coffee machine and Gage sang off key with the song on the radio. Sadly, the bell over the door rang just as the song finished and two sets of excited eyes found mine.

"Oh my, God. I didn't think we would see you before Christmas!" Danielle called as she ran around the counter, launching herself into my arms. Feeling the touch of my dearest and longest friend, the tears returned and brought the sobs with them.

"Oh, honey, what's wrong?" She cooed, concern and love flooding her voice and eyes.

"It's over, I ruined it. I broke the cardinal rule of dating a made man." Danielle and I had laughed at other women who had failed to gain the trust of the Matriarch of the Family. We knew, without her approval, the relationship is doomed.

"Come on, tell me all about it. I bet once you get it off your chest, we can find a way to fix it."

"Trust me, there isn't enough glue or tape in the world to fix this. I called her a bitter old bitch."

"Well, was she?" Danielle asked over the top of her cup of coffee as thunder boomed overhead. The lights flickered twice but held on.

"A bitch?" I clarified. "Absolutely."

For the next few hours, as the rain continued to come down in buckets, I sat at a table with Gabe and Danielle, telling them about my exotic trip of epic failure, leaving out the gun casing and the Malloy's, but warning Danielle to keep an eye on Finley.

"As soon as this rain quits, I'm going over to Dancing Zorba's and talk with Mr. Nakos. I need to ask a favor of him."

"Wait," Danielle placed her hand over mine, looking at me through excited eyes. "The place six blocks over with the too hot for words Greek God?" Danielle had been smitten with Stavros Nakos since she first laid eyes on him. But his mum, who worked in the kitchen, had given her a look of death and Danielle hadn't been back.

"Yes and don't forget the super scary mum who makes you piss your pants."

"What kind of friend would I be if I didn't help you move on? Besides, maybe you can get a job over there, instead of moving to Boringville."

Danielle cried with me when I shared my plan to move out of the city. It was the best thing for me, and I hoped she understood.

"Fine, you can come with me, but don't get your hopes up, 'cause I know they hire family only to work in the restaurant."

"Who said anything about working in the restaurant? I want a piece of Stavros."

Danielle and I made plans to meet at Dancing Zorbas the following night, enjoying one final meal together before I left for good. The rain slowed to a drizzle as I rounded the corner grocery by my apartment. Stepping inside, I grabbed a few items for dinner and asked if they had any empty boxes I could have. With both hands full, I made my way to my apartment, determined not to cry, as this could be my last trip to this store. Packing my dinner inside our tiny refrigerator, I took a good look around at the only home I'd ever known. Black marker lines on the doorframe documented how much I'd grown over the years. The magnets littering the refrigerator, something my father enjoyed collecting, made me smile as I recalled him bringing them home.

"It's just an apartment," I reasoned with myself out loud, as I opened the first box and began packing. The sky was dark when I took my first break, having cried tears of both joy and sorrow as I went through drawers and cabinets. I found a box full of my baby teeth and an old tin of my father's tobacco, the smell bringing me to my knees. A knock on my door makes me sit up straight, wipe the tears on the back of my sleeve and stand up. Looking around at the mess I had created, I considered not answering out of embarrassment. Assuming it was Jamie coming to retrieve his key, I marched over and opened the door.

"Hey, I heard about you and—" Words failed me as I came face to face with a set of green eyes, ones I wished I would never see again.

"I know I am the last person you ever want to see, but please, hear me out. When I'm finished, you can toss me out one of your windows if you like."

"I'll save you the trouble, you have nothing to say that I want to hear." Moving to slam the door in her face.

"What about this?" Holding the box, which held my parent's ashes, my mum's ring resting on the top. "Don't you want to know why I have one on my finger too?"

CHAPTER TWENTY-SEVEN

IAN

"IAN, there are things even you cannot control."

Mum had been less than helpful as she reminded me of my limitations. Mother Nature had chosen today to piss on my world, closing several airports as she pelted New York with torrential rains. We were rerouted to Virginia where we wait out the storm.

"Easy for you to say, Mum. The love of your life doesn't hate you right now."

"Oh, I'm certain your Heather wishes me dead. I assure you, we will straighten this up and someday you will look back on this and laugh."

On the plane ride from Edinburgh to Virginia, Mum attempted to tell me the story of the ring, and its significance. However, the amount of scotch I consumed, combined with the stress I had endured during the fight, made my body shut down and I fell into a deep sleep before our wheels left the tarmac. I'd begged her to tell me as we waited inside the hanger, but she refused, closing her eyes with a content smile on her face.

"From your lips to God's ears."

Cadan had called ahead, arranging for one of my cars to be waiting when we landed. As we taxied down the runway, my cell rang. Hoping it was Heather, I answered without looking at the screen.

"Heather?"

"Nah, man. T-Bone."

"What's up?" I demanded, not in the mood to talk business.

"My boy, who watches over your shorty's apartment said he saw her carry empty boxes into the building and wanted to know if she was moving in with you or if she had a new crib?"

"Have your boy keep an eye on her. I'm on my way there; have him stop her if she tries to leave."

"Everything all right?"

"I sure as fuck hope so."

"No worries, dog. I got a homey who can hook you up if you need a new shorty."

"Thanks for the offer, but I'll pass." I end the call as the door to the aircraft opened. Not waiting for the pilot to welcome us to New York, I charge out the door and down the steps. A member of customs stands waiting with a clipboard and bad comb-over. Before he can speak, I'm handing him my passport and denying I have anything to declare.

"Mind if I have a look on board?"

"Does it require me staying here while you do it, Doug Myers?" Looking to his name badge as my mum and Finley came down the steps.

"No, sir."

"Then be my guest."

Forty minutes later as the rain reduced to an annoying drizzle, I parked the car outside Heather's apartment. Mum sat in the passenger seat, holding onto the black box she insisted Finley bring.

"Such a long way from Arthur's Seat." Mum sighed as she bent over to look at the tall building through the raindrop-covered window.

"What is the significance of Arthur's Seat? Heather wanted to head out there the other day." Turning her face in my direction, "This is a story for Heather, you can listen in if she wishes."

I never cared for the building Heather lived in, not enough security or amenities for my taste. As I unfold myself from the vehicle and turn to help Mum, I'm clinging to a sliver of hope she will change her mind about being with me, after she hears what Mum has to say. As we near the front entrance, a couple with three small children are leaving, the chubby man smiling as the woman holding a baby reminds him to stop at the grocery store. Holding the door open for the couple, the woman appreciates me up and down with her eyes.

Pungent odors hit me in the face as I push open the door to the stairwell; a combination of shit, piss, and wet dog lingers in the air. Taking the steps two at a time, I race to the fourth floor, my heart beating fast from more than just exertion. Using the few minutes it took for Mum and Finley to climb the steps, I tried to think of what to say to her, tell her how sorry I was and how I would do anything to make it right with her. I hadn't been this nervous since the first time I saw a girl naked. I forget her name, but it doesn't matter as the last girl I ever want to be with is on the opposite side of this door.

Finley walks down the hall as if she has done so a million times, marching up to the door and knocking as if the woman on the other side doesn't detest her. I've seen Finley talk her way out of some situations, but thought she would strike out when it came to Heather.

"You have five minutes to tell me about my mum's ring, as you can see I'm busy packing." There was a bite in her words, anger strangled by hurt and regret.

"Fair enough." Finley started, but Mum placed her hand on her shoulder.

"Finley, this is my mess, and I should be the one to clean it up."

Finley bowed her head and took a step back, placing the black bag and box of ashes on Heather's coffee table.

"But first I must apologize to you, Heather, for my behavior. I was dreadful to you, treating you like a second-class citizen, when in fact you are so much more."

Heather stood her ground, crossing her arms over her chest as she stared at my mum. "May I sit down? It was a long flight to get here."

Something flashed in Heather's eyes, as she lowered her arms and moved to clean off her sofa. "Of course, I apologize for the mess, but I have little time before the rent is due again. Let me put the kettle on, and we can have tea." Disappearing into what I assumed was her kitchen without a sound. Several minutes later she returned carrying a tray of tea and what I knew to be American cookies.

"I hope no one wants lemon; I don't usually keep it in the house. I suppose I can run down to the market if anyone wants some."

I wanted to rush to her, hold her in my arms and take away all the nervousness she had coming off her in waves. She sat down on the sofa, rubbing the palms of her hands up and down her thigh.

"Finley says you judge people on how they make tea. Mine is most likely too simple for your taste." Her eyes shift to mine and linger for the briefest of time.

"I find simple to be the best when it comes to good tea. Finley tells me you make some of the best she has ever tasted."

Heather isn't swayed by pretty words or compliments. "Why do you have my mum's ring on your finger?"

"Well, to tell you where I got my ring will require more than five minutes. Would you prefer to have us come back, or can we go beyond the allotted time?" This was the Mum I knew; patient and kind, full of motherly love and affection.

"Please, tell me the story."

My leg bounced as my need to be near her increased, to comfort and assure her everything would be okay.

"Well, you heard from Ian how I became Lady Greer; granted the title and land from a long since dead King. Years later, when arguments sprang up among other property owners who wanted to throw the McLeod's off our land, two families came to our aid. An agreement was created to keep the bonds solidified and the royal lineage alive and well. So, for hundreds of years, the three family's: the Malloy's, McFarland's, and the McLeod's, shared the lineage by marrying female McFarland's to the leaders of the McLeod and Malloy clans. As time passed, the Malloy's chose to branch out, taking their family and moving to the States. Returning to the land only when the leader of the Family chose a wife. The McFarland's and the McLeod's stuck with the tradition, mandating the agreement remain intact."

I'd heard this story my whole life and had McFarland girls paraded in front of me like Miss America contestants. Knowing how cutthroat they could be to one another, I had refused each of them, until the dreadful day when my Family demanded I take a wife.

"I apologize for waving Erin in your face; there was never an arrangement between her and Ian. Knowing what I do now, I'd rather claw her eyes out than let her near my son." Heather's eyes widened, but she remained silent as Finley and Mum shared a laugh.

"Anyway, as I was saying. When I was of age to marry, my mum and father took my younger sister, Bridgette, and me to a party which Shaw, Ian's father, his friend Thomas Malloy, and his brother Scott were attending. Shaw took one look at Bridgette and fell in lust. However, she didn't even notice Shaw as she fell hard for Scott. Since Shaw was the next in line to take over the McLeod Family, our father tried to force Bridgette to marry him. Scott told her not to worry as he and Thomas had a plan. Some time goes by, and Shaw becomes more insistent, demanding my father keep his end of the bargain and give him Bridgette. Thomas and his father happen to be at the house when Shaw came calling, and as soon as he left, Scott came back and took Bridgette in the middle of the night."

Mum's voice cracked as she spoke of her sister, someone she and my father refused to talk about.

"Scott took her to Ireland, married her in a private ceremony and lived in a house owned by the Malloy's. When Shaw found out, he sent a group of men to kill Scott. Thankfully word got to them first, and they escaped into the still of the night, leaving everything behind."

Something stirred in my memory, a conversation I had with Declan Malloy. He told me how he visited a home on his family's property when he was in Ireland before marrying his Katie. How he had walked into a house which looked as if the people had left in the middle of having tea. This had to be what my mum meant. The Malloy's had protected the couple, celebrated their love.

"Mum worried Shaw would cause trouble with our lineage and ask the King to take back the title and the rights to our land. She and I requested court with the King, showed him our documents and he agreed to split the title, allowing Bridgette, and I to both have the rights once she returned to Scotland. Shaw demanded a wife, so my father made me marry him instead."

Finley wrapped her arms around my mum, kissing the top of her head as she handed her a handkerchief.

"Ian spoke of how cruel Shaw was, I'm sorry you had to endure his wrath, but this still doesn't explain how my mum's ring and yours are the same. My mum's name was Mallory, not Bridgette."

Finley let go of my mum; grabbing the black bag which contained all the paperwork she had shown me earlier. Mum scooted closer to Heather, handing her each document as Finley had done earlier.

"In the hours before Shaw's death, he brought Ian and I into his room; he shared secrets he kept with each of us. He told me how Thomas Malloy confessed to helping my sister and Scott escape, but wouldn't tell where they were or if they had any children. Had Shaw shared this when it was told to him, I would have used every dime we had finding my sister, and ultimately you." Heather studied my Mum's face, her brows furrowing as her mind mulled over what she had heard. As she reached for the pot to pour herself a cup of tea, she gasped, dropping the pot back on the tray, her hand flying to her mouth.

"Oh my, God!" She exclaimed, jumping from the sofa and staring wide-eyed at me. "If Bridgette was my mum, that makes her your aunt." Pointing a trembling finger at me. "Then we're cousins, and we —you and I, several times."

Mum jumped from her seat, wrapping her arms around a hysterical Heather.

"Calm down, Ian thought the same thing." Mum held tight to Heather's shoulders, pulling her attention to her eyes.

"Listen," Mum's voice was calm and even. "In this family, there are secrets we hide, even from each other. What I'm about to tell you is my atonement for keeping this secret and hurting two people who have the purest of love for each other."

Heather began shaking her head back and forth, hostile tears storming down her face. "You have to breathe for me. I need you to calm down, or you won't be able to hear what I need to tell you."

I couldn't stand it anymore, leaving my place against the door I moved to sit behind Heather as she lost her battle to her fears. "Please, Heather. I know what you're feeling, but you have to calm down." Squeezing her as tight as I could without hurting her, swaying her back and forth as her sobs stilled.

"When my mum was expecting her third child, one of the maids found herself pregnant, without a husband. Now, back in those days, this was not something families took as well as they do today, so she hid the pregnancy from everyone. The night my mum went into labor, my father called for the doctor. On his way back, he found the maid having her baby in the garage. He carried her in, but by the time the doctor arrived, our maid was having complications. Back then, fathers weren't welcomed in the delivery room, so when my mum gave birth, the baby was stillborn. The doctor wrapped the little boy up and placed him with my aunt who took him out of the room. The maid who was close to delivering hemorrhaged, and when the doctor couldn't stop the bleeding, he delivered her baby girl as the maid passed away."

As she spoke of the loss of life, Heather pulled away from me, wrapping her arms around my mum and Finley.

"Everyone believed the story my mum told them. How the maid and her son died in childbirth, and she had given my father another girl, Bridgette. So you see, beautiful Heather, your Mum may not share my blood, but she was my sister none the less and my best friend, and I will miss her every day until I see her again in heaven."

CHAPTER TWENTY-EIGHT

HEATHER

"Dɪᴅ my mum know she wasn't a McFarland?" Taking the ring from the top of the box and turning it around between my fingers. "I mean, I'm grateful Ian isn't my cousin, but it also means this ring didn't belong to her."

Lady Greer wraps her fingers around mine, encapsulating the ring in our joined fist. "Your mum may not have been born a McFarland, but she earned this ring a million times over. She loved your father enough to leave everything she knew behind, willing to do anything she had to in order to protect you. That alone makes her more of a McFarland than myself or Finley."

Shifting my gaze to Finley who sat quietly with a black box in her lap. "So, if my mum was Bridgette McFarland, then that makes you and I...?"

"Second cousins. My mum was your mum's cousin, but I'd like to be your friend too if you can ever forgive me." Finley had been amazing until the last few days; she was important to Ian and my new family.

"I'd love that." Leaning over and giving her a tight hug, I felt as if the weight of the world had been lifted.

"Oh, I nearly forgot the best part." Finley jumped, severing our embrace. Raising the lid off the black box she had on her lap, handing the top to Greer. "Since Lady Greer was smart enough to have the title split, and your mum was never able to return to Scotland, all of her holdings fall to her only daughter. Heather McFarland, this is for you." Finley placed the box on my lap. "Malloy." I corrected her, "since my father was a Malloy, I'd rather take his surname."

Ian wrapped his arms around my middle. "For now, Heather, for now." His breath tickled my neck, and I wasn't sure I wanted to allow myself to even hope for a future with Ian. Especially one which included a white dress and a promise of forever.

Inside the box were folders upon folders of official looking documents. "What is all of this?"

Ian reaches into the box, pulling out a square leather-bound book. "This, my love, would have been the money my grandfather set aside as a dowry for your mum, or as it would now appear, you."

Flipping back the leather cover, I found several pages full of numbers. My heart stopped as I saw the last column and balance. Never in my life had I seen so many zeroes and commas. "Wait, this is in pounds, not dollars, right?"

"Not only is she beautiful, but she is brilliant. Yes, Heather, this is in pounds, but don't forget the conversion rate. I'm certain your banker will be happy to do the math for you. If you would like, we can have our accountants take care of this for you. No pressure, it's your money to do with as you wish."

Greer patted my hand, giving me a reassuring smile. I'd never had an abundance of anything besides love and affection from my parents, believing my whole life it was the three of us against the world. Now, I have a huge family, one I looked forward to getting to know.

"You know, Mum used to tell me how one day I would wear her

ring, and she would tell me how special it was for our family."
Glancing over to the mantle where her picture rested. "Unfortunately,
she died before she got the chance."

Greer stood from the sofa, crossing the room and taking my
mum's picture in her hands."When I saw you for the first time, I saw
my sister in your eyes." Running her finger over my mum's smile, "I
pushed away any thoughts I had of you being a part of her as I
assumed she never had children."

Carefully placing the photo back on the mantle, kissing the tip of
her finger, and then gently placing it against the glass of the frame. "If
you would allow me the honor, I'd be happy to tell you why the ring
is so special."

Rising to my feet and clearing the distance between us, I hold up
the palm of my hand, the ring shining in the center."Please," I
pleaded. "I'm ready to hear where I came from."

Lady Greer nods her head, taking the ring from my hand. "When a
McFarland girl is of the age and maturity to be considered for
marriage, her father will arrange a meeting with the current head of
the McLeod family, to see if they are a match."

Turning to look over my shoulder and catching the bright blue
eyes of Ian looking back at me, his smile broadens as he jabs his
thumb at himself.

"Which would be me. You name the time and place, and we can
certainly discuss how well we match." Wiggling his eyebrows in a
suggesting manner.

"Not so fast, Ian." Greer cautions, and I can feel the story shifting
gears. "With both your parents deceased, the closest relative would
need to arrange the meeting, if you so desired."

Ian rose from his spot on the sofa, stepping around the packed
boxes scattered around the floor. "Mum, I have the perfect place to
have this meeting. With your birthday in two days, how about we
have it then?"

Lady Greer holds her hand out, pushing it into the center of Ian's chest. "Hold on, son. You forget she is a Malloy, with many living male relatives."

Ian holds both hands up in surrender, taking a step back he heads across the room, pulling out his cell and searching for something.

"As I was saying, an agreement is struck, and the father places the ring on his daughter's finger, much like a pre-engagement ring. Then the leader of the Family is permitted to pursue her, per the agreement. Once the wedding occurs, the dowry is paid, and everyone lives happily ever after."

I admire the ring between her fingers and compare it to the one resting on her right hand; the two of them are identical.

"Wait, if this is given to the daughter in acceptance of marriage, why does Finley have one?"

Finley clamps her hands tight, and I notice her ring is not quite as detailed as Greer's and mine. "Oh, Finley and my two other guards have rings specially designed for them, as will the women you choose to guard you."

"Wait, why do you need a guard?"

Finley and Greer share a look, one I'm not sure I want to know about. "Heather, I know you understand what type of business Ian is involved in."

"Yes, I'm well versed in what he does."

"Then you understand the danger being with him places you in." Confirming what I already knew made me think of things my father said, how he spoke of missing his old life and the great adventures he had.

"So many things my father said when I was a girl now make sense. I always loved listening to him talk of the adventures he took. I thought they were just stories, but it appears it was all true." Looking around the room, the chair where I curled up in his lap still as he left it. "All this time I thought I was alone, when in fact I was related to the Malloy's."

"Yes, Heather. Your father was to be the next leader of the Malloy Family, but he chose the love he had for your mum over his duty. The position then fell to his brother, Thomas, who by Malloy custom should have killed Scott for not wedding an Irish girl. Instead, he let word reach his brother's ears of the hit out on him, giving him the opportunity to take his wife and flee Ireland."

My vision blurred as I considered what she said. I needed to sit before I made a fool of myself and passed out.

"You said the Malloy's chose to marry outside of the agreement, but my father wanted to change this. Is that why Shaw objected so much?"

Ian sat beside me taking my hand in his. "No, my father was a selfish bastard who was broke as fuck. Thomas offered him the money for the hit, knowing how big his mouth was and sloppy his work tended to be. The only reason he accepted my mum's hand was because of the size of her dowry. He very nearly squandered all of her inheritance, but she was too smart for him."

My heart broke for Lady Greer, and I felt awful for how I had spoken to her. With everything she had endured in her life, she has every reason in the world to be as bitter as she chooses.

"I'm sorry, for what I said. The terrible name I called you."

"Why on earth should you be sorry? It was the truth, I am bitter, but hopefully, in the next few weeks, I'll feel a lot better." Spiking a single brow, silently suggesting something sexual. Greer was a beautiful and recently single woman; something told me her holiday was not spent alone.

"Mum, if it makes you feel better, you can go ahead and put the ring on her finger. I'll accept any terms you ask."

"Who said I was talking about the two of you?"

"Who else would we be discussing? Heather is a McFarland and a

Malloy, which qualifies her on both sides of the family, giving you no room for argument as this continues the lineage."

"Ian," Greer stepped closer to her son, placing her hands firmly on his chest. "I know you have formed a new alliance with the Malloy's, but this isn't an agreement to help ship goods, or to come to their aid when an enemy threatens. Heather is Patrick Malloy's niece, one he knows nothing about. Consider how he is going to feel when he learns of his father's actions. Permitting you to marry Heather is going to be the last thing on his mind."

I wouldn't have believed it if I hadn't seen it for myself, pure anguish covered Ian's face as he considered what his Mum had said. Lowering his gaze to the floor, he excused himself and said he would wait for them downstairs in the car. Everything in me wanted to chase after him, to tell him the truth of how I felt about him.

"I will give you the same advice I gave him. Give him a minute to get himself together."

Finley and Greer hugged me goodnight after I agreed I wouldn't make any decisions about moving away without talking with them. I thanked them both for returning my parent's ashes as I said goodbye.

"When you come back to Scotland, I'll take you to Arthur's Seat straight from the plane," Greer swore as she kissed my cheek one more time.

"Wait, what is the significance of this Seat, anyway?"

"It's where your parents kissed for the first time, and where he placed this ring on her finger."

After they left, I was too keyed up to go to bed; everything had changed for me in the blink of an eye. I couldn't believe how fate had stepped in; placing me in the exact moment Ian was walking in the door I was leaving. Discovering I had this new family, including the Malloy's.

A soft knock at my door chases away my brief meltdown. Looking at the lateness of the hour, I nearly called Ian to have him come back to see who was on the other side of the door. Checking the peephole this time, a frazzled head of dark hair blocks my view. Opening the door, I find Ian with one arm leaning against the doorframe, the other reaching out for my face.

"Heather, please tell me I didn't lose you? Tell me you need me as much as I need you."

* * *

"OKAY, LET ME GET THIS STRAIGHT. YOUR MOM WAS SOME SCOTTISH princess?" Danielle questioned as she speared a piece of her Greek salad, bringing it to her mouth and hovering the dripping chunk of lettuce just outside her lips. Having been the first person I called after Ian left, we agreed to keep our original dinner date while Ian and his Mum talked.

"A Lady, not a princess." I correct her for the tenth time. "And wipe your mouth, here comes Stavros."

Danielle dropped her fork like a bad habit, sat up straight and pushed out her chest. It was nice to see her attempting to get someone, besides Joe's attention.

"Hello, ladies. Is everything okay with your meals?" Stavros Nakos is exactly as Danielle describes him; a too hot for words Greek God. With his olive skin and dark hair and eyes, he certainly didn't lack for any female attention.

"Everything is wonderful." Danielle praised under her thick eyelashes. "As usual."

"I'm glad to hear it; we are trying out a new cook." He admitted as he motioned with his head to the kitchen.

"Oh, your mother isn't cooking anymore?"

"No, my mother went to live with her sister in Florida. The New York winters are too much for her."

Danielle's smile brightened as she took a quick glance toward the kitchen. "Oh, that's a shame. I'm sorry to hear she's gone; I always enjoyed her cooking."

She was such a liar, Danielle steered clear of this restaurant, as she feared Stavros's mom would try to poison her.

"I'll be sure and tell her when I see her next week." Stavros returned her smile with a bright one of his own; the two seemed to melt together.

"Listen, I was hoping you would stop by; otherwise I would have come to the coffee shop in the next few days. I've asked around to a few people, and they say you are single. Would you consider having dinner with me after I get back from Florida?"

Danielle shoved a piece of hair behind her ear, something she did when she was nervous. "I would love to have dinner with you."

Stavros slides into the booth beside her, but I couldn't tell what they spoke about as the front door to the restaurant opened and in walked Ian and Greer, both with serious faces as they scanned the room looking for me. As our eyes met, the severe lines vanished replaced by the smile he had left me with last night. As the pair neared our booth, Ian caught sight of Stavros sitting beside Danielle, cocking an eyebrow in question.

"There you are, I was wondering if you two would show up?" Standing from my seat, I leaned over to kiss Greer on each cheek as Stavros stood to shake hands with Ian.

"Oh, you know how he is, always on the phone about business."

"I do, but it's necessary." Ian and Stavros exchanged pleasantries, discussing the more substantial stuff in Greek. I was grateful Ian was willing to take extra steps to protect me even if it meant from himself.

"Are you ready to go? Did you get enough to eat?" Ian pointed at my plate as he tossed several bills to the table. Last night when Ian came back, I assured him nothing had changed between us, and how I wanted him to be a big part of my life. We sat on my couch as he held me tight, thanking me over and over for being so wonderful. He admitted his apprehension for the call to Declan he needed to make but assured me he wouldn't let anything happen to me.

As he got ready to leave, he took my hand and made sure I understood if I did decide he was good enough to marry, he wanted me to keep my dowry and use it to buy whatever I wanted. When he turned to leave, I pulled at his elbow, stopping him letting him know I had something I had wanted to do for a long time and I wanted him to be with me when I did it.

Ian helped me into his car as we waved goodbye to Greer and Danielle, who fell into a comfortable friendship over coffee this morning and planned a shopping trip on Greer's favorite street. I offered Danielle money, but Stavros had intervened.

"Okay, love. Where does this dream of yours begin?"

CHAPTER TWENTY-NINE

IAN

PATIENCE IS a characteristic I was never blessed with, waiting for most anything is like nails on a chalkboard for me. So when Heather asked me to wait outside the admissions office at Columbia University, she placed me in a position I don't care for. Heather was a bright and beautiful woman who wanted to attend college more than anything. When her parents became ill, she placed her dreams on hold and stepped up to the plate to take care of them. Now that she had her own money, and plenty of it, she could do anything she wished.

Still, as I stare at the brick and mortar building, its stark white letters spelling out admissions over the arched entrance, I can't help the feeling of pride I have for what she has chosen to do with her inheritance. Most of the McFarland women I know would have hit the designer stores, filling their closets with the latest fashions, buying shoes and purses they may never use. Even though Heather insists she is a Malloy, the few of them I have been acquainted with are the same: love shopping and busting the Malloy men balls. Not that I would mind her attention to the set of McLeod's she already owns.

Glancing at my watch, I groan when only a few minutes have

passed since last I checked. Several young adults walk past my car. Some, mostly guys, lower their sunglasses to get an unobstructed view of my car. On any other day, I would shoot them a boastful grin, taunting them with the knowledge I could snag the beautiful girl beside them if I wanted to and fuck her on the buttery leather seat beside me while the bastard watched. Not today, not when I can see the back of one of Heather's bodyguards' head through the window. I listen as he tells me she is finished and how many young males have checked out my girl.

"Ms. Malloy is headed out."

Duff McCord, Cadan's oldest brother, speaks into his microphone. Having security for the women in my world has never been a luxury, but a necessity. My mum, Finley, and now Heather, are all aware of the men they see guarding them, but what they don't know, and I hope they never will, is the additional set of eyes following them. A hand-picked team of the toughest men I know, all willing to do anything to protect the women who mean the most to me. Sitting up straighter in my seat and reaching over to turn the ignition, I watch Heather's smiling face push the glass and metal door open. With an arm full of folders, and a genuine smile on her face, I know this is what she is supposed to do.

"I'm sorry I took so long." Ducking into my car, leaning over to place a kiss on my cheek, much to the dismay of several people walking by. "But my counselor kept rattling on about financial aid and work scholarships."

Shifting the car into gear, checking over my shoulder for oncoming traffic, "You will get used to it. Let them assume you don't have the means; it creates less of a target on you." I didn't want to scare her, but life, as she knew it had changed the moment her identity was discovered. She would have opportunists crawling out of the word work, all proclaiming to be her long-lost whatever. Trying to prey on her generosity and kindness.

"Where to next?" Reaching over to collect her hand, my need to touch her growing rapidly. "Aroma, I keep forgetting to drop off a key for a friend of mine."

"A key? To your old apartment?" I was trying like hell to keep my jealousy at bay. The thought of her with someone else was not something I wanted to explore. Last night she had assured me her feelings for me had not wavered and she saw her future with me.

"No, my neighbor's. He caught his wife cheating, kicked her out of his apartment and asked her to leave the key with me. Since I always see him at Aroma, it's better to leave it there."

"Okay, Aroma's it is."

As I drove through the city streets, glancing over at Heather, I noticed her smile fade and her face take on the look of worry. Squeezing her hand to get her attention, "Hey, what's wrong? Talk to me." Shifting her head toward me, a speck of shock colors her face and then disappears. "I want to ask you a question, but worry what your answer will be, or you won't be able to answer."

I pause long enough to change lanes, then turn my attention back to her. "If I can tell you the truth, I will answer anything you ask. If I must lie to you, I won't say a word." Heather was no stranger to this life, now that I knew who her father had been and the extreme measures he had taken to protect his family, she understood sometimes answers would not be possible. Silence was sometimes the key to staying alive.

"Stavros Nakos asked Danielle out for dinner. She likes him a lot," Heather turned her gaze back to the passing sidewalk. While she hadn't asked me a question yet, I felt the need to help her along.

"According to him, she caught his eye some time ago, but circumstances weren't right, now they are."

She remained silent, carefully choosing the right words. Something I have no doubt Scott Malloy taught her.

"I know when you see him, you respect him enough to address

him in Greek, or maybe you're protecting me, perhaps both." As I
stop at a red light, she turns her body to face me, taking a deep breath,
"Do I need to worry about her, distract her with spending more time
with Greer? Or is he a solid guy?"

I hated the look of worry which marred her beautiful face,
drawing hateful lines where whispers of smiles should be instead.
Kissing her lips, trying to convey what my answer never will. "Did
you know his cousin is a SEAL?" As the light turns green, I press the
gas, taking her hand in mine.

"His Mum moved down to Florida so she could be closer to her
sister, who is working overtime trying to get his cousin married off."
Heather was smart enough to know the reason I spoke to Stavros in
Greek had nothing to do with respect and everything to do with
keeping the code. Several years ago, Patrick Malloy stumbled upon
information the FBI sent their people to learn several languages,
except for Greek. He shared the information, and my father sent me to
Crete to learn first hand. While I was there, I ran into Stavros and
struck a deal with him and his Family, outside of the watchful eye of
my father. Stavros and I have made a fortune in the gun trade, using
his ships as transport. Last year, his primary supplier wanted to jack
the price up three times the agreed on rate, claiming he had a new
buyer who was all too willing to pay the higher prices. We both knew
who this new buyer was, so we stopped buying from him, and I
opened a factory underneath the distillery my Family owns. It took
time, but now we produce more guns than our old supplier ever could.

"Stavros has been in a position to take a wife for some time, but
his Family has some of the same rules the McLeod's do for marriage.
So, it took time for him to find the right girl."

I could never tell Heather how deep Stavros had to dig to make
sure Danielle was the right girl for him. I couldn't tell her how he had
to stand before his Family and prove how innocent she was, or how
much he had to pay Joe Ferrezzio to keep his hands off her.

We pulled up to the shop at the same time Cadan parked the car, packed with shopping bags and two joyful women. Danielle jumped from the car the second she notices Heather next to her.

"Everything okay?" Mum whispered as she faked pulling something off my jacket. Lady Greer had been the financial backing when I went into business with Nakos. Needing to replenish the money my father squandered, she sank most her inheritance into the business.

"Absolutely perfect."

Last night after I left Heather, I placed a call to the Malloy's. Mum and I agreed it would benefit everyone to make them aware of what we knew as soon as possible. Patrick, of course, demanded to have proof of our claim, asking for a few days to allow his men to look over the files Cadan sent over. Declan, however, didn't share in his father's apprehension and gave his permission as leader of the Malloy Family to pursue Heather as I requested. My mum wasn't as easily swayed and insisted on sitting down with me as Heather's aunt, and not as my parent. After our informal meeting, which included my single demand of Heather keeping her inheritance, but also permission to ask for a long engagement. She asked me to speak with Nakos and make him aware of Heather's position.

"Danielle mentioned something about school. How do you feel about that?"

Taking a deep breath, hooking my hands on each side of my hips. "Mum, I love her to death, and I want her always to be happy. If going to school for the rest of her life does that, then I'm happy." Mum looks at me with such pride, the single most important thing I've always tried to see reflected in her eyes. "You know, I think that's the first thing I've ever heard you say as the true leader of this Family?"

The excited squeal from the girls behind us captures my attention and ends the conversation. Danielle is jumping up-and-down, with her hand over her mouth as if she's just told a big secret.

"Nakos is going to have his hands full with that one." Mum chuckles, and she too falls prey to their laughter.

"Aye, Heather was worried about Danielle and Nakos's intentions toward her. Asked me if she should have you spend more time with her, distracting her from him." During the time, I spent forming a friendship with Stavros; Mum formed her own with Diane, Stavros's mum. While it's true, Diane had moved to Florida to be with her sister; she had taken a side trip to Spain with my mum. Diane had been against Stavros's choice in pursuing Danielle, but after a few conversations with Lady Greer, she changed her mind and now looks forward to grandbabies.

"Well, I guess my work here is done. I have my son, who has the love of his life, and my best friend has a gem in her future daughter-in-law."

Pulling her in for a hug, I know I'll never be able to thank her enough for swallowing her pride and telling the truth of Heather's lineage. "I love you, Mum."

Heather approaches us, a smile on her face and a sparkle in her eye. Danielle is fast on her heels and much too giddy. "Ian, I'm just going to leave the key inside, be right back." A male voice calls her name from behind us before she can take her first step. Out of habit, I'm ready to pull my gun as if this man poses a threat. Standing three feet away from us, dressed in an NYPD uniform, is a man with his arm around a blond, whose face is downcast to the ground.

"Oh, hey. I was just going to leave your key inside." Heather steps around me as she reaches into the pocket of her jeans to retrieve the item she spoke of. As I take in his features, I recognize him from one of the conversations I had with his partner Joe, as a favor to Stavros.

"I'm glad I caught you. I haven't had a chance to go by the apartment, not that I want to see her again." This poor bloke has a belly full of hate for whoever this woman is as he can't even say her name.

I've known hatred like that, looked my father in the face every day and hated him more and more with every breath he took.

"I'm sorry about what happened. You're a good guy and didn't deserve to be treated as you were."

"Thank you; you're a kind person for saying so." As the man takes the key from Heather's outstretched hand, he looks at the girl standing beside him. "Heather, you remember Cindy, don't you?" The officer squeezes the shoulders of the blond, bringing a smile to her lips and her face into view. What appears to be melted skin covers the left side of her face, it's clear she's endured a significant trauma.

"Yes, of course. I'm sorry to hear about your sister's death."

"Thank you; she's in a better place now. Away from all the poison those men were feeding her."

Reality slaps me in the face as I realize this is Bethany's sister, the one Heather said introduced her to the lifestyle she died from. I ponder whether the lifestyle was also responsible for the destruction of her face?

"Please, let me know if there's anything you need. Jamie, I'm glad to see you happy, you deserve it."

Just when I couldn't love her anymore, she says something so touching and honest.

"Son, if you don't marry that girl and soon, I swear to God..." Mum whispers in my ear, the raw emotion cracking her voice as she pats my back.

Heather introduces the couple to Mum and myself, recognition flashing in Jamie's eyes, but he says nothing. As they walk away, Heather curls herself under my shoulder, wrapping her arms around me.

"Did you notice the way Jamie looked at Cindy? All the love in the world floating in his eyes as he stood close to protect her?"

"Aye."

"It's as if all he can see is the perfection of her soul and not the scar on her face."

Spinning her to face me, laying my finger under her chin, brushing my lips against the shell of her ear, I whisper. "You asked if you needed to worry about Danielle with Stavros? Would it help to know he looks at her the same way?" Tears well in her eyes as she nods her head, the joy, and the emotion battling so fierce she cannot express them with words.

"Jamie isn't the only one who looks at the woman he loves like that."

Joy wins out as laughter falls from Heather's mouth. "Oh my, God. You get your subtlety from your mum."

"Be that as it may, you still haven't told me what you have planned for the rest of the day."

"Well," drawing the word out with a hint of seduction in her tone. "There is one thing in the city, I've always wanted to do."

CHAPTER THIRTY

HEATHER

"Love, you are aware I have a multimillion dollar penthouse not far from here, where you can sleep tonight for free, correct?" Sitting in the valet line, outside of the Plaza Hotel, Ian is about to break his steering wheel in half as the line hasn't moved in two whole minutes. Generally, I find him irresistible, but his inability to wait for anything... not so much.

"Ian, when I was a little girl, I would walk by this hotel with my mum and dad. I assumed it was a castle and just like every little girl who dreams of her prince charming, this was the place mine took me to. Now, I know it's not a castle because I've been in yours, but I still want to know what it feels like to live inside those walls. If only for one night."

Shifting the car into park, he turns to me as the valet opens my door. "Fine, but since I'm the prince in this fantasy of yours, I'm paying the bill." `

Majestic black and gold doors open just beyond the red carpet, white stone separating each window along the front of the hotel. San Francisco style streetlights adorn each side of the entry, giving an adult feel to my childhood fantasy. A tail-coat clad older gentleman opens the front door, tipping his hat as we walk through the entrance. Marble floors welcome us into the majestic space, overwhelming me with the grandeur of the room. Circular settees in cream and blue border the main walkway, giving the introduction of the colors chosen for the hotel. In the center of the room sits an elongated wrought iron table, two massive flower arrangements on each end. Ian squeezes my hand, pulling me along toward the reception desk. Craning my head back as I take in the painting on the high ceilings, the resemblance to Lady Greer's dining room is uncanny. A manly laugh to my right draws my attention to the mahogany and glass front of the bar. With its rich tones and friendly face of the bartender, I assume it is a cozy place to enjoy a drink.

Ian glides to the desk as if he's done so a million times; perhaps he has in his numerous travels. My breath is stolen when my eyes land on the massive chandelier. Thick chains secure the crystal masterpiece, allowing its warm glow to illuminate the brass lettering behind the desk, spelling out the world-famous hotel's name.

Behind the desk stands a tall man dressed in a pressed white shirt and dark vest. A gold-plated name tag rests over his heart. Salt and pepper hair hint at his maturity, confirmed by the pair of reading glasses sitting at the end of his nose. His smile is warm and welcoming as he motions for Ian and I to come forward.

"Good afternoon, Sir. Do you have a reservation?"

"No, but I hope this will help." Ian removes a gold card from his wallet, the hotel's logo printed in the center.

The gentleman takes the card, swiping it in a slot on his computer keyboard. His impressed eyes flash back to Ian before he clears his throat and leans across the desk.

"Of course, Mr. McLeod, but I regret the presidential suite is occupied."

At first, I'm confused, but realization hits; this is the hotel he stayed in when he was with Bethany. Granted, according to him the interlude was brief and didn't last all night, the thought of her touching him brings a wave of nausea to my stomach.

"I'm sorry, excuse me." Placing my hand on Ian's shoulder, swallowing down the bile that threatens to come out. "I've changed my mind; your penthouse sounds much better." Regret resonates in his eyes as he nods his head in silence. Thanking the man for his time, he leaves the card behind informing him he no longer needs it. "We can go to my castle in Edinburgh. I can have the plane ready in an hour, tops."

Waiting as the valet brings his car around, the sounds of the busy street somehow calms and helps rid me of thoughts of the two of them together. "I can't fault you for having a past, Ian. Besides, it was a stupid fantasy created by a girl with big dreams and no money." Ian pulls me to him, ignoring the valet who waits patiently for a tip. "It isn't a stupid fantasy, it was important to you and if I could change what happened here, I would. All I can do is make every day, for the rest of your life, a dream come true." Where his words are eloquent and the subject of romance novels, they're also from his heart. This wonderful, incredible, powerful man is willing to do anything he can to make me happy.

"I love you, Heather. With everything I am and everything I will ever be, I love you." Tears spill down my face, an explosion of joy and happiness my body can't contain.

"I love you, too, Ian. And I can't wait for my future with you."

* * *

THE BEAUTY OF HAVING A PENTHOUSE AT YOUR DISPOSAL IS THE ability to start removing clothing the second you get in the elevator. There's no worry of anyone else getting on at any of the floors as you make your way to yours. There are no do not disturb signs you have to remember to post outside your door, or bed linens you have to second-guess whether or not they contain the body fluids of the previous guest. While Ian's penthouse looks nothing like a castle, he most definitely is my prince charming. But the best part, the one I secretly happy dance to, there is no memory of any other women here.

"You have no idea how often I've pictured you in this bed," Ian carried me from the parking garage to the elevator and began undressing me as soon as the computer welcomed us. "Spread out before me like a delicious temptation of forbidden fruit." Relaxing into the mattress, I allow my arms to float gently to my side, Ian knows how to bring me to orgasm just by playing with my nipples. Pushing the pair together, his tongue lapping between the stiff peaks, nipping with his teeth on the very tips, making my body jerk with pleasure. Not wasting a moment of our time, or perhaps he's as eager as I am, he descends lower, removing the last scrap of fabric on my body as his tongue parts my folds. In and out, up-and-down, round and round, and then repeat. In the short time we've been together, he has mastered my body, and I am grateful he's such a quick study, as I cry out his name with my second orgasm.

Moving his shoulders up from between my thighs, leaning back on his heels, he lifts my legs behind my knees, places my thighs against his chest and enters me in a quick motion. Ian was blessed with many things, substantial girth making the top three. Licking the thumb of his right hand, he places it against my clit as his eyes lock with mine.

"That's it, baby. Your pussy looks beautiful with my cock in it." His focus changes to where we're joined, his bottom lip becoming a prisoner between his teeth. I can feel him growing inside me, and I know he's close, but so am I.

"Heather, I need you to come." I can feel him holding back and won't have it. He deserves all the pleasure he's giving me and so much more. Reaching down, I remove his finger from my clit and replace it with my own, increasing the speed and crying out his name as he collapses on top of me.

As the sun disappears behind the building across the street, Ian and I enjoy takeout from the Thai place around the corner. He paid the owner a hefty tip to have it delivered, which earned him a blowjob here on the couch. As he feeds me a bite, his cell phone across the room begins to buzz. Jumping up from his relaxed position, he apologizes and swears it will take only a moment.

"Aye?" He barks into the receiver, and I cringe just a little for whoever's on the other side. "When?" I don't care for the way his tone changes. Something has happened, and it must be bad. As Ian turns to face me, his fingers buried in his hair, his eyes squinted, and something tells me someone has died. "Get the jet ready. We'll be there in half an hour." Ian ends the call and crosses the floor, picking up the remote and pointing it toward the television. Silence is golden in a situation like this, and I remain quiet until he's ready to tell me what's wrong. He changes the channel several times until he lands on a national news station, the tagline at the bottom scrolling with the news of a man's death.

"Funeral services have not been announced, but a spokesperson for the Kumarin Family inform CNN they will cooperate with federal authorities in the apprehension of those responsible. Some of you may remember earlier this year when officials announced plans to reopen the investigation into the death of Kumarin's first wife, and mother to the now head of the Family Andrey Kumarin..."

Ian silences the television before the reporter can finish. "Love, I hate to end this, and I swear I'll make it up to you, but I need you to get dressed. We have a plane to catch."

Jumping to my feet, I walked quickly behind him to the bedroom "Can I ask where we're going?" Ian doesn't slow as he walks into his closet, selecting a tailored suit from the rack. "Russia." He responds as if it were a trip across the street to the corner store.

"Does this have anything to do with the news report?" Standing in the doorframe of his closet, watching as he pulls several suits from the rack, tossing them into a garment bag he retrieved from behind one of the large doors.

"Yes. Kumarin is a friend of mine, and we have to pay our respects for his loss."

Ian moves to the center of the room where an island-like cabinet sits. Entering a code into a panel on the side, a single drawer opens, and Ian removes a ring, placing it on his middle finger. My mind flashes to the photo I saw of him and the other mafia leaders, the ring on his hand I couldn't make out.

"What's this?" Crossing the room, I lay my hand on his arm as he reaches back in for a pair of cufflinks.

"My Family's crest. All the men in my world have one; it's given to the leader when he takes the reins."

"How come you never wear it?" Closing the drawer, he turns in my direction, wrapping his open hand around the back of my neck.

"Because I hate wearing it. If I could, I would destroy the fucking thing as my father used to make everyone kiss it, showing him the respect he never deserved." I could understand Ian's distaste for the ring, and hatred he felt for the man who hurt so many.

"Well, maybe one day, someone will give you a ring you will want to wear. One that will make you smile instead of feeling the need to hide it away in a locked drawer."

* * *

AS WE BOARD THE PLANE, I FIND NEARLY EVERY SEAT IS TAKEN; FACES I hadn't seen, but suspect are members of his security detail. Lady Greer was dressed in black, a beautiful set of pearls around her neck.

"Heather, come sit with me, love. Let the men discuss business." Sliding into the seat beside her, the stewardess inquires whether I would care for something to drink. As I decline her offer, I catch a glimpse of the grin on Greer's face.

"Did I say something funny?" I lean in to ask, as there are so many conversations going on around me, I don't want to shout.

"Oh, no lass, this is not amusement on my face. If I could get away with it, I would be in tears, that's how happy I am."

Instead of answering, she taps her manicured finger against the top of the ring on my right hand. After Ian loved me into oblivion, he pulled out my ring and asked if I would accept it.

When I quizzed him as to why he had it and not Lady Greer, he admitted it was one of the conditions they had agreed on.

"You know the engagement will be long? I want to live life a little, get used to this new world."

"Aye, you never know what can happen in the future." Her eyes dance with something mysterious, and I wondered if somehow she was a psychic and knew something I didn't.

The trip to Russia was solemn at best. I'd heard of Kumarin, saw Drew's photo when he attended the Malloy wedding. From everything I've heard, his father, Viktor, was a ruthless tyrant, allegedly responsible for the deaths of his own family. This trip, as Lady Greer explained, was a show of solidarity; a union among the Family's Declan Malloy had been responsible for bringing together. We would attend the wake and show our respects, and the leaders of the Family's would find out who was responsible for Viktor's death.

"Not that anyone will mourn the loss of him, but we're here for Drew. He's a good boy with a level head on his shoulders, much like your Ian." Lady Greer's assignment of Ian being mine, not hers, did not get past my ears. This was my life, and I love the people who are in it, especially my Ian.

Landing in Russia, I expected to be greeted by customs, grilled as to the nature of our business, as our plane was full of large men, with equally big guns. However, the only thing on the tarmac is the convoy of black SUVs, and wind so cold it took my breath away.

* * *

I WASN'T CERTAIN WHAT TO EXPECT AS I'VE NEVER ATTENDED A WAKE before. When my parents died, there was barely money to afford a coffin, much less a party such as this. Tables a mile long, covered in every food you could imagine. Three bars, full of top-shelf alcohol, sat in each corner. A sea of people standing shoulder to shoulder, ladies wearing expensive furs stood beside a well-dressed man who puffed on cigars, creating a cloud above our heads.

"My husband tells me you have good news." I'm startled by the feminine, yet familiar voice of Christi Malloy. "It appears we are family."

She doesn't give me a moment to respond, pulling me into a tight hug and whispering in my ear. "You'll be good for Ian; he needs someone with your strength to balance him."

I understand what she means, men such as Ian, Declan, and even still Patrick, carry the weight of the world on their shoulders. Sometimes they need someone they can lean on, one who won't judge them if they show a moment of weakness.

"Perhaps the next time we are together, we will have reason to celebrate, perhaps your wedding." Her eyes flash over my shoulder, and I can feel Ian approach before I see him. Turning to look over my shoulder, I catch a glimpse of the reason for her silence as Ian, and Declan approach with the man I recognize from the photo.

"Drew, I want to introduce the newest lady of our Manor and my future bride, Lady Heather."

Drew Kumarin is a handsome man, with dark hair and ice blue eyes even more intense than Ian's. He's a man of taste, clearly defined by the clothes he's chosen, and the cigar which rests between his fingers.

Holding out his hand, with a slight bow of respect. "Pleasure to meet you, Lady Heather, I apologize for the circumstances."

Circling my hands around his, I step forward and say, "I'm truly sorry for your loss, I know what it feels like to lose a parent. You have my sympathy."

Kumarin squeezes my hand, shoots a side glance at Ian as he responds, "You are too kind and far too good for the likes of this bloody Scotsman. My father was a bastard and doesn't deserve your sympathy. The only regret I have is I didn't get to kill him myself."

I can't hide the shock or take back the gasp that leaves my lips. I knew Ian hated his father, but Drew is in a league all by himself, and I cannot imagine the torture this man has endured.

"My apologies, Lady Heather, for my crass words. My body and mind are tired, and it will be some time before I can rest." Wrapping my hand tighter around his, I try to send as much warmth into his cold skin as I can. It's clear he has suffered many years of neglect, and I can see he has built up quite a fortress around his heart.

"Too good she may be, but the deal has been sealed, and she wears the ring. Only the king himself can stop this union." Ian teases as he wraps an arm around Drew's shoulder.

"The king gets to stand in line."

Patrick Malloy stands beside Declan and who I recognize as Caleb Montgomery, who's face looks brighter since the last time I saw him in Italy.

"And you," addressing Ian." Haven't formally come to me and asked my permission to marry Heather. But that is a conversation for another time." Patrick extends out his hand for Drew to shake, drawing him in, the pair embraces, and Patrick says something into his ear too quiet for me to hear.

Declan moves into the space between us, wrapping a single arm around me as he places an envelope in my hand. "Give my father a little time to forgive my grandfather for his deception. Then be prepared to be welcomed properly into the Malloy family."

Nodding as I pull away, a tight smile on my face. Disappointment fills my chest as I had assumed I would be welcomed news for the Malloy's. I don't have to look at the envelope to know it is thick with money, perhaps a buy out to stay away from them. Before I can allow myself to drift too far into despair, Greer pulls me back to the conversation with Drew.

"Heather, don't let him scare you. This man is doing a world of good in Detroit I hear." Death affects us all differently, and I suspect Drew hasn't come to grips with his father's passing. I'm grateful for Lady Greer's interruption, pulling me back and severing the hold Drew had on my hand.

"My apologies again, Lady Heather, I did not mean to frighten you. And Lady Greer you are correct, I've purchased the hockey team in Detroit, and have plans to build a new stadium. There are several buildings I have my eye on and have hired a consultant who is helping me build my empire."

"What of your home here in Russia? Won't you miss your family?" Christi Malloy's voice is so somber and loving, her question genuine and not meant to be prying.

Drew swallows hard as he blinks away what I worry are tears he refuses to shed. "My family died when I was a boy, my father, and his greed took everything, including the only girl I will ever love." His voice cracks as he utters the last few words; more pain than I can comprehend rests on his shoulders. My heart hurts for this man, and I have little power to stop myself as I close the distance between us and wrap him in a tight hug.

"You're never alone, Drew. Don't ever forget we will always be here for you." I swallow the sadness my words bring me as Drew returns my hug and whispers into my ear.

"Make sure he treats you well, or I will come find you." A chill runs up my spine as I suspect what he said was not meant for me. Rubbing his back gently, I pull away and step back into Ian's embrace.

"I expect an invitation to the wedding."

As quickly as the emotions came, he swept them away. I wonder to myself how often he has had to do this, mask his pain behind his fury?

"Of course, as soon as I can convince her to set a date." Ian pulls me close; his warmth welcomed as the chill of the room returns.

"Take my advice, Lady Heather. Don't wait too long; tomorrow is never guaranteed."

"You're right; I will. Thank you." I add although I'm not sure why.

"If you will excuse me, I have other guests I need to speak with," holding out his hand he shakes each mans hand. "I expect to see you all in Detroit for the first hockey game of the season, as my personal guests."

His demeanor changes as he speaks of the sport, a brilliant light in his eyes, which chases away the dark. Something tells me this move to Detroit will bring so much more than business success, but an opportunity to live his life for once, experience the joy truly living can bring and the hope of finding his special someone. A girl with a heart strong enough to take away his pain.

EPILOGUE

Iᴀɴ ᴡᴀs ᴄᴏʀʀᴇᴄᴛ, Arthur's Seat was an odd spot for my parent to call special. Greer and I stood at the edge of one of the cliffs as the brisk wind ruffled my clothes and tossed my hair. Shadows of the clouds above skirted along the terrain below, creating dark patches along the tiffs of grass.

After the funeral, Drew called a meeting between the Families. Ian was reluctant to go, but when Cadan tapped his ring, he knew this was more than drinks and cigars. It was a formal change of power, one requiring many witnesses.

Greer and Finley huffed when Ian promised he would return in a few hours, reminding him how long the meeting lasted when he took the ring from his father. At first, he suggested shopping but was met with three faces full of contention. Next, he offered to send us to a spa but quickly took back the suggestion, kissed me and said to have fun in whatever I chose to do.

"I'm going to have to do a lot of apologizing once Ian finds out where we are."

Greer turned to face me, a motherly smile on her face, "I doubt that. He loves you and wants you to be happy. Besides, with my sister gone, I feel as if I need to be here with you, delivering her ashes to her final resting spot."

I contacted Danielle, having her go to my apartment and grab the boxes containing my parent's ashes. Greer arranged for a courier service, and in less than twelve hours we had boxes in hand and were in the air back to Scotland.

"When your mum first laid eyes on your father, she swore she saw the future in him. Both of us knew the rules the Malloy men followed, but she held out hope some miracle would keep them together."

Greer stood with her heavy shawl hugging her body, tiny tendrils of hair flapping around her face.

"The first time he came calling for her, she begged me to come with them. Afraid she would lose herself to his charm and let him go further than she was willing to go." A happy smile pressed on her lips as she pointed to a mound of rocks across the way.

"I sat on those rocks, Scott's jacket tucked around me, as the two of them sat at the edge of this cliff, holding hands and kissing. He was perfect for her, and she him. I worried someone would find out, and separate them before their love had a chance to bloom."

A single tear rolled down Greer's cheek as her eyes settled on the rocks, her memories as fresh as the day they happened. "We promised one another the night she left we would find a way to keep in touch." Her voice cracking and her sobs breaking forth as she spoke the last three words.

Tucking my box into the crevice of my arm, I pull her close and hold tight. "If I know anything about my mum, she never stopped trying to find a way to speak with you. She wasn't one to hold a grudge."

Greer's sobs turned into a laugh. "No, she did not hold anything against anyone."

"And just as she forgave me for the anger I felt when she died, never seeing the children I will have in the future, or help me with the planning of my wedding..." My throat closes with the emotion bubbling in my chest. "Or my father's funeral."

Swallowing hard and forcing the tears to retreat to where they came from. "You have to believe she loved you and wanted you in her life, it just wasn't possible."

Placing a kiss on her temple, I pull back and open the lid of my box. "Come on now, let's send them home."

I remember the night my mum took her last breath, my father and myself each holding one of her hands. She made me promise to take care of him, even encourage him to love again, although we all knew he wouldn't look at another soul like he did her. As the snow fell outside, she hummed as she took her last breath, the pain she had suffered leaving her face and relief settling in its place.

As I watch the cloud of ash dance in the wind, carrying the last remains of the woman who gave me life, I whisper the same words I did to her as she closed her eyes for the last time.

"I love you, Mum."

* * *

I CANNOT RECALL BEING SO TIRED, SO MENTALLY AND PHYSICALLY drained. Greer's head rested against the seat back, her eyes closed and breathing shallow for the last half an hour. I could not find the ability to give in to my exhaustion. I missed Ian and his warmth, his ability to scare away the bad and make me feel good.

The car jerked slightly from side to side as we pulled into the gates of the castle. Rain fell in sheets, keeping the staff from showing Lady Greer her required greeting, but as the car circled the drive, I saw the tall man standing under the eve of the front door.

Tossing off my seatbelt, I didn't wait for the car to stop as I bolted out the door, running as fast as I could into Ian's waiting arms.

"Baby, why didn't you wait for me?"

"I'm sorry, I should have. But I needed this time, and frankly, so did your mum." Looking over my shoulder, a still sleepy Greer was being ushered from the back seat, an umbrella protecting her from the rain. At first glance, I assumed it was the driver who was assisting her, but a closer look revealed a man of advanced age, with his silver hair and black-rimmed glasses. As I was about to ask who he was, Greer reached up and placed a not, so PG-rated kiss to his lips.

"What the—?" Ian started to step away from my embrace, but I held fast, pulling him back to me.

"Ian, your mum is a beautiful, *single* woman. You need to get used to men being interested in her." Encouraging him to watch as the man wrapped Greer tight in his arms, the look of contentment flush on her face. "Look, she's happy, just as you make me happy."

Blue eyes drop to mine, "Are you? Happy, I mean?"

Spending time with Greer and the memories of my parents has shed new light on the world around me. They sacrificed everything to be together, including my father leading one of the most notorious Family's. For years they lived in secret, hiding who they were, spending holidays and birthdays alone, never knowing what was happening back in Scotland. They chose to be together, living every day as if it was the only one they got.

"I am, but I know how you can make me happier."

Pulling me out of the elements, closing the massive wooden door behind us. The warmth of the fire blazing in the fireplace chasing away the chill which had crept in.

"You know I would give you anything, all you have to do is ask."

My mum chose to run from everything she knew, leave this house for the man who held her heart. How often in life will fate present you with everything you never knew you wanted? Giving you the gift of an everlasting love, one romance novels are written about.

"There is only one thing I want from you, at this moment anyway."

Wrapping his hands around my shoulder, lowering his face to the same level as mine. "Tell me, Heather, and it's yours."

Searching his eyes, joy and elation mixed together, overflowing in his blue orbs. He claimed to lack the patience it took to heat a cup of hot water in the microwave, so I knew my silence was killing him.

"Your name, Ian. I want to have your last name. No waiting, no big ceremony with people we don't know or like, drinking your scotch and hanging around too long. I want to live a life as my parents did. Take the love we have for one another and let the world see what true love looks like. I don't want to waste any more time trying to find myself, or waiting for life to pass me by. I want to wake up with you, go to sleep beside you, sharing everything with you, including the same last name."

I waited what seemed like an eternity as Ian's eyes searched mine. As the silence grew between us, I worried something had happened in Russia, making him change his mind.

"Ian? What do you think?"

A slow smile crept across his lips, the flames from the fireplace dancing in the reflection of his eyes. "I think you were right when you said someday I would have a ring I would want to share with the world. I just can't believe it's going to happen tonight."

* * *

THE LAST TIME I STOOD IN THIS ROOM, I FELT UNWELCOME AND angry. Having been shunned by the woman who now holds my hand as I walk across the room to where Ian waits for me. Greer was beyond thrilled when Ian gave her the news of our impromptu wedding. Her excitement grew as she introduced the handsome man as Alberto Estevez, a shipbuilder she had been keeping company with for many years. During one particular argument with Shaw, she had packed a bag and escaped to clear her head. While having dinner at a restaurant, she and Alberto were seated next to one another, and a friendship blossomed. Over the years, their love developed, and Alberto was there for Greer when things got rough with Shaw. Alberto moved several of his holdings to Scotland in order to be closer to Greer, including purchasing the building where the registrar's office of public record was housed. Which meant he could not only officiate, but also file the paperwork for Ian and I to marry.

As I reached the end of the room, the gold-framed paintings I once glared at as I assumed the love I had found had slipped through my fingers, now stood bright and welcoming, like the joy I felt. Greer's hold on me increased and then released, as we took the final steps, kissing my cheek as she handed me off to Ian. I'd asked her to walk with me, stand by my side in place of the two people who could not be here for me.

The surrounding room faded into silence as Ian, and I joined hands. His eyes glisten with tears as I swore to love, honor, and obey him. Fusing our lives together as we kissed for the first time as husband and wife.

As we lay in our bed, covered in sweat and rumpled sheets, the first rays of the new day broke the horizon. We hadn't bothered with sleep; too busy wrapping ourselves in the essence of one another, celebrating our union.

Gilly left a tray of breakfast outside our door, knocking politely, and then disappearing before Ian could crawl out of bed. I watched as his naked body crossed the floor, grabbing a towel we had used to dry off after showering together sometime after three this morning. He picked up the tray, the smell of coffee and sugar filling the air, causing my stomach to grumble with hunger.

Ian insisted on making me a cup of coffee, rationalizing I had made my fair share, and he could do it for once. But as he crawled between the sheets, my cup of hot coffee balanced in his hand, the mattress dipped, and the coffee splashed onto the sheets. Ian moved the cup to the side table, an oath leaving his lips as he worried he had burned me.

"It missed me completely, I swear." Reaching for another towel to help absorb the mess, Ian stills my hand as he kisses my lips.

"Leave it, Heather. When it comes to us, spilled coffee is good luck."

I HOPE YOU HAVE ENJOYED IAN AND HEATHER'S STORY AND WILL JOIN me as I spin another twisted tale in this series. Turn the page to enjoy a preview of Family Secrets.

PART 1

PREVIEW OF BOOK SIX: FAMILY SECRETS

Giovanni Vitale has it all; good looks, money, and a notorious family name which can open any door he chooses. He's poised to take the reins of his Family, provided he complies with his father's conditions. While his life is privileged, it's foundation is built on generations of secrets and carefully constructed lies told so well they blur the truth. What happens when one of those secrets is unearthed, one so dark it stands to change the course of his life? Can Gino discover the truth before it's too late, or will the past repeat itself?

Elizabeth Smith is the stereotypical girl next door, living barely above the poverty level in the middle of America's Heartland. Surviving on hand-me-downs and thrift store bargains, she's no stranger to the ridicule and hushed conversations the townsfolk inundate her with. With no options for friendships, Elizabeth turns to social media, living vicariously through a woman who seems to have it all. What happens when tragedy strikes leaving Elizabeth at a crossroads? Will she choose the safe and certain path? Or the one too good to believe, despite the odd rules?

CHAPTER ONE

ELIZABETH

Elizabeth laid facing the wall in her garage-sale-find-bed, the digital clock on her bedside table read a few minutes after three in the morn- ing. Her heart stalled, the sound of her front door creaking, shattering the silence of the night. Holding her breath, she waited for the tell-tale sign of who'd stumbled through the door, friend or foe.

Elizabeth released her breath when a loud thump, followed by a hissed oath, reached her ears. Covering her mouth with her hand in an effort to conceal her silent celebration of the pain inflicted as a result of her grandmother's rearranging the living room furniture. Elizabeth almost felt guilty for hoping Jonah, her boyfriend of far too long, had broken his toe this time. It would serve him right for trying to sneak in, knowing how often her grandmother changed the house around.

Gripping her pillow tight, she readied herself for his entrance, something after all the nights he'd stumbled into her room he should have perfected by now. But not Jonah Kelley, that boy should come with a warning label; brains not included or common sense unavailable.

Elizabeth's body bounced as Jonah's heavy form fell into bed beside her, the smell of cheap beer almost masked the stagnant cologne of his latest side girl. Karen Miller, whose perfume, a designer knock-off and three years past expiration, filled the small office she and Elizabeth shared every day.

Seconds later, Jonah's obnoxious snores filled the room, putting an end to any hope of Elizabeth falling back to sleep. Feeling defeated, Elizabeth reached into her nightstand for her noise canceling headphones, letting the sultry voice of her favorite singer drown out the lawnmower beside her.

Pain in the middle of her back, combined with the screeching sound of her alarm, pulled Elizabeth from the little sleep she was able to manage. The brief rest wasn't long enough to produce a single dream, something she looked forward to every night. Pushing back the covers, she slid into her fluffy slippers, a birthday gift from her granny a few weeks ago. Standing to her full height, she reached for her robe at the foot of the bed, finding Jonah's dirty work boots, the laces untied and his feet still inside holding the terry-cloth hostage. The manners her grandmother instilled in her would dictate she not disturb the sleeping man, but her lack of sleep combined with his continued disrespect, those guidelines were forgotten as she shoved his feet to the side. A grunt sounded from his sprawled-out body taking up over half the bed and the reason behind her aching back.

Shuffling her feet down the hall, she dropped her tired body into the worn cushions of the couch, retrieving her laptop from its new hiding place. The second-hand piece of equipment was the most expensive item she owned, something she'd snatched up at the end of last semester when her community college purchased new computers. She wished she could upgrade her cellphone as easily, but money was tight and if she wanted to take classes when school resumed, she would need every penny in her savings for tuition.

Typing her password, her heart soared at the familiar ding of a waiting Facebook message. Even without looking, Elizabeth knew it's from her friend Mona Lisa, or Lisa as she'd asked Elizabeth to call her, and would save it for later, giving her something to look forward to in her projected dismal day. As she scrolled through the list of her friend's posts, she allowed herself to pretend she's a part of their lives, celebrating birthdays, anniversaries, and new babies. While her life is far from boring, she wouldn't mind having something worthwhile to celebrate and share with her handful of friends.

Opening the app for her email, she scanned the list of advertisements for everything from fifty percent off storewide clearance to penile implants available near her. Shaking her head, she considered forwarding the latter to Jonah; Lord knows he could use some help in *that* department.

A noise from the hall forced her to close the lid and store her computer back in its hiding place. No one, not even her granny, knew of the purchase she'd made. If Jonah found out, he would demand to see it, tinkering around with it until it didn't work anymore. He was one of those people who knew everything about nothing, believing there was nothing he couldn't do or invent. His parent's front yard was littered with his brilliant ideas and money-making scams, piles and piles of someone else's fault as to why his idea didn't work. Elizabeth recalled the last time he'd gotten ahold of her computer, how her heart sank as she watched it bounce off the kitchen wall, landing with a broken screen and keys flying in a million directions when he got angry at a game he was playing. She would have killed him, had she not kept all of her files on a thumb-drive, including the term paper she needed to print and turn in the next morning. He'd sworn to replace it, but just like his promise she was the only girl for him, he'd lied.

"Why isn't there any coffee made?" Jonah's husky voice, thick with sleep, which used to ignite something primal deep inside Elizabeth. Now it grated on her nerves.

"I don't drink it." Elizabeth shot back, her lack of sleep sharpening her tongue.

"Who the fuck doesn't drink coffee in the morning?" He argued, his voice raised much too high for the early hour.

"Watch your mouth, Jonah. You wake up my granny and you'll have more issues than lack of caffeine." Elizabeth hissed, chancing a glance toward the closed bedroom door.

"Birdie loves me," he boasted, shoving a handful of dry cereal into his mouth, several pieces dropping to the floor, another mess she would have to clean. Jonah was right, like most of the women in this dinky town, her granny, Birdie Campbell loved him. Ironically, it was the single reason Elizabeth hadn't dumped his ass.

"I have to get ready for work," Elizabeth stood from the couch, ignoring Jonah's grumbling about the lack of decent food in this house. He was right again, most of the food in their pantry was off brand or on sale. Money was tight, always had been, but between granny's social security and her job at the County Co-op, they managed to keep the lights on.

Twenty minutes and a hurried shower later, Elizabeth rounded the corner to find her granny and Jonah sitting at the kitchen table, a cup of coffee and an empty plate in front of him.

"Aren't you going to be late for work?" She deadpanned, not caring to know the answer.

"I need gas money." Jonah demanded wiping his face, then tossing a crumpled-up napkin onto the table.

"Then I suggest you get to work."

Elizabeth wasn't about to give him another cent, having not been paid back for the last chunk of money he'd conned off her. She'd watched enough episodes of those reality court shows to know not to loan more money when he'd failed to pay her back. She knew how much money Jonah made, she sent the deposit to his bank every other

Wednesday after her boss approved it. It wasn't his lack of earning, but his inability to budget.

Jonah shoved his chair back with such force it put a dent in the drywall. "Now see," pointing an angry finger in her direction. "You wouldn't be such a bitch if you drank coffee."

Anger burned hot in her belly as her granny cringed from Jonah's raised voice. "And you wouldn't smell like the perfume counter at Rite Aid if you didn't spend half the night screwing around with Karen Miller."

Elizabeth moved with purpose and determination in her step as she pulled open the front door, swinging her free arm in invitation for Jonah to leave, shooting him a raised eyebrow when he failed to move.

"No man likes a smart-mouthed woman, Lizzie." Jonah started, picking up his cup of coffee and stepping around the table. "I blame those snooty bitches over at that college you go to." He tossed at Elizabeth as he passed by her. Elizabeth ignored his jab about her education as Jonah took every opportunity to make her feel bad about wanting more. The joke was on him, as his cruelty had the opposite effect, fueling her desire and making her work harder.

"Birdie, thank you for the breakfast, though the eggs were a little runny," Jonah began his back-handed compliment, but Elizabeth slammed the door in his face, silencing any further foulness he had for the sweet old lady who'd raised her.

Opening the refrigerator, Elizabeth removed the container of leftover casserole from last night's dinner, shoving it, along with some utensils into a grocery bag. She heard the shuffle of Granny's feet against the linoleum behind her, the elderly woman needing a hip replacement for years.

"You have such pretty hair, just like your momma's." Birdie stood behind the little girl who'd blossomed into a beautiful woman, "Same sharp tongue too. She had some colorful words when she brought you into this world."

Turning, Elizabeth took her grandmother's face between her palms, staring deep into the sadness that clouded her blue eyes. She knew how much it upset her grandmother to speak of her mother, the agony of losing a child something no mother should have to endure.

"Careful with your tongue, Lizzie. Jonah may not be a prizefighter..."

"Are you kidding, Granny? He isn't even the water boy."

"Be that as it may, Sweetheart, Jonah isn't much, but he's your only option in this town."

Elizabeth knew her Granny spoke the truth. Middleton was twenty minutes from everywhere, yet failed to catch the eyes of any business developers who opened stores in towns all over Kansas. With a population of less than three thousand, Elizabeth didn't see prosperity knocking on Middleton's door anytime soon.

"Speaking of prize fighters..."

"Way ahead of you, Lizzie. I've got two beers I saved from my bridge club meeting I'll put in the fridge to get nice and cold."

"Granny, you holding out on the fine ladies in the church?" Elizabeth teased, picking up the grocery bag and slinging her purse over her shoulder.

"Considering there ain't a lady in that church," Elizabeth and Birdie spun in the direction of the now open door, the surprise fading from their faces as they recognize the woman standing in the open door.

"Rose, I didn't hear you come in." Elizabeth greeted as she stepped around her granny's neighbor and best friend. Rose was a gem of a woman, kind-hearted and funny as they come. She and Birdie had been instant friends since the moment they met when Rose moved in next door thirty years ago.

"I'm not surprised," Rose leaned over to kiss Elizabeth's cheek. "Probably deaf from all that snoring I heard last night."

"And on that note, I have to go or I'll be late for work." Stepping to the side, she placed a kiss to Birdie's cheek. "I'll be back in time for the fight. You, me and the devastatingly handsome Kane Cavallo and some other guy we don't care about."

Birdie loved to see the excitement on Elizabeth's face as she shared her love of boxing. She wished she could afford to take her to a live event, but with their limited funds, the best she could do was the overpriced internet cable service Elizabeth worked a little extra for each month.

"Have a good day, Sweetheart. And make sure you hide your lunch, can't have you coming home hungry because of a thief."

"That thief has a name, Granny. And not to worry, I have a way of keeping him out of my food." Elizabeth sent a wink in Rose's direction, never more grateful for the devious side of the sweet old woman who had more tricks up her sleeve than Houdini.

"You ladies behave today, don't want to hear about the Sheriff showing up because of your shenanigans."

Birdie watched Elizabeth back down the drive and then pull onto the road behind the wheel of her ancient Chevy. The car was older than dirt when she gave her the keys for her seventeenth birthday, but Elizabeth worked hard and kept the car clean and running, just as she did everything she touched. Birdie knew Elizabeth was meant for bigger things than this one-horse town, but she feared what would happen if she ever left to pursue the dreams Birdie imagined ran through the young woman's head.

Gripping the edge of the sink, it was time to tell her the truth. Tonight, she vowed, tonight she would tell her everything. She prayed Elizabeth wouldn't hate her.

CODE OF SILENCE SERIES
THE BAD BOYS OF THE MAFIA.

Shamrocks & Secrets

Claddagh & Chaos

Stolen Secrets

Secret Sin

Secret Atonement

Family Secrets

Buried Secrets

Secrets & Lies Coming soon

SOUTHERN JUSTICE TRILOGY

WHEN THE GOOD GUYS FOLLOW THE BAD BOYS RULES. KU EXCLUSIVE.

Absolute Power

Absolute Corruption

Absolute Valor

STICKY-SWEET ROMANCE

Crain's Landing

JUSTICE
REVENGE REALLY IS BEST SERVED COLD.

Justice

BILLIONAIRE ROMANCE

Hostile Takeover

ANGEL KISS
A PARANORMAL ROMANCE

Angel Kiss

ABOUT THE AUTHOR

Cayce Poponea is a USA Today Bestselling author.

A true romantic at heart, she writes the type of fiction she loves to read. With strong female characters who are not easily swayed by the devilishly good looks and charisma of the male leads. All served with a twist you may never see coming. While Cayce believes falling in love is a hearts desire, she also feels men should capture our souls as well as turn our heads.

From the Mafia men who take charge, to the military men who are there to save the damsel in distress, her characters capture your heart and imagination. She encourages you to place your real life on hold and escape to a world where the laundry is all done, the bills are all paid and the men are a perfect as you allow them to be.

Cayce lives her own love story in Georgia with her husband and her three dogs. Leave your cares behind and settle in with the stories she creates just for you.

Made in the USA
Monee, IL
20 February 2024

53825472R00193